KATYN

KATYN: The Yugoslav Camp

~

A Historical Novel

By

Mark H. Glissmeyer

Gradina Books

This book is a work of historical fiction. Apart from the well-know people, places and locations mentioned, all other names, businesses, places, locations and people are imagined and are used fictitiously. Any resemblance to actual persons living or dead is purely coincidental.

Paperback ISBN-13: 978-0-9985416-1-7

Hardcover ISBN-13: 978-0-9985416-2-4

This historical novel is dedicated to Heinrich Glissmeyer. He was born in 1890 in Egestorf and died in Buchenwald concentration camp on 7/16/1938.

CONTENTS

CAST OF CHARACTERS

Dayan Costovar - son of Goritza and Thomash
Goritza Costovar - mother of Dayan
Thomash Costovar - father of Dayan
Andrey - grandfather of Dayan
Theodore - uncle of Dayan
Dimitrye - uncle of Dayan
Auntie Vida - aunt of Goritza
Auntie Stephanie - Nashko's mother and aunt of Dayan
Vidak Montenegrin - grandson to Uncle Dimitrye
Nashko - son of Auntie Stephanie
Lazar - a young Cablo villager
Tobo - a Danube fisherman
The Sexton - sexton of the St. George Church in Cablo
Aladdin - son of the church sexton
Perun Novak - Cablo outcast and thief
Dr. Nikola Vedrano - Gradina High School Director
Herr Pushinger - Hamburg Import-Export Inc.
Angelica Moravaz - student in Gradina
Auntie Sandra - old neighbor in Belgrade to Angelica
Margaret Neuman - Biology representative
Yana - Cablo villager
Liuba - Cablo shepherdess
Veselinka - Cablo shepherdess
Comrade Rocka - female Russian spy with a temper
Comrade Edo - Comrade Rocka's right-hand man
Tell - an old Yugoslav soldier
Paul - former soldier from neighboring village
Max Barrack - Serb handyman and spy
August Vogel - Volkssturm Unit guard in Fugen
Cornelia Bechter - German niece of August Vogel

Emil Harder - Gestapo official in Fugen
Antonio Laguna - editor of *The Progressive Voice*
Dabovich - mayor of Gradina
Mr. Winfield - sleazy Western journalist
Major Hillarich - Commandant, Garrison of Gradina
Colonnello Mortellini - Italian town-Commandant
Colonel Obradovich - camp leader at Bad Aibling
Major Renard - stationed at Camp Jenbach
Captain Michelet - officer of French troops
Captain Tucker - American soldier
Captain Radovich - Serb guerrilla soldier
Mr. Bronton - Director of UNRRA
Mario Santucci - Italian soldier
Aristides - Greek shepherd with a flute
Mankiewitz - a Pole prisoner
Budovanich - evil interrogator
Lieutenant Pavlovich - drunk Serb soldier
Lieutenant Greenshield - uncaring British soldier
Professor Veletsky - Polish microbiologist and historian
Vukovich - District attorney of Gradina
Alexey Duboroff - Russian engineering specialist

REAL CHARACTERS AND GROUPS IN YUGOSLAVIA

King Alexander - Yugoslav King assassinated in 1934
Prince Paul - took over as regent of Yugoslavia in 1934
King Peter - underage son of King Alexander
Josip Broz Tito - communist leader of Partisans
Draza Mihailovic - royalist leader of Chetniks
Chetniks - guerrilla anti-communist group
Partisans - guerrilla anti-fascist group led by Tito
Ustashis - Croatian Nazi-fascist group

0

Yugoslavia 1939

The Costovar family lived in Cablo, a small village in Yugoslavia scattered up on a plateau and located westerly from the nearest town of Gradina. Its distance from Gradina was measured by three or four hours of walking, three if unburdened, and four if a person carried a load on their shoulders. An ash tree forest covered Cablo's rocky hills, yet there was an open view down towards Gradina, which most houses in the village could see in clear weather. In summer, when the tops of the ash trees were veiled in a morning fog, they knew they'd have rain that day, but a light one without any wind.

Plowmen and shepherds from many surrounding villages looked towards Cablo's pride, the St. George Church. Centuries ago, the peasants of Cablo had worshipped under a great oak tree which, according to legend, was planted by an Orthodox monk, an ascetic, to offer the people a better gathering place than his poor home in a forest cave. He told the peasants that when the tree was large enough to where all the worshippers could stand under its limbs at one time, this would be the signal to build a church dedicated to St. George.

At that time the Turks ruled the province, but Serbian guerrillas stationed in Cablo attacked the Turkish garrison in Gradina. In reprisal the Turks cut down the ash trees, however a denser forest rapidly grew back. This offered better shelter to the guerrillas, and the story became a part of the poetry and beloved legends of the Serbs. For this reason the Turkish Pasha forbade the building of the church.

The story goes that he was later bribed with silver and gold, coming from items donated by the neighboring communities. This proved enough so that he finally granted permission to build, but stipulated that the church must be constructed in a single night facing east. As a result of the villager's haste to finish construction, the church ended up with crooked walls. Another condition of the Pasha was that it must be painted the color of light green leaves—as a sort of camouflage—so that the Turks in Gradina wouldn't be reminded of its presence as a Christian symbol.

1

When A War Starts

It was customary in Cablo for a young man, on the eve of his departure for the army or to a foreign country, to bathe in the creek at sunset under a nearby waterfall. If while doing this he heard goat bells from the nearby fields, it was regarded as a good omen.

"But I'm not going into the army, Mother," Dayan protested. "Neither am I going to America, I'll just take an ordinary bath like..."

"Going to a university is the same! This is the last thing for today," Goritza insisted. "Stay until you hear the bells while under the waterfall." She handed him a small towel and a piece of soap. "Don't leave the soap there," she warned, "the crows will fly off with it in the morning. Now hurry, and listen for the bells. Lazar heard them last year. Nashko too."

Dayan took a shortcut through the woods and soon found himself under the chilly, splashing waterfall to bathe. He shivered there for a while, inwardly scornful for participating in such a backward village custom.

Then he dried himself as fast as possible with the towel and dressed quickly. He raced through the woods to meet Thomash, who was at the church cemetery waiting to discuss the design of grandfather Andrey's monument. It was still nothing more than a huge block of granite which was pulled from the hills last year using all the available oxen in Cablo.

Reaching the cemetery, Dayan stood outside the stone wall, jumping up and down. He stayed outside because he knew such behavior wasn't proper within the churchyard.

Thomash, his father, was already there leaning against the low stone fence. "Heard the bells, did you?" he joked.

"I couldn't even think of them," Dayan said, continuing to move and rub himself, trying to get warm. "It's so cold there. To hell with..." He started to vault over the wall.

"Go back!" Thomash ordered, waving both arms. "Such language—and in a holy place."

Dayan was almost over the wall of the cemetery and went back. He lifted his eyes to the church tower, whose golden cross reflected the last rays of the sunset. "Forgive me, Father," he said. "It's the cold water that got to me." He looked at Thomash, requesting permission now to enter the cemetery.

Thomash crossed himself, then nodded to his son, who vaulted over the stone barrier. "Just tell your mother you heard the goat bells," his father said. "All the boys do."

Dayan smiled and nodded cheerfully. Then they began to discuss the details of the monument and stayed in total agreement on everything, until they came to the question of Andrey's inscription.

"Father," Dayan began, having both hands pressed on the great chunk of granite. "Please wait! It's too soon to be adding the words."

"Too soon for the words?"

Dayan hesitated. "I mean—grandfather wasn't the only one to sacrifice," he said reluctantly, "but he needs something special to reflect that forever." He felt as if his hands were anchored to the granite so he couldn't move them. Finally, he went on, "I think the surface for the letters should be as large as possible. I'll have a design from Belgrade to show you when I come back."

"Then don't wait too long," Thomash said, "my eyes get weaker every day. But I'll prepare it like you said, now let's go home."

After giving their customary respect to the dead and the church through their silence, that silence continued even as they walked home, with the only sound coming from the metallic click of Thomash's crutch hitting the rocky path. Then through the dusk they saw a line of lanterns moving slowing towards their cottage.

"They're coming to see you off! Let's hurry," Thomash urged.

Dayan moved ahead of him, hanging the damp towel around his neck. "Watch the white towel," he instructed his father. "It'll keep you from falling down."

Thomash laughed at such caution. "Even my crutch knows every inch of this path," he said. "I don't need eyes for it."

At the threshold of the cottage Dayan barely paused, looking in at the old men now sitting around the hearth. "I heard the goat bells all right," he announced as he entered. The old men were pleased.

"That must have been Yana with her goat," Goritza said, smiling happily.

His mother was in the corner packing his belongings, while Dayan began to check through the addresses Goritza had collected for him. Meanwhile, the old villagers lingered, although they knew Dayan had to get up early the next morning before the first roosters.

They were eager to know what kind of school he was going to, and would he see the young King in Belgrade? If he did, would he ask him to build a better road up to Cablo? And would he arrange for some crippled old soldiers to be put into a hospital?

There were many other requests, and much advice was offered too. After all, they'd known Thomash since he was born, let alone Dayan; they considered themselves privileged to offer what wisdom they had.

Uncle Dimitrye, considered one of the sages of the district, eventually beckoned to Dayan, who obediently went to his side. Although the old man had never traveled far away himself, he was full of information about unpleasant things that had happened to others in foreign countries. He also whispered a warning that Dayan should stay away from young women. There were some, he said, who could encircle a man's body seven times with their arms.

Dayan kissed his hand in thanks, and promised to follow the advice. He went to the door and lit the lanterns for the old people as they prepared to leave. But first, Thomash and Goritza asked them to witness the fulfillment of Andrey's last wish.

Goritza opened a carved trunk and took out a big bundle. Slowly she unrolled it. Excitement grew as everyone watched the long piece of cloth, it kept turning and turning. And finally, from within, they saw a golden ring fastened by a leather strap. In the center of the ring, a diamond shined brightly back. Carefully Goritza untied it.

Then, asking Dayan to put out his left hand, she slipped the ring on his finger. "For you, our son." They hugged each other as Dayan teared up looking at the ring, and Thomash put his arms around the shoulders of them both.

After the three of them separated, the old men took turns one by one, and clasped Dayan's left hand as tightly as they could, trying to hide the tears in their eyes. After the last one said good-bye, Dayan escorted them all as far as the corner of the property, waved a final farewell and ran to the orchard, where he climbed part way up one of the tallest cherry trees.

He watched as the line of burning lanterns moved slowly through the night. The only sound to be heard was that of their many canes beating against the rocky path, as the old villagers of Cablo found their way home.

The superstitious villagers believed that any young man leaving home shouldn't look back towards Cablo, not until he'd passed the stone bridge on the way into Gradina, otherwise he'd be needlessly delayed when he returned home later. Even slightly looking back was sufficient for this belief to happen.

Dayan might have defied this the next morning had it not been for Thomash, who was following behind him while leading Uncle Theodore's donkey along on a rope.

This still provided many opportunities for Dayan to peek back since the animal stopped frequently, either out of stubbornness or to obey nature's call. But he didn't risk it, and at reaching the stone bridge, the same beggar was waiting as they'd seen there the last time. First Dayan, and then Thomash dropped a coin into the blind man's hat.

"Now you can look back," Thomash said.

"Right now I wouldn't if the devil told me to!" Dayan retorted.

Chapter 1

The beggar blessed them and started to sing about a lonesome wayfarer who wondered; is that snow or a forest fire that shines so brightly in the high mountains at night? It was neither, but rather the glow of some young girl's faces. The wayfarer then sang out to the girls, and ran up there to meet them.

Dayan jotted down the words to the song on a small piece of paper. "If it wasn't for mother's wish," he said, "I would've looked back a thousand times. But now you can tell her the truth tonight, it will make her happy."

"That's my son," Thomash said approvingly. "An old man shouldn't have to lie."

Still, Dayan couldn't understand why one was forbidden to look back towards the place dearest to him. But Goritza came first, and if she could stay at the threshold of the cottage as she had this morning, shedding no tears, then he too could make a sacrifice for her.

And what about poor Nashko, he thought. His mother, Stephanie, had heard stories from a fortune teller that the oceans almost covered the world, and warned her that they're as dangerous as the nearby canyons. Why hadn't he been able to look back?

"The world is bigger than you think," Thomash told him. "So take a good look forward. Always forward." He spoke with the authority of someone who'd traveled a lot, while Dayan knew the world only from a map.

"I'll see it from the train," Dayan promised. "And I'm certainly going to do something about all these superstitions," he assured himself.

His thoughts went to St. George, Cablo's patron Saint, and Saint Sava, patron of the Serbian schools. The people believed that both had saved them from dragons and darkness, and became saints and martyrs due to their enduring sacrifice and devotion to others.

No matter what Dayan might do in the future, he'd always remember Goritza's final wish this morning for him to buy a watermelon in Gradina to quench his thirst on the train. To her, water on the road in such strange places had a magical power. She'd heard that a single glass of water offered to a traveler by a young woman could drive him crazy enough to marry her, so that he never returns home. This had already happened long ago, it was said, to a villager who'd gone on a trip to South America.

"Father, you know better than I do when a watermelon is ripe," Dayan said. "You get one and put it on the donkey's pack between the loads."

The animal was already burdened with a suitcase of woven willow strands filled with his books. And on the other side was a wool sack which held a pair of new shoes, plus some winter clothes knit by the shepherdesses. There were also some smaller packages in the sack that contained various dried fruits and a wooden jar filled with butter, all given as gifts from various Cablo families.

Permission to postpone the draft until the completion of their education was automatically granted to the regular students in Yugoslavia. All they needed was an application. Dayan was on his way to the military commandant to get one, while Thomash went out shopping for the watermelon Dayan needed for his trip.

They'd arranged to meet later at the main entrance to the park near the railroad station. Dayan was glad to comply with Goritza's wish, for he knew there'd be many steps and actions in his life she wouldn't approve of if she knew. He was thinking that if some young woman really did encircle him seven times with her arms, as Uncle Dimitrye had said, he'd encircle her too. What more could they expect an unmarried young man to do?

He was only worried that Thomash would follow Goritza's request and buy the largest watermelon in the market. What would he do with it all on that narrow-gauge train to Belgrade? Maybe he could eat some of it and share the rest with the other passengers—as soon as he boarded the train. The less he had to eat, he thought, the more he'd become hungry and thirsty, not only for a glass of water from a young woman, but for both of her arms to encircle him.

Chapter 1

Thomash was leaning against Dayan's belongings at the park gate. He was listening along with one of the gardeners to a soldier reading aloud from a newspaper. The donkey, free of its load, grazed peacefully along the fence.

"Everything's fine, Father," Dayan interrupted them, displaying a slip as proof that he'd applied for a postponement of the draft.

But Thomash shook his head. "No, it's bad!"

"You mean not ripe?" Dayan said, referring to the watermelon. If so, he was glad because then he'd just eat the center of it out on the train. Maybe there's something to these superstitions helping him after all, he thought.

"Here—read this, you won't believe it," Thomash ordered him.

Dayan took the newspaper and read at the place Thomash pointed. *"Inside Poland, the bitter resistance of the Polish Army is still holding back the well-equipped German troops that attack in all sectors."* Dayan gasped, his mouth half-open. He dropped the newspaper. "But this means—it's war. This is war. Oh, no...NO!" He stomped the ground with his right foot. "It can't be. Only last year Chamberlain had said with certainty—*peace in our time!*"

The soldier picked up the newspaper and handed it back to Dayan.

"It's a shame," Thomash said soberly. "Go on reading, and think of your grandfather."

Fearfully dreading the next words, Dayan looked down at the newspaper cautiously again. His voice faltered as he read in a low voice: *"England and France, in accordance with their pledge, have declared war on Germany!"*

"Well, that's what matters now. The great Western powers will never let their allies be defeated," Dayan said, as his voice grew stronger. He then made a threatening motion with the hand that held the slip of paper postponing his draft into the army. "This is what the Nazis should get." He turned back to the paper to read more. *"Destruction of Warsaw. The mass air raids with German Stuka planes has destroyed a greater part of the city of*

Warsaw." This was even worse than he'd thought. He looked up at the sky. "It's unbelievable! What about the Hague Convention?"

Thomash gave him another newspaper. "This seems to be the latest news."

Dayan shook his head in defiance. "No, there isn't time, Father. I have to quickly take back my application for deferment. I'll join the army now, like Grandfather would have wanted me to. Where did you get the paper?"

"From the fruit vendor, to wrap up the watermelon. But I don't think you've read it all," Thomash urged. "Go on."

"According to a secret pact concluded between Hitler and Stalin, now known as the Ribbentrop-Molotov Pact for the partition of Poland, Soviet troops have crossed the Polish border and are on the march towards the west to meet the Germans."

"That makes it even worse," Dayan exclaimed. "England and France will have to declare war on the Soviets as well." He turned to the soldier. "Did you know about this before?"

The soldier shrugged his shoulders, then the park gardener said in sympathy that he'd heard rumors, but nobody knew the truth. There were so many proclamations coming from the authorities these days about Yugoslavia's neutrality. They were also trying to avoid panic among the peasants, who numbered about eighty percent of the country's population.

Thomash and Dayan asked the park gardener to watch over their belongings and the donkey until they returned. From there they traveled the shortest path through the park, and made their way into the recruiting office. Dayan spread out the newspapers on the table and explained to the seated officer why he'd returned.

The officer looked back at him, puzzled.

"He's hard as granite," Thomash assured him, interpreting the officer's hesitation as a doubt of Dayan's strength. "I'm a stonecutter and I know what granite is. Look!" He pounded Dayan on the shoulders. "See? He doesn't so much as move. You could give him a cannon right now!"

"I don't understand," the officer finally replied, looking at the crumpled newspapers. "Where did you get all this?"

"A fruit vendor gave them to my father," Dayan explained, "to use when I slice the watermelon on the train."

"Then you should use them for that," the officer demanded. "And I want to know where you got all these crazy ideas from? Panic! War! By the way, who is this with you?"

"I'm his father, Thomash Costovar, sir. Thomash Costovar, from Cablo."

From Thomash's voice Dayan recognized the state of his concern. He showed the slip of paper to the officer, then tore it in two. "Deferment isn't for me anymore."

"Hey, you can't do that with an official paper!" the officer warned. "It's against the law."

Thomash took the two pieces from Dayan. "Is it also against the law to make four pieces out of them?" He then tore them in half again. "And what about eighths? Or sixteenths?" Both times he tore the pieces again, then let them all fall on the table—just as Major Hillarich entered the office.

"God damn it," Hillarich shouted, "never had such a hard one." He threw a folded newspaper in front of the officer. "It sounds like the name of a mountain peak, but it's probably some kind of fish." Moving a pencil over a large crossword puzzle, he came to the spaces for the word in question. "See what you can do," he challenged.

Then he turned to Thomash. "I'll bet you came for Perun Novak. Nothing doing. There's new evidence against him."

"I came for my son, sir."

"Why him? Did your son pull out Perun's teeth?"

"No, I want to give him to you to serve in the..."

The officer interrupted Thomash. "I don't understand, Major. Half an hour ago his son here applied for a school deferment, and now he's back to be drafted."

"Things have changed," Dayan tried to explain. "In the village we didn't know what's been happening these past few weeks."

"What's he talking about?" Hillarich asked the officer, who was shaking his head in disbelief.

Thomash prodded Dayan gently. Encouraged, his son answered for the officer. "I'm talking about the attack by Hitler and Stalin on freedom-loving Christian Poland."

Hillarich stared.

"You could take both of us too," Thomash suggested. "I can make crutches for the soldiers."

"But we're neutral, strictly neutral. Our government's stance is neutrality," Hillarich reminded them, then he faced the officer. "Did either of them give the oath to King and Fatherland?"

The officer made a weary, negative gesture. Something was wrong about all of this, and he wished he was out of it.

"Please, may I have my application back, sir?" Dayan politely asked the officer.

"It's already been forwarded. As an official paper, it belongs to the country now and not to you. About the slip, you and your father just tore it up into many pieces."

"But I want to belong to this country too," Dayan asserted.

"Even after you gave that dreary speech on world peace earlier this year?" Major Hillarich asked Dayan. "Do you think we'd accept you after that lecture you gave us? Just send us your address and if we need you, we'll look you up." And to Thomash he said, "By the looks of the crutch you have, you don't make many. The army can't even hobble around on that. Now let's not discuss this any further."

Realizing they were dismissed, Thomash and Dayan left the office in disbelief, leaving the door open on the way out. The officer then closed it after them.

"It's easy to recognize these peasants," Major Hillarich said to the officer. "They either smell of hay or wet earth. And they have no sense of scale, always imagining something huge out of the smallest of events."

"And yet, they have their strengths," the officer commented back. "They'd sit naked on red-hot iron for the things they believe in. Imagine all of them united against our government, they outnumber us many times!"

This briefly put Hillarich on the defensive. "Don't forget," he retorted, as he tapped one heal against the other, "we've got enough bullets in our ammunition depot to take care of every one of them."

The officer suppressed a smile as he gathered all the tiny pieces of paper Thomash had torn.

"Wait a moment!" Major Hillarich said, suddenly remembering why he came in. "For God's sake, try to find the name of that damn fish I need, will you?"

2

The Train Rides Along

Dayan was still reading the newspaper outside the station in Gradina when the train pulled in. "Look here," he said to his father, pointing to a column on the first page. "Stalin has sent some notorious German communists back to Hitler as proof of their friendship and the pact they signed. Some of these men fled Germany after the Reichstag..."

Thomash interrupted him. "Just look to see if the paper says the Poles are brave people. Because they are."

"It only says we're strictly neutral."

Thomash pretended to spit across his left shoulder, as he did when annoyed.

"There's something more, Father." Dayan took Thomash's right hand in his, then lowered his voice, embarrassed. "I'm not going to marry Yana, but Lazar will as soon as he returns home from the army. That's why she hurried to learn how to read and write; she wanted to correspond with Lazar."

He kissed Thomash's hand in farewell. "Please tell Mother," he said. "Maybe now she won't mind so much."

"I knew all about that," Thomash replied. "Don't worry, just send your new address to the military command. They might be needing you."

After the train left the station, Thomash waved while he was still seeing Dayan, and Dayan in return waved his newspaper back from the train window. Finally, Thomash put his fur cap on the end of his crutch, and holding it overhead like a flag, went on waving towards the train—until it disappeared and everyone else had left the station. Assured he was finally alone, he brushed away tears from his eyes and slowly mounted his waiting donkey.

Dayan remained at the window long after Thomash's figure was out of sight. He threw large sheets of the newspaper out; he wanted other people to read and learn the horrible truth about the war. Thus occupied, he missed his last look back at Cablo, and was sad when he eventually realized it.

Sitting down in his seat, Dayan opened the sack he'd brought with the dried fruits, the little gifts from the villagers. Breathing in the fragrance of the sun-dried fruits brought his village near again, perhaps closer than seeing it with his own eyes. He almost felt like it wasn't right to look at this with the same eyes he'd read those detestable words of war with today—the news of Warsaw's destruction. An entire nation being crucified by the swastika, and the hammer and sickle.

In his mind, he saw these two monster symbols intertwined, appearing in the shape of an enormous scorpion whose claws and tail held large pouches of poison. Pouches that swelled larger, growing bigger and bigger. He shuddered.

"Bad dreams?" asked the passenger sitting next to him kindly.

"No, oh no!" Dayan couldn't talk about his vision, especially to a stranger, so he turned again to look out the window. The train was passing a large vineyard where many grape pickers were working, their hands holding large clusters of dark-blue fruit.

"Maybe you're sick?" his neighbor asked. He had deep set eyes and a face covered with many wrinkles.

"No, not at all," Dayan answered. He was grateful for the old man's interest but wanted to be left alone.

As darkness came, he began to feel at ease and even glad that he hadn't taken a last look at Cablo. He visualized the sharp peaks of its hills topped with clusters of bright stars, even larger than the grapes he'd seen that afternoon. Those were stars of happiness for all of God's creatures in Cablo—except for the scorpions.

As he gazed out of the train window at the darkening hills it seemed to him that the stars here were moving down into the forest. Also the faint tinkle of goat-bells could be heard as the train moved more slowly here, and there was the sound of laughter mingled with the bells. It was coming from young people, shepherds and shepherdesses, lying together in the lush green ferns near the tracks.

He wished they could all go to St. George Church to be married. And then to the attics above the stables surrounding their cottages to spend their wedding nights, where for centuries their ancestors had spent theirs. And the children created by these joyful unions would be born beneath the lucky stars he saw now, which must be shining down through heaven.

Suddenly the train gathered speed, the click of the wheels became louder, and Dayan came back to the present. The conductor was proudly explaining to some country passengers that railroad tracks are as long as the whole world.

And so are my desires, they're even longer! Dayan thought.

He also wished for the children—conceived and born in those attics on straw pallets covered with warm lambs wool. They should have as much honey as they want from the big oak in front of Cablo's church, where he imagined every limb of the tree had a big hollow of bees.

If that newly-created scorpion, that monster born of the swastika and the hammer and sickle, could grow those large poisonous bags at the end of each claw, then why couldn't the oak tree, which had been serving Christianity for centuries, grow honey for the children born like Jesus? The train was moving very fast now as it went noisily along a rocky hill.

Dayan remembered an old saying—be a victim for the sake of the victims and be a child for the sake of the children. He whispered, "Grow fast, my beloved oak! Grow fast! Let the honey flow from your hollow, for the children."

His neighbor's voice interrupted. "You ought to cross yourself before you sleep," he suggested. "You've certainly been having some bad dreams."

This time Dayan confessed. "You're right," he said, "I will cross myself." After a moment he asked, "Do you ever have any longings—any wishes?"

"Wishes at my age? Of course not." But then the old man corrected himself. "Well, right now I have only one—to get home safely."

Dayan nodded. Such a wish was easy to understand, especially in these times. Suddenly he asked, "Sir, do you know anything about scorpions?"

"Scorpions?" the man repeated, astonished. "Why do you ask me that?"

"Because I'm a young scholar," Dayan answered seriously. "I've been wondering what's the best way to kill them."

"Then smash them," the passenger said with certainty. "Smash them to bits or the pieces will grow together again. And watch out, they move mostly in darkness."

Here again Dayan and the peasant were in agreement. The youth looked at his seat-mate with respect. "Did you know," Dayan asked, "that in some countries there are scorpions with a large bag of poison on each claw?"

"That sounds more like the teeth of a vampire," the man replied doubtfully.

"Well, yes, in a way. But those monsters poison human blood first, and then they drink it. Many people don't feel it happening, and others finally feel it, but only when it's too late." Dayan sighed, then looked into the passenger's eyes solemnly. "Do you think such beasts could be killed with thorns?"

"Only with blackthorns. And then the branches must be sharpened, as for any vampire. You have to stab them in the heart with it. Like this!" He jabbed his index finger towards the window. "Remember, you promised to cross yourself," the peasant reminded Dayan as he gathered his belongings. Privately he was thinking this lad has too much imagination for his own good.

Dayan began repeating obediently, "In the name of God, the Son and..."

"Here's where I get off," the peasant interrupted him. He pressed a calloused hand on Dayan's shoulder as he turned and trudged down the corridor. Dayan then remembered the watermelon, and placed it in the empty seat he left behind. He slowly started to cut a slice from it using the knife from his sack.

Chapter 2

Meanwhile, back in Cablo, Goritza was still worried about Dayan like all mothers tend to worry. She thought of things she could do to help while waiting for news, any news, of where he was. Dayan was away and that's all she thought of for now.

"Cut it down!" Goritza begged. "It's old anyhow. And when Dayan comes home, he'll plant another one."

"Chop down the best cherry tree we have?" Thomash protested. "Next spring is its turn to bear plenty of cherries."

"But I can't sleep until you cut it, Thomas. I keep seeing his bloody nose. I hear him crying in the night."

"Oh, all right, all right," Thomash said reluctantly. "But all the boys fall down from trees, lots of times. Remember Lazar's elbow that I put in the cast? It will always be thick there from that time he fell out of a pear tree."

"I only ask you this one thing," Goritza begged.

"Far from it. Every day you ask if a letter came. Then when one does—you want to know when the next one will come. Why aren't you like Lazar's mother and the others?"

"I am like her," Goritza said, "and the others too. You don't know it, Thomash, but they cry too. We all cry together." His wife looked at him, the tears still in her eyes waiting to drop.

"So that's what you women do when you get together," Thomash said.

Finally, he reluctantly promised to cut the cherry tree from which Dayan had fallen when he was a seven-year-old, but with one condition: Goritza wasn't to constantly talk about Dayan and ask for his letters.

Thomash did this out of love so the villagers wouldn't make fun of her as they did Stephanie. She was always saying she wouldn't worry about Nashko drowning if he was only as tall as Lazar and Dayan were—as if his height mattered compared to the depths of the ocean.

Despite the abundant harvest this year, there was a sudden and sharp drop in the villagers' prosperity in the whole district. Everyone became more cautious—so they saved, polished and repaired everything they'd bought in town. Fewer weddings were planned and in Cablo they'd have only one wedding, that of Lazar and Yana, which would take place when he returned home from the army.

Nobody understood what had happened to the economy. The townspeople blamed the villagers for not bringing their produce to the market. The villagers in turn protested that they didn't trust the money, for a lot of it was rumored to be counterfeit and worthless.

The Gradina weekly newspaper, *The Progressive Voice*, reported many accounts of people being interrogated by the police, and others who were simply brought into court. Amidst all this confusion, the worst blow to Cablo was that they stopped the delivery of ash wood to Gradina. This was criticized every week in *The Progressive Voice,* for it meant the city would be shivering without firewood, and winter was fast approaching.

To the villagers they saw the skies turning dark; there were threatening black clouds, and with it came the smell of disaster.

3

All Torn Up

In an office at the Belgrade military command, Dayan stood before the desk of the chief investigator, who was looking at a page in a file lying open before him.

"Just listen to what is says," the investigator said sternly.

"After a thorough and repeated search, it's been proven that Dayan Costovar from the village of Cablo has neglected to apply for a deferment of his draft."

"If the accused is able to provide written proof that he has, indeed, made such application, then the charges against him will be dropped immediately, and this command will withdraw its accusation. Otherwise, the prosecution will be carried out to the fullest extent of the law."

"Signed, Major Hillarich"

"February 7. 1940 Commandant, Gradina"

The investigator looked up at Dayan. "Well?"

"I was in their office before coming here to Belgrade," Dayan said calmly, while hiding his nervousness. "They must have seen me..."

"What they saw is that you obviously didn't send in the application, or this investigation wouldn't be taking place. But they're willing to drop the charges provided you have some written proof of this, which I doubt."

"It's the written proof that created the whole problem," Dayan began.

The investigator interrupted him. "Rather, problems. But yes, I agree with you."

"The fact is, I put the application in personally. My father could testify to that."

"A father can't bear witness for his son, according to the law." The investigator looked back at the file, and then shuffled through some of its pages. He found the one he wanted and read: *"Neither Thomash Costovar nor his son Dayan ever gave their oath to the King and Fatherland."*

He closed the file and folded his hands on the desk, looking at Dayan cynically. "I hope you don't expect me to take your word over that of Major Hillarich, who swore twenty years ago to give his life for his country if needed."

"But we also offered to serve our country," Dayan said. "I asked to be drafted, and my father wanted to make crutches for anyone wounded in war."

The investigator smiled cynically. "War, you say? It says here you gave a speech that no one wants war, you only believe in world peace."

"That's right," Dayan answered quickly. "I also believed and trusted in an umbrella too. It's exactly why I'm here, because of the war that's going on in Poland. When I read about it in the newspaper, I tore up the receipt showing I'd made application for deferment–right in front of the recruiting officer. My father, God bless him, tore it up some more."

The investigator laughed. He picked up a blank piece of paper to show Dayan. "It's all torn up like this one?" He tore the sheet several times and tossed the fragments into the wastebasket.

"It was a demonstration, sir," Dayan replied with dignity. He spread out his arms. "We were showing our devotion to our country, to Poland, and to the Western powers."

"Whatever, whatever," the investigator said impatiently. "The point is you failed to comply with the law." He gave Dayan a wary, suspicious look. "We now hear you've been spreading panic and rumors at the university lately."

"To the contrary," Dayan retorted. "I only have one thought, and it fills my whole being. Just one single idea, that of peace. And peace by all and for all, nothing less."

Chapter 3

The investigator shrugged contemptuously and gestured to the policeman standing by the door. "Take the troublemaker away." To Dayan, he said, "Try to learn the ways of the real world, you can't live on hope. Now that's my free advice, for what it's worth to you."

Three days later Dayan was summoned before the recruiting officer at the Belgrade military district office, where he was informed that the charges against him were being dropped.

"Therefore, you're going to be drafted next month," the officer said. It seemed to Dayan that he was almost being spiteful to him. Regardless, Dayan was still shocked by the news, especially when he learned that his garrison would be near Belgrade; it was what he'd wanted earlier. He was instructed where to report for duty when he came to the capital headquarters when ordered.

"Your unit actually belongs to Belgrade," the officer told him. "But it's detached for security reasons. Remember that—and be careful!" He shook hands with Dayan and dismissed him.

Meanwhile, back in Cablo, Goritza had kept her promise to Thomash. She rarely asked when Dayan's next letter would be coming. She bragged about her courage, although she admitted to Thomash that the reason she didn't cry was because no tears would be sufficient to express her grief over Dayan's absence.

When Uncle Dimitrye prophesied that all the boys in the village who were away would return when the first blossoms appeared in the orchards, Goritza was the first to cover the young branches with rags and straw to protect them from frosty nights. Other hopeful mothers followed her example, a few even covered the trees with old furs, anything to ensure their son's future home-coming.

Letters from the young men in service began trickling into the village again shortly after Dayan reported for duty in Belgrade. They were addressed in Dayan's handwriting, and everyone recognized it. The villagers all told Thomash and Goritza they couldn't understand how he'd managed it. Nashko wrote that he'd learned how to swim, but he had no opportunity to practice because from now on his service would be on land.

"Dayan saved him," Stephanie beamed. "He went all the way to the young King and asked him to take my boy out of the water. God bless him!"

Unlike the few letters they'd sent in the past, now the soldiers described the mild winter and talked about their warm uniforms. There was good food now and they were having fun, especially when they had leave from the garrison and could go into the villages for dancing and corn-husking.

They talked about the pleasant, colorful celebrations they had over Christmas and into the new year. Meanwhile, the mothers were counting the weeks and months on their fingers, while the fathers kept busy stocking dry firewood. They wanted to be sure the homecoming fires wouldn't get smoke in their returning hero's eyes.

But there still wasn't any word as to when they'd arrive, although military terms of service were finished for some of them. Many at home wondered why the military was preventing their return, but nobody knew the answer.

When the first maple buds appeared along the creek, anticipation gave way to anxiety, which nobody wanted to admit. Finally a letter came from Uncle Dimitrye's grandson, Vidak Montenegrin, saying that he wouldn't be coming home. His unit, like many others, was being activated even though his term had expired.

Don't ask me to say more, the letter ended. It was signed, *Your real Montenegrin*. This was a nickname his grandfather had given him because he'd been shy as a child, and Uncle Dimitrye wanted to encourage him to be robust and brave, like a real Montenegrin.

Neither the priest, nor the old teacher in the neighboring village, nor any of the old warriors of three, or even four, Serbian wars knew what the term *activated unit* meant.

"Never mind, I'll find out," Thomash said one night at a closed meeting held with fathers in the Costovar cottage. "That school director in Gradina will tell me. Dayan says he knows everything."

"Maybe you should see Aladdin," somebody suggested.

Some of the villagers thought the sexton's son Aladdin had all the answers to their problems. He'd left the village and settled in town to get away from the nickname attached to him when he was a child.

He worked as a janitor in a big office building which included a law firm, so he had access to various papers and books which he pretended to understand. Just the same, Thomash first went to Dr. Vedrano for the information, only to learn that he'd also been called away into an *activated unit,* and that no civilians were allowed into the military command. So Thomash reluctantly had to look up Aladdin after all.

At first the sexton's son was fearful of the strange phrase, but when Thomash explained that Dr. Vedrano himself was in an activated unit, that information gave Aladdin a clue. He searched through some law books in the attorney's office and came up with an encouraging explanation. The phrase, he said, meant a type of unit which protected the king on a battlefield, marching with flags and music as his troops moved into the captured enemy's capital.

Having delivered this pronouncement, Aladdin commented on the shameful Soviet attack on Finland that winter. "The Finns," he said, "were giving the Russians plenty of trouble."

When Thomash returned home that same day, he learned that Yana had read Goritza a letter from Lazar. He was to have a short leave at the end of spring so he could return to Cablo for their marriage. Goritza passed the word to Stephanie, and news of the approaching wedding spread quickly throughout the village.

The real significance of Lazar's letter mentioned that he was at the Yugoslav-German border monitoring Nazi soldiers, just as Vidak Montenegrin was watching Fascists at the Yugoslav-Italian border.

The splendor of Cablo's blooming orchards during an early spring in 1940 was scarcely noticed by the villagers, let alone enjoyed. The pride of many homes had been the big oxen they'd always owned, having long, wide horns. But the oxen had followed in the same tracks as the horses did earlier, and were now requisitioned by the military—leaving behind crying children and rusting plows. Now their owners had to resort to shovels and hoes to do the hard work. There was no more singing, and no more time for siestas. Even the smallest patch of land had to be productive.

Farmers who had suffered through previous wars gave advice as to what was best to plant, and their counsel was strictly followed. Rye and barley were recommended because the bread made from these grains would last longer. Pumpkins and turnips replaced watermelons. *Wheat is for sick children and Holy Communion* was a slogan repeated by the villagers, who'd heard it from Uncle Dimitrye. He said that in some rich countries they even made pies out of pumpkins.

Now that the people had lost confidence in the value of money, there was no incentive to take produce down to the market in Gradina. They mainly bought only salt and petroleum. Dry caves in the hills were checked for possible food storage locations, while the nervousness spread because of the news in Lazar's and Vidak's letters.

It was also becoming a bad time for Thomash, whose eyesight was failing more and more; this made him work slower while woodcarving. Because of his poor vision—he relied increasingly on *seeing through his fingers*.

A recent line of communication the villages had with Gradina came from the youths who reported there for the draft at the prescribed age, and they were surprisingly being told to go back home and wait. Since they were never called to duty, they became unpopular with the girls, who considered it a bad sign if a country boy wasn't drafted on time.

Aladdin had told some of them there was sabotage in the government administration, but nobody in Cablo understood what he meant. They understood well enough, though, when news came about Hitler's invasion of France. This was a blow to the villagers, who already had heavy hearts. The daily greeting between them now was, "*Vive la France!*" A saying brought back by veterans who'd fought shoulder to shoulder with the French during the First World War in Greece.

When Paris fell to the Germans, Cablo went into a seven-day period of mourning, marked by the ringing of the bell at St.

George Church three times a day. Lazar returned home at this time for his seven-day furlough to marry Yana, but the wedding was postponed until the mourning for Paris was over. This left the newlyweds only one day together before he was to return to duty.

The wedding was a solemn one without much celebration. Lazar had brought news that all of France would be lost in a matter of days, and the villagers were in no mood for festivities. The next morning some young people escorted Lazar back to Gradina with Yana, and later brought back news of the fall of France to the Nazis.

What was the Yugoslav government going to do to prevent the same thing from happening to them? The Cablo villagers could only talk, and wonder.

4

Surrounded By Scorpions

At the contests played to celebrate the completion of his company's long training period, Dayan came in second to the eventual champion Tobo. He was standing apart for a moment resting, when his sergeant approached him.

"I'm sending you to Belgrade in charge of the transport carrying old shoes and leather goods to the repair shop," he told Dayan. "I'd send the winner Tobo, but that fisherman is still too clumsy. He may know all there is to know about the Danube, but as a soldier he makes a terrible impression. When he salutes a general, he sways like he's pulling a net out of the water!"

Dayan laughed and nodded back.

The sergeant went on to praise Dayan's strength and competence. "I'm sure you'll do a good job of it," he said. "The sacks will all be sealed, and you'll only need to make one trip a week. If the government hadn't sold all of our rawhide to Germany, we wouldn't have to go through this silly business of repairing old leather things. It's ridiculous," he said. "But," and he shrugged, "it has to be done."

After his second trip, Dayan was hoping he could quit. He was exhausted from loading and unloading big sacks of leather, some even containing heavy saddles. Meanwhile, Tobo had begged him to bring back some smoked fish from the city. He was feeling homesick and fish caught from the Danube river would bring him closer to it.

"You'll find lots of Poles there," Tobo said.

"Poles? Where?"

"At the Danube wharves. Lots of them. And some already speak Serbian. Please, Dayan, I'm dying for some smoked fish. I promise if you bring me a batch I'll never beat you again at rope-pulling or log throwing."

"Okay," Dayan said, smiling. "It's a bargain. But I wasn't planning on losing again anyways."

Dayan went to the sergeant and volunteered to take more sacks to Belgrade over the weekend. "We'll save the government time," he pointed out. The sergeant accepted this gladly.

It was easy enough to recognize the Polish refugees at the Danube waterfront. Their eyes were full of hate—hate for both their German and Soviet oppressors. Though they showed this suffering they'd gone through, they also reflected hope for the eventual return of freedom to their homeland. These were Polish fighters who resisted venturing along the Mediterranean or out to the west; they wanted to stay closer to their enslaved Poland, waiting for a day of revenge.

What Dayan learned from a few of them on this single Sunday made him ashamed of himself and his country. He thought of Major Hillarich—with his eyes the color of green algae, expounding in favor of neutrality, and his feverish search for a single word in a crossword puzzle.

He remembered being questioned by the chief investigator at the military command in Belgrade, and how the man had made such a point about Major Hillarich taking his military oath some twenty years earlier. This he would have done with his hand on their military flag, where the words—*With Faith in God* and *For King and Fatherland* were beautifully embroidered. Now listening to the Polish fighters, whose eyes were alight and burning in their gaunt faces, Dayan wondered about the significance of those words.

Going back to his garrison, he was glad that the award for his essay on world peace had been refused, although he was convinced of the truth he'd stated in it—about how the human heart really is the arsenal of the most destructive weapons.

Tobo hurried to help him unload the heavy sacks of harnesses when he returned. When they had finished, he looked at Dayan expectantly, but said nothing. Regretfully, Dayan answered the unspoken question. "Sorry, I forgot your fish because I was so busy. Next time, I promise."

Tobo looked disappointed, but sympathized. "You don't like to go. It's such hard work."

"Don't worry," Dayan assured him. "I'll go back, and you'll get your smoked fish."

Nothing, in fact, could keep him from returning. A Polish refugee had promised to tell him more about what had been happening, and he was anxious to hear what might be better news. But his hopes were dashed the next week, when later the same refugee pulled out a large map of Poland.

"Look here," his new friend said, indicating the westerly side of it. "From this area the people fled from the Nazis, going towards the east." His finger traveled in a second the torturous miles, the mountains and valleys and rivers the refugees had stumbled over for weeks with bleeding feet. Now his hand moved to the other side of the map.

"From here," he said, "people fled from the Bolsheviks, going towards the west."

He stopped, clenched his hand into a fist, and pounded the map with it, then looked into Dayan's face. "And finally the two groups met—exhausted, hungry and thirsty—with many dying. Everyone tried to find out where they were going, but nobody could answer. They were blocked, pushed and smashed from both sides by the two enemies."

Dayan felt sick. Still, the Pole's information didn't surprise him. Rather, it confirmed bloody fantasies he'd been carrying in his thoughts already. "But only the scorpions should be smashed and destroyed—they were surrounded by scorpions!" he cried.

The Pole didn't ask what he meant by scorpions. Though he couldn't know the symbolism of the intertwined swastika and the hammer and sickle, the word alone told the story. He only nodded somberly.

"A peasant in a train told me that—when I was going away from home," Dayan said. "It's the scorpions," he repeated, "not the people!"

They were in agreement, and continued talking about the histories of their two homelands, and how both had been soaked by the blood of their respective people for centuries. "And yet," said the Pole, "it is out of such anguish and suffering that great epic poems are born." He pointed to the line where the Nazis and Bolsheviks met. "A great poem will spread from here, until it covers all of Poland."

"One day," Dayan said, "I would like to translate that poem."

The Pole put a hand on Dayan's shoulder. "You must. So you're a poet?"

Dayan was momentarily silent, remembering that his only poetic creation so far was the poem he'd composed for Goritza, *I will return, Mother*. But since Goritza barely read, Dayan hadn't even written down the words, let alone gotten them published. Still, if Goritza loved them, that was enough. Finally, he said, "In some ways."

The Pole started to say something, but Dayan interrupted quickly. "Let's talk about religion," he said, "I mean prophets, or prophecy."

"Such as?"

"The old prophecy about the coming day when the people fleeing from both sides will meet, as you Poles did. Does that mean the end of the world?"

"I agree this is a downfall of mankind, the failure to destroy those who smashed the people from both sides; the shame of those who stood by, or turned their backs and let it happen. The sociologists would think the same. You, as a poet, must interpret this and see more than just the facts. You must see it as the priests, or as the prophets, would."

Dayan felt the Pole was entrusting him with more responsibility than he was ready to shoulder. "Let's go for a walk," he suggested, searching for a way to change the conversation.

But the Pole wasn't to be distracted. "From now on," he said, "the historians and poets should join forces, should look with the same eyes at these victims whose fate I have seen."

Dayan realized again that the Pole was thinking of him as a poet or a priest, for the old man continued. "Those whose blood soaked Warsaw, and those who were there when the victims of the Nazis and Soviets met, have seen far worse. And the world must be told." He shook his head slowly and closed his eyes for a moment. When he opened them, he looked directly into Dayan's dark, troubled ones. "Worse things have happened—things almost impossible to believe!"

Dayan looked at him fearfully now, being afraid of what would follow.

"Those thousands who vanished," the Pole murmured in a low voice, almost to himself, "also vanished from under the eyes of Almighty God Himself."

Dayan's mouth felt dry. He was dizzy, and the old man's face seemed to blur. He swallowed and took a deep breath as his companion continued. "Your countryman, Princip, assassinated the future Austro-Hungarian Czar in 1914, and the world knew where he was—what prison he was in. Now, not even God knows the place where tens of thousands of our people, Jews and Poles alike, have been taken. They've dropped out of sight completely. Gone. Vanished!"

"Impossible!" Dayan proclaimed.

"Yes, so it would seem. But it's true. I myself escaped twice from among them." He sighed briefly to pause. "I was lucky when I got away. And that's why I'm nameless. Now I have to be." He turned, taking Dayan by the arm, and they began walking.

At the pier they paused at the fishmonger where Dayan had wanted to buy Tobo's fish last week. The owner had sold some since then, but made up a new package, which he assured Dayan was of the highest quality. "I have only the best for a soldier, a Pole, or a refugee!"

With Tobo's treat tucked safely inside his largest pocket, Dayan turned to say good-bye to the old man, since his nameless friend couldn't go with him through the town. He was forbidden to fraternize with military personnel and wisely avoided it anyways.

All the way back to his garrison Dayan thought of the Pole's words. His entreaty that the fate of the vanished people be made known to the world drummed in the young man's ears—and was indeed to shape his entire life. He was awed by the task he faced. For this wasn't a matter of chanting a happy song from the branches of a blooming cherry tree under which Goritza sat, placidly spinning lambs wool to knit his socks. This message was a bloody one, a message of terror, and one which carried a threat to the person delivering it. All this Dayan knew, but he confronted the knowledge without flinching.

Disregarding the bumps and jerks of the baggage train where he was with the leather equipment stacked around him, Dayan pulled out the map of Poland the old man had given him from his pocket and began to write on the back of it. The words on the page were irregular and some were blurred, but what they said was crystal clear. Dayan had written not a poem, but a letter—one which would cost him much suffering.

Back at the garrison he was reprimanded for giving the fish to Tobo, who was in trouble now. "It must make him want to get drunk," the sergeant complained. "As a result, he swiped a bottle of wine this past hour we'd been saving from the King's birthday celebration. You'd better find him before we do."

Dayan went out and guessed where to find Tobo, out by a potato pit behind the stables. There he was as Dayan had predicted, avoiding others while happily eating his fish.

"Finish your meal," Dayan told him. "Then you better give the wine back to the sergeant, he's looking for you. There's also something I want to show you. I want your opinion."

Tobo swallowed his bite and carefully wrapped up the remaining fish. "The wine, and you want my opinion too!" he exclaimed. "My God, why me? Who am I? But go ahead—fire away!"

Dayan smiled as he pulled the map out of his pocket, knowing the fisherman was full of pride at being consulted. "Here it is on the back of this, maybe I'd better make copies, then you can read it first and pass it along to the others."

Tobo hesitated. "You know I don't read too well, or even write any words—they always look like chicken-scratches." He stuffed the packet of fish into his tunic pocket and shrugged, looking up at Dayan eagerly. "But I can learn by heart! I'm real good at that. Then I could say it aloud in the market, if that's what you want."

Dayan shook his head. "That won't do."

"But why not? You know what a big voice I have. I even scare the hell out of the mules when I shout at them. My voice flies clear across the Danube, like the birds!"

"This is different, Tobo," Dayan said seriously. "It's written to be read. And, the person who wrote it might be thrown in jail."

Tobo was startled.

"It's happened before," Dayan told him somberly.

"Oh, come off it!" Tobo laughed. "Scholars don't get thrown into jail. Only drunkards like me."

"Scholars, too," Dayan insisted. He clutched the paper in his hand, shaking it gently. "But for this I wouldn't mind it."

Tobo shook his head incredulously. "Right now thrown in the jail, then maybe stuck there until winter? Listen, if they put you in I'll break the wall down, so help me! We'll escape to the river. Lots of willows and huts down there. We can hide. Now read."

"Okay," Dayan said, "but remember, a man must never escape nor weep. My father told me that many times."

"He's wrong about escaping," Tobo asserted. "You must escape. But I've never wept."

Dayan decided to drop the question for now. He began to read from the text about the people killed in the Nazi air-raids on Warsaw, and about the people who fled to the east and the others who fled to the west. Then of their meeting together in hopelessness and despair, and the unknown fate of those who'd vanished from among them.

Tobo was shaken. He asked Dayan to show him where Warsaw was on the map, and crossed himself, kissing the place Dayan indicated. "Where are they now—the lost people?" he asked sadly.

"Who knows! Maybe some are in Siberia and Germany, and others were buried." Dayan looked to the north, where the hazy silhouette of Belgrade could be seen against the sky. That same Belgrade, now seat of a supposedly neutral government. Meanwhile, Tobo's damp eyes were concentrated on the map showing the pillaged country of the victims now devoured by two aggressors.

The fisherman began to walk away. "Let's go," he said, while grabbing Dayan's arm. "We'll tell them, tell everyone about what's happened."

Dayan pounded him on the shoulder. "But look at you. You're almost in tears!"

"Nobody's ever told me anything so terrible before, so frightening. If it happened to them, it could happen to us too."

Dayan took his arm in a reassuring gesture. "Pull yourself together, Soldier." he said. "How will you recite at the market otherwise?"

"Don't worry, I can do that. I swear I can, my professor." Tobo quickly wiped his face with the sleeve of his tunic. Then he knelt down and began digging into the bottom of the potato pit with his bare hands. Finally, he gave a little exclamation and rose with something in his hands. He held it out to Dayan. "Here!" he said. "Give it to the Sarge, otherwise some of the guys won't get their Christmas leave."

It was the bottle of wine the sergeant had complained about. Dayan took it, and Tobo settled down to finish eating his smoked fish. Dayan found the sergeant at his desk neatly inking a new column in the company's inventory book. "They want me to put down the exact number of holes in all of the harnesses and reins," he complained. "It's sabotage! When are we going to be trained to fight for our King?"

"The King doesn't need you, Sarge. But something does."

"Yeah? Like what?"

Dayan pulled the wine bottle from his military blouse. "The lost is found," he said. "You seemed to be worried about this?"

The sergeant reacted happily at seeing the wine bottle. He reached out for it and held it against his chest protectively. "Naturally," he said, "we need it for Christmas. Where did you unearth it?"

Dayan was secretly amused at the aptness of his question. "Never mind. But how would you feel if thousands of people disappeared. Would that worry you?"

"Of course. It would worry anyone."

This response was as encouraging as Tobo's reaction had been. Dayan took the map from his pocket and, while sitting at the sergeant's desk, wrote a letter to his troop commander asking permission to establish a military newspaper, like the American soldiers had done during the First World War. He said he'd illustrate its front page with a reproduction of *The Massacre of the Innocents* by the painter Karel van Mander, which would illustrate the atrocities committed against the conquered European countries.

He'd also write a poem, he said, about the vanished Poles to be published in the paper. All this, he summed up at the end of the letter, would serve as a warning to his own country. It's the most important service he could render now, until the time came to fight in defense of Yugoslavia.

He handed the map to the sergeant and watched eagerly as the man read it. But this time the reaction was disappointing. The sergeant sniffed disdainfully while he scanned the words quickly. "I can't put this through," he said. "In the first place, it smells of fish. Besides, you'll probably have your Christmas leave cancelled when the higher-ups take a look at it. They might even put you in jail for it."

Dayan pointed to the text of his letter. "But I state clearly that I accept all responsibility. Please try."

Two weeks later Dayan got his answer when he was summoned before his troop commander and informed that he wouldn't be sent to Belgrade anymore. He was also instructed that he could only make requests orally, and that senseless requests would be denied. Finally, he was told his Christmas leave was postponed for one month. Dayan was left stunned.

5

And Back At Home

The tranquility in Cablo during a late January evening in 1941 was disturbed only by the sound of Dayan's army boots crunching into the hardened snow, and by the howling of a lone wolf up in the forest. When Dayan eventually saw the light shining from his parents' cottage, he became worried. *They don't know I'm coming, so why are they up so late?* He ran the last quarter-mile and rushed up to look through the icy window.

Inside, he saw both Thomash and Goritza sitting by the hearth keeping themselves warm. After his father threw some sticks on the fire, Dayan saw in the flickering light that his mother was knitting.

Then he heard her ask, "Do the soldiers wear their socks high, to the knees?"

"Could be," Thomash replied.

Goritza measured the sock's length by the span of her palm. "I wonder if he's grown taller in the army?"

"Probably. At his age, they usually do." Thomash threw more kindling and the flames shined brightly out through the window, reddening the snow in the yard.

Dayan stood for a moment, watching. Then, so as not to startle his parents too much with a sudden entry, he walked back to the orchard. From there he began singing Goritza's song, the one he'd created for her—*I will return, Mother*.

Goritza jumped up and hurried to the door with her face radiant, the knitting instantly forgotten in her hands. She flung her arms around her son's neck and embraced him with tears in her eyes. Thomash followed her just as pleased, but was slightly restrained due to his worsening health. The questioning which went on when they were all settled by the fire was easy for Dayan. The theme they both asked him was the same: *How have you been? How do you feel? Do you get enough food? Are you warm enough?*

After things settled down Goritza measured the sock against Dayan's foot, from his big toe to above his ankle, to see if it would fit properly. "All right. Never mind!" she said to Thomash when he laughed. "You're not a mother, you don't know how we feel!" This was her old refrain, and Thomash knew better than to continue mocking her, no matter how lovingly.

Finally, they lit the gas lamp and sat around the table. The questions now became more specific from his mother: *Who mends your socks? Does the rain trickle down your neck? Do you have a proper coat? Do they have fires and hearths in the army? Have you been giving any speeches like that time in Gradina?* Patiently Dayan replied to all of these as best he could.

Now it was Thomash's turn. His questions were strictly military: *Where are the armies now of the two dogs, Hitler and Mussolini? What makes them so powerful? What will England and America do?*

He was interrupted here by Goritza asking, "Why do the soldiers on Gradina's training grounds keep running in circles?" Then she wanted to hear again about the food in the army. But before Dayan could repeat his answer to this question, she jumped up. "You must be hungry from your journey. I'll make us something to eat."

While his mother prepared supper, Thomash finally had his son to himself. He wanted to know about the young King: *Do you ever see him? How does he look? Have you ever marched before him? Does this young King talk to the soldiers like his father and grandfather did?* These questions were harder for Dayan to answer, since the thousands of holes in the harnesses he'd counted as punishment during Christmas were still parading before his eyes.

But now supper was on the table and Goritza offered Grace after the three of them sat down together. "Thanks, Lord, for blessing us all here tonight. Welcome back home, Son!" It was kept brief since she'd noticed Dayan's hair was missing its usual thick, bushy waves. She leaned towards him and tenderly touched his short-cropped hair.

"We've stayed up each night ever since Christmas, waiting for you," she said. After supper it was agreed that Goritza would go to bed, while Thomash and Dayan could talk for a while longer—on condition that they watch the fire carefully; Goritza had heard about a child being almost burned last week. Another condition: Dayan must devote most of tomorrow to answering more of her questions—she hadn't even started yet!

Dayan sensed how they looked forward to tomorrow, and would enjoy it all the more after a good night's sleep. Still, there were things he wanted to do for himself.

"But tomorrow I want to go to Gradina," he insisted.

Goritza almost shouted, her tone and indignation shocking him. "What! We've hardly seen you tonight. You haven't even taken your boots off, and now you talk of leaving!"

"Only to Gradina. Tomorrow is the celebration of Saint Sava at the school, I was thinking," Dayan said, "that I might give another speech. Mother, you remember the last one?"

Thomash said gruffly, "Let our son go."

Goritza, softened by remembering her pride when she'd seen Dayan giving his speech at the Gradina High gymnasium, finally relented.

"I'll be back the day after tomorrow, at dusk," Dayan promised eagerly. "Be sure to keep the door open. I like to see the firelight shining outside."

"Then you'll stay until your hair grows longer?"

Dayan laughed. "Not so long as that girl you saw at the school two years ago."

Goritza looked searchingly at her son. "So that's why you're going to Gradina?"

But Thomash came to his rescue. "Leave the soldier alone," he said.

Goritza gave up. She blew out the lamp, said a prayer before the icon of Saint George, then warned Dayan once more like he's a three-year-old to carefully watch the fire, and at last went to bed.

Now Dayan and Thomash sat by the fire again. When he was especially curious about something, Thomash threw more kindling on the fire as he asked a question, so he could study his son's expression in the brightened firelight. He did this when he repeated his question as to whether Dayan had marched in any parades before the young King. As the fire slowly died, Dayan was relieved.

He asked Thomash if there was any progress on his grandfather's monument, and his father said there was, but having the inscription design would make it go faster.

"I've thought a lot about it, Father," Dayan told him. "One idea is to have a cross with the words—*IN HOC SIGNO VINCES*—engraved underneath it. This became the Emperor Constantine's motto after he saw a vision of it before a battle he'd won."

Thomash said nothing, but his expression showed he was curious.

"He was the first Christian Emperor," Dayan told him. He poked the logs in the fireplace so they formed a cross, while Thomash tried carefully to say the Latin words.

The burning logs cast sufficient light for the young man to draw a cross, with the words written under it, on a piece of paper he took from his pocket. "We'll do it exactly like this. I'll write out the words for you." He looked up at his father, whose intent eyes were concentrated on the design.

"*IN HOC SIGNO VINCES*, what does it mean?"

Dayan drew in a deep breath, as this was a very important moment for him. While Thomash was now gazing at him, he slowly exhaled, then looked into the fire, and then back into his father's eyes.

"It means," he said at last, "*Through This Sign, Thou Shalt Conquer.*"

Then, though his heart was pounding and his face flushed by the significance of those words, he made an attempt to appear matter-of-fact. Raising his right arm, he stretched it out above the hearth. "I think the cross should be about this size on the monument," he told Thomash.

He could see from his father's expression that the meaning of the words, and the drawing on the little piece of paper, hadn't been clear to him. With a gesture of resignation, he threw the paper into the fire. It made a small flame that formed a halo around Thomash's head, but Dayan was reluctant to look at his father now. "I'll make a better drawing when I come back from Gradina," he promised.

"Do. And make it larger," Thomash said. "We'll light the lamp for that."

The next day Dayan was the first to appear in front of Dr. Vedrano's office in Gradina, and gradually others gathered there as well. At last Dr. Vedrano came to the door. He nodded his head, acknowledging the greetings of the waiting people in line. Since Dayan was at the front, he was the first to enter and be seated.

His former school director wore the wrinkled uniform of an anti-aircraft private. His boots were muddy, and he looked tired and sleepy. The two soldiers greeted each other warmly.

"You'll be welcomed by the senior students at the dance tonight," Dr. Vedrano told Dayan.

"Thanks, I'll be there, of course." He then hesitated. "Dr. Vedrano—why would you be drafted?"

Dr. Vedrano smiled ruefully, shaking his head. "It wouldn't be so bad, but I haven't enough time for it. For example, I've got just this one day's leave to arrange for the Saint Sava celebration. But you, you're lucky. At least you're in a position to be learning something."

Dayan lowered his head. The doctor looked surprised.

"Well, aren't you?"

"You might call it learning," Dayan replied. "Counting holes in leather equipment." He laughed wryly. "You'd be surprised how many holes there are! I carefully enter them into the inventory books."

Dr. Vedrano smiled. "So that makes two of us! And I'm the one lying in the mud by the cannons counting stars."

"Well, at least you're outside in the night, under the sky."

"Ah, and you're still a poet!"

"I want to be. I need to be," Dayan replied quickly. He sighed. "There are things I couldn't tell my father last night. I tried to, but...if only you'd listen..."

"Of course I will!" Dr. Vedrano said warmly. "Go ahead, my boy. Talk!"

Dayan was relieved. He was glad he hadn't succumbed last night to the inquiring expressions on his father's face when he asked those questions about a parade.

"I particularly didn't want to talk about parades," he told Dr. Vedrano.

The doctor looked puzzled. "Parades? Some people find them impressive," he said. "There are all sorts, after all. For some, they provide excitement, even romance. Perhaps your father is one of those."

"I mean military parades," Dayan said intensely. "Something happened...I saw something...or maybe I didn't actually, but it seemed like I did." He sighed.

"Tell me about it," Dr. Vedrano said, realizing that the young man was troubled.

"It was a crystal clear day," Dayan began slowly. "This parade was to honor a new general. The soldiers' bayonets were held tight against their shoulders, pointing at the sky in the normal way. Except that..."

"Yes? What happened?"

Dayan's face contorted. "It seemed to me that some dark clouds hovered over those pointing bayonets, and blood began coming down, all around. To me it was Plutarch's *bloody rain*. I was sickened—horrified, and my face must have revealed it; maybe I looked like I was in pain. Actually, it was pain, but not in the way they thought." He shrugged. "To my officer, it appeared that my boots were on too tight. He ordered me out of the ranks."

"And did you tell him what you'd seen?"

"Oh, no sir." Dayan said somberly. "I knew better than that. They later punished me for not having the sense to wear proper shoes for the parade."

Dr. Vedrano nodded thoughtfully. "Dayan, I believe you're right when you say you *must* be a poet; you've been charged with a solemn duty." He cupped his chin in his right hand, in a gesture of deep concentration. "Only the poet sees blood before it's been shed." The director spoke slowly, groping his way through the words. "The poet—and also as any mother does. The others only recognize the tragedy after the fact, for they were concerned solely with day-to-day routines as life follows a normal course year-after-year through the centuries. For these people, the poet must act as their eyes and ears—and yes, even their heart as well. Only then can dying men become entities, and not merely statistics to be written down and forgotten."

Greatly moved, Dayan turned from Dr. Vedrano to look at the volumes of books contained on his shelves. He was giving himself time to swallow the lump which had grown in his throat—time to see through his eyes which held tears. Dimly he perceived that one of the books appeared to be new. It was titled: *Diocletian versus Christians.* At last he had control of himself and turned to confront the older man.

"But I'm not a poet—not yet," he said. "I might be to my mother, or some fisherman from the Danube. But not like you are," and he nodded his head toward the professor's diploma on the wall, which credited him as the author of a dissertation on Virgil and Pindar.

"To me," Dr. Vedrano said seriously, "you're as much of a poet as I am."

Dayan searched in his mind for a word of significant respect. He felt that the word *professor*, which Tobo the fisherman had applied to him, wasn't eloquent enough for this occasion. Finally, he said, "Thank you, my *teacher*," and as he spoke the word he was grateful and confident that he'd chosen it well.

It was a proud night in the gymnasium. At the small hall the first senior class dance was in progress, under the supervision of certain parents who'd been assigned as chaperones. While in the big hall the professors along with civilian and military dignitaries were gathered with the parents, who were free to enjoy themselves. There was much going back and forth as people strolled from one hall to the other. Major Hillarich, resplendent in a uniform reserved for such gala occasions, led off the King's Circle as the music began in the big hall, offering his right hand to the wife of Gradina's mayor. His own wife was at his left.

Others joined in, forming a large circle. Dr. Vedrano, in his role as host, now dressed in a black tuxedo, took the center with his wife. When the dance was over Hillarich thanked both ladies, kissed their hands, and led them to their seats. Then he approached Dr. Vedrano, whose greeting to him with something less than joyful. Hillarich knew quite well why this was, and hastened an attempt to vindicate himself.

"Some wretch who should have known better fouled things up, Dr. Vedrano," he began, with every appearance of honest regret. "Obviously, you didn't deserve to be drafted. And believe me, whoever was responsible is in for it!"

Dr. Vedrano listened without replying, having a sardonic smile on his face. Meanwhile, Dayan had become the center of attention among his former schoolmates, who wanted to hear all about the university and military life in Belgrade; they were more interested in this than in dancing to the music coming from the aging phonograph.

"If you'd put it all in the form of an interview," one student suggested, after listening to Dayan with wide-eyed interest, "we could feature it in the next issue of the school newspaper, for all to read."

"Okay," Dayan promised. "Be glad to."

The student happily hurried away and returned with a girl he described as the secretary of the literary group. Dayan eagerly began to introduce himself, and thus didn't catch her name before the others went off to dance.

Someone had put a tango record on the phonograph and the lyrics were typical of such music. *You'll fall in love when we meet...Cause this hot blood boils in you; Then the world's all nice and sweet...As your wildest dreams end up true.*

Dayan asked his companion if she'd like to dance, but her expression told him she was too shy. Instead, she took a pencil and some paper from her pocket like a mature reporter, and with an attempt at formality, she asked: "How do you feel when you wear that uniform, are you ever afraid?" Then she stopped, as they both spotted Major Hillarich waltzing past them with Senora Laguna, wife of the editor of *The Progressive Voice*, the weekly newspaper in Gradina.

"Did you know," Dayan's companion whispered, "that Hillarich is now the commandant?"

"And what if he is? I'm not afraid!" Dayan replied strongly while faking surprise. He found her shyness to be attractive, and wanted to show off. "Miss...?" he asked, looking down at her.

"Moravaz. Angelica Moravaz. I'll be graduating this year." She glanced rather wistfully at the paper in her hand. It was still blank, but she hesitated to ask any more questions.

"Here," Dayan said, "I'll give you an interview." He stood up straight, stroked at an imaginary beard and began talking in a mock-serious tone, with a solemn expression on his face.

"The influence of environment in rearing the younger generation cannot be over-emphasized. Its importance must never be neglected by society and the educational world. It's their common duty to create a proper climate." Here Dayan looked to see if she was keeping up with him; she was scribbling as fast as she could.

He continued, "It has long been my observation that the difference between the intellectual attainments of a country youth and one raised in the city is that the first, out of necessity, contributes while he learns to the environment in which he lives. In fact, the more he gives, the better for him. His own scholarship is thereby enriched and stimulated—if he teaches the shepherdesses how to write by scratching words on rocks in the hills."

"You're talking about your own life!" Angelica interrupted eagerly, forgetting her shyness.

Dayan smiled. "How did you know?"

"Well, ever since you gave that speech two years ago, we all know it, and your father's story too."

Dayan was glad that she was at ease now. The tango record had ended and since they were standing near the phonograph they turned it over. It was another tango: *Have you ever been lucky to love or be loved?*

"Please—let's dance," Dayan urged.

But Angelica pretended not to hear him. She was looking towards the small hall.

"Angelica, tell me something about yourself." He'd given up trying to persuade her to dance, at least for the moment.

Finally, she looked up at him, smiling faintly. "What's there to say? Let's see. Well, my father is a teacher. Soon we'll move to Belgrade."

"To Belgrade! What district?"

"I don't know really. Father says it's *the teacher's colony*." She looked rather fearfully back at Major Hillarich, and then quickly looked away again. "Is it true that he can put half the town in jail?" she asked in a low voice.

"Of course not!" Dayan replied with a conviction he didn't really feel.

"Well, I know he can draft anyone he wants, he drafted you and Dr. Vedrano. Everyone knows why, too. Because of the ash trees near your village."

Now Dayan looked around cautiously before he replied. "But nobody's selling ash trees anymore."

"Thanks to Dr. Vedrano, but it's too bad Cablo is so poor again."

Chapter 5

Dayan wished she wouldn't be so serious. He didn't want to think about solemn, unhappy things tonight. He tried to grasp her hand. "Come on, Angelica, let's dance! Everyone does it in my village, even though we're poor."

She stepped back.

"It's a tango, easy," he urged. "Just follow my steps."

Still, she held back, shaking her head. "I've never danced with anyone—except along with my family," she told him.

"No? But you're at a dance, don't worry," for he made a move to take her around the waist, when they were interrupted by a loud voice.

A young lieutenant in dress uniform shouted: "Any military men around? We're all on alert to return!" He swayed as though he'd had several drinks too many.

"Here, sir." Dayan reluctantly stood at attention.

"Good! Get me back to the barracks at Gradina, there's a good man," said the lieutenant. He staggered and Dayan put out a hand to steady him. The young officer smiled rather foolishly. "Thanks," he said, "come on." Turning to Angelica he said, "Don't worry, pretty one. He may be back soon if it's a false alarm. By the way, I'm lieutenant Pavlovich. Just call me Bora-Flute." He leaned on Dayan's arm.

"See you later," Dayan said hurriedly to Angelica as he started out. Over his shoulder he called to her, "I'll have to come back and get the phonograph—to return it. Please tell them, will you?"

Angelica nodded. The music had stopped and the officers in the group were leaving slowly and quietly.

"Get a move on, you're ordered back to duty!" Major Hillarich shouted while rushing up to the men, and now they began to hurry out to the street, where a line of carriages were waiting to take them back through town. When Dayan came up to one of them with his drunken lieutenant in tow, intending to ride back and see him safely to his quarters, one of the officers grabbed at his charge and pulled him rather roughly up towards a seat. At the same time another officer shoved Dayan back as he attempted to climb into the carriage.

"You'll walk back to the barracks," he ordered.

Dayan stepped back to the road and shrugged. He preferred to walk in the night air anyways, and his dignity wasn't offended simply because the officers were opposed to sharing a vehicle with a lowly private. He strode forward, breathing deeply.

At Shark Street he found the area still packed with soldiers and non-commissioned officers, busy leaving the various bars and dim rooms from all directions. This was continuously followed by calls directed at them from women at nearby windows. Some were complaining, others were cheerful and inviting, and others got insulting. Remembering his earlier experience here, Dayan moved past with guilty thoughts swirling through his mind.

Upon reaching the large training grounds in front of Gradina's garrison building, he encountered a large gathering of officers, animals and equipment now forming. The officers, still in dress uniform, mounted their horses and were led by Major Hillarich. Quickly they all took their places in front of their units. It was bitter cold; the sky was bright with stars.

Dayan joined a small medical unit near the gate, where he found the same drunken lieutenant he'd put into the carriage. Too confused to find his own unit, the lieutenant was bragging loudly about his subordinates: "Those bastards had the time of their lives on Shark Street!" He then began to sing an indecent song about Hitler.

Major Hillarich brought the entire formation of troops to abrupt attention with a sharp command: "Soldiers! Attention!" he roared. "Dark clouds at this very moment are hanging over us all!"

The listening men shifted uneasily, their boots crunching on the hard ground. Others were still arriving, creating confusion as they sought to find their units. There was the sound of clanking and rattling metal as equipment was shouldered or sometimes dropped. The horses beat the frosty earth with their hooves, and from everywhere came the sound of heavy coughs, the result of miserable winter colds.

Chapter 5

Despite all this racket, Major Hillarich's voice was clearly audible as he bellowed his speech, lauding the troops for their quick response to the alert and boasting that even a potential member of the Academy of Science had joined forces with them.

If he expected an enthusiastic response to this announcement—none came, so he hurried on, demanding a general salute of *three shouts for the King*. "And I want that salute to be so loud that the stars fall down and the moon trembles! Come on, now. Long live the King!"

Obediently the troops roared in echo to the major's shout: "Long live the King! Long live the King! Long live the King!"

Dayan's voice wasn't part of that tribute. He was whispering to himself over and over again the same words: *Teacher's colony—Angelica Moravaz.*

Major Hillarich was dissatisfied with the salute the men had made. "That wouldn't even bring a blossom down from a peach tree," he said angrily. "Now, let me hear a real salute to our beloved King!"

Only a handful of soldiers heard him, for the first salute had frightened the horses, who were rearing up on their hind legs and neighing or blowing through their noses. Some of them even tried to throw off their riders and gallop away. Disregarding this commotion, Major Hillarich then ordered still another third salute, an order which nobody paid attention to.

Those not busy quieting their horses were absorbed in watching a drama they didn't quite understand. Bora-Flute, the drunken lieutenant, was now being carried away on a stretcher by Dayan and three members of the medical team. The soldiers closest were watching anxiously or curiously, and their concerns were transmitted to others who couldn't see. But this didn't bother Dayan; he was more than happy to accomplish what the horses couldn't do, and escape—before this farce of an assembly got any worse.

At dusk the following day, preparations at the Costovar cottage in Cablo had already been completed. Firewood was stacked neatly by the door, wine was poured into bottles, and the lamp was filled. Expecting a large crowd of villagers, they'd borrowed extra chairs from neighbors, and these were arranged around the room.

"Oh, I wish the night would come," Goritza exclaimed. "Then he'd be here already!"

"He'll be here, don't worry," Thomash told her.

"And I wish Yana didn't go and marry Lazar. She could serve the wine."

"You complain, even when our son is returning?"

Goritza quickly covered her mouth with her hand, showing that she took back her words.

Thomash reminded her of the poem about a Serbian Czar on whose right shoulder stood Saint Michael the Archangel, caressing the Czar's face with his wings while he served the guests. But when the Czar sat down with his guests, the Archangel became angry and slapped the Czar's face before flying away.

"That won't happen to me!" Thomash promised, excited at the prospect of being host to their friends on this joyful occasion.

Goritza agreed, adding that she'd help him serve the wine. "Oh, it's going to be such a fine party!" she said. She looked the happiest she had since Dayan left. Thomash was glad he'd been able to divert her momentarily, so the time would go faster until their son arrived.

"It's getting darker," she said. "I'll watch from the door. He always looks so big with the long shadow behind him!"

Uncle Dimitrye and Theodore were among the first to arrive. Auntie Stephanie followed them with a full basket of dried fruit, insisting she was as happy as if Nashko was coming home. All the guests had found an excuse to come early, and everyone followed Uncle Dimitrye's example by refusing to accept wine until Dayan arrived.

Goritza scarcely had time to answer people's questions about Dayan. Pretending to watch over the fire, she kept running back and forth to the kindling by the door, bringing back just a few sticks, pausing each time to peer hopefully into the darkness.

Finally, she turned from the doorway. "Thanks Lord! Now he comes!" she announced excitedly. Then she added in a worried voice, "But he's not alone. Hurry, Thomash! Light the lamp!" She held the door wide open.

Everybody got up to make room for the expected guests while Goritza stood by the open door. They all heard a loud voice and the tread of heavy boots in the snow. "This cottage is the furthest from Gradina," an authoritative voice announced. "And has the worst road," added another, in a somewhat milder voice.

Then they appeared in the light; two gendarmes from Gradina wearing heavy overcoats and with scarves wound loosely around their necks.

"Good evening," said the loud-voiced one. "Is this the Costovar home?"

His partner made a general nod in the direction of the gathered villagers.

"Good evening, gentlemen," Thomash replied, as he placed the unlit lamp back on the table. "Yes, so long as we live, this house bears our name. Why do you ask? Is there something wrong?" He spoke firmly and with dignity, but his heart was beating fast.

"No, nothing's wrong," the loud-voiced one replied. "So you're Thomash Costovar?"

"That's right. Will you sit down?" Thomash looked over his shoulder anxiously; Goritza had rushed to St. George's icon. She stood before it, moaning, with her hands crossed over her chest. Auntie Stephanie and another woman were trying to comfort her.

Thomash turned back and walked closer to the two gendarmes, waiting politely for them to continue.

The two men looked into his face intently, but without revealing their thoughts. After a pause, the spokesman said, "Your son Dayan has been sent back to his garrison. Belgrade, I believe. The orders may have come by telegram."

"Telegram? Belgrade? But why?"

"The country's in danger of..." the other, apparently gentler man began, but his taller companion stepped on his foot.

Goritza had left the icon and walked trembling towards the doorway. "What—what's happened?" she asked falteringly.

"There was an alert of some foreign planes," the shorter man began, but he was stopped once more by his superior, who stated: "He wants to say—we're only doing our duty."

"Yes, yes, of course," Thomash replied. He pulled himself together. "Will you have a glass of wine?" he asked politely, drawing Goritza back towards the table and gesturing to the men that they should enter.

They both did so, then accepted a small glass of wine, and praised it as the best in the district. They remarked on how helpful a nip was in this cold weather, then thanked their hosts and departed, leaving a stricken silence behind them. It went on, with nobody saying a word, while the flames of the fire flickered out and died. The villagers sat with their heads bowed, some with their faces covered by their hands.

Finally, Thomash put some dry wood on the fire and the flames leaped and crackled again. The people slowly lifted their heads, their somber faces glowing in the rosy light.

Thomash went up to Goritza, who was half-supported by one of the women in front of the icon. "He's gone," she keened. "My son is gone."

"You didn't hear what they said," Thomash told her. "The country is in danger. They sent a telegram for him to report. Maybe the King himself gave the order. We should all be proud!"

"Of Dayan? Yes, but..."

"But what, woman? He's *needed*. The wires are still humming all across the mountains and into the valleys. Humming and singing the name of Costovar, for everybody to hear. Dayan Costovar, our son, called to defend his country." Thomash handed his wife a bottle. "Here. A toast to all! To King and Country!"

Goritza tried to drink and the villagers, their faces shining in the warm glow of the fire, watched her. "I'm sorry, I can't swallow," she said.

Chapter 5

The villagers stirred, but no one spoke. Then Uncle Dimitrye said, "Yes, we should all prepare! Time to go home everybody," and people rose and followed him out. They listened to his instructions that they must obey any order from the authorities in Gradina to deliver hay and oats for the military horses, as they had on the eve of the last war.

After the brief farewells and the sound of their footsteps had died out, a new silence descended on the Costovar cottage. With his crutch—Thomash made a cross with the logs in the fireplace as Dayan had done two nights before. He could hear Dayan's voice: "*Exactly like this. I'll write out the words for you.*" Only two nights ago, and now he was gone.

"Say something," Goritza begged.

"I can't."

"And you're a man."

"It's because I feel guilty. I told him to go."

"You sent him away? After we'd scarcely seen him or talked to him?" She began to cry again.

"No, not just now," he told her. "Long ago. I told that major in Gradina to summon him if the country needed him. And me too." Thomash then turned his face from his wife, and watched the crossed logs in the fireplace as they slowly burned.

Goritza put her arms around him. "God sent him away," she said, "and He'll bring him back."

"Yes, yes!" Thomash said, relieved at her change of mood. "Now let's make a toast to Dayan!"

Quickly Goritza handed him the bottle. She lit the lamp, whose beams were reflected on St. George's icon, and put a big pile of dry wood on the fire. Then she opened the door wide.

They began to drink the wine, while the bright firelight filled the house as it danced on the walls, and then it fanned out through the open doorway far into the darkness. Soon the voices of Thomash and Goritza could be heard singing in unison: "*I will return, Mother!*"

6

They Dance In Circles

It was a pleasant Sunday to start off spring when Dayan Costovar met Angelica Moravaz, her father Philip and her mother in front of the Pavilion of Arts in Belgrade. This was their first meeting since Angelica's family had moved to the capital. The Pavilion was holding an art exhibit today displaying paintings done by Yugoslav artists who'd studied in France, with the proceeds from ticket sales to be spent on behalf of French prisoners in Germany.

In order to avoid offending the German and Italian embassies, the exhibit was simply called—*The Annual Exhibit*; this ambiguity made it possible for one of the King's delegates to appear at the opening.

As the two young people and her parents attempted to enter, they were stopped at the door by a man in a blue uniform. "This isn't the thing for soldiers," he told Dayan. "Too many civilians. Better come another day."

"The King's delegate is a soldier," Dayan said.

"Sure, but he's a general!" The doorman moved his head in the direction of a nearby park. "Why don't you go sit in the sunshine over there? Boy, I wish I could!" He motioned Angelica's mother and father to go in.

"You go ahead," Dayan told them. "I'll wait here."

But her parents didn't want to leave Dayan, and neither did Angelica. The four people clustered by the entrance, looking around undecided, and this bothered the attendant. "There's a spring dance today," he told the young people. "Why don't you go to it? Much better than staring at paintings."

Dayan sensed encouragement from Angelica's parents. He asked quickly, "Well, where is it, and how do we get there?"

"Just outside the city limits. Take the tram to Opera Plaza, then go to the end of the line and walk a couple hundred yards."

During this exchange Angelica had read in her parents' eyes that it was all right with them. There was but one condition: Dayan must bring her home before sunset. With this agreed upon, the elders went to look at the paintings and the two of them started off together quickly.

As they passed the Monument of Gratitude dedicated to France by Yugoslavia for its help in the First World War, they saw an old woman selling violets from a little cart. Dayan bought two bunches, and gave one to Angelica. The other he placed gently at the foot of the monument, beneath the words chiseled in the stone: *WE LOVE FRANCE AS SHE LOVED US.*

Turning back towards Angelica, he saw that she'd put some of the flowers in her hair and was looking down at the fragrant cluster in her hand, her eyes shining. This was the first bouquet anyone had ever given to her. Lightly Dayan touched the blossoms in her hair.

"Beautiful."

"Thank you. I'll keep them even after they fade. My first."

Looking back in time, Dayan realized that these were the first flowers he'd ever bought or given to a girl, not counting the wild lilies he'd gathered in the hills near Cablo, nor the violets he'd brought to his mother from the woods when he was a child.

"They're my first too," he told Angelica.

She smiled, and they continued walking happily side by side. He had an impulse to grab her hand, but thought better of it. Besides, soon they'd be dancing.

Outside the opera house there was an announcement for *Aida*, a performance on Easter Sunday which wasn't far off. "I'll take you to it, Angelica, if you want," he told her. "You'll love it. A perfect choice for your first opera, another first!" He was delighted to be outside in the clear sunshine with a pretty young woman.

But much of the country, including the capital, now seemingly encircled by the Axis powers, was in a different mood. It was present in many people's voices as they discussed world events in the streets, and it could be seen in their faces, with their frightened eyes and tight-clenched teeth. Some were even seen protesting while yelling: "*Better a grave than a slave, better a war than a pact.*"

Thankfully Angelica's face, framed in her abundant hair with the purple violets in it, seemed to be serene and unaffected. In a way Dayan was sorry she'd come to this city, with its long history of destruction and tragedy. He had an impulse to tell her about it, but didn't want to spoil her day so he stayed positive.

"How lucky we are, Angelica!" He smiled at her. "It's spring, and we're going to a dance!"

Actually, it turned out to be more of a carnival than a dance once they arrived, having many large tents and stands displaying tempting merchandise. But there was a small orchestra as well, playing Gluck's *Spring Festival.* And inside were gypsy bands playing and young people dancing in large circles.

Angelica had never seen this sort of dancing, and Dayan told her, "The hora dances are very old. The Greeks danced them, and the Slavs too. Pindar's choral dance-songs are famous. Look!"

She followed his gesture, watching the dancing men as their dark hair and full sleeves swung and billowed, while they jumped agilely to the music that grew faster and faster—in rhythm.

"They look...almost wild," Angelica exclaimed as the dancers flung themselves ever more violently into the patterns of the *hora.* "The ground's shaking under their feet!"

"You're right," Dayan replied, happy at her interest and response. "These dances were created by suppressed people, who worked out their resentments against their oppressors this way. The dances grew out of suffering, like Schubert's melodies."

He laughed suddenly looking at Angelica, who put her hand nervously to the violets in her hair. "No, your flowers are fine. I'm not laughing at you. I was just remembering what we said in Gradina, that the major could never arrest half the town. You see now how right I was? It's the spirit of the people that counts when they stick together. Don't you agree?"

"I do, I do," Angelica said quickly.

"Half the town means people," Dayan continued. "And look at them. These are the people!" The dashing male dancers were now joined by women who wore flowers in their hair, just like Angelica's. They all looked as if they could give Major Hillarich a run for his money—all were laughing, healthy, strong and unafraid.

"Lincoln was right," Dayan said half to himself. Angelica looked at him curiously. "You know about Lincoln, Angelica?"

"Not much," she admitted. "He was an American President."

"Yes, but much more than that. He understood the people, and felt for them. Come on."

She followed by his side and they began to go from tent to tent, looking at the items for sale. They also were listening to the vendors shout angrily about the dancers keeping their customers away. In front of a tattoo shop the owner was standing tall with an eye out for a likely victim. Spotting Dayan, he sang out: "Half price today for the soldiers! Any tattoo you want. Extra cheap. Any design!"

He lifted the flap of the tent and invited Dayan to enter, while Angelica remained outside, looking a little bit frightened by it all.

"Now," said the tattoo artist. "Do you want it all woman? Or maybe you'd like half-woman, half-fish—a mermaid. Take your choice," the man said jovially, pounding Dayan's shoulder with his fist. "Or how about an ugly monster instead?"

Dayan shook his head while taking off his military blouse. He held out his right arm, looking at it as if he was already envisioning the finished tattoo on it. "I want a book," he said. "An open book with a burning candle in the middle of it."

"A book? That's a new one on me! I've never heard of such a thing! Are you sure?"

"Don't worry. I'll show you how it should look. Just give me a pencil and some paper." Dayan then drew the open book with the burning candle and the tattoo was started. The fledgling tattoo artist was glad to enlarge his repertoire and accepted only half-payment, since Dayan left the sketch for future customers who might select it. "Now I can appeal to the intellectuals in our midst," the artist boasted.

Chapter 6

Meanwhile, Angelica had waited patiently outside the tent. She was relieved when Dayan rejoined her. Noticing a number of soldiers wandering around rather aimlessly, she asked, "Why don't those soldiers join in the dancing?"

"They're probably just afraid. I'll get them into it, but first let's take a look around."

"Dayan, when were you last afraid?"

"I remember once when I was a child, at my grandmother's grave. The priest was wearing a robe embroidered in gold, with crosses and angels. How afraid I was!"

"Surely not of the angels?" Angelica said, surprised.

"Yes—of the angels too! The priest, who was holding a big book and chanting, said the angels would take my grandmother away. I was afraid they'd take me away too, because I loved her."

Angelica smiled.

"After all," Dayan said, "I was only seven."

"No wonder then."

"My father said the priest knew how to chant because he could read that book he held. I loved chanting so I was determined to learn how to read. And later, through books, I came close to people and their languages too—whether dead or alive; even the crosses and the angels."

Angelica's attentive listening stimulated him. It was a long time since he'd been able to express himself to such a sympathetic listener. "Through the books I learned to hold out my hands, to be willing to go, no matter where, with the people I met through them."

"But not with the angels?"

"Yes, with them too! You take, or you get taken by what you love. This is God's design; it's not selfish." He paused for a moment and Angelica looked at him expectantly. "Listen!"

"I am listening."

"No—not to me, it's the *March Slav!* Tchaikovsky dedicated it to the Serbian soldiers." The music was coming from the same orchestra which had played Gluck's *Spring Festival.* Dayan put his hand on Angelica's arm. "Let's get these poor soldiers into the dance. Angelica, maybe you will..."

He was interrupted by an authoritative voice: "*Line up, men! Line up! One, two, three! Hurry up! You too!*" It was coming from the leader of the military patrol, who saw Dayan and said: "Back to the garrison! You had no business leaving it!"

"What do you mean? I was..."

"City limit is garrison limit. No time to talk now," the sergeant said harshly. "One, two, three, up!" He signaled the soldiers to enter a military truck. "Get in!" he shouted at Dayan.

Dayan held back. "No! I can't leave her!" He turned quickly. Angelica was screaming as two soldiers advanced towards her with fixed bayonets. Then she calmed herself somewhat, although the soldiers continued to move forward. "Go Dayan, Go!" she implored him while trembling. The men were still some distance away. Dayan looked quickly to the sky. It was at least an hour until sunset. He grabbed Angelica's arm.

"Remember," he whispered, "your streetcar stops at the teacher's colony. Go straight there."

"Yes, yes. Don't worry."

With regret he entered the truck and when he looked back—Angelica was gone, lost in the crowd. But some of the partygoers at the fair, sobered by the incident, had clustered around the military truck and were shouting objections to the soldiers being carted away. "What's the idea?" they yelled. "Just like so many sheep!"

"I'm only carrying out my orders," the sergeant said. He explained that even the lowly typist at their officer's quarters knew war might be declared at any moment. As the truck moved away, Dayan glimpsed Angelica as she hurried towards the streetcar stop. He leaned out and shouted, "Get out of Belgrade! Save yourself!"

Evidently she understood. She waved her hand before disappearing from his view.

Chapter 6

"You!" said the sergeant to Dayan. "Over to the other side!" He took out a memo pad and jotted something down on it before the truck sped away.

Back at the garrison in Belgrade, the sergeant took Dayan inside to be questioned by the intelligence officer on duty.

"Now, what's the girl's name?" the officer asked in his office.

Dayan shook his head grimly.

"Here, have a cigarette."

"It won't work, I don't smoke."

"So you know that cigarettes are offered when possible spies are questioned?"

"Frankly, I know quite a lot, but I didn't know that. Spies, I've been told, are offered ropes around their necks. It happens that I don't smoke anyways."

The officer leaned his elbows on the table. He shrugged. "Okay, so you know a lot. Then tell me something, what were you up to out there?"

"Very simply," Dayan replied quietly, "I'd promised the parents to get her home before sunset."

"What a story! Parents and sunset. How about moonlight? You some kind of a nut—a poet?" The officer smiled in a muted way.

Deceived by the easy pace of the questioning, Dayan relaxed. "Well, everybody is to some extent, depending on how and what he loves. Pindar, for example, must have loved Thebes as you and I love Belgrade."

"Good God, I was only kidding. I don't give a hang for your Pindar." The officer leaned forward and his tone became grim. "I want to know—who's that girl working for? Hitler? Mussolini? Or maybe Horthy?"

"You're crazy!" Dayan shouted.

The officer stayed angry and grinned unpleasantly. "Sure," he said, "like a fox. Now, suppose you tell me what you both were up to?"

"Nothing at all. We went to the dance, and then the trucks came. The sergeant here said war is expected at any moment, and I wanted to save her. That's why I yelled: *Leave Belgrade*. At least he leveled with us. Too bad the government isn't doing the same."

At this expression of overt defiance the officer reacted with visible hostility, while the sergeant looked rather uncomfortable at the compliment Dayan had given him. Meanwhile, at a signal from the officer, the guards took Dayan away to lock him up.

After he was led away, the intelligence man turned to the sergeant. "What can we expect from a coward like that? *Leave Belgrade!* He said that, didn't he?"

The other man nodded.

"Do you think the girl's actually a spy?"

"What else? He told her to leave Belgrade to save herself. What from, if not a rope around her neck?"

When the guards returned, the officer took a bundle of photographs from his desk drawer and spread them out. The sergeant studied them. At last he said, "None of these."

"So much for that. Then we know she's not German. You say she's a brunette?"

"Definitely, sir."

The officer gathered up the pictures and put them away. He spread out another batch. "Let's try the Italians and Hungarians."

Again the sergeant studied the photos, putting aside a few over which he spent more time. Finally, he shrugged. The officer sighed and beckoned to the soldiers standing back from the desk. "Come and take a look. You saw the girl. Find her here!"

Obediently they looked carefully at the pictures, but they remained silent.

"What's the matter, can't you talk? Aren't you proud to have such an honor—to discover a spy? You'll get a decoration from the King if you find her."

The men shuffled uneasily, looking down at the pictures and then back to their superior. "She...she had violets in her hair," one said finally.

"All the women dancing had flowers in their hair too," the other chimed in hesitantly.

There was more silence and then one of the soldiers said, "The violets were on the left side. I noticed when I approached her with my bayonet."

"Yes, and she screamed," the first soldier said. "As soon as she saw the bayonet."

The intelligence man looked at them disgustedly. "And that's all you can do for your King? Violets and she screamed?"

"Christ, all women scream when they see a bayonet coming towards them," the first soldier said doggedly. "She covered her face with her hands."

"That's enough! Just remember what a big, fat help you've been on this case when someone else shows up with a gold medal on his chest." He made an impatient gesture, ordering them dismissed.

As the men shuffled out quietly—they heard him mutter angrily: "Save yourself. Leave Belgrade! The selfish coward!"

7

Attacked By Planes

It had been ten days since Yugoslavia's government was overthrown by a putsch that abolished a pact they'd signed with Germany on March 25, 1941. The free world had praised the putsch. Many people were happy when young King Peter was declared of age to take over the new government from Prince Paul. Winston Churchill said, "The Yugoslav nation has found its soul."

The members of the successful coup d'etat—including King Peter, stressed a policy of strict neutrality, while Churchill's words were received coldly by many inside of Yugoslavia. They wondered what he'd meant, asking: *If we never lost our souls, how could we ever find them?*

Dayan had been determined to be unsuitable to serve near the capital by the military authorities. He was now into the second day of a trip out to a fortification unit along the Adriatic coast. The charges against him were still unresolved, pending an investigation into the identity of Angelica Moravaz.

Tobo, the strongest man in the company, had been detailed to escort him to the new garrison. On the way he admitted to Dayan that he'd volunteered for this duty because he wanted to learn something from his *professor*. He was most interested in learning the alphabet, so Dayan had carved all thirty Serbian letters on a board taken from the company fence. The half-illiterate Tobo was instructed to copy them with the sharp point of his bayonet before they reached the coast.

At a crossing their train waited for one carrying military equipment to pass through; it was a small station about twenty miles outside of Sarajevo. The clerk on duty apologized to the passengers for the delay.

He turned on the radio in his office and music from Belgrade came on outside through some loudspeakers; they were playing a fiery hora dance. Some of the passengers, bored with the monotony of travel on the narrow-gauge train, couldn't resist. They started to dance, and Dayan was happy to join them. Tobo paid no attention, but continued to carve his letters with care.

Suddenly the music stopped and the radio crackled and hummed. A loud voice said excitedly:

"Attention! Attention! Germany attacked Yugoslavia this morning without a declaration of war. German planes heavily bombed Belgrade, destroying residential areas. The number of victims appears high. Fighting continues. Everyone report for duty. The country is now at war! Attention! Attention! Germany attacked Yugoslavia this morning without any..."

At this point the passengers reacted with panicked outbursts and cries, and the radio announcer's voice was drowned out amongst them.

"Impossible! It can't be!" people were shouting.

One voice was heard saying excitedly: "Why just yesterday the press announced the wedding of a daughter of one of the leaders of the putsch. Would they be holding a marriage ceremony if we were at war?"

"Of course not," another voice said. "The putsch is to show our allegiance to the West. Nothing to do with war!"

Now a third voice joined in: "But we're neutral, they said so themselves."

Dayan was silent and stricken, and in his head ran the words: *Destroying residential areas...the number of victims appears high.*

The only armed man in the group was Tobo, who held his rifle in his right hand and the precious alphabet board in his left. "They lie," he shouted. "Not Belgrade—it's strong!" He lifted his rifle. "No war. More generals in Belgrade than fish in Danube. Never sleep. Watch all the time. Watch even me—how I salute."

These disjointed sentences nevertheless were reassuring coming from a soldier, who the people thought certainly should know the military situation. Even Dayan felt somewhat reassured. He ran to the clerk's office to telephone Sarajevo.

Rushing into the crowded little room, he grabbed the phone and shouted quickly into the mouthpiece: "Hello? Hello?"

"Save your breath," the clerk said. "Line's dead. Probably sabotage."

On the station platform people were gathering around Tobo, who, because he was a soldier and armed, had become at least temporarily their hero. But they quickly dispersed when Stukas appeared low overhead, flying towards Sarajevo. They ran back to the comparative shelter offered by the train as the last Stuka machine-gunned the area in short bursts while on its way through.

But Tobo hadn't sought shelter. He'd stood scarcely believing his eyes as the planes flew overhead. As the last Stuka attacked again with a stream of raining bullets, Tobo's body suddenly jerked as he was hit. Blood quickly spurted from his neck and arced over his right shoulder. His legs moved while his body swung towards the right. By the time Dayan reached him, the blood was bubbling all over and he'd lost enough that a small puddle was forming under him.

Tobo's right knee was on the ground and he was trying to creep forward with the left one, which moved awkwardly. "Don't cry...my professor." His voice was faint and the words were half-mumbled. A shoulder bone seemed to be smashed, and there was a larger wound close to his neck.

Dayan tried to cover both wounds with his hands as Tobo's body sagged towards him. He was still conscious and trying to say: *Don't cry*—but couldn't. The sound he did make was garbled with the gurgling blood in his throat and the scratching of his left foot on the hard ground. Dayan continued supporting Tobo's huge body with his own, to keep the dying man from completely falling.

Trying to call for help from the people huddled around the train, Dayan heard his voice drowned out by the sudden explosion of a bomb—the work of the same Stuka which had shot Tobo. Now heavy black smoke was rising and someone yelled they're bombing in the direction of Sarajevo. Dayan noticed Tobo had stopped breathing, so he gently let him slide down his legs to the ground and crossed his arms over his chest. He then ran over to the train and joined the others hiding—until the last Stuka finally left the area.

After it was all clear and the shock of what had happened wore off, Dayan's concern turned to Tobo. He couldn't just leave his dead friend where he was, or even move him somewhere else without giving him a proper burial. Dayan noticed the gentle slope near the railroad tracks had aspen trees, which were putting out new green shoots. They could be Tobo's new casket, enveloping his corpse in its uniform. It was the best he could do under the circumstances, so sadly he picked out a spot.

He had the clerk help him carry Tobo over to this final resting place. They both dug a shallow grave, and after placing him with his arms crossed, they said a prayer so he may *Rest in Peace*. Then they placed his bayonet along his flank, and the board with the carved alphabet as a covering over his face. Lastly, they covered him completely with dirt and made a small pile of rocks as a headstone.

At dusk the train with some damaged cars turned back towards Belgrade, carrying with it a number of fleeing passengers. The others not on the train chose to continue towards Sarajevo on foot, walking as best as they could.

Dayan was confused about which direction to take like they were: Where did his duty lie? In seeking Angelica beneath the ruins of Belgrade, which was now a second Warsaw, or in continuing towards the Adriatic in obedience to his military instructions?

The clerk had already clambered on his bike and peddled away towards his home, leaving Dayan in the cold darkness of the station to contemplate this. Before leaving, he'd warned Dayan to look out for any poisonous snakes, since they'd begun to come out of their winter hibernation. Dayan told himself that his heavy army boots, studded as they were with nails, would be useful to crush the head of any viper, crawling or otherwise, which showed itself.

He wandered back over to Tobo's grave, where silence and the night blended together despite occasional flashes from blacked-out Sarajevo, punctuated by the sound of gunfire. After a while Dayan went back to the station and tried to sleep, but he couldn't.

He remembered how Uncle Dimitrye, telling stories by the hearth in Cablo during the evenings, would sometimes nap with his head falling forward and his big mustache covering his chest. Whenever he snored, Dayan would laugh. This awoke Uncle Dimitrye, who reprimanded him by saying: "Never mind, young man! I'm just making up for all the sleep I lost during the war."

Restlessly Dayan tossed back and forth—and finally got up to go to Tobo's grave again. After the third trip he'd beaten a little path to it. "That's good," he whispered. "The more visible and worn the path, perhaps the more people will come to visit Tobo's grave. Children will come from Sarajevo with flowers. Peasants will come from far away villages to walk this trail in their moccasins. There will be veterans with flags, generals with shiny decorations and music—and all will follow behind Tobo's weeping mother!"

When he'd walked back and forth twelve times, he thought of the twelve Apostles. This was his commitment—to beat a path to the grave of an illiterate fisherman who was a victim and a hero, one of the first Bosnian casualties of the war. As he stood facing the slight mound created by Tobo's body under the earth, Dayan thought how close the dead are to us and how much they're a part of us. He'd also left his own boots in front of the station, feeling like a pilgrim he should show his respect and be barefoot for Tobo.

"Yes," he thought, "we owe the dead recognition, since they can't speak for themselves."

Nearby, there was a slight crackling sound as a budding birch tree stretched after its long winter sleep. This reminded Dayan of something missing from Tobo's grave: *A cross!* He berated himself for not thinking of it sooner. A cross—like the one Thomash had shaped in the glowing logs in Cablo—like the one he wanted Dayan to form with his own arms after he died. Dayan knew that birch trees were good for making crosses; strong and glowing white in the dark, it would be a nightly reminder to those who see it.

Working quickly and carefully under a faint moonlight—he cut branches from a nearby tree and formed a cross. He then managed to carve an inscription on the bark: *A soldier, April 6, 1941*. He carefully pounded it in with a rock at the head of Tobo's grave and walked back to the station in his bare feet.

Now, at last, he was exhausted enough to sleep. He sank onto a bench and in moments was oblivious to the world. He was awakened by some of the first refugees from Sarajevo, who had fled from the city on bicycles and in carts pulled by horses. They brought sobering news—Italy, Albania, Bulgaria and Hungary had joined with the Germans in sending troops against Yugoslavia. One even said the Hungarian statesman Count Csaky had betrayed everyone.

Belgrade was almost totally annihilated with 38,000 dead and many more wounded. The young King and leaders of the putsch were fleeing towards Bosnia. Meanwhile, treason and sabotage by former Austro-Hungarian officers was causing dissension and turmoil in Sarajevo, as committees had been established to welcome the Nazi troops.

All during the day refugees streamed by, and towards evening there were crowds of them around carrying bundles and packages, with babies on their backs and children getting towed by the hand. They told Dayan that the Italian fleet had taken the Adriatic Coast after heavy bombing, and that members of the Croatian Nazi-Fascist group known as the *Ustashis*, who until now had been operating in Italy and Germany, were on their way to Croatia.

It was a matter of hours, they said, before a proclamation might be issued to create the satellite state of Croatia. And the train that had left earlier had returned after failing to pass through a blown up tunnel. It spent the night carrying swarms of refugees on only ten miles of usable track, all that was left to help shorten the long eastward trek for those refugees fleeing the fighting.

The next day around noon a cavalry platoon, their horses white with sweat, galloped up to the station to the applause of the people gathered there. A lieutenant spotted Dayan in uniform carrying Tobo's rifle. He signaled, and Dayan followed him into the clerk's office.

"Good to have a soldier here," the officer said, studying Dayan through half-closed eyes. "Where are you from?"

Dayan gave him a plausible, but fictitious answer, naming his unit and his division. He was praying the man wouldn't want any details. Then the lieutenant coughed—a cough coming from deep inside his chest. Fortunately, this created a diversion. "Damn cough," the lieutenant said, "can't seem to shake it off!"

"Your trouble is you need some sleep. The only way to cure a cough is rest," said the clerk.

"Yes, rest," the lieutenant repeated cynically. "Fat chance I have of getting any rest with this war just starting."

The clerk clucked sympathetically and Dayan tried hard to look noncommittal, like a good soldier. The lieutenant informed them that he was assigned as security commandant for the area, since the King and his government might arrive at any time. "We must take all measures for their safety."

"The King? How come?" asked the clerk. "What does that mean?"

"A decoration for you if you're smart," replied the lieutenant. "Pow!" He made a *pull of the trigger* gesture with his right index finger and went on to boast about his role in the putsch. "Those devils who opposed us, they hate the Anglos," he said, "and there are plenty right here among these so-called refugees. Go ahead and shoot them!" he told Dayan.

This was the first admission Dayan had heard that everyone hadn't welcomed the putsch.

They listened eagerly while the lieutenant brought them up to speed on what's been happening. Taking a map from his pocket, the lieutenant traced the recent course of events he'd been told. The Turks had marched through Bulgaria and the British through Macedonia to meet in Belgrade. The British had also mined the Danube Iron Gate gorge.

"Later, the plan is to flood the north of Yugoslavia, including whoever's around, especially the Nazi troops and tanks if we're lucky! It's all God's plan," the lieutenant continued. "Hitler should find his grave in Serbia, like Potiorek did in the Great War." He looked up now, his expression serious. "Keep all this under your hats," he warned them.

Then the lieutenant lowered his voice, so there was no one within possible hearing distance. "The King with his entourage are scheduled to go through Montenegro—they're still free. We'll push the Nazis and Fascists right into the Adriatic—into the Danube Basin, where it's flooded and then..." Here he picked up the two sides of the map showing the area he meant, and brought them together with a slap of his open palms. "Pow! The war will be over!"

"God—let's hope so," the clerk agreed.

"Right!" said the lieutenant. "But as for those Anglophobes who insist the putsch was organized and paid for by foreign powers, we'll settle their hash, believe me." He made a throat-cutting gesture. "Right now, though, we'd better take care of the present."

He instructed Dayan how to salute the young King when he arrived, proclaimed the area under martial law, and ordered Dayan to establish a military court. "You'll be the court president," he told Dayan. "All executions in the name of the King. Show no mercy—just shoot them!"

Then he rejoined his soldiers and the platoon galloped away in a cloud of dust.

Dayan sat down and considered everything the lieutenant had just said. It was logical for the King to travel through Montenegro, as that seemed the only possible route he could take right now. But it wouldn't be as simple as the lieutenant, who was riding off now in search of Anglophobes, had said—especially about the flooding portion, that seemed impossible and made up.

He was concerned too about the lieutenant's orders for court martial, then execution, show no mercy, and above all, the instructions to *shoot them*. Shoot whom and why? That couple carrying two babies who just passed by? Or the Jew with a dismantled bike on his back and a small box, who had told Dayan he was fleeing not only because he was a Jew, but as one of the best interpreters of the Talmud in Sarajevo?

Maybe, Dayan thought, the lieutenant had heard them as he'd heard others, saying that people wanted neither a pact nor a putsch. One was the cause of the other; the pact was imposed by fearful statesmen and the putsch was the result of ambition. All just men filled with empty pride, ignorance or vanity. Dayan wanted no part of such a war. The opportunity he'd sought to help the brave Poles and to give the last drop of his blood, was now so remote that he felt betrayed and ashamed.

He visualized a huge threatening monster forming, but it wasn't like one of those devils the peasants believed inhabited the deep caves near Cablo. They have heels where their toes should be, who legend said were to be discovered only at night and against whom the only weapon was a black-handled knife. No, this was a different threat, for it came from ordinary places, from big cities with decorated palaces, churches, conference buildings and banks with deep vaults full of gold.

This threat spread like the tentacles of an octopus, reaching its cold, slimy feelers out, aiming especially for the human heart and mind to destroy their humanity and fill them with apathy. Dayan was afraid. What if this monster was to penetrate his own heart and mind as it must have done to the protagonists of the pact and the putsch? And, he thought, it could certainly happen if he followed the military instructions he'd received from the dashing lieutenant—who had already cantered off with his fellow soldiers.

He took a long, last look towards Tobo's grave and crossed himself. Then he shouldered his rifle, along with the sixty cartridges now stowed in his pocket, and joined the stream of refugees headed eastward.

As he trudged forward into the seemingly endless line of human beings, he thought over what the lieutenant had said about pushing the Germans out of Montenegro and into the Adriatic. As impossible as the idea sounded, he couldn't help but become attracted to it in a different way. He remembered a poem Thomash had recited to him when he was a child, which told that the Montenegrins fought so fiercely, they even set the sky on fire. Ever since then he'd wanted to see that area and someday be part of such a glorious battle! And now, it seemed, if he eventually circled to the southwest, he might get that opportunity to fulfill his dream.

There was no one there to encourage him, but he thought of this as his proper assignment. This new *duty* would be honest fighting, not merely killing or executing in the name of the King. Now he'd defend the brave Poles and all the vanished people—the moment of truth was no longer remote, but here and now!

Dayan felt like he could follow such a way of life, but he admitted secretly that the very moment before a battle might prove to be difficult for him. Montenegrins are quick to pull the trigger, saying that a rifle isn't a distaff. If it's in a man's hands, it's to be used. Well, there was no one to give him strength. He must rely upon his own courage and he wouldn't disgrace himself.

Stimulated and exhilarated by these thoughts, he remembered William Washington's sacrifices and Lord Byron's struggles for Greece. To hearten himself—he chanted some verses from Tennyson's poem, *Montenegro*.

They kept their faith, their freedom, on the height,

Chaste, frugal, savage, arm'd by day and night.

8

Selling Wine Bottles

As Dayan headed eastward, he'd become like the thousands of other refugees fleeing inside of his homeland. To him it was a repeat of the story he'd heard from the Pole on the banks of the Danube. He remembered the stranger's very words—*from this area the people fled from the Nazis, going towards the east*—and his fingers had moved across the map, passing over its many mountains, valleys and rivers.

And here Dayan was—all cold and hungry, moving painfully across that same map. Even though he knew he was headed in the wrong direction, for now there was no other choice. *Am I in a safer place than others are elsewhere?* He wondered. What of the people back in Cablo and Gradina? What's happened to his parents, and to Perun Novak, who'd had eleven teeth pulled out to escape the draft? And what of Major Hillarich? Which side was he on now? If Dayan knew what was happening back home, perhaps he'd react differently.

Looking back to the day before Hitler attacked Yugoslavia, Major Hillarich had held a party at the Officers' Club in Gradina in order to give recognition for some war games they'd conducted. Civilian authorities, merchants and civic leaders were all in attendance, and there were many toasts to the success of the putsch and to the western world.

The newly appointed Mayor Dabovich greeted Hillarich as the first commandant who would enter Vienna at the head of the victorious units, and march upon the skulls of Hitler's troops. He sent his police chief to inform the nightclubs on Shark Street that they could stay open all night for the non-commissioned officers and soldiers, but warned them not to overcharge for the drinks they served.

Everybody in fact drank a lot that night and the party got quite boisterous, so much so that nobody was aware of when it ended, nor what went on into the early hours the next morning. They were all socked in, sleeping off the effects of their overnight debauchery.

But a detached anti-aircraft unit on a hill had rudely woken them up by shooting down an Italian plane, part of an attacking squadron flying over Gradina dropping bombs. The plane crashed near the bridge, and the sleepy population started to flee from the city in all directions. Then came a proclamation stating the planes had been there by mistake, and were suppose to be headed to Greece, which was already at war with Italy.

The people remembered a similar incident from the prior year when Italy had bombed the Yugoslav city of Bitola—also by mistake—followed by some apologies and promises to pay for the damages done to the homes and for the people that were killed. Still fearful this time, the residents of Gradina eventually returned in the darkness, but their questions and doubts remained.

The answer they got later was brief. *Details will follow as soon as lines of communication, which are being interrupted through some technicality, become re-established.* This wasn't very comforting, and some residents were more inclined to trust rumors started earlier by a German-speaking waiter on Shark Street. He said that Germany and Italy were on the march across the entire Yugoslav border.

The more the authorities warned them not to panic and listen to rumors, the greater the tensions grew amongst them. They'd already divided themselves into two factions: those for the putsch and those against it. They only joined forces to fulfill their Christian obligations for the quick funeral of the two Italian airmen, along with burying the civilians killed by the plane's bombs.

After sunrise their fears were no longer of the unknown: German parachutists took over command of the lumber yard near the railroad station, where the ash trees purchased by Herr Pushinger of Hamburg Import-Export Inc. were stored. Before the garrison had even spotted them, squadron after squadron of Stukas flew over Gradina.

Their noise and that of the air sirens, plus the roar of approaching German tanks, paralyzed the confused city. Before any brave action could be taken in the name of the King and Fatherland, the German flag was hoisted over Gradina city hall, and the local military was disarmed. They were placed under strict discipline, and were reminded of the cost for any insubordination.

The Germans also decided to intimidate the ordinary citizens of Gradina. They efficiently marched off all the captured officers except for lieutenant Pavlovich, who was allowed to play *Gladly Goes A Serb Into The Army* on his flute before being executed along with six random civilians taken from the main street. This was done at the city hall as a warning to everyone.

The soldiers they'd captured were then forced to load all the ash tree logs, weapons and materiel into freight trains. After this work was finished, they were shipped off to be used as labor at a distant work camp. So was Dabovich, the old Mayor of Gradina, as an ardent Putschist. He was replaced by the German-speaking waiter from Shark Street, whose rumors had turned out to be true after all. The invaders even broke into the newspaper offices of *The Progressive Voice,* where the printing press and equipment was smashed and dumped into the swollen Mista river.

Satisfied with their job, the German troops then moved on towards Greece and were replaced by an Italian force as the new occupying power of the area. The Germans left only their liaison officers in Gradina and the new Mayor named Singer, the former waiter.

Cablo learned about Yugoslavia's unconditional surrender, which happened following ten days of war, when guerrilla leaflets appeared on trees bearing a crude skull and crossbones. They described the young King's safe exit out of Belgrade, and were hopeful of a guerrilla strategy that would bring about their eventual liberation from the invaders. They ended with the words: *Freedom or Death,* a traditional symbol of Serbian warfare against the Turks.

New leaflets then appeared week after week, filled with optimistic predictions about the state of resistance to the Axis powers. One said the King was already directing the opposition fighting along with his government-in-exile, while another urged the young to join the guerrilla units, and asked the population to sabotage the enemy occupiers whenever possible. Young men were inflamed by this propaganda, and one after another they disappeared and were never heard from again.

Obviously the leaflets were emanating from Gradina. *The first acts of sabotage*, a typical leaflet told them, *should be to cut off all ties with the cities, and to destroy every crop so the enemies can't use them. There's no need to worry about any food for the winter, since large shipments of wheat are coming from America and Canada.*

The villagers who attempted to follow these instructions found it difficult because the wheat, barley and oats were still green, and wouldn't burn properly. All they could do was cut these crops down and leave them to rot.

There were rumors of a sharp disagreement between Hitler and Mussolini as to their respective zones in the Balkans, especially Dalmatia and Montenegro. The dictators were also said to be quarreling over the Trepca gold mine and the Bor copper mine in Serbia. These mines had been used by the British and French before the war; now they were under Hitler's control.

Meanwhile, over the radio came news that Yugoslav Colonel Draza Mihailovic, called the first guerrilla leader of Europe, and his Chetnik fighters had been giving the Germans a hard time on the main communication line between Belgrade and Salonika, an important artery through the heart of Serbia.

Then, into this confused state of affairs, suddenly that rascal Perun Novak showed up back in Cablo. Because he'd avoided the draft, he was now a minor hero to the Italians, who'd given him the job of a dishwasher in the newly opened Officers' Club. There he appeared resplendent in a black Fascist shirt around which he wore the white belt of a carabineer, and in his cap he proudly flaunted a marksman's fluffy feather for everyone to see.

Chapter 8

While on a break during his second day back, Perun took an Italian mule carrying empty Chianti wine bottles into the small village square. "Fine bottles for exchange," he said to the Cablo villagers. "The best Italian wine bottles. Think of all the good uses at home for these gems. You can have some for only a dozen eggs."

The local villagers only stared back at him with antagonism on their faces. After a while Perun's mood turned ugly and he started to shout. "You'd better do business with me, or the Italians will do business with your daughters!"

There were murmurs of both anger and fear from everyone watching him.

"Look here!" Perun shouted. "Look at this!" He held up a document stamped with many seals. "This paper can bring the big guns and tanks up to Cablo. Roman power is strong, you know that by now. So just pray that your chickens have laid some eggs by the time I come back."

Scowling, he grabbed the mule's bridle and strode off, heading back to his soft job in the kitchens. There was a silence as the villagers watched his squat figure move away, stopping sometimes to kick at the mule and curse. For a long moment—no one moved. Then Auntie Stephanie summed up the general reaction when she spat forcefully, turned, and walked quickly in the direction of her cottage.

***

"Bologna University, the oldest in Europe, is proud to have you as its graduate," said Colonnello Mortellini, the Italian town-commandant in occupied Gradina. He was addressing Dr. Vedrano in an office which was part of the former Gradina chamber of commerce. "Ever since we took over here a couple of months ago," Mortellini continued, "we've been most generous, despite the crimes you've committed against the great Roman empire. That's because we realize your importance to these miserable Balkanians, for whom our Duce has great sympathy."

"Or great interest," said Dr. Vedrano.

The colonnello chose to ignore this interjection. He continued pompously, while striding up and down the narrow room: "And if you stress in your book that our coming to this country has created a new Renaissance for the Balkans, you'll be granted honorary membership in the High Forum of the Party."

Dr. Vedrano nodded with only a half-smile on his lips.

The colonnello now became more enthusiastic. "Il Duce himself is very much interested in such a project. And I'll guarantee that your manuscript will be preserved amongst our greatest treasures —in Florence." He gesticulated with his hands in the Italian way. "You'll be assured of a place in the New Europe for which Il Duce and Der Fuhrer are striving."

With the same half-smile, Dr. Vedrano bowed slightly.

Mortellini drew a deep breath of satisfaction. Taking out his cigarette case, he opened it and offered a smoke to Dr. Vedrano. "So, you accept then?"

"No thanks," Dr. Vedrano said, as he made a gesture refusing a cigarette.

Surprised by this—Mortellini stared at him, suddenly aware that things weren't going his way.

"By no thanks, I mean no to both things," Dr. Vedrano added.

"No to everything?"

"Exactly."

Mortellini began to sputter. "But you can't—do you realize this book would be translated into every important language? Think of the Italians in America—of the world of Islam—of our Asiatic friends. New movements are sweeping over Asia at this very moment—and since the Bolsheviks can't win them over, we will! And once we have won the war..."

"But you won't win it," Dr. Vedrano interrupted.

Colonnello Mortellini stood facing him for a moment, his expression a mixture of incredulity, shock and rage. Suddenly he spun around, and with a few jerky, short steps—he marched to the desk and pressed a bell. In a few moments the door opened and a chronic coughing could be heard. The man who entered had lanky, dark hair. He was tall and thin, and walked with his shoulders hunched.

"Signore Laguna," Mortellini barked. "Take over. This assignment is now in your hands. You will interpret for Dr. Vedrano."

"I don't need any interpreter," Dr. Vedrano said serenely. He turned to Laguna. "I'm a doctor of your university—as Signore Laguna knows very well."

"That may be," Mortellini cut in angrily. "Nevertheless, the rules of occupation require that you have an official interpreter. I already made a concession in speaking to you directly."

Dr. Vedrano began to go into his little half-smiling bow and Mortellini yelled, "And don't say no thanks again, damn it! This isn't a game, Signore Vedrano, although you may think so. Don't forget that you killed two of our boys with those anti-aircraft guns of yours. The only sons which their parents had."

"Along with those scores of innocent civilians your side murdered." Dr. Vedrano reminded him.

Mortellini, who'd sat down momentarily, now jumped up again. "And I suppose it wouldn't be inhumane if the British dropped bombs on our Italian cities tomorrow?"

"Of course it would be. Whoever kills innocent people is inhumane."

Laguna, who was still standing near the door, began coughing again as the colonnello rifled through some papers in a folder on his desk. It contained the accusations against Dr. Vedrano, neatly summarized on the final sheet:

1. Responsible for the deaths of two Italian airmen, as commander in charge of an anti-aircraft emplacement on a hill above the city of Gradina.

2. Wrote letters to Queen Helena of Italy, making accusations concerning the behavior of Italian troops.

3. Neglected to carry out the school program as prescribed by the occupying powers.

4. Sabotage of Il Duce's plan for establishing a new post-war order in Europe.

After reading these off in a solemn, accusatory voice, Mortellini looked up triumphantly at Dr. Vedrano, who laughed.

"Concerning the guns," Dr. Vedrano said, "I don't even know which of the guns hit that plane. My military knowledge is zero. In fact, I've never been told why Hillarich drafted me for that duty, but doubtlessly he had his reasons."

"Doubtlessly," returned Mortellini sarcastically.

"However, there's one thing I do know," Dr. Vedrano continued calmly. "You will lose the war," he said, while looking straight into Mortellini's eyes.

"Oh? And what makes you so sure of that? I hope you're not putting any faith into that guerrilla leader named Mihailovic?"

Dr. Vedrano said nothing back.

"Because if you are, I've got something to show you." The colonnello rummaged through the right-hand drawer of his desk and finally pulled out a newspaper, which he handed to Dr. Vedrano. Someone had outlined an article in heavy red ink that included a photograph of Hillarich wearing a German uniform while standing beside a heavy gun.

"This great friend of yours is going to give Mihailovic a run for his money—including his Chetnik guerrilla friends all hiding together up in the mountains," Mortellini said. "When Hillarich is through with them all, they'll be, as our friend Herr Hitler would say, kaput!"

Silently, Dr. Vedrano studied the picture and read the article. Then, contemptuously, he threw the newspaper on the floor. Laguna stooped rather painfully to pick it up.

Mortellini was pleased at Dr. Vedrano's reaction. "No need to get excited, Doctor," he practically sang. "You haven't seen the best of it yet—here!" He displayed another newspaper which showed a still larger photograph of Hillarich. Here the turncoat was leading a Croatian unit composed of Bosnian Muslims. They were parading before some dignitaries on a platform which was decorated with a framed picture of the Grand Mufti of Jerusalem.

"You know what that means, don't you Doctor? Global war—that unit is volunteering to fight the Bolsheviks. In fact, it seems everybody's getting into the fight, but you, Dr. Vedrano."

Dr. Vedrano made an uncertain gesture, wiping his forehead with his handkerchief. He was obviously shaken.

Mortellini looked at him, smiling ironically. "Well? Any questions, Doctor Vedrano?"

"Perhaps," Dr. Vedrano hesitated.

Mortellini listened carefully.

"It's not that I'm against those poor Bosnian Muslims," Dr. Vedrano went on. "If only I could be for them."

"Then do!" cried Mortellini. "Be for them! Join with us!" He was almost pleading now.

"No. No. You don't speak my language as I do. Neither did Hillarich."

"What do you mean? The important thing is we'll give you a chance—give you freedom."

"God keeps me free."

"We can give it or take it away. We can even send you to a prison camp in Albania as a political rebel—if you refuse us."

Dr. Vedrano shrugged.

"You wouldn't take it so lightly if you realized what could happen to you there. Those Balkan cannibals would eat you up in one night. Think it over. Come to us and you can introduce that educational program which we've prescribed."

Dr. Vedrano was now tired, and too tired to think clearly. He shook his head wearily, like a man trying to clear away the cobwebs.

Mortellini recognized his symptoms of fatigue. "You don't need to decide right now," he said almost kindly. "I'll give you another chance. You can let me know later."

After Dr. Vedrano had left, Mortellini turned to Laguna. "You have it easy, Signore Laguna," he said. "You didn't have to translate a single word. I wish I had a job that simple."

"I know my way around," Laguna said before smiling. But the colonnello's expression made him nervous, so he coughed again.

"Anything wrong?"

"No, nothing," but he continued to cough nervously while the sound echoed out through the long corridor.

"Oh, Santa Maria!" exclaimed Mortellini, who was looking through Dr. Vedrano's dossier and noticed where he'd unveiled a plague during a high school ceremony last year. He grabbed the telephone and spoke into it. "Viva Duce! Majore Donadio," he began, in almost a pleading voice. "Send men to the high school gymnasium—send lots of them! Give them orders to break up the American Red Cross plaque inside! Break it into many pieces—a thousand pieces! Smash it completely! Gracie! Gracie, caro mio!"

He hung up the receiver and sat while looking at the telephone. "Gracie, caro mio!" he said to himself again with a laugh.

9

Without Any Salt

The war going on continued to rage elsewhere, while in Cablo it was still relatively calm. News from leaflets and the youth who'd joined the guerrillas recently had stopped arriving, along with the rumors that some of them were killed. There was no way to find out the truth anyways, so people stopped repeating reports which occasionally came into the village.

However there was one message they heard that meant a great deal to everyone; Aladdin, the sexton's son, sent word that Dr. Vedrano had been sent to a prison camp in Albania. People were very worried about the school director, for whom they had great affection and respect.

The Radio-London news came rarely, usually filled with demands for greater sacrifices in the struggle for the future of mankind. With this Cablo had responded as best it could by sending young men to fight with Colonel Mihailovic, and by cutting off all ties with Italian-occupied Gradina. There was little else the village could do, even when the wife of a government member spoke from exile in London. She urged all Serbs to perish fighting the Nazis rather than let the exiled Putschists lose face before their great Western Allies.

Another speaker was quoted as saying, "The Serbs are like grass; the more you cut them down, the more they will grow." Colonel Mihailovic and his Chetniks were praised for postponing Hitler's march towards Russia. No other conquered European country had received such acclaim. In Gradina the Italians were settled in. They had barbed wire encircling the town and its airport, and were protected by heavy artillery, so they felt safe and secure.

The last demand that arrived in Cablo via Radio-London said to again continue burning the crops to make them useless to the occupying forces. These appeals were now ignored by the villagers at Uncle Dimitrye's command. "It's against God's will," he announced defiantly, and the people evidently agreed.

Perun Novak had left Cablo towards the end of spring bound for Gradina, and minus four more teeth after a quarrel with some neighboring villagers. His business venture of trading empty wine bottles for eggs had been a total failure. Maybe he'd do better in Gradina, he thought, where there was more scope for connivers and rascals.

Constantly worried about the fate of their sons, and still concerned about not letting down their exiled government representatives, the villagers in Cablo now had another problem to deal with. Thomash sent word to gather for a meeting under the oak tree, it was to discuss an epidemic of skin rashes spreading amongst the children and young girls.

Goritza had already sent word throughout the village that this disease was happening due to a lack of salt in their diet, and she'd learned this supposed fact from her newly arrived *daughter*. It was an open secret that Angelica Moravaz, who'd fled from the bombardment of Belgrade, had arrived safely later in Gradina. From there she'd gone to see Dr. Vedrano to tell him about her mother's death by German planes, and about the injuries to her father, along with her last encounter with Dayan in Belgrade. This gave Dr. Vedrano the idea of having her stay as a daughter with Dayan's parents up in Cablo.

So now the villagers had to decide where to acquire enough salt to end all the rashes. This wasn't easy for Cablo, as the only nearby source with sufficient salt for them was in Gradina, and Cablo had already cut off all ties with that town earlier in the year.

"But we can't wait for the war to end," Thomash said to the villagers gathered beneath the great oak tree. "With God's help our boys will come home by then, and how will our poor girls be able to face them, with ugly, broken-out faces and rough skin?"

"And don't forget about the little ones that are just growing up!" someone called out.

Everyone agreed that Cablo was in danger of becoming a village of spinsters—and they'd always been proud that all the girls became married. The villagers decided they'd have to get enough salt from Gradina one way or the other, and Thomash volunteered to try.

"Why you?" Goritza protested. "You, who needs a crutch? Let a younger man go."

"I am who I am," Thomash said. "They might arrest a younger man, but what good would I be to the Italians?" He lifted his crippled right leg, and tapped it with his crutch. The villagers all applauded. "And remember," Thomash told them, "only you can proclaim me a traitor for doing this. Not the King—and not London."

"Long live Uncle Thomash!" they shouted until it echoed back from the surrounding hills.

"I'll be back," Thomash promised, "either with salt or with medicine."

In Gradina he got in touch with Aladdin, who told him that Colonnello Mortellini was in charge of issuing salt to the villages. Leaving five donkeys with packs and empty bags in front of the former chamber of commerce building, Thomash limped through the entrance way.

A sentry told him to halt. "Here—give me your crutch."

"But I can't walk without it."

"That's too bad," the soldier said coldly, "but orders are orders. No armed civilians allowed."

"Armed? With a crutch?" Thomash protested.

"Sure—armed! You could kill a man with that thing."

Thomash laughed unbelievably, but handed over his crutch and a soldier supported him into Mortellini's office. The colonnello was busy inside looking important at his desk. He glared irritably at Thomash as he stood awkwardly before him.

"Well?"

"We need salt in our village," Thomash said, after identifying himself. He explained everything about the skin outbreaks.

"You come at a very inconvenient time for the Roman empire," Mortellini said. "We're dealing with huge problems—our ships can't transport enough troops for the final battle against the Anglo-American plutocrats and the Bolsheviks. Yet Il Duce demands that we end the war pronto so we can get busy solving the postwar problems of the world. And with all this on our minds —you ask us to worry about a skin outbreak of children in a tiny Balkan village, one so small that it doesn't even show up on any of our maps?"

The interpreter, Laguna, translated all this while Mortellini shuffled some papers impatiently. But as Thomash assumed defeat and turned to go, the colonnello suddenly said, "Hey, wait a minute, I haven't finished—"

Thomash turned back and almost stumbled. Laguna put out a hand to support him.

"This village of yours, Cablo, it was the first in the area to cut off all ties with the cities." Thomash said nothing, so Mortellini continued. "Tell me, how many houses are in Cablo?"

"Thirty-seven."

"Hmm. Thirty-seven houses and twenty-four guerrillas fighting with the Plutocrats and Bolsheviks. I've got a good mind to make you pay for them all right now—if it wasn't for your good boy."

Thomash was astonished. "My boy? My good boy?" he stammered. Could the colonnello mean Dayan?

"I mean Perun Novak. He's from Cablo, isn't he?"

"Oh, Perun! Sadly, yes. But he's not my boy," Thomash began. "I'm ashamed—"

Laguna pressed his shoulder cautiously, and didn't translate the last words.

"In our files on Perun we found that you're known to have helped him before the war. It's your good luck," said Mortellini. "It gives you a decent record, even though your son is out fighting with the Bosnian guerrillas."

This time Thomash knew the colonnello was referring to Dayan. "My son? You mean he's alive? Oh God, Dayan!" He closed his eyes and counted on his fingers. "Twenty-four weeks and five days. No, six days! Twenty-four weeks and six days. He left early that morning and not a word from him since. You say he's alive?"

Mortellini didn't answer, but instead launched into a lengthy tirade about his generosity towards the people, and how he'd never allow anyone, especially little children, to suffer. He finally got around to saying he'd even help out the villagers of Cablo. "But strictly on a cash and carry basis. You understand me?"

Thomash was puzzled.

"Look," said Mortellini, "you've got a forest of ash trees around your village, don't you? Well, we need that wood badly. Next winter our soldiers will bring their children to learn your language and to be your friends. You don't want them to freeze, do you?" He shivered dramatically.

Thomash, being the good sentimental man that he was, responded as Mortellini had expected.

"Children freeze? God forbid—never."

"Of course not," Mortellini said approvingly. "And neither will we let yours be disfigured all of their lives. All you have to do is get us the wood, then you'll get the salt you need. Lots of it, even medicine. And after we win the war, we'll all be friends."

It all sounded fine to Thomash except for that part about them winning the war, but he overlooked it for the moment. "That's wonderful," he said. "Outside I have ten empty bags on five donkeys. That'll do for a start."

"Wait a minute! Evidently you didn't understand what I meant by cash and carry, as it's an expression we learned from the British. You see, after our conquest of Ethiopia we had to pay in gold before each of our ships could pass through the Suez Canal." He sighed reminiscently. "Believe me, that lesson taught us something!" Noticing that Thomash still hadn't followed him, he decided to cut it short. "In other words," he added briskly, "when we get the ash wood, you'll get the salt—and not a minute before."

Now Thomash understood. "But we have better wood for making fires," he said. "Wood that doesn't smoke. It makes the children's eyes run when the wood smokes, sir. You must know that."

"There!" Mortellini beamed. "You see? You're already thinking about our children's welfare. We're starting to be friends, in spite of your twenty-four guerrillas. That's how Il Duce wants it—the Europe of tomorrow."

"Yes, yes." Thomash nodded and, deciding the interview was over, looked around for his crutch in order to leave. But he'd forgotten the sentry at the entrance still had it as a weapon. Since there was nothing more to translate, Laguna left the room, and in a few moments Perun Novak showed up to hand Thomash his crutch. His former friend took it without looking at the gap-toothed opportunist.

Goritza and Angelica were anxiously waiting for Thomash at their cottage with news of what he'd learned, and they met him at the door with questions in their eyes. Once inside he quickly gave them an account of his conversation with Colonnello Mortellini. "And listen to this. He said that Dayan is somewhere in Bosnia!" The two women were overjoyed at the news of their beloved.

"He's in Bosnia? That's wonderful! But where is Bosnia?" Goritza asked.

Angelica took a piece of paper from a shelf, and with a pencil drew a map of Yugoslavia. Goritza watched eagerly as she made a circle. "See? Right here. That's Bosnia."

The older woman stared intently at the place Angelica had outlined, as if she expected Dayan to somehow appear and walk right out of the paper. "Dayan—in Bosnia!"

"And here's where the others are," Angelica went on. She drew another circle showing the location of the villagers who were with Mihailovic, in Serbia.

"If only Dayan was with them," Goritza said. She wiped away a tear with the back of her hand. "It'd be easier for us all."

Thomash had been watching and listening. Now he spoke urgently. "Remember—say nothing of this to the other women in the village. Not a word! It wouldn't be fair since they have no news of their sons."

Goritza nodded. "You're right, we're lucky!" Then she hurried to the door and looked outside.

"What's the matter now?" Angelica called.

Goritza answered with her head out the door. "I'm only looking to be sure there's plenty of dry wood—just in case he comes home to surprise us."

Towards the end of summer Italian troops arrived to begin hauling away the local ash tree lumber. It was an ordinary day like any other, and Thomash had been working on the grave monument. He'd washed his hands at the well and was saying his prayer, when Perun Novak appeared with fifteen armed soldiers having red stars on their caps. They jumped over the church fence, called to Thomash and ordered him to open the church.

Reluctantly, Thomash started up the path. "But why didn't you come through the gate?" he grumbled. Even for Thomash with his limp, he was walking more slowly than usual, when a young soldier made a gesture with his gun—*Get a move on!*

But Thomash continued his uneven gate without quickening his steps. The soldier took aim at him with his gun.

"Go ahead—shoot, if you're a man!" Thomash yelled angrily. He opened his shirt, showing his bare chest. "Go on—what are you waiting for?"

At this Perun Novak approached the youth and pulled him away. They all ran through the open door of the church, which Perun ordered Thomash to lock after them.

Meanwhile, Italian soldiers appeared from behind the hills, and it was evident that their course would lead them right past the church. Thomash decided to wait until they arrived via the narrow village paths, so he returned to his work.

The troops had with them many large mules loaded with ash tree logs. Some carried machine-guns and mortars, and there were even soldiers carrying logs on their shoulders. As they trudged along, they sang in Italian. When they came up to Thomash busy with his stonework, one soldier dropped back and threw the log from his shoulder.

"Buon giorno," he said pleasantly.

Thomash nodded noncommittally. The Italian troops were still filing past in a long column containing soldiers, officers and mules.

As Thomash watched, the soldier picked up his chisel from the ground and started to polish the big piece of granite. In Italian he asked Thomash what's wrong with the church—why are the walls so crooked? Dayan's father just smiled at the young man, not understanding his words.

The Italian pointed to himself. "Mario. Mario—lo Mario."

The older man pointed to himself. "Thomash."

"Tomas. Tomas," the soldier repeated, giving it the Italian pronunciation. He fished in his military blouse and extracted a photograph which showed a whole family—first a short old man with a mustache like Thomash had. "Padre. Luigi Santucci."

Thomash nodded his understanding.

Mario pointed at the plump woman standing next to his father. "Madre. Donata." Then the young ones. "Pia, Esperanza, Domenico." There was a pretty young woman at the right. "Mi...mi..." but he couldn't bring out his wife's name, for by this time he was quietly sobbing.

Thomash came to his rescue. He pointed at himself, then at Luigi. Then he pointed to Donata, the mother. "Goritza," he said.

Mario had blown his nose and wiped his face with the sleeve of his tunic. "Si, si." He then looked at Thomash expectantly.

Thomash hesitated, then patted the young Italian's shoulder. "Dayan. Dayan."

Again the soldier nodded and pointing again to his wife's picture: "Clara!"

"Angelica, Angelica," Thomash responded. He looked at the church and crossed himself, and Mario did the same. Then they both lifted their eyes towards the cross that's above the church bell. Suddenly they heard gun shots from within the church. Those inside were shooting through the altar window at the Italian column—as it disappeared down the path.

Chapter 9

Mario threw himself to the ground. "Mamma mia! Mamma mia!" He was trembling. Thomash signaled him to lie down behind the granite monument, and not to move.

Somebody from inside the church was pounding on the door. Thomash went to open it. "Shame on you!" Thomash yelled as he did so. "Shooting from the altar. And besides, to shoot at people's backs. Cowards!"

But the men inside paid no attention. Brushing past him once the door opened, they leaped over the stone fence and quickly disappeared into the woods on the other side.

The Italians fired machine-gun bursts back up the hill in retaliation. Bullets whistled high over Thomash's head, while there was silence from the men hiding in the woods. Then the machine-guns started again. By this time, many of the villagers had been coming fearfully and curiously in the direction of the church to find out what was going on. Thomash warned them to go back to their homes because bullets were grazing the branches of the orchard trees. One bullet even hit the church bell, which gave out a high, clear sound like a prayer heard amidst the gunfire.

A few minutes passed and mortar rounds started, causing dogs to howl throughout the village. When two small planes arrived later, they strafed the village and dropped bombs, which set a stable and two cottages on fire.

As night fell heavy artillery shells began to explode in the hills and down around the village.

Thomash and Mario had taken shelter in the church; it had remained too dangerous to try and get home, Thomash decided, but he prayed that Goritza and Angelica were safe. The artillery hitting the area was coming from Gradina, Mario said, pointing in the direction of town. "Gradina—boom, boom!"

Thomash nodded, then they both looked towards the church door opening—all of a sudden it was getting lighter inside. It was from the muffled gleam of a lamp someone carried, being partly shielded by a cloak. A solemn file of villagers entered as two men each carried a body—with eleven bodies in all. They laid them down gently on the floor near the altar, and the women mourned their loss with tears and prayers, while some men outside dug a common grave for those killed.

The burial service was brief. Then, silently weary, the villagers returned to their homes. Those without homes were taken in by others. Thomash brought food to Mario and they both returned to his cottage, where Goritza and Angelica were still huddled with only a small fire for light and warmth. Later they helped other women boil cloth in water mixed with ashes. This was cut into pieces and spread over a thin layer of warm beeswax to cover injuries—for those people left wounded.

At last, the village slept. But in the early morning, still exhausted, they were aroused again by roaring planes overhead. This time they dropped leaflets which warned that any resistance would mean total annihilation of the area.

Around noon a new column of Italian soldiers from Gradina entered the village. With Laguna acting as interpreter, an order was issued for everyone to gather in the churchyard. After being assembled there together, fearfully on the part of most women, defiantly on the part of many men, ten people were selected and lined up against the church wall before a firing squad. An officer, stiff and forbidding, confronted the villagers.

"One of our soldiers is missing," he said in a slow, threatening voice. "Name—Mario Santucci." He paused and looked searchingly towards the faces in the crowd. No one moved. Pointing at the ten men—husbands, fathers and grandfathers, he said, "These men will be shot—here and now—if..."

Suddenly there was banging on the church door from within, and a frantic voice shouted, "Aprite! Aprite!"

The officer jerked around. He wheeled, stalked to the doorway, and kicked it with his heavy boots. The door flew open and Mario emerged. His hair was wild, and his face was contorted with fear. He knelt before the officer, grabbing at his legs while babbling in Italian. His superior listened contemptuously, then gave a signal to the firing squad, which lowered its guns. Meanwhile, the officer motioned to Mario, who followed him back into the church. There was a tentative stir from the villagers as they listened to the sobbing voice speaking rapidly in the foreign language.

Just as the two men emerged from the church, Thomash appeared on the path coming from his cottage. He limped up to the cluster of people and looked warily at the officer, then exchanged a glance with Mario—who was more calm by this time.

"Who's the chief of this village?" the officer asked, his eyes darting here and there amongst the huddled men and women, some carrying babies, others with toddlers clinging to their skirts or trouser legs.

"I am," said Thomash in a firm, clear voice. He held up the key to the church as proof.

Mario ran up and shook Thomash's hand. "Grazie—grazie tanto!"

The officer scolded Mario for this, and ordered him back in line.

Regrettably, Thomash patted Mario on the back as he left. They'd agreed that Mario would remain inside the church overnight; he was planning to desert from the army when the troops moved out. Thomash thought there was a fair chance of escape had he left earlier.

The Italian officer turned to the villagers. "Anyone here by the name of Costovar?"

"That's my name," Thomash replied with dignity.

"So? And what about Dayan? Dayan Costovar?"

"He's my son." Thomash looked towards the church, as if to seek a blessing from it for Dayan.

"Well, where is he now?"

"My son's safe in God's hands."

The officer looked at Thomash angrily. "Sure—sure. Aren't we all, or hope to be." He strode away while gesturing to some nearby soldiers, who grabbed Thomash and lifted him onto a mule's back.

Dismissed, the villagers straggled back to their homes, while Thomash was taken to Gradina—with the two tallest soldiers in charge of helping him. When the rocky road became steep and

Thomash was close to falling off, they'd put out their hands to steady him; he was a valuable cargo.

Ushered finally into one of Mortellini's offices, Thomash was questioned by a member of his staff. "Tell us who's leading those rebels and you'll go free," the investigating officer demanded.

Thomash said nothing back.

"We'll give you plenty of salt, and medicine too—anything you want from us."

Still Thomash remained silent.

Another officer in the room settled his monocle, and then looked coldly at him. "Was it by any chance, Perun Novak?" he asked. When Thomash again failed to respond, the monocled one sighed heavily and shook his head. "No—surely not!"

At this, Thomash shook his head too, meaning he agreed that it hadn't been Perun.

"It couldn't have been," the other man said. "Perun Novak was kidnapped by your own son."

Now Thomash straightened up. His expression, which was that of a man under careful control, changed to one of amazement combined with fear. "Dayan—my son? What do you mean?"

"It's very simple. Dayan was there in the church, wasn't he? Shooting at our men from the altar? Isn't that why you're keeping quiet about it—to protect your own son?"

"No, that's not so at all!"

"Then why won't you talk?"

"They're my people. I won't betray them."

"Very well then." And with that he was taken away.

The sentence of the military court in occupied Gradina read: *Thomash Costovar, as the leader of Cablo, was instrumental in ordering his village to cut ties with Gradina based on Radio-London propaganda. He assisted his son Dayan Costovar, a wanted rebel fugitive, with the capture of Perun Novak for clandestine purposes. Therefore, he is hereby sentenced to serve one hundred years at hard labor while in a prison camp. This sentence is immediate and will be carried out to its fullest extent.*

10

The King Leaves

While Cablo underwent its hardships and Thomash was being hustled away to begin his sentence, Dayan continued on his journey through the monstrous Independent State of Croatia created by Hitler and Mussolini.

His worry about holding his own as a warrior among the fierce Montenegrins was long past, for actually he never reached Montenegro. That mountainous area was further from where he'd traveled than he thought. After circling around to the west he was now traversing deep forests with paths leading nowhere, or over steep terrain without any paths. There were gorges that stayed dark until noon, and rocky mountain peaks which seemed almost as distant as the Alps.

Towards dusk one day he stopped in a small village to rest and buy a few supplies, and was told by a priest that King Peter and members of his government had passed by close to Sarajevo, then had flown from Montenegro's only available airport en route to Greece and then to exile in London. Space on the plane was limited so the King, who was English-educated, was ready to act as an interpreter for the non-English speaking members of the government. It was also rumored they'd taken the last of Yugoslavia's gold reserves along with them.

The Independent State of Croatia was having its troubles too; the cities that were occupied by the Germans and Italians remained relatively disciplined, but out in the villages there was unrest due to the massacres of Serbs carried out by Nazi-type party *Ustashis*, along with the establishment of concentration camps used for torture and executions. For this the opposition guerrillas reacted violently, and they grew in strength and resistance. The situation assumed the dimensions of a mass rebellion. Warfare indeed was sweeping the area as never before seen, even in the historically turbulent Balkans.

Meanwhile, a handful of old Montenegrin isolationists also proclaimed their own independent kingdom under Prince Michael, the grandson of their last king. They'd already chosen cabinet members with the approval of the Italian Royal Court, Mussolini, Hitler and the occupying troops. It seemed everybody was in favor of their choice except for the people and the western-oriented Prince himself. At this time he was still imprisoned in Germany, and after rejecting the offer said he preferred his imprisonment over ruling their puppet throne!

All this confusion was augmented by increased conflicts of an ideological and regional nature. And when Nazi Germany invaded the Soviet Union, new communist guerrilla units, called *Partisans,* were activated in Serbia by Josip Broz Tito, their new leader.

The Germans added to the local threat by making a promise; for every German soldier killed by any Serbian guerrillas, one hundred Serbs would be killed in retaliation—and they abided by this resolution as best they could.

Already shaken by the massacre of Serbs by Croatian Ustashis, everything was now shattered by the additional conflicts between the two guerrilla movements themselves; the Chetniks and the Partisans.

Meetings were held between their individual leaders, Colonel Mihailovic and Tito, in late 1941 to form an alliance, but these talks broke down and turned into new bloodshed, leaving the occupying powers in observance of a full-scale civil war. Mihailovic and Tito made mutual accusations—Tito charged that the colonel was the puppet of London, and the colonel in turn insisted that Tito was a tool of the Kremlin.

These counter-charges had reached the Kremlin and the country's exiled government in England. The confusion and disharmony even reached as far as the New World, dividing Yugoslav immigrants in North and South America and Australia into almost as many factions as there were in the old country.

Traditional devotion to the West and to their democratic principles assumed widely romantic proportions among Mihailovic's guerrilla followers. New slogans were carved in wood bark and new odes to the West were created and sung, with flags held high on even the most remote mountain peaks.

This fiery band of Chetnik guerrillas wanted the shame to be made known to the whole country. The isolated Chetnik units at the Adriatic were always the last to be informed, and the only means of spreading the word to them was by individual couriers.

Under the circumstances Dayan didn't regret not getting to Montenegro, for almost every square foot of Yugoslavia outside of the cities had become a battlefield, where poetic courage—as well as fanaticism and brutality—were being displayed daily. He was still carrying Tobo's rifle, yet the sixty cartridges—which he'd once considered sufficient to kill off all the world's trouble-makers and bring peace to mankind—had long since been spent.

He couldn't remember how many times he'd filled and emptied his cartridge bags, nor could he recall the time when the words *killing* and *fighting* had come to mean the same thing. Sometimes he was aware that he'd become caught up in violent turbulence, but he never asked himself why. This was no time for questions, except for one which kept haunting him—why has he survived it for so long?

But this question couldn't be answered either and so he let it go, along with all the confusion and senselessness he was going through. And just as his grandfather had given Thomash life twice, Dayan had new life almost every day too thinking of them and the others back home, forgetting he might be killed at any moment—just as the other guerrilla fighters around him could, and were.

For this reason he didn't hesitate to volunteer for the Adriatic area as a Chetnik courier. It was to carry the message about the next phase of open conflict with the Partisans.

"But not as a soldier," Captain Radovich instructed him. "Carry no proof of identity, and you must go alone." Radovich was a former Saint-Cyr military student who had acted as interpreter in Mihailovic's headquarters until the British military mission was called off. "Better go to communion before you leave," he advised

Dayan. This was customary in the Serbian army before undertaking a dangerous mission.

However Dayan refused; he was confident and thrilled with the assignment. After all, he was the one who'd carved the most slogans on wood bark, and even written an ode to the Western powers. Yet Radovich's words, *not as a soldier,* sounded strange to him. He'd been wondering lately if he could ever be anything other than a soldier, one who's used plenty of cartridges and to whom each experience had, so far at least, granted him a new spiritual life. But he was happy now not to be a soldier, even if it meant handing over Tobo's rifle to a newly-recruited man.

The next day Dayan started out on his secret mission, and for a week made good progress towards his objective further west. He was careful to avoid the areas he knew might be dangerous to cross, but only one moment of indecision was all it took, and just one wrong turn—when suddenly he was captured!

"So your real name is *Mutan*?" asked the Partisan named Edo, who had rimmed glasses and a mustache like Stalin's. "That's strange. Mutan means someone who can't talk, but you manage it quite well."

"It's what Auntie calls me," Dayan answered, hoping his expression wasn't visible behind his eight-day growth of beard.

"Your Auntie? Well, what did the others call you in school?"

"Never went to school." He managed to keep his face blank. "She calls me Mutan too."

"She?"

"Rosa. Damned Rosa." He hit his hands upon the rock he was sitting on.

"Is she your girl?" The man laughed. His shoulders were bent as Dayan's had been when he was a student. "And why *damned* Rosa?"

"She hit me, threw mud on me. And she ran away with a gendarme." He put his head down upon his folded arms, thinking about how to answer the next question, while Radovich's words—

not as a soldier—hummed in his ears. He looked up. "They also handed me over to the Germans."

"Would you kill that gendarme if we gave you a gun?"

Dayan clenched his fists and looked as bloodthirsty as possible.

"Well, it isn't necessary, we'll give you a knife. However, to become a party member you'd have to kill with your bare hands. And the person killed must be someone related to you. You have no parents?"

"Never."

The man lifted his mustache and laughed, showing many gold teeth.

"Yes. Me and Rosa. I'll kill her like this—like a goose!" Dayan brought his clenched hands close, as though twisting the neck of a fowl.

Suddenly the man jumped up and came close to him. "What's this? A gold ring? Gold—in these times?" He grasped Dayan's hand with the tenderness of an orthopedic surgeon examining a patient. "And with a diamond in it!" he said jealously. "A big one!"

Not as a soldier, you're not a soldier—hummed in Dayan's ears. Aloud he said, "Stole it from Rosa. Damned—"

"Don't beat that rock anymore, you might hurt it," Edo chided, then he got up and whispered to the guard.

Dayan was glad for the focus being on the ring, rather than on his face. He looked towards the railroad tracks in the distance; it's where he'd been captured that morning by Tito's Partisans, after a train loaded with fruit had passed to the north. From the high mountains, a fresh breeze still came down from where he'd descended last night.

"Come on," said his guard, and he led Dayan back amongst the armed Partisans standing around the former school building.

"Did you find out his real name?" someone asked.

"We'll call him *Mutan*," his guard replied. "After all, Comrade Tito goes by another name: *Nikitin*. So does our father, Stalin. Lenin also had one—and even Trotsky."

He took Dayan into the building where they supplied him with an English military blouse and belt. *Thanks to Stalin*—he was told. His companion tightened the belt around his waist. He wrote Dayan's fake name and the unit to which he was assigned on a small piece of paper, and handed it to a woman—who began sewing the identification onto the collar of the blouse.

The man with the eyeglasses looked again at Dayan's ring and patted his shoulder affectionately. "We'll teach you how to write," he promised. "You're my good recruit!"

That evening a report was ready to be sent out via Radio Free Yugoslavia: *Tito's Partisan units have liberated an entire transport of forced laborers from a German train, killing all the Germans aboard. The train was totally destroyed. All laborers have voluntarily joined our units.*

Dayan's friend with the Stalin mustache was just signing the report, when they heard shouting from outside. "Comrade Edo! Comrade Edo! Comrade Rocka's coming."

The thunder of horses' hooves came from a distance and Edo quickly ordered all the Partisans to line up in the schoolyard, Dayan among them. Comrade Rocka, with blonde hair cut short, dark gray eyes and a thin mouth, galloped up to the gathered men and reined her horse to a halt. She sat erect on the horse surveying the crowd of soldiers, her arrogant expression helping to disguise the words which she finally yelled: "Comrades! I bring you greetings from our great father and savior of mankind—Comrade Stalin!"

"Long live Stalin! Long live Lenin!" the men shouted back.

"Shut up, fools!" Rocka's horse jerked forward a few steps and she angrily reined it to a stop. Evidently, there was no love lost between the horse and mistress. "Idiots," the woman shouted, "Lenin is dead, Stalin's our leader. Stalin! He sent you his greetings through Comrade Tito, and Comrade Nikitin got them from Tito, who sends them through me."

Those greetings certainly travel around a lot, Dayan thought to himself, taking care to keep his face blank while in the role of Mutan.

Chapter 10

Suddenly, as the men stared at Rocka while shuffling with uncertainly, Edo broke the silence. "Long live Rocka!" he yelled. A long, blank silence followed.

Hurrying to fill the void, Rocka began speaking rapidly in a rather hoarse, unpleasant voice. "Listen up everyone! Now for the big news! We've learned that the Western powers aren't coming to the Balkans. Instead, they will foolishly supply us with whatever we need—Stalin has seen to that. From now on, our fortress of socialism won't be built on the lives of our best comrades. No more. Let the bourgeois sentimentality of the Western plutocrats pay that price!"

This news caused a stir amongst her listeners, but it's impossible to gauge whether it was because of approval, surprise or skepticism. Rocka continued, "There's no need to spare ammunition because the West will send us plenty. Liquidate your class enemies and you don't have to be careful with just one bullet to the back of the neck. Shoot the works—three or even four bullets. Seven if you want. But kill! Kill!" She was working herself up into a hysteria. She began galloping back and forth in front of the Partisans. "Kill! Kill!"

Then she turned her horse, galloped across the schoolyard—and disappeared beyond some buildings.

Edo had informed Dayan that he was scheduled to take a loyalty oath that morning, and attend the execution of some *People's enemies.* For the loyalty oath he was brought to the former house of a schoolteacher, where Rocka was quartered. An armed guard, who called himself *Tell*—remained outside as a sentry.

Dayan entered the room and was confronted by Rocka. She looked more relaxed than when she'd been exhorting the Partisan troops. Beckoning him to approach her, she held out her hand. With inward reluctance, but an impassive face, Mutan shook it. Her long, cold fingers reminded him of small snakes.

"You're a good soldier. And strong, too. The priest would say *God made you*, but our thinking is nature made you. For there is no God. You hear me?"

He heard the words, but he really noticed the sounds which came from the second floor above them. It was the loud moaning of a man, and it seemed to be a peasant's voice. Then he heard blows hitting toughened flesh, which brought increased moans and cries. Looking away from Rocka's intense face as her eyes attempted to probe him, he saw the silhouette of a man outside the window. Dayan recognized him as the Partisan known as *Tell.* In the growing dusk his figure loomed large.

Rocka then motioned Dayan to sit, and they faced each other across a worn wooden table, part of the former school equipment. Dayan imagined the children sitting there. *To eat their lunches? To make things with paper or clay?*

"Tell me your story," Rocka said in as gentle a voice as she could manage.

He made an apparent struggle to speak.

"What's the matter? Afraid to say something?"

"Un uh." Dayan answered more by the movement of his shoulders.

"Then—ashamed? But why? You're a man, as nature made you. Are you cold?"

"No." This time his voice was clear and loud.

"Have you no story for me?" she asked. "About your childhood —you must have been poor?"

Dayan had been waiting for a good entry into this treacherous interview to help avoid suspicion. Now he grasped her question eagerly, by keeping his expression impassive—and he hoped stupid. "Yes, poor, poor! My girl Rosa too."

Rocka looked pleased. "Well, I'm not poor, Mutan. I'm from Belgrade. There I have a big home with many baths." She looked at him for a reaction, but there wasn't any.

She tried again. "My job, Mutan, is to fight for ideas. Do you know what that means?"

He shook his head, trying to shrink into himself and let her do all the talking.

Chapter 10

"One day we'll go to Belgrade—along with the Russians. I'll take you to my home. Rosa too. You'll sleep with her in a very large, soft bed. How would you like that? You'd like to sleep with a woman, wouldn't you Mutan?"

From above there was heard a loud scream from a different voice than before. This one sounded like it was a young woman, and she pleaded: "No! No! Don't touch me! I'm engaged—my fiancé is a prisoner. No, you swine. Don't!"

Dayan's muscles tensed. He wanted to rush out of the room and away from this crazy person, to rush upstairs and—*what?* Get shot like a dog before he could so much as lift a finger to save the screaming woman?

The screaming above stopped abruptly when the sound of something heavy hit the ground outside by the window, followed by pistol shots fired over and over. Dayan counted six shots. It must be the tall woman with long blonde hair he'd seen under guard with other peasants in the school room. He longed to avenge her—right now! But the words—*you're not a soldier*—still rang in his ears like the gunshots he'd just heard. His mission as a courier was at stake, with all that meant to the forces waiting for his message. However, how long could a man sit still? He wanted to jump at Rocka and squeeze her neck as he'd demonstrated earlier—just like you'd squeeze the neck of a fat goose.

Every muscle in his body was tightening now, preparing for action. *You're not a soldier, you're not a soldier.* When that phrase ran through his head once more he'd leap at his victim. Then those words were followed with—*but you're still a human being.*

Only a swine, as the dead woman had said, would kill a woman. From outside now there was silence, except for the small sound being made as Tell threw his rifle from one hand to the other—with perfect skill. Should he take a chance and try to rush Tell? No, he realized it was an impossible feat. Besides, the tension was gone from him now. All he knew was that he's *still* a human being.

It was fortunate that he'd hid behind the *Mutan* mask, for all these murderous thoughts which ran through his head hadn't shown on his face at all. Rocka had been studying him, and had little suspicion of what was going on in his mind. In fact, she seemed to imagine she was making great headway.

"What a foolish woman she turned out to be," Rocka said contemptuously. "She even denied us free love. We'd given her a whole week to change her mind. I hope you're not stubborn like that, Mutan." She gave him what was intended to be an inviting smile, then stood up and walked to a corner of the room, where she took a small bottle out of a rucksack. Dayan watched as she sprayed herself with it, and the strong odor of a musky perfume drifted into his nostrils. He pretended to swoon from the heavy fragrance.

Encouraged, Rocka sprayed some on him. "It makes you feel fresh," she said, "and young." She looked at him hungrily.

Dayan was repelled by her clumsy tactics. She certainly went at seduction with a lack of finesse. Compared with her methods, the experience he'd had at Shark Street seemed like a rosy picnic. *If I spat three times to cleanse myself of that memory, how many will this one take?*

He wished for a chance at a sudden attack on Tell, who was still tossing his rifle from hand to hand. Tell was older, but that didn't matter, Dayan thought. He needed to do something.

Rocka had sat on a bench and was pulling at her boots. "I can't get them off," she complained. "This English trash!"

This was his signal to approach her and help to pull her boots off—and then? Sickened, Dayan half rose, still undecided if he'd attack Tell first—when suddenly Edo ran across the yard with two guards following him.

"Comrade Rocka!" he shouted. "Sector bulletin to read!"

Rocka rose and took out her pistol. "You wait here," she said, and then pinched Dayan's neck.

As soon as she left the room, Dayan moved swiftly to the window. Edo, with the two guards on either side of him, stood at attention as Rocka appeared. He offered her the bulletin, but she waved it away. "Read it," she commanded, and then she listened attentively, with her head cocked towards her right shoulder as he began: "*It's been learned that the couriers of Colonel Mihailovic have managed to pass through our territory on a highly secret mission. They carry no identification.*"

Watching, Dayan saw Rocka lift her head and look quickly towards the window behind which he was crouching. She said nothing, and Edo continued reading: "*All suspicious persons must be arrested and sent to headquarters immediately. Death to Fascism! Freedom to the People! Signed—Nikitin.*"

Now Rocka, her face furious, sprang forward. "I knew it. I knew it!" she screamed. "Come on!" They all rushed towards the schoolroom to find Dayan where he'd been previously. But he was standing up now. Standing tall!

The two pistols, Edo's and Rocka's, were aimed at him as they entered. The guards carried rifles, which were also trained on him, and Tell stood in the doorway. Rocka marched up and confronted Dayan. "He's admitted to everything," she said in a low, cold voice. "But we'll let him tell us again. You know what to do, take him away. Search him first."

The *search* didn't take long, for one of the first things the men discovered was Dayan's tattoo, with the open book and burning candle on his right arm. That was enough! It told the story—it certainly wasn't a tattoo a *Mutan* would have on him.

They wasted no time. Within a few minutes he was hanging on an apple tree by a rope around his chest, barefoot and with his hands tied—while surrounded by armed Partisans. It was dark outside, except Rocka and Edo sat at a table which had many lighted lamps. The blinding light made Dayan's eyes ache. Behind Edo and Rocka stood Tell, his rifle at the ready.

Dayan, while squirming as little as possible, couldn't control turning his head away from the glare of the blinding lamps.

"So, you can't face a people's court?" Rocka smiled scornfully.

Dayan couldn't reply back if he'd wanted to. His breathing was reduced by fear, pain and the squeezing rope.

The woman commander signaled to the surrounding men, who approached and each hit the prisoner with whatever was handy—

mostly sticks and pistol butts. Then they withdrew some distance and began throwing rocks at him.

Dayan began counting. *One, two, three*—until he reached *sixteen*.

Meanwhile Rocka and Edo watched intently, but even in the midst of his pain, Dayan noticed Tell's eyes seemed to be looking out into the darkness of the fields—somewhere beyond the circle of light. It was that light which hurt Dayan almost as much as the blows, and the rope around his chest.

Then, for a moment, Dayan thought he felt his feet touch the ground, but it was only a pile of straw they'd placed there. They laughed as he scattered it while moving his feet. Now Edo gave a signal and the Partisans, still in the same order, came up with branches of a thorn tree and hit his feet. "How's that?" Edo asked jovially. "Had enough yet?"

Dayan shook his head. He wanted them to hit him until his feet bled. Edo signaled again, and the men each took another turn. Dayan bent his shoulders, trying to ease the pull of the rope. He'd lost all sense of time and soon he lost consciousness. His eyes closed.

Eventually he became aware of light beating down on his closed eyelids, and when he opened them—he discovered it was sunrise. He was still surrounded, but these were different soldiers than last night. All except for Tell, who was fast asleep with his head down on a table snoring, with the ends of his mustache swaying on either side of his chin. In spite of his condition, Dayan managed a slight smile.

Suddenly he heard a stir and some suppressed murmurs from the crowd of men. Rocka appeared. She too was surrounded by different soldiers, and ordered two of them to take Dayan down from the tree. His body was so stiff when untied that he fell into the remaining straw they'd thrown under his feet last night. There his muscles contracted and he drew himself into a protective fetal position, with his face pressed into the straw. The smell of it was the only sensation he had—sight, sound and touch were muffled or almost non-existent.

Chapter 10

In a numbed, trance-like state he thought of the straw in the attic rooms above the barns in Cablo, where newlyweds spent their first nights and where their first children were conceived. *Am I asleep now—dreaming?* Suddenly he heard a woman's voice say to someone—*"Congratulations!"*

But there's no reason to congratulate him. He'd failed to accomplish his secret assignment. Angelica might be dead and will never know about the new poem he'd promised to write someday. His body felt warmer now, the fragrance of the straw was stronger, bringing him back to the present. He opened his eyes again and saw the sun over the mountain tops. He was lying on the ground and there they were, the new Partisans, fresh for another day of torture by stick beating and rock throwing.

Then he heard the same voice again. *"Congratulations!"* It was Rocka's voice. She stood above him smiling down. "What a strong man you are—our big, brave Apache." Rocka went on: "That's the kind of man we need." She signaled and he was pulled to his feet, then helped into the building. Once inside they sat him down at the same table as before, which was now set for breakfast.

There were cans of food with labels in English. "From Stalin," Rocka said proudly, "now eat up!" She offered him the food, but Dayan couldn't eat anything. He drank some tea though, and it was pleasant smelling like the straw had been. His nose, it seemed, was the only part of his body which wasn't aching—somehow it had escaped the beating he'd taken last night.

Rocka had buttered a slice of bread on both sides, then she dipped it into her tea. "You know America, Mutan?"

He swayed his head from side to side and took a sip of the hot tea.

"Well, they have Indians there—savages. In the old days they used to torture anyone who wanted to join the tribe. If he didn't break down because of the pain, he was accepted." Rocka swallowed the soggy bite of buttered bread. She looked at him, smiling. "That's what we do, Mutan—and you succeeded. Congratulations, you've survived it!"

He pretended not to understand, so she repeated, "Congratulations, I said!" Dayan kept his expression noncommittal, but as the woman began to speak again they were suddenly interrupted—to Dayan's relief.

Edo came in, stepping with assurance, his Stalin-like mustache neatly brushed and his eyeglasses gleaming. He handed Rocka a piece of paper to sign, which she read quickly. It was going to be sent to someone named *Sector Commissar Nikitin*. The message was brief.

Your bulletin's been received. We have caught and interrogated a courier who confessed to everything before the people's court. Investigation details to follow. Death to Fascism, Freedom to the People!

Rocka then signed the communiqué and rose to go out with Edo. Dayan heard what sounded like an argument between them, and it carried out into the hallway outside. Evidently, there was something Edo wanted. Then he heard the woman say: *"Take it—take it then! I have plenty of rings."*

Dayan fingered the gold ring which was his legacy from Thomash's father, the same ring that'd pleased Goritza so much when she'd handed it to her only son. Dayan sat quietly, thinking now of the orchards back home. How far away Cablo was now! Then Rocka returned with Edo, who was armed with an English submachine-gun, and Tell, who carried his rifle. The two men tied Dayan's wrists together with rope, though he struggled to resist them.

"Don't be a fool," Rocka chided Dayan, "it's only to show Comrade Nikitin how you escaped from the German transport. You're wearing a military blouse and belt we supplied for clothing, aren't you? We're taking you to see Nikitin. He'll admire your strength."

"Then give me my moccasins," Dayan said, "if I'm to be marching."

"Oh, the Apaches made their members walk barefoot all the way from Texas to Mexico. You've heard of Texas, haven't you?"

"Never."

"Oh well, there's no time to explain it. Get going." She motioned to the three of them to go, but detained Edo to whisper, "Bring at least four and be sure they're young ones. I'm sick of this food already."

"Yes, yes," Edo assured her. Then they pushed Dayan out the door, and set out across the fields together. The two Partisans seemed to know where they were going; they never hesitated, but walked confidently along one path and then another. The ground under Dayan's feet sometimes felt soft, sometimes hard and sharp, but when he looked down it all seemed the same.

Everything around him—the trees and shrubbery—seemed to be moving, swaying. Even the horizon was in motion with large vibrating ribbons of rainbow colors, which danced and shimmered as he watched.

He'd heard about such experiences from buddies who had similar illusions when they faced death in battle. If this was the way it is, he thought, even death has some charm. Strangely though he felt like he wasn't touching the ground. Perhaps he was being carried on death's wings to those magic colors at the horizon. But suddenly he felt something soft and silky under his feet, so he looked down. A thick braid of golden hair was visible above a pile of freshly turned soil.

It must be the young woman who'd fallen earlier with a heavy thud, from the window of Rocka's schoolhouse headquarters. Dayan stared in shock, saying to himself—*Forgive me for not doing more.* All around him he saw more piles of fresh soil. *To all of you as well,* he whispered.

Edo and Tell had continued forward without turning their heads. Now they came to a small settlement. Edo waved at Tell and went off towards a nearby cottage. A few moments later there was the sound of shooting, then children crying and Dayan heard a commotion of roosters and hens.

As they approached, he saw a peasant woman standing in front of a chicken coop armed with a pitchfork. She was confronting Edo angrily and cursing as she brandished her weapon. Tell hustled Dayan away until they came to a crossing of two paths, and for the first time Tell hesitated. Either he didn't know which path to take or he was expecting to meet Edo here. He looked up towards the mountains again as he had last night.

"Is that where you live?"

Tell nodded, looking at the distant mountains with longing. "Yes, far away."

"My home is much farther away than that," Dayan said in a friendly voice. "Tell," he said, "Tell...is that what your kids call you?"

"No, they call me Papa."

Dayan smiled. "That's what I call my father." Tell was beginning to relax a little. "I'll bet you're a great sharpshooter."

"How'd you know?"

"You should be, because of your name. There was a famous Swiss marksman. Did you ever hear of him? William Tell? He was a hero."

Tell looked pleased, but was somewhat confused. He wasn't sure what the word *hero* meant, but evidently it was good. Dayan went on, talking partly to win Tell's confidence and partly to win back his own. The sight of the fresh graves, along with the golden hair gleaming out from one of them, must be put out of his mind for now until he could avenge them.

"It's a well-known story," he told the old man. "Schiller wrote a drama about him and Rossini an opera. Ever been to Switzerland?"

"Maybe," Tell replied. "So many countries, in the army."

"You must have served in Austro-Hungary, and maybe Italy, Yugoslavia, Croatia, and now here."

Tell shrugged bitterly and nodded. He wasn't impressed with his career as a soldier, always being in so many different countries. The fighting was all the same. It was only a little worse or a little better, a little colder or a little hotter, the food was either bad or worse. The days and months were endless and gray.

As if sensing the man's feelings, Dayan said, "I feel sorry for you, Tell. You've killed many in the name of a few. Do you remember the last time you killed?"

"Some Germans."

"And?"

"We retreated."

"Then what?"

Tell scratched his gray hair and lowered his eyes. "The Germans burned the village."

"The real Tell wouldn't let them. He'd be brave. He must be cool-headed too, because when the time came to hit the apple on his son's head—"

Tell had been looking towards the mountains again. But now he looked at Dayan in surprise, wondering what's this about hitting an apple?

"That's what the other Tell did to save their lives. Both him and his son's," Dayan said quickly, "and if you're weary, you may not have peace of mind—so you might miss."

"Miss!" Tell was indignant, defensive. That's a word he knew and denied about himself. "Never! Nobody can make me miss!"

"Don't be so sure. And when you fail, you'll just be a small killer, so everyone will blame and curse you. It's the big killers who get rewarded and praised. The little ones have to pay. You'll pay, as I pay now."

"What do you mean?"

"I know what's going to happen to me. After all, my hands are tied."

"Oh, shut up." Tell was uncomfortable. He wasn't suppose to carry on conversations with a man who's destined to die by his hand after an interrogation.

"No, I won't shut up," Dayan pursued. "My spirit will haunt you, Tell. Just when you try to hit that apple on your son's head."

"Stop it!" The old man was angry and pointed his rifle towards Dayan.

"I can't stop now. I must try to help you, Tell."

Slowly, looking into Dayan's face with a mixture of hope and distrust, Tell sank into a crouching position, laying his rifle across his knees. Dayan sat down on a boulder. The countryside here was strewn with dark blue, slate-like rocks.

"This is much like my own country, Tell, we're also rich in rocks and tragedy. Hand me one of those slates and a small rock." There was authority in his voice and Tell responded to it.

With his tied hands, Dayan carefully wrote on the slate. He made a small cross, under which he printed: *IN HOC SIGNO VINCES*. He put Thomash's name and address at the bottom and showed the slate to his companion. "Give this to my father one day and my ghost won't haunt you," he promised.

Tell looked over at the flat stone. "That's a cross."

"Right—and I'm a Christian. Those words mean that you win by the cross only, and not that rifle."

"I'm a Christian too." The old warrior sighed and cupped his head in his hands wearily.

Dayan looked compassionately at the tired soldier. "That's not what the others call you."

"No, they call me bourgeois, I think." The man's head was nodding to his knees.

"You mean proletarian."

"Maybe."

"You're tired," Dayan said gently, "but you'll be happier from now on if you stop killing." He saw the man's shoulders heaving, ridding himself of all his burdens. "Relax, relax, slowly, slowly—Papa," Dayan repeated gently, as if he's soothing a baby in a cradle.

The soldier's manners showed what resulted from the heroic products of Radio-London and Moscow—a tired, miserable old man and a veteran of many battles. He'd fought in Austro-Hungary, Italy, Yugoslavia, the satellite Croatia and, most recently, as a loyal Partisan soldier for Tito, who still hadn't managed to teach him how to distinguish between the proletarian and the bourgeois. This all weighed on Tell, who shrank into the frame of his old bones—weary, bitter, and haunted by the thoughts of some terrible fate which awaited him.

Dayan was ashamed to betray him, but Edo might be coming at any moment. So he quickly threw the slate into a bush, and with a few leaps—had hidden himself behind a big rock. Tell remained with his head down on his arms, lost to the present as he was lost to the future.

From his vantage point Dayan suddenly saw Edo appear behind the old man, in each hand carrying two chickens by the legs. Silently, Dayan moved away further while crouching, and then ran a few steps to find shelter again. As he slipped away, he heard a gunshot—but it couldn't have been aimed at him, he thought, for he heard no whistling sound.

God rest his soul.

Dayan continued running, this time towards the Adriatic.

11

While Playing A Flute

There were more freshly dug graves seen in the woods, some were still empty and others were filled and rounded over. From one grave a man's callused hand, large as a plowshare, stuck out. It reminded Dayan of the peasant he'd met on the train when he first left for Belgrade—the one who'd told him that scorpions must be smashed and any vampires stabbed while using a sharpened blackthorn branch.

The Ustashis from Sarajevo had devised this system where the victims dug their own graves, and employed it in the destruction of the Jews. This practice spread quickly.

As Dayan continued walking he saw great clouds of smoke high beyond the hills. It was probably farmers burning the stubble and orchard trimmings, as they did in Cablo when autumn drew near. He hoped somebody there could cut the rope which bound his hands, and maybe he'd also find some moccasins to help him on his way. Now he hurried as best he could in that direction, even though he was barefoot and sore.

When he neared the area, the smoke driven by the wind reached him, and he sniffed curiously. The color and smell were unfamiliar. He could scarcely see, and as he stumbled through the acrid, dark clouds of smoke, he heard dogs howling.

Still, he hurried on, for Edo stalking forward in his stout English boots might be right behind his own torn feet. Rocka's right-hand man wouldn't slow down at those graves—he certainly knew of them and had doubtlessly helped to fill many of them. He'd fire twenty rounds from his Tommy gun and that'd be that. One shot might be enough, but to be badly wounded would be worse for Dayan than to be killed outright.

Now there was a red glow, and he came to a burning house. The sparks had kindled areas around it and he managed to burn the rope which bound his wrists together. This would make it easier to run through the only shelter he had—the heavy smoke. There was something ahead of him behind a hedge, it seemed to be dancing in the air. Cautiously, with the sound of his footsteps being muffled by the crackling of the fire, he drew nearer, until he could make out an ox, reddish in color and with only one long horn. The other had been broken off, apparently by a bullet close to its head.

The ox was turning around and around, senselessly with fright. Rocka's horse had wheeled and turned like that last night while she was exhorting on the comrades. Dayan held out his hand, trying to coax the terrified animal towards him.

"Halt!" A shiny object suddenly appeared in front of him—a German bayonet. Dayan stood motionless, but his hand remained outstretched. The ox moved forward and began to lick it. The soldier motioned with his weapon and Dayan limped in front of him, passing groups of men in green uniforms. He was thankful he didn't have to run, for his feet were hurting more and more. The ox had accepted him as a friend, it was following behind his captor willingly. At last they reached a military truck loaded with peasants in the back, which he was instructed to enter.

Once inside, Dayan greeted them in the customary way—"God help you!"

For this he heard an angry grumble from all sides: "What do you mean—God? Listen to him. You don't have God, you bloodthirsty communist!"

"No—you're wrong, so help me. I'm not. Believe me!"

An elderly peasant spat at him. "How about that English blouse? They're not handing them out for us to wear, mister."

"Yeah. How about that?" Another peasant slapped him in the face, and now they all joined in. It seemed that every peasant's hand was raised against him as large as a double plowshare. Dayan had no will to strike back at them even though his hands were free now. He used them only to shield his face from the ground when they threw him out.

Chapter 11

The Germans, laughing, drove the peasants back from him; even with his eyes almost closed, Dayan still saw their rough and hairy hands stretched out eagerly to hurt him some more. Big, strong hands, like those that stuck out from the graves in the hills, like those of the Saints. The same hands now rolled him to be carried in a coarse blanket, one man at each corner, to the nearest railroad station. The men with bayonets followed behind.

As they trudged ahead with their burden, the man holding the blanket to the right of Dayan's head spoke to his fellow comrades: "Some way to turn us all into proletarians." He was obviously the spokesman for the quartet. "Just put some dynamite under the railroad tracks, kill the Germans—and run. That's their heroism."

The others mumbled their agreement with his irony.

"When have we Serbs ever fought like that?" the same man continued. He was talking to Dayan as much, or more than he was to his comrades. "Then the Germans burn the village—more heroism. You should be ashamed of yourself—the whole country's nothing but a large grave now!"

Dayan covered his face with his hands.

"Slaves of fanatical masters," the speaker went on. "Such slaves shouldn't be allowed to fight. They're like toy robots. Wind them up and they fight, without knowing for what or why. Take your Comrade Stalin—"

"He's not mine, any more than he's yours," Dayan replied. He had uncovered his face and turned to look at the tall, gaunt man who was accusing him. Big hands or no, this man wasn't a peasant. His speech was that of an educated man. "Who are you?"

"Never mind my name. I'm now a broke lawyer. I was there at the station yesterday, trying to find some food for my children. I saw your heroism; four freight cars loaded with plums and squash derailed by the Partisans like you." He raised his voice. "And now the Germans are burning a village and its people in retaliation. Such heroism—a hundred Serbs lost for each German—or six thousand to fourteen, as in Kragujevac. Are those the percentages you like?"

"Of course not," Dayan said indignantly. He'd forgotten he was being carried through smoke on an improvised stretcher. Forgotten about the guards behind him with raised bayonets. He wondered briefly why they're even allowing this conversation, and then realized it's a gesture of contempt. These creatures weren't speaking in perfect German, they thought, but were babbling in some foreign tongue, and were therefore unworthy of their attention.

The broke lawyer was becoming reckless—he'd been bottled up, with no release for his indignation, hatred and frustration; now he had a listener who might understand him. "And why won't you ask your fat Churchill to send dynamite and weapons to those English islands these foolish German have occupied. I wonder how many Englishmen were even shot? Or did they manage to do away with a few of the enemy? Yes—ask your Churchill about that one!"

"That's impossible!" Dayan knew it was useless to reply, but he couldn't stop himself. It was galling to be accused like this and have no defense.

"Why so? Haven't you got plenty of English radio stations? Why, every damned prostitute following Tito's units is seen wearing an English uniform." The angry lawyer looked at Dayan's torn feet. "And by the way, how come Churchill didn't send you some boots to wear? You aren't a very successful slave, are you?"

"I'm not a slave at all!" Dayan wanted to shout it at the top of his lungs, but what was the use? Instead, he covered his ears with his hands; he couldn't take any more of this.

At the railroad station a German officer was separating the younger peasants from the old ones for transport to Germany. He confiscated Dayan's English military blouse and belt as captured war materiel. Taking a woolen jacket and a pair of moccasins from an old peasant who was being sent home, he gave them to Dayan and put him into a boxcar—which was divided down the middle by barbed wire.

One side was for goats and the other side was for some people from the Southern Balkans, mainly peasants they'd captured wrapped up in sheepskin coats and coarse blankets. At least it was a relief not to be among the ones who wanted to beat him with their hands, while wishing they had something harder to use like sticks and iron rods.

"Want to play this?" It was dim within the boxcar and Dayan, startled, looked at the flute, then at the young man who was offering it to him. The boy's fingers were as slender and fragile as a bird's skeleton.

"Thanks, but no."

"All right then, I'll play something instead. Know this song—*Shepherd Kiros. Shepherdess Marika*?"

Dayan nodded. "That's a good one."

It was a bucolic song in which Kiros and Marika asked if they can graze their sheep together, promising that if her mother punishes the girl, Kiros's door will always be open for her. The thin, dark-haired young man played it well. When he'd finished, he wiped the flute and tucked it back into his pocket. "What's your name?" he asked. He seemed as simple as a child, although he was probably not much younger than Dayan.

"Mutan," Dayan answered.

"I'm Aristides. Those are my goats over there and they're thirsty. The Germans gave them wheat—that's nice. Now if they'd only water them."

He wore a large mantle, bordered with many embroidered crosses on his shoulders. In his Macedonian dialect he told Dayan that he was a shepherd from northern Greece. He'd been caring for some villagers' goats and three of his own, when the Germans captured him and the goats two days ago and put them into this boxcar. Then the train started off while taking in more people along the way.

Dayan noticed his own hunger as the train started moving, and then all the wheat scattered about under the goats. He reached under the wire and took a handful, putting some of it into his mouth. Aristides struck at his hand, spilling the grains of wheat. "You must be crazy. That's no good for you. Here!" He took out a piece of homemade bread from his pocket and gave it to Dayan.

He showed him how to bite off small pieces and soften them in his mouth before swallowing it, since the bread was hard and old. "Eat all you need," Aristides encouraged him. "There's plenty until Athens."

"We're going to Athens?"

"Sure—my uncle is there. I'll see him." The Greek youth looked questioning. "Is anything wrong?"

"No—nothing's wrong." Why make him unhappy beforehand?

"That's good. Then I'll play some more." He played another Greek song using his flute, and long before he'd finished it, Dayan was fast asleep.

"Attention! Attention!"

It was morning and a loudspeaker was blaring as they stopped at the German border. The subdued hum of activity in the boxcar—people moving around stiffly, stretching, and eating from meager stores of food—was stopped as the captives strained to listen to the recorded announcement. It came after a railroad clerk pushed a button on his desk, and it was broadcast twice in all the Balkan languages:

"Attention! Attention! In the name of the Third Reich and our Fuhrer, we welcome you! Congratulations on your decision to participate in building a new Europe!"

The announcement was followed by a recording of Schubert's *Military March.*

"Wake up. Mutan—wake up! We're lost!" Aristides was digging into Dayan's back with his toe.

Dayan was only half awake. "Don't worry, they'll be all right," he murmured. "The Germans will water them." He closed his eyes again and went back to sleep.

"No—no. Not just the goats! The whole train is lost. Did you hear me?"

Now Dayan began to wake up. "What's wrong, Aristides?" He rubbed his eyes, sat up and yawned.

"Those aren't my goats. If I lose them my father will have to pay for them. And we're very poor." Aristides was close to tears.

Chapter 11

Still fuzzy with sleep, Dayan was oblivious to his panic. "You're richer than I am. My father only has two goats—and yours has three. Why don't you play something?"

The young man tugged at Dayan's sleeve. "I can't play now—we're lost. This isn't Athens, it's not even Greece. They said there'd be better pasture for my goats near Athens. They told me I could visit my uncle when we arrived."

Dayan motioned him to be still as an official appeared. They were checking the train; locks on the boxcar doors were tested and instructions were issued by the border patrol. Dayan tried to divert Aristides attention by playing a song on the flute about girls in Macedonia who'd cursed the Shara Mountains for luring three shepherds into its abyss. "Do you see, Aristides, how much luckier you are? Now play a happy song, why don't you? You're better at it than I am."

The young Greek, like a child who's been comforted, smiled and took the flute from him.

While he played, officials came loudly into the boxcar and frightened the goats, making them move about in agitation—along with the ringing of their bells. The sound of the bells complemented the hora dance Aristides was playing. This song was about young people dancing outside a monastery. A monk, watching them from within, was tempted to leave his cell so he joined them, taking his place between two lovely girls.

Listening to the music and the merry ringing of the bells, Dayan was able to forget the immediate present, even though the German guards were clumping in and out with their heavy boots, looking sourly at the musician and his companion.

After all, didn't the Germans love music, and even pride themselves of this fact? Besides, he wanted to reassure Aristides, who, although he continued playing, looked fearfully at his burly captors. He had trusted them, and they'd deceived him back. His mother had taught him to tell the truth; so something was wrong. He finished the song and put down the flute.

"How wonderful!" Dayan praised him. "And the goat bells with the music—like Liszt. Ever hear of Franz Liszt?"

"Did he keep goats?"

"No, but he came from this area, so he probably loved them."

"Mutan, when will we see the peak of Olympus? The Germans said—"

"No one's ever seen the ancient one. No one but God. Surely your father's told you that."

"Oh, I suppose he did," Aristides said vaguely. "But God's in heaven now—far, far away. And we're lost."

The train was moving slowly again and Dayan thought they must be in the mountains somewhere. But where? "No, we're not lost," he assured Aristides. "God's leading us through the country of Hegel. He was a great friend of Greece."

The Greek shepherd brightened. "Maybe we'll see him when we get there."

"I'm afraid not. But don't worry about it."

"I do worry about you, Mutan. You're my friend, so here, have the rest of the bread. Eat it all. We'll find Hegel and ask him for more, and we'll ask him to send my goats back because my father can't pay for them. You'll help me find him, because you're not foolish like me."

Now the train was picking up speed, as it rushed through the alpine valleys.

The Vienna-South Station they arrived at later was blacked-out due to an air raid. Hundreds of people were milling about it while dressed in cotton garments labeled *East* on a big stripe fastened to their backs. The guards moved around with dim lights trying to create order. The boxcars of the train were disconnected and put onto various other tracks. "Achtung!" A guard motioned the people in Dayan's boxcar towards the exit at one end, and obediently they shuffled forward.

As Dayan stepped into the stuffy, dim interior of the station, he looked back and saw a reddish ox with one missing horn being prodded forward across the entrance ramp at the other end. Not you too, Dayan thought.

Suddenly Aristides, who was just in front of him, stopped. "My goats!" He started to turn back, but some soldiers pushed him with the rest of the people into a boxcar on the opposite side.

There was an open window in the new boxcar, and Aristides managed to get to it. He stood playing his flute as loudly as he dared. From the open car on the other side his goats bleated pitifully back, their bells jingling as they tumbled and bumped against each other, trying to find their master. But even Aristides could see now that it was hopeless; they were lost to him. Listlessly his hand fell, dropping the flute outside of the boxcar.

A workman was sweeping up debris, where the flute was gathered with other trash to be thrown into a dump truck and carted away. Dayan hadn't seen what'd happened to the flute; he was trying to discover what's in store for him, Aristides and all the other miserable, confused people inside the station. It was impossible to detect a pattern in what was happening; some of the cars loaded with people remained in the same place, while others were moved forward.

Now the boxcar in which they stood was suddenly encircled with guards carrying strong lights, which they shined into the doorway and through the windows. Everyone was ordered to leave, then they were pushed and prodded out of the vaulted station into the darkened streets of Vienna, where they formed into a long column and started forward. *Where will it end?*

"Mutan, don't leave me!" Aristides was trembling as he spread half of his mantle around his friend's shoulders, clutching half around his own. "You'll help me find that man—that friend of Greece," he whispered.

"Yes, yes," Dayan said to quiet him down. "Don't worry." In spite of the dreadful circumstances, he had to briefly smile; what would Georg Wilhelm Friedrich Hegel have made of the present events, and those of recent years? All this was a far cry from the serene purity of Ancient Greece!

"Can he bring back my goats?"

Dayan patted the shepherd's shoulders. "Everything will be all right."

Thomash used to tell Dayan, *Vienna is so beautiful at night—thousands of lights, and as bright as Cablo at noon.* Yet tonight it was dark, with the only light coming from the torches the guards held, and signs glowing against the wall in phosphorescent letters saying—*The Enemy Is Listening.* Above them were pictures of some creepy-looking men, and hung in-between were human bodies titled: *The Destiny of a Spy*—a warning.

As they passed these phantoms, Aristides trembled and clutched Dayan's arm. Silently, except for the shuffling feet and shouted commands, the column marched until it reached a wide road which ran by a canal of the Danube river lined with trees. Here more human bodies were hanging from the branches. Aristides looked at the smooth surface of the water, which reflected the cloudy night sky. It was silvery and appeared flat, like a field in the moonlight.

"Look, Mutan," Aristides whispered. "What's that?"

"The Danube—a river," Dayan answered in a low voice.

But a guard had heard. "No talking or I'll shoot you!" he threatened.

"Pasture? Did you say pasture?" Aristides whispered.

Dayan pantomimed drinking a glass of water, but Aristides didn't understand him, and looked over to the canal. Suddenly he pulled the mantle from Dayan's shoulders, flung it around himself and leapt into the water. There was a loud splash and a cry of terror, as the shepherd realized that the smooth, inviting surface he'd seen was really water—and not a field of wheat.

Horrified, Dayan saw his lifted arms break the surface of the canal, which was lapping with waves made by his falling body. The arms disappeared at the same time that the guards, alerted to an escapee, machine-gunned Aristides' mantle floating on the surface. Then the waves subsided, and again the water became smooth and silvery, like a field of wheat in the moonlight.

Reaching a complex of tall buildings, the column was ordered to throw their sheepskin coats, moccasins and heavy wool blankets into a huge incinerator. Then everyone was given a short haircut, and sent into a collective bath using some big showers.

Unaccustomed to public nudity, people waited uncomfortably for the disinfected clothing to be handed out, averting their eyes from the naked figures around them.

"Nothing to be ashamed of," the sanitary personnel told them. "It's better than being full of lice, isn't it?"

By the following morning the peasants from the Balkans, now cleansed and wearing disinfected clothing, emerged as working members of the Third Reich. At this time their immediate troubles became the heavy wooden shoes to which they were unaccustomed to wearing, and the fact that they didn't know where they were going.

Dayan was summoned from the others by a field-garrison and taken into an office, where he was confronted by a man in civilian clothes sitting behind an old desk. Recorded music came from a corner of the room: it was Strauss's *Voices of Spring*.

"I'm told you've lost a friend," the thin man said. He wore pince-nez eyeglasses, which gave him a scholarly air about it.

"You have, too," Dayan replied while standing. "He told me the Germans are good people, since they fed his goats." He'd also planned to tell him how Aristides had wanted to find Hegel—but the man opened a large drawer and pulled out the English military blouse and belt given to him by Rocka. He then tapped his finger on the identification sewn into the collar.

"This is you—*Mutan*?"

Dayan nodded, his knees trembling.

"Well, Mutan, I welcome you as a fellow scholar. You've heard of the Rosenberg Institute for Eastern Europe?"

Dayan hoped his expression was blank. He shook his head stupidly.

But the plainclothesman behind the desk overlooked this, and went on in a confident voice as to an equal. "We've got tremendous power, as you know. We can convert the most dedicated communist into the most ardent supporter of Nazism. And I don't mean just individuals—whole nations! Take the Russians for example."

The record went off and stopped playing. Herr No-uniform put on a new one titled: *Tales from the Vienna Woods*.

Dayan stood by and stayed silent. He was thinking how wrong this professor-type was. The Russian masses, he knew, had of their own accord turned against communism. But Rosenberg's brutal methods had sent them back into the orbit of the Reds, since nothing else was left for them. In the same way, most of the Serbs in Croatia had been thrown into the Partisan camp by the Ustashis.

The new music made a pleasant, deceptive background to the conversation which followed, a game of hide-and-seek with words. "So to sum up," the thin man continued, "what Rosenberg did for the unhappy Russians can also be done for you. Congratulations!" He rose up and went to Dayan with his hand out--stretched.

Dayan, fearing he'd be hit by it, protected his face with his arms.

"Come now—there's no reason to be afraid. Haven't you been baptized?"

"I think so," Dayan answered.

"Under the name Mutan?"

"Well, it's my name."

"You're a Christian?"

"Maybe yes, maybe no." His heart was pounding.

"Maybe yes, maybe no," the man mimicked back louder, suddenly discarding the pretense of friendliness. "Would you draw a cross on a message if you weren't a Christian? Or write a strange quotation if you weren't a scholar?" He was standing directly in front of Dayan now, and since they were of equal height— he stared directly into his victim's eyes.

Dayan tried looking away while his mind was racing. The Germans must know about the message scratched on the slate that he'd shown to Tell, the cross with the words—*IN HOC SIGNO VINCES*. Had Tell betrayed him? And what had become of Tell himself?

Chapter 11

As Dayan was escaping across the mountain that day while hearing a gunshot, he'd thought it was certainly coming from Edo's rifle. To the contrary, though he wasn't to learn this until later, it was Tell in disillusionment who'd shot Edo—thinking he was a German. Then Tell had fled too, only to be captured by the real Germans later. He'd actually ended up on the same train as Dayan, after telling them about the piece of slate on which the strange man had written a message—the man who wore an English military blouse and belt, and was called Mutan.

Yet not knowing this now, Dayan couldn't think of something, anything to explain things away. Luckily the interrogator signaled a waiting soldier to take him away; it's the same soldier who'd threatened Dayan and Aristides the previous night. He handed Dayan over to some field-gendarmes, who put him into a truck. The soldier returned to the office, finding his superior sitting behind the desk again, angrily writing out a report. He looked up.

"How many times did that Greek fool call him Mutan?"

"All the time—I didn't count," the soldier answered.

"He must have been crazy!"

The soldier nodded. "Otherwise, he wouldn't have jumped into the Danube."

"Bring me an interpreter."

The soldier saluted and went out. He was back in a few minutes with a short man who wore glasses with thick lenses, and whose stubby hands were covered with dark hair.

"Tell me, does the word *Mutan* really mean one who doesn't talk well?"

"Definitely, sir," the interpreter replied. "All professors of Slavic languages could tell you that."

"Professors. Ha!" Apparently he couldn't have made a worse suggestion. "Damn them. They'll stick to the Slavic Bolsheviks, in spite of the Fuhrer's statement that Slavs are only good for dung. Professors! A bunch of romantics who've spent too much time in the Balkans." Furiously he dismissed him.

The truck Dayan was in wandered after leaving, first in one direction and then another, sometimes fast and sometimes slow, so that Dayan lost all sense of orientation. Eventually he was delivered to a house which seemed identical to all the others in the block. There was a long guarded hallway which ended in stairs leading to a basement.

"Well, here you are," said the field-gendarme in charge of him. "I only hope they devour you tonight."

"Devour?"

"That's right, your comrades. All Slavs like you. The intelligentsia." The officer touched his temple. "The crazy ones. They'll eat you alive."

He opened the door and pushed Dayan inside, slamming it after him. Dayan found himself supported by men who'd been waiting inside to catch him. As they steadied themselves, he heard a key turn in the lock. The men led him over to a large round table and told him to sit down. Someone had given up his chair, and there was a moment of confusion while they shuffled around until everyone was settled again.

Dayan looked at the faces of the strangers who apparently were his fellow prisoners. They didn't look crazy, he decided, but they had a look about them of men who were aging long before their time. When they were all settled in, a white-haired old man climbed up and stood on his chair. He began to recite to them—evidently continuing a speech interrupted by Dayan's arrival.

"And finally they met—those from the east and those from the west. They were blocked, pushed and smashed from both sides by the two enemies."

The men nodded and smiled tiredly. It was evident they'd heard all this many times before. The speaker now got down from his chair and placed it upside-down on the table. Dayan saw that a map was drawn on the chair's bottom in charcoal. The old man pointed to a place marked with a cross. "A great poem will spread from here."

"All right, all right, Professor. Why don't you go to your bed and rest for a while," a man named Mankiewitz half suggested and half demanded.

"No! Please let him finish," Dayan said. Ordinarily, as a stranger in a new group, Dayan would have hesitated to assert himself. But there was something different in this place, as if ordinary rules of behavior didn't apply. For instance, nobody had asked him why he was here, where he'd come from, or what his name was. Perhaps those were unimportant matters, he thought. Perhaps these men were looking for solutions instead of compiling statistics.

Whether he was correct or not, the group decided to let the old man have his say. "As a professor of history," he then continued, "I call this the downfall of mankind." He indicated to the map on the chair's bottom, his finger marking the place with the cross. "You, young man, should look at what happens in the world with the eyes of a priest, or those of a prophet."

"Okay, that's enough now, Professor," a Pole objected. "The stranger doesn't know what you're talking about."

"Let him talk," Dayan begged again. He recognized his words, which he'd spoken long ago by the Danube. But the man's eyes were now sunk so deep into his head that they could barely be seen, and a long scar above his left eyebrow crossed the temple and led behind his ear. What terrible things had happened to him?

At last, wearily, the old man trudged off to a corner. He laid down on his improvised cot, but held his body stiff and straight, almost like a corpse, with his face turned upward towards the ceiling.

"Poor Professor Nameless." It was Mankiewitz, the same Pole who had spoken earlier. "He bothers everyone. You can just take so much of it."

"He doesn't bother me," Dayan protested.

"Maybe not yet. Just wait and see—if we live long enough!"

Dayan glanced towards the corner and unconsciously lowered his voice. "Please tell me about him. It's important."

"Well, first of all, the Nazis have listening devices around, so they hear a lot of what we say," he whispered. "Not that it matters. Ever since they discovered the massacre of Poles in the forests around Katyn they've kept us alive for some purpose. As far as the professor goes, don't ever call him by his real name or he'll break a chair over your head."

Dayan nodded and looked around. "Still, I must know about him if you can tell me," he whispered. "The old man speaks my language."

Other people sitting near them had been listening to this quiet exchange, and now one of the Poles joined in to give Dayan the old man's background. The professor was a former European luminary. He'd escaped death from the Germans and Bolsheviks while fleeing inside and outside of Poland, where he was later captured by the Soviet invaders and thrown into a prison work camp. There they discovered his real identity as Professor Veletsky, and sent him away to work on secret programs instead.

"You saw his scar?"

"Of course. Nobody could miss it," Dayan shuddered.

Mankiewitz nodded, sighed, and then shook his head as if to deny the inhumanity such a scar reveals.

"He got that here after a few days when the Nazis interrogated him repeatedly as a member of the Polish intelligentsia. They have interrogated all of us, but he got it the worst. They almost cracked the side of his skull trying to get him to talk, and he barely survived it. The poor old fellow, God knows there's more suffering and misery here than the mind can comprehend—but his went deeper. Perhaps it's because he was so brilliant—and in some ways he still is."

"I believe you." Dayan rose. "Think I'll go talk to him."

"He'll be glad for an audience. We have all heard it so often, and fond as we are of him, as I said—you can only take so much of it."

Mankiewitz turned to the other men and they all plunged into a discussion which appeared to be pre-arranged, as if they took turns teaching each other. Dayan had counted secretly; there were sixteen of them, not counting the professor.

Seeing Dayan approach, the professor, who was still lying stiffly on his straw pallet, immediately turned his chair upside down to show the charcoal map, and began: "...finally they met." He repeated the same recital Dayan had listened to long ago on the banks of the Danube.

When the professor came to the part about the *great poem*, Dayan interrupted: "I'd like to translate that poem some day, Professor."

The professor turned his sunken eyes towards him. "You're a poet?" The same words he'd spoken before, and from then on the conversation was a repetition of their earlier conversation back then. At first he sounded almost normal, but when he mentioned the *vanished people,* he covered the scar on his face with his hands and chanted: "No-no-no-no-no-no."

Dayan gently grasped his hands. The muscles were so tense beneath the tightly-stretched skin, one could almost imagine seeing the bones pierce through it. Then, when his hands were placed back in his lap, the professor rewarded Dayan with a surprisingly coherent: "Thank you, my boy."

The session around the table now with the other Poles had the character of a lecture given by a Russian on the subject of Stalingrad. His premise, as much as Dayan gathered from the snatches he heard, seemed to be that the battle of Stalingrad would be unique in history because it was won by slaves; that is, by Russians, already enslaved by the Bolsheviks, who'd fought with a newly awakened national spirit in the hope they'd achieve real freedom following their victory.

"If the West," the speaker concluded, "fails to realize the importance of this victory for themselves, with their moral obligation to grant freedom to the Russian people from the Bolsheviks, they'll pay dearly for that omission here on this sinful earth, long before they meet their God."

Comments and questions followed. Why, his comrades wanted to know, did the speaker have such doubts and fears about the future of Southeastern Europe?

The lecturer moved his head, indicating the corner of the basement where Professor Nameless was now sound asleep, snoring gently on his straw pallet. "Too bad he can't explain it to you. He could make you understand everything in ten minutes."

Dayan was proud to hear this tribute to the man who'd already lost his brilliant mind because of his devotion to the vanished people. Since he'd rejoined the group around the table, he sensed a difference in their attitude towards him, which until now hadn't been actual hostility, but rather was guarded with judgment withheld.

And as he found out, the seventeen men were considered to be survivors of the Polish intelligentsia, and known to be anti-communists. The Nazis had been actively hunting them after their invasion of Poland, and had killed off thousands of them. The Soviets had been just as ruthless with them after they'd invaded, sending many to the Soviet Union to be massacred in the areas around Katyn. Chances were these seventeen Poles wouldn't survive the war or even the next few months, but being intellectuals meant they couldn't idle away thought.

The four days Dayan spent amongst them, listening to them, learning from them, before he was sent off to a labor camp in a town named Fugen in southern Germany, were the greatest revelation of his life.

12

The Leaflets Fall Down

With the Allied invasion of Sicily in July of 1943, a special program was carried out among the occupying Italian troops in the Balkans with the purpose of elevating their spirits, and to convince the conquered people of the inevitable victory of the Axis powers. This attempt wasn't a roaring success, but it worked well in at least two areas: for singing and lighting.

The Italian songs *Vinceremo* and *Viva Duce* were sung with equal enthusiasm by grooms taking military mules to the rivers, and with the generals and field officers gathered at the gaming tables with their mistresses. The same words were posted around the garrisons, including the one in Gradina, which was illuminated by hundreds of gas lamps every night.

The peasants were delighted with all the lights. They sneaked in at night to steal the lamps, which were useful for trading in other areas. But their business suddenly fell off when Mussolini was ousted at the end of July and *Viva Duce* no longer applied.

However the slogan *Vinceremo* was still popular. Marshal Badoglio, who'd replaced Mussolini, declared that the war against the West would continue—but fortunately it didn't go on until the last man was left standing. With Italy's surrender as the Allies crossed the Straits of Messina, the Italian troops in the Balkans found themselves under two commands. One by Badoglio with the Allies to surrender, and the other by Mussolini, who'd already been rescued by Hitler's parachutists. Il Duce ordered them to continue fighting to their last breath.

All of this confusion had its effect on the detachment in charge of a satellite prison camp in Albania. The guards were instructed to trust to their weapons when in doubt. "Whatever happens," they were told, "remember, you're soldiers—and military courts are in full operation."

On one night in particular there was a thunder of planes over the camp, and the guards were quickly shooting into the air to destroy the thousands of leaflets released by the Allies. The bullets shredded them until they fell down like snowflakes.

There was chaos everywhere. In some quarters rebellious shouts rang out: *"Basta guerra!"* Some soldiers cursed, while others sang. One group ran out and scooped up some leaflets from the ground, then brought them into the barracks and passed them out. The propaganda was issued by the Allied command, and spoke of a coming freedom for everyone with a quick end to the war.

The prisoners read the leaflets eagerly, but many were dubious as to their contents, others were apathetic, and still others were cynical. And why not? By this time, what sensible person in a prison camp could hope for peace with any conviction?

In the morning, they were ordered to hand over the papers or be denied food for the whole day. Obediently, but with secret hatred, they turned the leaflets in by the hundreds. But the numbers returned didn't satisfy the officers, who then conducted a search. This was interrupted by the sound of heavy ground fire nearby.

"The English are coming! The English are coming!" The cry swept among the many barracks like flames in a forest. Wildly the frenzied inmates hammered down the doors and broke out the windows, oblivious about the outnumbered guards and their officers. Under pressure from the storming mob, the gates eventually gave way and they all ran out, only to find themselves confronted with a long column of roaring tanks. The monsters formed a large arc facing the prison camp.

The prisoners, not yet daunted, pressed close together and shouted: *"Long live England!"* With their voices almost drowning out the noise of the tanks, nobody heard the bursts of machine-gun fire aimed over their heads. *"Long live England!"* they shouted over and over, with some even waving the leaflets they'd managed to keep. But now the shooting could be heard more clearly.

Suddenly there was a new cry from the crowd, some of whom had noticed a few swastikas painted on the tanks. *"They're Germans!"* Now soldiers appeared from the tanks and started walking towards the mass of people, machine-guns at the ready. The crowd fell silent, with the men standing like white skeletons, their brief joy extinguished, and their scant energies spent.

Then, a tiny figure detached itself from the others. It was Dr. Vedrano. He walked silently up to the German soldiers, who eyed him suspiciously, sullenly, while the crowd watched it in fear. Dr. Vedrano introduced himself with dignity. "I wish to speak to your commandant," he said calmly, addressing a soldier from one of the tanks. The soldier looked at the frail, white-haired man in astonishment. But the professor had an air of assurance and some authority to him.

For a while there was silence, except for some muffled conversation and whispers, the crunching of the hard earth underfoot and coughs—everywhere the rasp of coughing. Meanwhile the prisoners waited anxiously, while shivering in their thin clothes and skin. Those in the back had to rely on rumors passed from the people at the front who could at least see, if not understand, what was happening.

Then there was a crackle from a loudspeaker and a weak but familiar voice came to them; it was that of Dr. Vedrano. He requested them all to return to their barracks and wait for further information. The professor was known to many, and his reputation had spread throughout the camp. They trusted him. Obediently, and in good order, they began to file back through the gates and into the hated barracks.

While the prisoners continued filing slowly inside, a tank moved closer followed by two limousines filled with officers. They stopped in front of the camp's administration building, known to the inmates as *Palazzo Chigi*—mimicking the name of Mussolini's palace in Rome. An honor guard of Carabinieri, in gala uniform, stood before it. A German major ordered them to lay down their weapons and sit, holding their arms above their heads.

Meanwhile, time dragged by in the barracks, until at last the weary prisoners were ordered to assemble in front of *Chigi*. As they were gathering the major in command appeared, standing above them on a balcony. With him was his aide along with Dr. Vedrano, who was acting as an interpreter. He wore no shirt, but a light jacket which was open and revealed his bare chest.

The major stood silent, while looking down into all the miserable ragtag and undernourished people huddled below him. Gradually the noise of their assembling died down, and at last he spoke in a clear, rather deep voice: *"Achtung! All of you gathered here are representatives of your people. If this weren't so, you wouldn't be here in this camp. And in the name of the Third Reich, I greet you. If there are any among you who wish to receive a certificate attesting to the time you've spent at this camp, you may apply for one in the office. You're all free now to return to your homes."*

Dr. Vedrano translated all of it, except for the last part: *you're now free to return to your homes.*

"What's the matter?" the major asked impatiently. "Go on and tell them. Translate everything I've said!"

"No."

The major's aide pulled out his revolver and pointed it at Dr. Vedrano.

"You can kill me, but I won't lie to my people," Dr. Vedrano insisted.

"You're being foolish," the major told him. "You know we'll be fighting the Anglo-Americans one day, so we'd be fools to feed these thousands of nobodies like this in the meantime. They're nothing but skeletons, just look at yourself."

The opportunism of this statement rang true and somehow convinced Dr. Vedrano that the Germans actually intended to release the prisoners. Rather freely he translated what the major had just said, but the people continued to stand looking up to the balcony, while not moving. They were still unconvinced that they could leave and expected to be shot if they moved through the gates.

Chapter 12

It was necessary for Dr. Vedrano to give them a long explanation before they grasped the truth, that the Germans simply didn't want to be bothered feeding them and sheltering them, no matter how inadequate that care might be. When this came through to them, they at last surged towards the outside world and into their unknown fates.

On the balcony the men stood watching the mass of emaciated, pale bodies pushing forward towards the walls. "Why don't they take their belongings with them?" the aide asked.

"They haven't any," Dr. Vedrano told him. Unconsciously he covered his naked chest by crossing his arms. His only property had been a shirt which he'd washed last night and hung up on a high fence pole to dry, but the gunfire intended to destroy the propaganda leaflets from the Allies had torn it to shreds.

By this time the first people in the crowd had reached the open gates, but some of them had second thoughts, despite Dr. Vedrano's assurance of the Germans' good faith.

"It's a trap!" someone shouted. The word *trap* was repeated by others and spread around in seconds. Then the same voice shouted, "They'll shoot us!"

Suddenly thousands of white phantoms stood motionless in the sunlight.

But now a short skeleton wearing a tattered rag as a bandage over an eye with a ragged scarf around his neck, leaned on his crutch and cried out, "Don't worry. I'll try it!" He crossed himself. "I have to get back to my village."

"Bravo, Uncle Thomash!" This cry was followed by a strange sound, like the crackling of dry bamboo sticks. It was produced by some of the thin hands beating together in applause. Now Thomash encouraged the crowd to follow him and they formed a long column on the dusty road, watched carefully by the bewildered German soldiers.

Meanwhile the officers with a civilian who wore thick glasses were busy looking through the files and cursing the Italians for allowing the inmates to starve, otherwise they'd have been transported to Germany and used as slave labor. Angrily they proclaimed the entire guard to be prisoners, and ordered them to occupy the newly emptied barracks. The major and Dr. Vedrano were still on the balcony, watching the gradual retreat of the freed men. Everything seemed to be going smoothly.

"Let's go in now," the major proposed. Then he turned around, startled, as a nearsighted civilian came running over. He addressed himself to the professor.

"Aren't you Director Vedrano, from Gradina?"

Dr. Vedrano nodded.

"Don't you recognize me? Hamburg Import-Export. I'm Herr Pushinger!"

Dr. Vedrano nodded again, impassively.

"Then why—mein Gott—didn't you say something right away?"

Dr. Vedrano looked at him contemptuously. "I didn't want to interfere with your duties."

"Oh, come now, Director. You didn't mind doing that before the war—you must remember that."

Dr. Vedrano was uncomfortable. With a slight motion of his eyes, he guided Pushinger to move aside so they could talk together alone. Pushinger complied. The major looked at the two for a moment, shrugged, and went through the doors leading away from the balcony.

"Now," said Pushinger as he leaned towards Dr. Vedrano, with the light shining on the heavy lenses of his spectacles. "Let's see if you know something. For example, who started the rumors I was paying the Cablo peasants with counterfeit money for their ash tree logs until no one wanted to sell any? And whose students were being encouraged to set fire to our lumber yard?"

Dr. Vedrano had a talent for needling people with his silence, so he used it now and looked calmly back at Pushinger, who had beads of sweat forming on his round face.

"You knew damn well what we needed that wood for!" he shouted. "Well, say something! Didn't you?"

Dr. Vedrano spoke calmly. "Not exactly, but I had a good hunch about it."

"Germany needed that for war materiel parts. Well, we got some out, but those damned Italians were such cowards. Somebody in Cablo shot at a few of them, and in retaliation they nearly turned the place into another Lidice."

The Cablo peasants filing into the churchyard and laying the bodies down on the floor of the church—and the women weeping. Yes, Dr. Vedrano had heard all about that. He shivered with revulsion when Pushinger grasped him by his thin arm and said, "Come along now, I want to introduce you around."

It didn't take a lot of strength to pull this last remaining skeleton of the camp to the main office where the German officers were gathered. Pushinger drew himself up as far as he could since he was a short, stocky man—and gave the Nazi salute. "Gentlemen," he announced grandiosely, "I wish to introduce to you the greatest brain in the Balkans, Dr. Nikola Vedrano."

"Ah, Kultur!" The officers rose in a body and solemnly shook hands with the newcomer.

"Famous," Pushinger proclaimed, "for his...."

"Studies in philology," Dr. Vedrano attempted to come to his rescue. Not accustomed to blowing his own horn, the professor spoke in such a low voice that Pushinger failed to hear him. A few of the officers nearest to him did, however, and nodded solemnly in admiration.

Pushinger sensed that he was holding his audience, although he misunderstood the reason why. He continued with aplomb: "This brave man, I've heard, even shot down one of Badoglio's own planes on the very first day of the war."

Standing, the officers somberly saluted the shadow-like human figure wearing a jacket which failed to cover his naked torso. They motioned him to be seated at the end of the table. Orderlies brought in cognac and glasses, and there were toasts to the Fuhrer, to the newly freed Mussolini, and to the hero who shot down the plane of the Fuhrer's treacherous enemy, Marshal Badoglio.

Unfortunately, the *hero* didn't join in this conviviality, excusing himself because of poor health.

"Is anything wrong?" the major asked him.

Dr. Vedrano turned to him and spoke in his faint, but clear voice: "I'm concerned about those poor people on the road. Their homes are so far away. If someone were to arouse the Albanians against them..."

Other conversations had died down and the other officers were listening to this dialogue. Dr. Vedrano attempted to raise his voice, in order to include them. "Balkan history," he said, "reveals a succession of enmities, of instigating one's people against another's. To the peasants of Albania, my people are as alien as the Italians, or..."

The major smiled faintly. He assured the professor that he'd send out instructions via radio, ordering soldiers to pick up the people from the road in trucks if possible. Then he left with the other officers, who were to check the suitability of the barracks for use by his troops.

Dr. Vedrano and Pushinger remained seated at the empty table while some orderlies quietly removed the dirty glasses. Pushinger poured himself another cognac from a half empty bottle. He then raised it over Dr. Vedrano's unused glass, and gave him an expression for an answer. But after the negative nod he gave a shrug, then settled back in his chair and crossed his thick legs.

"This is a hell of a job," he complained. "Always stationed in a foreign country while trying to help your own, and with everybody constantly barking at your heels."

"Even Major Hillarich?" Dr. Vedrano asked ironically.

"Not anymore," Pushinger said with hatred. "That bastard! He deserted at Stalingrad, taking a whole regiment along with him."

This was no surprise to Dr. Vedrano. His expression, however, was abstracted. He was still worrying about the army of ghosts plodding away from him along the dusty Albanian roads.

Pushinger looked at him while shaking his head slowly. "Der Fuhrer has stated that war is evil," he said, "and everybody in the whole world would believe him if they could see you, skinny as you are, a walking bag of bones. You'd be a great help to an anatomy class."

Getting no reaction to this quip he went on, "But just wait until we win!" He bent forward and peered into Dr. Vedrano's face. "Or maybe you don't believe we will?"

Dr. Vedrano sighed. This man was really obnoxious! "There will be no victory," he said. "There will only be an end, and that's what I'm waiting for."

Pushinger pounded the table. "No victory for the West, naturally. It's between us and the Bolsheviks! And since Der Fuhrer opposes the Bolsheviks, they can't win. He has appointed Rommel to take over the military command of your carved-up Yugoslavia now. Victory will be ours!" He looked around and then lowered his voice. "Yet you and I could reap great benefits by working together if you wanted to."

Dr. Vedrano shook his head, but Pushinger paid no attention.

"Listen, the district around Gradina is rich in bauxite," he whispered eagerly. "I have taken samples. It's there, scarcely beneath the surface, ready for the taking. In Cablo it's especially good, how about that? You and I could do it. Surely you see the possibilities."

But it was obvious Pushinger was making no headway with this stubborn scholar, so he decided to change the subject. "There was another bastard—that Mortellini. He nearly destroyed that whole damn village of Cablo when we were there. And for what reason?"

Dr. Vedrano pointed to the swastika on Pushinger's lapel. "He was one of yours, Herr Pushinger."

Pushinger made a negative gesture. "Ha! Eventually he went to Italy and planned to stay away to play it safe. But it didn't work, so Il Duce had him shot. What a coward the man was for sending so many men to this prison camp, including you and that chief of Cablo. Didn't I just see him leaving with the others?"

"Only what's left of him," Dr. Vedrano said. "At least his spirit is still unbroken."

Now they heard the German officers returning from the inspection, so Pushinger straightened up, listened for a moment, and rose to his feet.

The Germans were unhappy about the condition of the barracks, which they considered entirely unsuitable to house their troops in. Only the building *Chigi* was usable. The major said to Pushinger, "I hope we didn't disturb your conversation, we can't believe the deplorable state of this camp."

"Well, the men who've just left are in as bad a shape—if not worse," Dr. Vedrano bravely interjected. "The results of the tender loving care received from your allies."

"Come now, Herr Doctor," the major warned, while grabbing an empty glass. "That's going a bit too far. The facts contradict you."

"Which facts?" asked Dr. Vedrano. "Such facts as one hundred Serbs killed for every dead German?"

"Even more!" the major replied. "Thanks to your London and Moscow."

"I don't understand," Dr. Vedrano said with dignity.

"Look," the major told him. "According to the statistics, the ratio is one hundred and two Yugoslavs for every dead German. And do you know why? Because your people are killing each other off by themselves. And for that we don't hold ourselves responsible at all." He turned to his fellow officers. "Am I right?"

They all nodded in agreement.

"Not responsible? After the fire you threw amongst us?" Dr. Vedrano remonstrated. "Look at the Croatian Ustashis, they didn't create themselves!"

"True, but look at the Anglophiles and Russophiles amongst you," the major insisted. "London helped Mihailovic with propaganda first, until he had more guerrillas than he needed."

"He still has them," Dr. Vedrano interrupted.

"All right, true enough. But then London also helped Tito with arms." The major laughed sardonically and was joined in by the other officers. "That balances out fine for us. Tito has enough fanatical followers to murder as many of your own people as he wants—and its all to our advantage!"

Now Pushinger wanted to have his say: "The West is losing anyways. The people will never forget the butchery they suffered from the weapons used by their own allies."

Dr. Vedrano ignored him while looking through an open window, from which could be heard the newly-imprisoned Italians singing: *Mamma, son tanto felice.* This song was as popular amongst the Italian troops as *Lili Marlene* was to the Germans.

The men in the office listened for a moment.

"Do you have any family, Doctor?" the major asked.

"I have my wife and three children. They're in Spalato."

"So you want to join them, I imagine."

"Yes, and to go back to Gradina to reopen the school. The students have lost so much time lately."

Above the balcony of *Palazzo Chigi* the German flag was waving, and beyond it on a pole still hung the remnants of Dr. Vedrano's shirt, waving bravely in the wind as well. A young officer with a Leica camera was patiently waiting for the right moment to snap a picture of it. He wanted to show only the bullet-torn shirt waving symbolically over the building, but try as he might, it was impossible to get Dr. Vedrano's shirt into focus without also getting the German flag into the picture as well.

So perhaps it was fitting that these two banners would appear in the same photograph together; while unlikely companions they might be, they were nevertheless to share the same fate in the not too distant future, and that time was approaching faster than anyone could have guessed.

13

On Cracked Easter Eggs

"Eins—Zwei! Eins—Zwei!"

Dayan Costovar's guard from the local Volkssturm unit looked at him confidently before he handed over a pair of almost new ski-boots. August Vogel watched as Dayan tried them on—they were the right size. "Now, make plenty of noise when you pass her house," he ordered. "Beat to the ground with your boots. Eins—Zwei! Good and loud!"

Her house was that of his niece, Cornelia Bechter, the women's block leader in the town of Fugen. At a recent town meeting, she'd urged that the Volkssturm must compel all foreigners to march vigorously by putting their feet down smartly as they strode to work. This was to convince themselves they were part of a greater, powerful nation—Germany—and were doing their part for her continued success. The news of her country's impending collapse, Cornelia said, was absolutely false.

The boots Dayan tried on had belonged to her husband, last heard from four months ago in Sebastopol. Dayan was supposed to consider himself fortunate, not only because of the boots, but because he was assigned to a labor-commando with three other war prisoners from his native Serbia. This was thanks to the burgermeister's admiration for Serbia's heroic history, and also because August Vogel had requested a fourth man in order to build a small marching unit.

Dayan was therefore detached from the large transport of East European workers with whom he'd traveled from Vienna. Those people all wore a cloth marked *East* on their shirts and lived in moldy barracks. Instead, Dayan shared an isolated storehouse with his three countrymen which, according to rumors, had sheltered the last witch burned in Fugen centuries earlier. For this reason it was still called the *Witch House*.

But all these advantages failed to convince Thomash Costovar's son that he should march to the *Eins—Zwei* and go clip-clopping as loudly as he could with borrowed boots.

"What did the ground ever do to me that I should beat it?" he countered. He handed the ski-boots back to August. "I'd rather stay with my wooden shoes."

To him, the word *ground* meant the soil; something to be worshipped like a mother for its life-sustaining role in our lives, something merciful which never cracks under the weight of a person—no matter how sinful they might be. Besides, why should he march? He wasn't even classified as a war prisoner. He'd been told at the burgermeister's office: *We're only responsible for the future world after we win, so we can't be bothered with individual cases*. Thus he was classed as a *Balkan bandit* and had no protection from Geneva. He received no Red Cross parcels either.

This didn't bother his countrymen, who gladly shared their own parcels with him. But August was very disappointed since he'd counted on additional chocolate bars for his teenage daughters. Not that he didn't get enough as it was, but something extra was always welcome. All in all, the deal between August and the three Serbian prisoners was mutually satisfactory. The contents of the parcels were fine currency for obtaining fresh milk and eggs from local farmers, and Frau Vogel's bright cheerfulness every morning was attributed to her cup of real American coffee.

To top it off, when August managed to scrounge some schnapps for himself, he was another man—the son of Germany who already had given his left arm to her in Galicia during the Great War. He'd volunteered recently for the early Volkssturm at Cornelia's request. Besides, he thought of this duty as payment for his luck in being the father of daughters only, with no sons to bleed for Goebbels' false promises.

With the approach of Orthodox Easter, one week later than the German Easter, and the expected invasion in the west, Dayan felt more cheerful than he had for a long time. One morning as he marched to work he stared openly at Cornelia, and although her uncle August was watching, he made no objections. Cornelia was in the garden pruning some rose bushes, and she returned Dayan's look with a warm smile. *Imagine! A block leader, a Nazi Party member—and she smiled for a Balkan bandit!* This certainly didn't bear out the warning he'd had in the burgermeister's office, that any man who so much as looked at a German woman would end up with either a rope around his neck or a trip to the gas chamber.

A few days later, August turned up at the *Witch House* with a small box of fresh eggs and some coloring crayons. "For your Easter," he said, "but why in Himmel did you make it a week after the real Easter?"

"Aha!" Dayan laughed. "The question is whether your Easter is a week early, or ours is a week late!"

The crayons, August said, had been smuggled from school at great risk by his younger daughter Helma, as a present. And this was to be followed by an Easter surprise later, he promised. He then went away, while humming and patting his stomach, which was filled with many chocolate bars and American coffee.

"I'll bet the Anglo-Americans have already invaded," Dayan told the others. "That must be why August is being so generous." They devised a plan to bribe him with more goodies from their Red Cross parcels if he'd bring them a radio one evening. They wanted to hear from London and find out what was happening.

The Easter surprise was a great one indeed. The four Serbs were taken to a public bath, where they were allowed to have showers with plenty of warm water. Then that afternoon, August escorted them to the hills and while he busied himself chopping wood—they were allowed to wander around freely. Actually, they went only as far as the first big aspen tree. There, four faces still rosy from their recent bath were turned towards the east, radiating hope for a better tomorrow, with the Lord's Prayer on their lips and some Holy Bibles in their hands.

The Easter service began with Dayan officiating. "In the beginning was the Word, and the Word was God."

At hearing this August ceased chopping, picked up his rifle and approached the four men clustered beneath the big tree. He stopped a little distance away and looked towards them somewhat apprehensively, wondering what they were up to; Dayan was speaking in Serbian and the language sounded strange and frightening to the German.

"Brother in Jesus, Herr Vogel," Dayan said, turning to him and speaking in German now. "Please put down your rifle, and your cap too!" August obeyed somewhat awkwardly and joined the four men. The self-styled priest addressed him: "Blessed is the man that walketh not in the counsel of the ungodly, nor standeth in the way of sinners, nor is seated in the seat of the scornful."

"Amen," the four men chorused in low voices.

The short service ended with a sermon about the Babylonian King Nebuchadnezzar, who'd thrown three Jews into a fiery furnace. But as he watched them afterwards—they didn't burn, and neither did the smoke harm their garments. Instead, they walked safely together in the fire and the king saw a fourth man walking with them—it was the Son of God.

After this Dayan passed out the colored Easter eggs he'd made to the five members of this tiny congregation of Christians. On each one there was a drawing of the world as a globe, and at the top in tiny letters were the words: *May Peace Arise*. But one of the five eggs had cracked.

"Give it to me," said Michail. "Already I've had enough joy for today." He handed Dayan a recent letter from his wife in Belgrade, pointing to a paragraph:

I have made them shirts from the quilt. If the weather outside is nice I'll take them both to Easter services. We wouldn't have needed the quilt until winter, but by that time the war should be over! Then they say we'll get everything we need from...

"She means from England and America," Dayan whispered.

August was examining his egg. "Look how small you've made Germany," he complained.

"It's all to scale," Dayan answered. "That's the way it is, all in proportion."

August was turning the egg. "But see how big America is?"

"Neither smaller or larger than it is."

"England and Japan?"

"The same. Just as they are in size to one another. Nobody is big compared to the whole world. Only when all nations and all the world is seen together is it large."

August put the egg carefully into his pocket.

On Easter evening the *Witch House* was busy with preparations for a dinner guest—August. He was scheduled to smuggle a short-wave radio to them, luckily it ran on batteries since there was no electricity to use. For illumination at night they used tallow candles and this pleased Dayan; it reminded him of the cottage in Cablo where lamp light was only for special occasions.

Their guest arrived with a flourish, but rather late. "You poor unfortunate people!" August said by way of apology. "Late with Easter, late with friends." Smiling, he handed a wrapped radio to Dayan.

"Better late than never," Dayan said. "A friend is a friend."

"You bet!" August pulled a half-pint bottle of schnapps from his pocket and took a sip from it. "I'm your friend all right. But what about the Anglo-Americans?"

"What about them? We're not worried," Michail said.

"You'd better be—they destroyed your capital today, Belgrade. There were thousands of civilians killed by Anglo-American planes. Churchgoers mostly. They'll tell you all about it." He moved his head, indicating the radio. "Quite an Easter present, nicht?"

The four hosts attributed these remarks to August's drinking—he'd been working on the bottle steadily since he arrived. They went on calmly while preparing their dinner. August could drink a lot without slurring his speech. What he'd said about the Anglo-American planes bombing Belgrade was obviously nonsense.

However, they turned out to be wrong about that. August wasn't drunk and he was speaking the truth. He persisted: "A protest has been sent to the Red Cross in Geneva. And Radio-Berlin says..."

"Please, Herr Vogel. It's Easter—let's not have such unfunny jokes." Dayan turned to Michail, who was cooking. He put his hand on Michail's shoulder. "His family lives in Belgrade."

While he was talking, August had taken another long pull at the bottle, and that did the trick. He decided in a fuzzy way that the best idea was to let them find out for themselves, so he dropped the subject of Belgrade's destruction.

The Serbs had timed dinner so that August would be leaving before the Radio-London broadcast was aimed at Yugoslavia. However, due to his late arrival they hurried things up. This was fine with August, who was eager to reach home with his chocolate-stuffed pockets before Helma's bedtime. In fact, he was in such a hurry after having dinner that he only turned the key once in the door of the *Witch House*, to lock in his prized prisoners.

Then there was the sound of stumbling and a metallic crashing sound when his gun was dropped. This was followed by a low moan and some swearing—apparently he'd dropped it on his foot. Finally the sound of hurried-fading footsteps came to the listening men with the words: *You poor Balkans!* After that nothing more was heard from Herr Vogel.

At eight o'clock the four men gathered around the table where they'd placed the little radio. The dishes had been washed and the room tidied up. Dayan turned on the switch; there was a humming and then a voice came through clearly, speaking unemotionally and without emphasis, in the typical way of radio news broadcasters:

"The capital city of Belgrade in Yugoslavia was heavily bombed early today in fair and sunny weather by British and American planes. The air raid, deemed highly successful by military authorities, caused many civilian casualties..."

Abruptly the voice was cut off as Michail struck the radio with his fist. There was a confusion of squawks and static—and then silence. Murmuring the names of his wife and children, Michail then stared at his comrades blindly. Since they were equally stricken, being unable to move or speak, they were helpless to comfort him or themselves. They all sat like stone figures, silent and motionless.

Finally Michail said, "The weather was fair and sunny? That's what he said?"

Dayan nodded miserably.

"And her letter said she would go to church with the children if the weather was nice?"

There was a long pause. "Yes—that's what she said." Dayan wished the sputtering candle would go out so they could hide their faces—four men whose heroic past was admired by their captors—four men whose capital had just been hit by Allied bombs on Easter Sunday.

Finally, it was dark. They still sat around the table in silence until Michail, who had taken the broken Easter egg that morning because he'd had enough joy for today, suddenly jumped up. He struck the table, rattling the saucers in which the candles had burnt out.

"Die, London!" he shouted. *"London! Not my children!"*

14

Wearing English Uniforms

After the Germans released him from the prison camp, Thomash Costovar began limping towards home. He had no real reason to go through Gradina other than to get some salt, assuming his village still needed it. But as he later found out the skin rashes in Cablo weren't due to a lack of salt, they were from bed bugs that the children had spread. Regardless of this, he avoided Gradina out of safety and bypassed it on his trip back.

After long months of labor and near starvation at the prison camp, Thomash was amazed to find enough food when he finally arrived back home. This had been deposited out of superstition by a few villagers as advance payment; it was for work they wished him to do upon his return. There were frames to be carved for family pictures, and holy icons and wooden dishes to be shaped by his skilled hands.

At first he wasn't physically able to handle much work. Every bone in his body still ached, and every weak muscle he had was painful to move. Goritza lovingly applied compresses of dried garlic leaves daily, while Angelica gently massaged him. Slowly Thomash began to heal, and before the last snow had melted from the Cablo hills in 1944 he felt able to return to work, making the easiest of the things he was paid for in advance.

Later he felt strong enough to continue work on the monument, which he found upon his return just as he'd left it. He set to work cheerfully, glad to be working outside on it with his chisel and hammer again. Three days later around noon he saw a column of armed men emerging from the forest, walking slowly—almost stalkingly—towards the churchyard. Perhaps Dayan was among them!

"Come on, boys," Thomash called out to encourage them. He hated to see his son acting afraid. "No need to hide! They all left Gradina yesterday."

An explosion he'd heard from the prison barracks in Gradina had meant to Thomash that the Germans were evacuating. He compared it with the time in 1918 when they'd also evacuated, but yesterday's explosion had been much louder. Now a uniformed man rose up from behind a rock. He shouted in an angry voice, "Summon all the villagers!"

Thomash started up the path to the church where he intended to ring the church bell, the customary way to gather the villagers together.

"No, not that way! Stay away from the bloody church, reactionary! Call them yourself!"

Thomash stopped and stared at the man. Then he moved a little closer to be sure his failing eyesight wasn't deceiving him. "By God!" he exclaimed. The young man wore an English uniform and had an American machine-gun slung across his shoulders. "You're Perun! Perun Novak!" Again he moved a little closer, while still staring in astonishment. "By God!" he repeated.

"No. Stay back—or else!"

"You're not Perun?"

"Yes, of course I'm Perun! But there is no God! No God—understand?" Perun stepped towards Thomash threateningly. He pointed to the red star on his cap, which had a lot of greasy, black hair sticking out from under it. Thomash, who was now speechless, stared at the former Cablo villager. What a troublemaker he always seemed to be!

Perun now aimed his machine-gun towards the church bell. "This is the way to do it," he said, and a burst of gunfire made it ring, followed by a chorus of barking dogs and squawking roosters. In the distance a donkey brayed from the woods. Cautiously the villagers started to appear after hearing all this commotion.

The Partisan soldiers, about fifty of them with over half wearing English uniforms, now filed in behind Perun, and two stationed themselves to either side of him. Meanwhile, more villagers continued to show up, some of them were women carrying small babies, others held toddlers by the hand, and the old walked in slowly with the help of sticks.

When they'd all gathered, the man to Perun's right stepped forward and pulled out a printed paper from his pocket. Perun then motioned all the people to silence as his familiar lieutenant began to read, even though he was now accompanied by the hungry wail of a young baby:

"Excerpts are quoted from Karl Marx, as an introduction to the theory of dialectical materialism. Surplus in accumulated capital produces the chief problem of the bourgeoisie in overcoming difficulties resulting in unsuccessful efforts to survive the fatal social crisis during this crucial period."

Here the reader paused because the man next to him broke into a coughing fit from which Perun rescued him by pounding on his back. When this interruption was over, a growing murmur could be heard from the crowd. They were far from impressed by all the long words which to them were unintelligible.

"Look," some were saying, "That's Aladdin! Why, I remember him when he was just a little boy. And now look at him!"

Disregarding the inattention of his audience to his speech, the newly identified one continued:

"Comrade Kaganovich states that imperialism and plutocracy by themselves stimulated the revolution, since those ideas have no boundaries. Consequently, this newly-built socialism is the vanguard of the new world system as directed by our savior, Comrade Stalin."

"*Long live Stalin*!" the soldiers all howled, drowning out the reader's voice and forcing him to stop. In the sudden silence, a woman who didn't recognize the seriousness of this gathering asked anxiously, "Sir officer, can you explain why our sheep are all barren this year?"

Even if Aladdin had known the answer to this sensible question, he wasn't about to give it, as there was another noisy fit of coughing next to him. By the time this new interruption had been quieted, he decided to ignore her question and continued reading:

"Henceforth, Comrades of Cablo, you, as members of this new social system, will be subject to certain orders which will guarantee the success of our heroic struggle under the leadership of Tito."

Again, there was a shout from the soldiers: "*Long live Tito!*"

Aladdin waited rather impatiently for this commotion to die out and then he continued, but again, suddenly he stopped. He blushed and he tried desperately to get the words out, but they seemed to get stuck in his throat. The villagers watched with various expressions depending on how they were seeing Aladdin, for he once had been popular in the village. So the cougher, now calm and collected, quietly took the paper from Aladdin's hand and began reading further:

"Cablo must be proud that our hero Perun Novak spent his innocent boyhood here."

At this Perun gave a constrained smile, revealing two sets of golden teeth, both upper and lower.

"Heavenly Father!" shouted Auntie Stephanie, who was standing next to Goritza. She began edging her way through the crowd towards the so-called hero.

"No, wait!" Goritza pulled at her skirt, trying to hold her back. "Auntie Stephanie! Wait until our boys are safely at home. Don't!"

But it was no use. The old woman had succeeded in pushing herself to the front and was confronting the man with the golden grin.

"Tell me," she said seriously as she peered into his mouth like one does when looking down a well. "Tell all of us, Perun—who made your teeth?"

On this question, Perun, who'd been eyeing her nervously, drew himself up and thrust out his chest. "Our Allied friends," he announced proudly. "They sent me to southern Italy. Look here!" He pointed to a gold-colored ribbon pinned to his chest.

"Italy! Did you see my Nashko there?"

"Nashko the fascist? No." But seeing that she obviously didn't understand what the word fascist meant, he added: "Nashko is a traitor."

Auntie Stephanie knew very well what traitor meant. She spat at his face. Astonished at such insolence Perun was unable to move for a moment, and started wiping his face with his handkerchief.

But the soldier to his left stepped in front of him protectively. "Are you willing to die for disrespecting a party member?" he asked her. "Don't you know you have offended Tito as well as your own soil? See my uniform?"

"What about your uniform?" Auntie Stephanie retorted. "I only spat at Perun's face. But now—" Unfortunately Perun was out of her reach, for he'd moved back and was surrounded by other soldiers. "So go ahead—I'll die for him!" she said, spitting at the soldier's chest. "Now tell me—where is my son?"

At this all the women took up the same cry. "Our sons! Yes, our sons! Where are they?" Some of them quickly walked up and gathered around her.

Thomash was quietly leaned against the unfinished monument while he watched what was happening. He'd learned during his imprisonment that there are times when protest is useless, and in fact wasteful. But now he spoke up so as to save Auntie Stephanie and to point out another curiosity. "That man who's reading," he shouted, "it's Signor Laguna—from Gradina. Listen!"

"Your sons have been fighting for another social order—the one that the Anglo-American plutocrats and the warmongers both favor. We however have fought for the people's freedom; mankind's future."

"Then how come you're wearing those uniforms?" a burly man asked him.

"Never mind about that," Laguna answered quickly. "It was part of the struggle and it paid off, thanks to our party's wise leadership. Remember, your Chetnik boys fought for Churchill and Roosevelt as well, and ended up with nothing!"

"Cut that out!" the burly man retorted back. "You can have Churchill and Roosevelt. I don't want them!" He stepped forward with his fists clenched. "And that includes Stalin!"

Laguna retreated towards the soldiers who were lined up with their American machine-guns at the ready. He knew the temper of the Cablo peasants well, for he'd learned about it when he pronounced as unpatriotic their refusal to sell ash wood to Pushinger. That was in the newspaper he'd published in Gradina, *The Progressive Voice*. He'd experienced the meaning of clenched fists on his own skin, and realized that only being behind machine-guns made him feel secure. From there he decided to take a fresh tack.

"Good friends," he began, "the war isn't over yet." He paused for a moment as he surveyed the crowd to see any reaction, then continued. "We came to watch you elect one member from Cablo who will accompany us as your official representative to Gradina."

"Thomash! Thomash!" the crowd yelled until the sound echoed back from the hills.

Laguna's expression as he listened showed nodding approval. "So be it, a wonderful choice," he said.

He signaled—*at ease*—to the soldiers and directed them for light applause, adding to the unanimous election of Thomash Costovar, stone-cutter of Cablo. In the more defused atmosphere which prevailed, Thomash and Goritza approached Laguna and the two were soon joined by Aladdin.

Laguna looked to Thomash and said, "They made the right choice, I knew you were the man for the job. Unfortunately, we'd better get going, there's a lot to do in Gradina."

"Can't we wait, there's a commemorative meeting this weekend in honor of the eleven victims who'd been killed, including the church sexton. Besides, I need my wife to bring me my new moccasins."

"You won't need them," Laguna said. "You'll get the best American shoes in Gradina."

Thomash turned to Goritza. "Did you hear that? American shoes!"

"Oh—please save them for Dayan," she begged.

Meanwhile, some of the soldiers had entered the church and were carefully greasing their shoes with the beeswax candles from the altar. Other soldiers still outside wandered around looking for things, until one picked up Thomash's bag with its chisels and hammers sitting on the monument.

Thomash noticed this and objected. "Those are mine, I need them for myself!"

"Never mind him. You'll get new tools in Gradina as well," Laguna promised.

Thomash then asked in a hopeful voice, "Are they American?"

Laguna shook his head quickly. "Russian tools are much better for you, soon you'll find out. Now let's get going!"

A week passed in Cablo with no news from Thomash. One morning Goritza made a package containing his new moccasins, "I'll take these to him," she told Angelica. "He must save the American shoes for your wedding. Lucky you, to marry a young man with American shoes!" For although she hadn't heard from her son in so long, and despite the bombing of Belgrade, the occupation of Gradina, and all the humiliations and disasters suffered during the war, Goritza persisted in remaining hopeful of Dayan's marriage to Angelica.

On this day she kissed her *daughter* affectionately good-bye and set forth along the stony path towards Gradina, full of plans for the future. Learning that the Germans still held the town, she followed the route taken by Perun and Laguna with the soldiers, but lost track of it near the third village from Cablo. Here her brief journey was to come to an end.

While thirsty she'd asked a peasant woman weeding her garden for a drink of water.

"Here you are, and welcome," the plump woman, who was about Goritza's age, said as she handed the stranger a mug of cool water. "Sit down, won't you?" she invited politely, and thrust a wooden stool forward under the shade of a tree. The two women sat down and began to exchange news and rumors.

Goritza learned that three other villager leaders had been taken away as Thomash had been. But the worst news was that last night Aladdin had come to the old priest in her village, and had taken holy communion. He then hung himself on a dead tree at the nearby crossroads.

Goritza, greatly shocked by this tragic news, turned straight around and headed for home, although she was to find Cablo by no means a peaceful retreat when she arrived there. Young men with red ribbons on their sleeves were pouring into the village with written orders. There was much talk about the Soviet advance towards the Danube and the troubles of the Anglo-Americans after their invasion of France. It was said that Monte Cassino had become a graveyard for General Anders' Polish Army.

The young men wearing red ribbons had orders to organize the village so it could defend itself against *the people's enemy*. The villagers were told to elect various committees, even a cultural committee, which would include theatre, public speaking, music and dancing sections, and a section for *reeducation*. In fact, there were more committees to be established than there were adults in Cablo to fill them.

The villagers, confused and worried, waited patiently for things to sort themselves out. The only order they understood was the instruction to paint the St. George Church a darker green color. With the exception of the natural green of growing things, to them dark green symbolized Muslim dervishes, who wore green outfits and caps. So to Orthodox Christians, that color was regarded as unlucky.

All this, in addition to Aladdin's suicide was causing much anxiety in Cablo.

On a late summer day after a couple of months had passed, a worried Goritza again set out to bring Thomash his new moccasins. News had arrived that the Germans were at last out of Gradina. It was said that Perun and Signor Laguna were stationed there with an enlarged unit which included some observers and so-called war correspondents from the West.

Chapter 14

As she neared the town, Goritza found the bridge which had crossed the Mista river destroyed by the Germans. In its place was a temporary footbridge guarded by armed soldiers. Goritza thought they looked like some of the ones who'd been in Cablo—at least their uniforms were the same.

"Let's see your pass," a soldier with a red star on his cap demanded.

"Pass? I don't know what you mean."

The soldier explained that no peasant was allowed to enter the newly-liberated Gradina unless they had a pass issued by the local committee in their village. But as of yet, Cablo hadn't established such a committee.

"Committee?" Goritza said, after the soldier's explanation. This was a word she'd learned out of necessity in recent months. "So that's it! Well, my husband belongs to a committee right here in Gradina. Thomash from Cablo. Thomash Costovar."

The soldier saluted in acknowledgment of her statement, but then he said, "Still, I can't let you in without a pass."

"Then give Thomash this," Goritza said, and she handed him the package containing the new moccasins. "And tell him to send me the American shoes. I'll wait here. Remember—Thomash from Cablo."

The soldier then took the package and went off in the direction of town, while Goritza waited in vain for his return. At sunset, the other soldiers by the bridge advised her to go home. There seemed nothing else for her to do, so she turned and started back to Cablo from the same place where, five and a half years earlier on Saint Sava Day, Dayan had kissed her good-bye after being awarded honors for his essay on world peace. This time, as she turned sadly back towards Cablo, she heard the soldiers laughing at her, their voices clear and cruel in the early dusk.

Meanwhile, Thomash hadn't entered Gradina as an elected committee member as Goritza had thought, but entered it as a prisoner of the People's Liberation Army of Yugoslavia, together with one or two men from each of the other eighteen villages which the units of Perun and Laguna had passed through. They'd all been *elected* as Thomash had been: by acclamation, and as influential and respected persons in their village—that was to be their downfall.

They were brought into the same jail from which Thomash had been sent to the prison camp in Albania a few years earlier. But now there were iron bars on the windows, with small holes that admitted a minimum of light and air. It was also more crowded than before, and the nights were noisy with the screams of people being tortured.

At first nobody bothered Thomash and the other villagers who'd been brought in with him. They were informed that their election by their villages was proof that they'd shown *reactionary tendencies,* so they must be kept away in jail until the people had been reeducated on how to elect real representatives.

One day Thomash was taken away from his group and brought to an interrogation room. He was questioned as to Dayan's whereabouts and replied that he didn't know anything. Then he was measured from the floor to his lifted chin and thrown into a dark basement cell with a muddy floor and a rubber-framed door. Strangely, it had a hook set high into the ceiling.

"Welcome to *Tehran* cell," was his greeting from the other prisoners inside. The light was poor and he couldn't see too well, but Thomash guessed there were many of them since the air inside was stifling. Vukovich, a former district attorney was there, and two judges from Gradina. *Tehran* was an allusion to the Tehran Conference, at which the Western powers and Stalin had agreed to extend full help to Tito.

Suddenly a jet of water shot through a large hole in the wall. It was a thick stream, and the cell rapidly began to fill, the water rising from their ankles to their knees and then up further to their waists—and then to the shoulders! Thomash was terrified by it.

Vukovich supported him gently under his arms. "Don't be afraid," he said, "it will only reach to your mouth. You're the shortest one in here."

"Even the fascists didn't have something like this," Thomash said.

"Don't be so sure!"

"It's true," Thomash insisted. "I've been here before!"

The water continued rising higher, and the cellmates joined arms and formed a circle. Then they began singing: *When a hero Montenegrin is a captive in Istanbul.*

Thomash joined in the singing until the water reached his throat and then it stopped. But the rising water had forced out most of the air, stagnant and evil-smelling as it was, and the men stopped singing to save the little oxygen which remained. Slowly the water level fell, leaving a new coat of sticky mud on the floor and on human skin. The men shivered in their wet clothes, even though they were huddled together to conserve the heat of their collective bodies.

Later that night they were eventually returned to their cells, while Thomash was taken to the interrogation room. The interrogator now was flanked by four armed men. "I understand you have a son?"

"God has," Thomash replied.

"God? Did God sleep with your wife then?"

There was no answer back from the little skeleton shivering in his wet clothes.

"Or did you sleep with God?" At this quip all the armed men laughed merrily.

"I always stand when I speak His name," Thomash replied. "I live with Him."

"Listen to him, he thinks he's Jesus! That's enough of this nonsense for now. We'll see," the interrogator said angrily. "Take him away!"

As if this was their signal the four men began kicking and hitting Thomash, whose small body wasn't large enough to receive all the blows from the clenched fists and heavy feet wearing sturdy American military boots.

When he woke up in his cell the next day, his shirt and skin were *mixed together*—an expression used in ancient Yugoslav poetry about people who've been beaten and tortured. A sunbeam shined through the small window-hole in the concrete wall, dancing with puffs of dust. Painfully Thomash crawled to the beam and let it fall on the palms of his hands. He was comforted by the warmth and for a moment went into a daydream, forgetting where he was. Then there was a scraping sound, and the door was flung open.

"So, you tried to escape!" said a guard, handing him a piece of paper and a pen. "Here—sign this."

"What does it say?"

"That you admit you brought food to your son in the Cablo hills."

Without replying, Thomash held his hand into the warm beam of sunlight again.

"If you don't sign it," the guard warned, "we'll put you back to sing until the water reaches your mouth again."

"Then I'll sing," Thomash replied calmly.

And sing—he did, for three weeks. Each day he was taken to *Tehran* to sing with the other men until the water reached up to his throat. During that time the old priest who'd given communion to Aladdin also joined the group, and he contributed a new song to their repertoire: *I am not afraid—For I belong to Jesus*.

Finally, Thomash was brought before a different interrogator, and this time he was charged with *pan-Teutonism* on the basis that he'd arrived from Vienna forty-five years earlier.

"Vienna gave its full support for Hitler during this war," Budovanich reminded him. "I'm informed you brought tools and pencils, even papers, back from the city to use as propaganda. Pan-Germanism. How was that?"

"They were gifts from the students," Thomash replied. "Students from many countries, even some Americans."

"Don't insult our Allies."

"I don't, but you already have."

Budovanich shrugged contemptuously.

"Like when your troops shot at people from the altar of our church in Cablo," Thomash continued.

"You're crazy!" the investigator said. "But it was you who persuaded Aladdin to see the priest and confess, then hang himself."

"That's not true," Thomash said with dignity. "I didn't persuade him. That was God's work."

The other man was striding back and forth impatiently. Then he stopped close to Thomash, looking at him sternly. "I want just one thing from you," he said. "One thing. Your son. Where is he?"

Thomash crossed himself. "My son? Then he's alive? Why doesn't he come home then, the war is almost over."

Budovanich looked at him angrily, wondering what he could do with a simpleton like this. At last, Thomash was taken back to his cell.

The situation in the Gradina jail actually worsened when Belgrade was liberated from the Germans by Soviet forces accompanied by Tito's Partisans. The exiled King Peter had called on everyone in the country to join Tito in this fight for Belgrade, causing many Chetniks to obey and join the Partisans, which was a great disappointment to Mihailovic.

Now a series of daily ordeals began for Thomash with torture, blows and kicks. The only response he had was to be silent and cross himself, sometimes murmuring the single word: *Jesus*. His body was numb now, and mercifully it ceased to react. He was beyond his tormentors, whether they realized it or not.

In the Gradina jail's daily reports, which earlier stated the exact number of open wounds and broken bones, now only the number of gold teeth being taken was recorded, along with the number of corpses. The teeth were pulled out by the guards and taken to the empty vaults of the Gradina Agrarian Bank under local armed escort.

Formerly the job of burying the dead had been accomplished in the presence of priests, but the new authorities didn't trust the gravediggers until they'd undergone a reeducation course. The problem of burial was solved by the newly-formed militia; they bundled the dead into empty UNRRA sacks and threw them into the Mista river.

Thomash's numb condition, in which he no longer felt the blows and kicks to which he was subjected daily, gave one in the investigating staff a unique idea. Maybe they should wrap Thomash in the skin of a freshly-killed lamb to revive him. This method was rumored to have been used with interrogated prisoners jailed after the Sarajevo incident in 1914. Word duly went out to Cablo and the other villages, and sixteen lambs were brought in by villagers. They had no idea as to how the lambs would be used other than it was to help a fellow villager in need.

After dropping off the lambs they'd collected, two villagers from Cablo were anxious to see Thomash and to ask him for some advice; the bark of the fruit trees in Cablo was getting swollen with disease and only Thomash knew what to do about such things. But instead of being allowed to see him, they were greeted by Laguna from the balcony of the former chamber of commerce building. Reluctantly, they explained their problems to him.

"I beg of you, don't be concerned about a few bugs in your trees," Laguna told them. "Instead, think of the great duty entrusted to your fellow villager, Thomash Costovar, who was taken to Belgrade yesterday in a special American plane. Death to Fascism, Freedom to the people!"

Silently discouraged, the two villagers trudged away and went back to Cablo.

That evening Thomash was taken back into the interrogation room and placed in the corner on a chair. They hadn't used any of the lambs on Thomash since they were deemed too valuable for such a use. Instead, salt with vinegar was rubbed into Thomash's wounds to try and get him to react. However, he still only uttered the word *Jesus* from time to time while they tried this.

Next the investigator held a strong light in one hand and a stone slate in the other. He shined the light into Thomash's sunken eyes. "This has got to work," he told the others. "Now, where is he? WHERE IS HE?"

Thomash's eyes remained closed.

"Dayan! Dayan!" the investigator shouted, putting the stone slate into Thomash's hands. "Read it now. Your cross!"

Chapter 14

Thomash extended two skinny hands and pressed the slate to his chest. But his hands, arms and shoulders shook; his whole crushed body trembled and the slate fell down. He bent weakly to pick it up, but his tormentor was faster. He showed it to the watching guards. On the slate, scratched with the rock Dayan had used the day he fled from Tell in the mountains, were the words still clearly visible under a small cross:

IN HOC SIGNO VINCES
THOMASH COSTOVAR
CABLO, DISTRICT GRADINA

"Where did it come from?" a guard asked.

"From Bosnia—it was found in a bush after this man's son had escaped—the same day one of our officers was killed." The man now looked harshly at Thomash, putting it again into the old man's hands. "Here, read it! What does it say?"

Slowly Thomash brought the slate to his face and held it against his cheek. "It's warm," he said, and he held it against the other cheek. "Warm. Why didn't you write on paper, my son?" He kissed the stone, and made as if he wanted it under his shirt.

"Oh no you don't!" Budovanich yelled. He tried to snatch the stone back from Thomash, but this time when it fell back on the floor—it broke into many small pieces. "That was important evidence, and now you've destroyed it! You're guilty of aiding a criminal!"

Thomash didn't answer, but silently held out his hands trying to grasp the message from Dayan once more. From there Thomash was taken to the empty *Tehran* cell where they tied his ankles together, and hung him upside down from the hook in the center of the ceiling. Then they flooded the cell.

The next morning there were no gold teeth to report; neither was there a report of a corpse, except for one listed as *Jesus*.

That evening a banquet was held in the largest building on Shark Street, it had recently been remodeled. Here Laguna and Perun acted as hosts, in celebration of the advancing Soviet troops who were moving westward from Belgrade. Their guests were reporters and observers from the West. The menu consisted of sixteen barbecued lambs, courtesy of this newly-built socialism.

There were toasts to the Red Army, to the Lublin Committee in Poland, to the Greek Liberation Front, to Stalin, Churchill and Roosevelt. There were sharp accusations against the Polish General Bor-Komorowski for terming the Warsaw uprising an adventure of the dying bourgeoisie, and criticisms of General Mihailovic and the Greek monarchists.

Pictures of the lambs turning appetizingly on the spits were taken, and Perun Novak formed a bond of brotherhood with an observer-correspondent who that night sent by radio a report to the Westania Times agency about the miraculous economic recovery of the liberated areas in Yugoslavia. The report ended: *Meat is plentiful on such a scale that even America would envy us.*

15

And Displaying Flags

Angelica had decided to return to Belgrade in search of Dayan, her father and Thomash. Goritza was happy at hearing the news. "It's no good to marry here," she told the young woman. "So many are already dead, you'd better marry in that big city as no people are killed there." The destruction of Belgrade was unknown to her as Goritza's life was encompassed by the village and barely stretched out to Gradina.

"But Belgrade," Angelica said in a low voice, partly in fear.

"That's it, I forgot the name. Dayan's sure to be there in the school. Tell Thomash to quit that committee and come home," Goritza pleaded.

Angelica, who had deep misgivings about making the journey and what she'd learn from it, only nodded her head. Goritza went on cheerfully, "And make sure Dayan wears the American shoes Thomash was promised by that man, he must wear them for the wedding!" Again, Angelica nodded obediently. She kissed Goritza, picked up her little bundle of belongings and left the cottage reluctantly, but with timid hope.

Angelica's prewar knowledge of Belgrade was scarce and half forgotten. Her trip from Cablo to Belgrade was slow but simple enough, however upon arriving at the Belgrade railroad station, she inquired how to find the street where she'd lived earlier. The first person she asked pretended not to hear her; the next one shrugged to indicate he didn't know the language. A third laughed like a crazy man. Although Angelica didn't notice this, the fact was there were no two people in the street even speaking to each other.

After all this she gave up on asking for help and decided to find it on her own. She quickly noticed as she walked how heavily bombed the city was, only assuming it must have been done by the Germans. Then she began to remember a few landmarks here and there. After several hours of wandering, she at last came to the street where the Moravaz family had lived after leaving Gradina shortly before the war—but it had been bombed by the Anglo-American planes on Orthodox Easter the previous year.

Almost nothing noticeable was left of their house except for a gatepost. From the street where rubble still lay, Angelica stared at the place she'd known for a while as her home. She didn't have the courage to go through the ruins. What would she find in there? Better not look.

Then she saw a hand waving from a yard some distance away. It was their old neighbor, Auntie Sandra, who still clung to a sparse life in what remained of her property. Angelica ran to her and the women embraced. When they drew apart, the young traveler saw that the older woman was hardly recognizable. She had aged so much in such a short time. Instead of asking questions, Angelica joined her in weeping.

When they were more calm, Auntie Sandra wiped her eyes with a corner of her apron. "So much has happened here, Angelica. You can see it. But maybe you know this since you went to school, do the Anglo-Americans believe in God?"

"Of course. At least, many of them do."

"Then let's pray that He will forgive them."

Angelica nodded and started to cross herself.

"No—no! Not here! They'll shoot us." Auntie Sandra then took her by the arm. "Come inside." She led Angelica to the quarters she occupied like a person shipwrecked on an island, and pushed her into a makeshift chair.

She sighed happily, looking at the young woman whose presence brightened the shabby surroundings. "Ah, it's good to have you here," Auntie Sandra said, with tears still in her eyes. Then she began to bustle around near a little stove. "I'll make us some tea." She boiled water over a tiny fire and they drank the tea, which was weak, but sweetened with a little honey. Then they knelt together.

They prayed for England and America, with light coming through the walls and ceilings of one of the few shelters in the area left by the heavy bombers of the Anglo-Americans. Then they prayed for the souls of all the people killed by the bombs from those planes—including Angelica's father Philip Moravaz and Auntie Sandra's son Luka.

"I haven't prayed for them before," Auntie Sandra said. "I mean the Anglo-Americans. I didn't know if they believe in God. After all, it was Easter when they bombed us."

Angelica wanted to ask about her father, but was afraid to. Sensing this, the old woman pulled her into her arms and held her closely. "They were both ready to go," she said. "My son stayed with your father all the time; he was wounded when the Germans bombed us—when your mother died."

"Was he able to walk at all?"

"I'll tell you everything," Auntie Sandra said. Searching through a bundle of papers she came up with a letter and gave it to Angelica. "This was by his hand when he died."

It was an unfinished letter from Philip Moravaz, her father:

To my beloved daughter on Easter, 1944. Auntie Sandra is already in church. Luka is waiting impatiently outside, but I can't leave without describing the giant Anglo-American planes flying above me, which prove that our skies here are free at last. And it won't be long before our whole country is free, too. I can hardly wait to see you...

With a sob, Angelica flung herself into Auntie Sandra's lap. The old woman softly stroked the young woman's hair. She began reciting in a low tone: "To my beloved daughter on Easter, 1944. Auntie Sandra is already in church. Luka is waiting for me impatiently outside—you see, I know it all by heart. It's too bad he couldn't finish it. The bombs came suddenly." She sighed. "So many things were left unfinished on that terrible day!"

Angelica's sobs were controlled at last. She rose and sat facing Auntie Sandra, who said, "He wrote you many more letters and I've kept them all for you. I knew you'd come back someday."

She led Angelica across the rubble to the ruins of the Moravaz house. The concrete floor of the cellar and a part of the wall were all that remained of the structure. In a corner under some planks were several wooden boxes. "Look in there," she said.

"For the letters?" Angelica asked her, surprised. It seemed a strange place to keep them hidden.

"No, the flags, the flags!"

"What flags?" Puzzled, Angelica walked over and tugged at one of the boxes.

"There are British, American, and some French flags too."

The girl stared back at her, bewildered.

"We made them," Auntie Sandra explained. "All of us worked on them, for blocks around. We were going to put them in the windows to show the Allies how glad we were, but they didn't come." She hesitated. "That is, they did come—but with horrible bombs, and on Easter!"

The two women then sat down on pieces of rubble facing each other, and Auntie Sandra explained that Philip Moravaz had been in charge of counting the windows of the houses and then collecting the flags. Then they were carefully hidden away until the proper time came to display them with pride and happiness. Once, the Gestapo had stopped him for questioning, and discovered that he had a carefully drawn map showing all the streets in that section of Belgrade. But they could see he suffered from amnesia, and decided he was harmless—so they released him—and never learned that people were making the Allied flags, biding their time to show the victorious armies how welcome they were.

At last Auntie Sandra fell silent and the two women sat in the pale sunshine, looking across the blocks of devastation. There were distant sounds: a child laughed, a dog barked, a bird somewhere sang a few notes, a plane flew overhead. Angelica looked up and shuddered. A mother could be heard scolding someone, probably a teenager, and there was a hint of music from a radio nearby; even in the desolation some life here still remained. Angelica fell into a daydream of sorrow, from which she was aroused by the sound of her companion's voice speaking softly: "And now there are no windows, no houses. And on Easter they did this to us, mind you."

Chapter 15

Determined not to give way to absolute despair, Angelica jumped up with a show of liveliness. "Well, there's something we can do," she said. "We'll take those flags and decorate the graves with them." She'd managed to pull one of the boxes out far enough to get it open, and now extracted a British and American flag. "Come, Auntie Sandra," she said. "We'll go to the cemetery."

But Auntie Sandra was frightened. "Impossible! The Russians are there, looting. At first they only looted homes, but now they loot graves. Nobody goes to the cemetery anymore, it isn't safe! Come, let's go back to my place."

Once there she prepared a frugal meal and they spent the night together talking. Angelica listened sadly to the events which had taken place in Belgrade since the war started, when her mother was killed by the Germans, and to the present with Russian soldiers looting the graves.

There was pillage, Auntie Sandra told her, and rape. It was so bad that one of Tito's top aides even sent a letter of protest to Stalin over it.

Angelica realized that Auntie Sandra was trying to warn her to go back to Cablo for her own safety. "But there's a military parade tomorrow," she objected. "I heard them talking about it on the train. It's in honor of some general from Italy, and you know, a general always has many soldiers surrounding him. But perhaps the Anglo-American troops will come some day instead, just as the Russians did."

"We don't need any more troops. A few soldiers in each province are all we need and the people will take care of the rest."

"Just a few?"

"That's all we ask for. The American Mission with General Mihailovic thinks the same thing. Just so the people understand they're not communists."

Angelica was puzzled. "The Anglo-Americans aren't communists?"

"Haven't you ever heard of that old proverb, my child? Then listen," Auntie Sandra said darkly. "Whoever plants pumpkins with the devil will also break them over their head."

On the following day, early in the morning they both went to the military parade together. It was to honor a Western general recently back from the Italian front which was still active, and was being given as a gesture of appreciation for the great help extended by the West.

The Western general, some high-ranking Soviet officers, and officers of the Yugoslav People's Liberation Army stood together on a large platform erected along the newly named *Boulevard of the Red Army*. Huge portraits of Marx, Lenin, Stalin, Tito and various Soviet commanders were displayed. The bewildered and frightened masses stood pressed together on the sidewalks, all shivering in the chilly March morning. In front of them were dense lines of Soviet military police, and scattered among them were members of the Yugoslav secret police and the Soviet NKVD. Loudspeakers blared from the nearby trees and poles.

After hundreds of tanks had roared past them, next came a Soviet unit marching by, all majestic in their parade uniforms with many decorations and singing a happy Russian song. While the song continued the people applauded; then they kept their hands pressed together in a prayer position. This enraged the secret police who'd been taught, like Perun Novak, to deny the existence of God.

There were many incidents of fighting in the crowd. As the singing Russians passed by and marched down the boulevard, it became apparent that the sound of applause was being *piped in* via the loudspeakers strung amongst the trees. Tense as they were, this amused the people, and they began to laugh almost hysterically. Then came an announcement which was shouted into the microphone:

"COMRADES, we now welcome our fraternal troops from Croatia who were captured by our fraternal Soviet Army at Stalingrad, having been reeducated and prepared as dedicated members of our new social system."

Now appeared troops wearing the remnants of their former Croatian and German uniforms, but all in well polished Russian boots and with red stars on their caps. The only applause for them came from the platform where the dignitaries stood, and from members of the secret police scattered along the sidewalks. This caused more scuffling when they saw people holding up hands in pretend applause, but their hands were still; they were praying, or appeared to be.

To make up for the relative silence the recorded applause coming from the loudspeakers was stepped up in volume. Under the blaring noise people whispered to each other that the units marching by were actually units recruited by the Grand Mufti of Jerusalem and sent to Stalingrad three years ago.

Suddenly Angelica pointed to a marching officer with spectacles, a bulbous nose and a big belly. "Look!" she mentioned excitedly. "Auntie Sandra—look! I know that man. It's Hillarich, from Gradina!"

Auntie Sandra swiftly grabbed Angelica's pointing arm and pressed it down to her side. "Shh," she whispered.

"What treachery!" Angelica said hotly. "Hillarich, and there he goes, marching at the head of the unit. For shame!"

From under her coat Angelica took out two flags. She'd tied them to a branch taken from a rosebush her father had planted; it was found still alive near the ruins of their house. As Hillarich marched towards them, she waved the flags as high as she could over her head.

There was a stir in the nearby crowd. "Look at that—English and American flags!"

"Hey, get away from here," a voice protested harshly. "For God's sake, I just got out of jail yesterday." The man in his late fifties held up his hands, showing twisted and broken fingers, evidently the result of torture.

But Angelica was too excited to notice him. "I'm not afraid of Hillarich. Why should I be? Dayan never was." She continued to wave the flags violently back and forth.

"Here—give them to me," a pale, thin man next to her begged. "I'll wave them before the Western general." He gestured towards the platform. "Let him know what we stand for!"

"He's not worthy of seeing them," the man with the broken fingers replied back. "If he was, he wouldn't be up there with the rest of those ruffians."

"If only they'd come with a few soldiers, as Colonel McDowell had requested."

"Sure—but McDowell wanted simple soldiers, sons of the people, not sons of—"

Colonel McDowell was head of the American Mission with General Mihailovic. At the mention of his name spies scattered around in hopes of hearing just such comments, and went into action. A movie camera had already been at work; everyone within range took care to hide their face or turn away.

In the ensuing confusion, Auntie Sandra and Angelica managed to find their way out through the crowd and disappear. Meanwhile a new fist fight had started just as the rear column of the former Nazi unit recruited by the Grand Mufti was marching past.

On the following day, Angelica realized that neither Thomash nor Dayan were anywhere to be found in Belgrade, and having become frightened by everything she'd seen, she decided it was time to go back to Gradina. She took the two flags on the rose branch along with her, but before leaving she asked Auntie Sandra to place a bouquet of her father's roses on the ruins when they bloom.

"Yes, yes," Auntie Sandra assured her. "And spring will come soon. They can't keep spring away from us, that much is sure! And they can't keep the roses from blooming either."

When she eventually reached Gradina, Angelica was even more convinced of Thomash's probable fate. On the main street in a large window of the former chamber of commerce building, now occupied by the People's Committee, there was a visible display. It contained a Holy Bible on one side, and in the middle was a large cross turned upside down. On the other side was a bag with a chisel protruding out of it. All of these artifacts were labeled in hand-printed letters: *Tools of the Reactionary Elements.*

Angelica stared into the window for a long time—her thoughts were racing inside her head. She seemed to recognize the bag; it looked like the one Thomash had owned which was full of his tools, and was the same bag she'd packed her lunch in when she grazed Thomash's two goats in the hills above Cablo. That same Cablo where she was hurrying to now. Fearfully she wondered what she would find there.

Meanwhile, not too far away from her in the Gradina jail, a prisoner being held there was under questioning. "Some school director you are! Seven simple words—and you can't get them through your thick head." A heavily-armed guard was taking Dr. Vedrano from the cell formerly called *Tehran*—but now was named *Yalta*. "Death to Fascism, Freedom to the people!" The guard shook Dr. Vedrano violently. "Go ahead and say it!" By now they were in the corridor outside of Laguna's office, while Dr. Vedrano, his clothes soaking wet, could only respond with chattering teeth.

Laguna had his own interrogation office inside in addition to his regular duty as secretary of the District People's Committee. When the guard prodded him through the door, Laguna offered Dr. Vedrano a seat, which was refused. The doctor didn't want to sit down in his wet and cold clothes, which would then stick to his shivering body again.

Laguna began: "I didn't let the gravediggers do their job until after they'd taken a class in social reeducation. You, as a school director, obviously require an indoctrination course in it."

"Even after their reeducation," Dr. Vedrano said, "it seems you don't need the gravediggers after all. You're still throwing the dead into the river instead."

Laguna moved slightly in his chair.

Dr. Vedrano continued: "And inside of UNRRA sacks—of all things. Imagine! The Americans stuff food into those sacks to feed our people, then you stuff them full of the people's corpses."

"Don't get ahead of yourself, Doctor," Laguna warned him. "Better not try to be too brave here."

"I'm glad you recognize it," Dr. Vedrano replied calmly.

"Tell me—who changed the *Tehran* cell into *Yalta*?" Laguna leaned forward and pointed his finger at Dr. Vedrano. "And why?"

"In order to keep up with the fast-moving events of history," said Dr. Vedrano. "A more shameful name appeared to eclipse Tehran's. Hence—Yalta."

Laguna looked at him steadily for a long moment, then he sighed heavily. He wondered how he could get through to this man, surely he must have his price. "Look," Laguna finally said. "Suppose we make a deal. If you will—"

"No," Dr. Vedrano said sharply.

"Wait a minute. Don't be so sure. Let me tell you," and he began to speak quickly before he could be interrupted, "we only want you to write an essay proving that our fight under Marshal Tito is a continuation of the epic poetry of this country. Is that asking too much of you?"

Dr. Vedrano leaned back his head and laughed, a surprisingly hearty laugh considering his weakened condition.

"But wait! If you do, I personally guarantee you'll be promoted with a membership in the Academy of Science. Marshal Tito himself is going to be a member soon."

Dr. Vedrano ignored this promise of dubious honors and continued as though he hadn't heard it. "Heroic deeds you commit—throwing an old cripple's body from the bridge crammed into an UNRRA sack, after crushing every bone. And all because his son is a prisoner in Ger—"

"You're wrong about that!" Laguna interrupted. "He's hiding in the hills above Cablo. Don't worry—we know all about him." He shook his head in pretend pity, while studying Dr. Vedrano with cold eyes. "I hope," he said slowly, "that you didn't present this war to your students as a credit to the Western powers. Whose planes, by the way, killed your own wife and children. If you had any sense, you'd recognize how lucky we are with the fraternal Soviet Army at our side."

"I didn't present anything about this war to my students," Dr. Vedrano replied. "It's been the most dishonest war in history, the only truth lies with its innocent victims. If there's any doubt of this war's corruption, the fact that it has put you in power is proof enough."

Chapter 15

It was almost unbearably galling for Laguna to swallow such talk, but he had to since he couldn't afford to lose his temper. Dr. Vedrano's potential had been under discussion for the last month at meetings between the Regional Party heads, especially after the District Attorney Vukovich and two judges had died of either pneumonia or drowning in the *Yalta* cell. It had been determined that they'd bend Dr. Vedrano to their purpose, and it was Laguna's task to do so.

The committee's plan was to induce Dr. Vedrano to write a second essay after the one Laguna had been discussing. This one would deal with Greek epic poetry, on which Dr. Vedrano was a famous expert. Its purpose was to encourage and inflame the Greek Partisans who were engaged in fighting the Greek government and the Western interests in the areas around the Mediterranean. It was hoped that such an essay, referring to their glorious past, would serve to encourage them, since the attempt to assassinate Churchill during his visit to Greece had already failed.

For the moment, however, Laguna recognized a stalemate. It was obvious that Dr. Vedrano couldn't be broken by physical torture through the *Yalta* cell, so he decided to reach into him through his pride. For this Dr. Vedrano was assigned to clear rubble around Gradina under the supervision of German prisoners, and in the evenings he'd take course in social reeducation. This class was being held in the gymnasium building and was led by the ubiquitous Perun Novak.

Informed of this sentence—for such as it was—Dr. Vedrano said nothing. He held his head high as he marched out in the company of a guard. Observing the frail professor's dignified and erect stance, Laguna experienced a moment of misgivings. But then he told himself how foolish it was to worry about what the professor might do. After all, he was in command—Signor Laguna, who'd survived to ride the crest of the wave while so many lesser men had already gone under.

During the following week, and after another day of Dr. Vedrano's rubble-clearing job was over, Laguna was startled by an agitated knock on the door to his office. It sounded extremely urgent, so he strode across the room and quickly opened the door. A soldier in a dripping uniform stood outside without a cap, his wet hair plastered to his head. He was breathing heavily and the young man, ordinarily a well-trained guard, had forgot to salute.

"Here, sir! You better read what I found outside," the guard said shivering noticeably.

Astonished, Laguna took him by the arm, almost swinging him into the room. He closed the door, and as an afterthought, he turned the key in the lock. Then, forgetting to reprimand the guard for not saluting, he snapped. "Well?"

"It's Dr. Vedrano."

"Dr. Vedrano what?"

"He killed himself–jumped off the footbridge into the river!" The guard now thrust a piece of paper into Laguna's hand he'd picked up from where Dr. Vedrano had jumped.

On the note was written: *My end is due to those trying to rewrite this war using our poetic history, something I'd never present to the students in my school–and for that I'm very happy and proud.*

For three days Laguna suppressed the news of Dr. Vedrano's suicide–he was frantic–while the Regional Party Committee kept asking him how his negotiations with the professor were progressing. Was Dr. Vedrano going to agree to their demands? He evaded and postponed an answer. Meanwhile, he was becoming more and more anxious and distraught. So much so that when the chief of the Westania Times observing team in Gradina appeared at his door one day, Laguna jumped to his feet and gave the fascist salute.

The American appeared not to notice the faux pas. "I have come to you concerning a matter of utmost importance to our staff and our superiors," Mr. Winfield said in his flat, colorless voice.

I hope it's important to me too, Laguna thought miserably. But he remained silent.

"To us in the West," the American continued, "it starts with the individual and his rights, and in our society we protect those rights for everyone."

"Yes, I know. Of course!" Laguna agreed. What did the man have on his mind?

"But your society appears to have a different approach. You're concerned primarily with society as a whole, to which the individual is completely subordinated."

Now Laguna was relieved. If this was just to be a rigmarole about theoretical matters, there was nothing to worry about. He could double-talk, or even triple-talk with the best of them. He relaxed and smiled. "Please sit down, Mr. Winfield. Be comfortable."

"Thank you." Mr. Winfield was clutching a thick attaché case, which he then laid on the corner of the desk. "You understand, Tovarich Laguna," he continued, "that it's our strict policy being from another country that we never interfere in the conduct of internal affairs. In fact," and here he smiled faintly, "this is one of our chief exports, morally speaking."

"Indeed it is!" Laguna replied enthusiastically. His voice was now clear and full of self assurance. "And this cements our future relationship; showing our mutual respect for each other's opinions and systems."

"Precisely. And as you know, there are no strings attached when we offer help to our allies. And there never will be," Mr. Winfield said, while making an off-hand, generous gesture with his hand. But now he straightened up and his voice took on a more serious tone. "But as you doubtlessly know, not everyone in your country wishes to subordinate himself as an individual to the new society." Here he held out his hand, with the fingers outstretched. "You have a saying here, *not even the fingers of a hand are identical to each other*."

Laguna nodded, but he wished the man would get to the point.

The American looked around, and observed that the window was closed and so was the door. He moved his chair closer and lowered his voice. "Your Doctor Vedrano was quite a man," he said. "He was one of those people who adhered to the belief that individual rights should come first, as we Westerners do. His death was..."

"Death?" Laguna asked in apparent astonishment. "Dr. Vedrano is dead?"

Mr. Winfield gave him a cynical look. "Please, Tovarich Laguna, the point doesn't concern death as such, but whose death. In the case of Dr. Vedrano," he paused and Laguna listened with his heart beating wildly, "the fact is, I had a message meant for him from the Historical Society of one of our oldest universities."

"They must have wanted to spy on us," Laguna broke in, forgetting his pose of friendliness.

"To the contrary," the American replied. "However, even the greatest of minds sometimes go astray—especially the more sensitive ones. Like with Ezra Pound, for example. This case of Dr. Vedrano's death, though," he spread his arms widely, "it's a sensation—a sensation which..."

"But we don't want a sensation," Laguna said horrified.

"Perhaps not," Mr. Winfield said quickly. "But we do!" He opened his attaché case and extracted a paper from which he read: "*Prospective Academy of Science Member Commits Suicide —Fears People's Tribunal.*"

"Maybe that's true," Laguna agreed.

Mr. Winfield nodded and continued reading: *"Death came to Dr. Vedrano, eminent Yugoslav intellectual on April 1, 1945, when he threw himself into the swollen waters of the Mista river in the town of Gradina."* Here Mr. Winfield stopped. "You see, that's no good. A swollen river, melting snow, and rapids in spring. It's all so natural. But people now want sensationalism after a war, and that means money."

Laguna was curious, while forgetting about his own problem with Dr. Vedrano's death. "What's wrong if he jumped into the river? Isn't that sensational enough for readers?"

"Not nearly, but it can become so. Now listen to this: *Death was the result of his jumping into a water-filled crater left by heavy bombers.*"

"Whose bombers? German?" Laguna asked.

"It doesn't matter. The important thing is the picture it creates —no one will care whose planes dropped the bombs that made the crater. The point is the bombs were dropped because of a war, so subconsciously they will think he died due to it. Then they will hate war and love peace."

This statement about hating war embarrassed Laguna, who added, "Of course, it may have been he simply slipped in the bomb crater while bathing there and drowned as well. I hear those things happen out here, and if you want to report the sensational facts, then maybe we can do business together."

Mr. Winfield looked pleased. "I came to you hoping to become the exclusive reporter for this area out here, and as such I'd make it a point to report only the facts, along with your insightful tips, of course." He took another paper from his case and placed it before Laguna. "Your signature and it's a done deal," he said calmly.

The text was a typed contract which stated that Laguna, as the sole recognized authority in the District of Gradina, granted permission to Mr. George Winfield, U.S.A., to be the sole area reporter via the Westania Times newspaper, as an exclusive. Attached at the bottom was a check written to Laguna for 500 Swiss Francs. Laguna, who was closely watched by Mr. Winfield, didn't react at seeing the check, but continued reading the contract. It stipulated that Mr. Winfield could cover the entire Regional Committee area until his superior cabled for him to return home or he was reassigned.

"We want this paper to constitute a legal document, and I gather that you're the man who makes the laws here," Mr. Winfield said after Laguna had finished reading it. "We'll both sign it in a spirit of victory."

"And in a spirit of mutual cooperation in working for peace as well," Laguna concluded piously as he quickly removed the check and stuffed it into his pocket. "This also means that you have to report all the news we decide to give you. And remember Mr. Winfield, no contract is legal with us until certain words are written at the bottom. I'll write the first part, and you can write the last part."

Mr. Winfield nodded in agreement and Laguna wrote *Death to Fascism!*

Then Laguna continued:"It's a shame Dr. Vedrano accidentally drowned in that bomb crater. Just imagine, he'd just started to write essays interpreting Greek poetry and how our glorious victory under Marshal Tito will be a continuation of past Yugoslav poems. I'm thinking we have to include that in the story about him with a little more detail." Then smartly he handed the paper to Mr. Winfield.

And at his direction, Mr. Winfield carefully wrote in bold letters—*Freedom to the People!* Laguna then signed his name, and Mr. Winfield added his to bring Western journalistic ethics to the district of Gradina, be it for better or worse.

16

Is Off Limits

Tensions were growing in Fugen, Germany, ever since the Allies had crossed over the Rhine. This was due to the hostilities that erupted between the foreign workers and the rest of the population, so meetings were held about this inside the burgermeister's office.

Two plans were proposed to keep the foreigners under control —the first was to do away with most of their free time, and the second was to issue picks, axes and pitchforks to the townspeople as potential weapons. The local Volkssturm unit had declared itself inadequate to control the foreigners, especially after all the teenagers had marched off towards the Eastern Front one day, leaving them under-manned.

Then rumors began circulating concerning the plans made by the Russian and Polish workers. It was said they'd divided the area into zones, which at any given moment could be plundered and looted—even babies in their cradles, it was whispered, wouldn't be spared. Meanwhile, the retreating German artillery units were implored, in vain, to remain and protect this strategically important part of the war front.

Emil Harder, the sole Gestapo official in Fugen, described all the unrest as the circle of fear—without gaining much sympathy from his superiors. And although the apprehensions of the people were mainly focused on the Russians and the Poles, the four Serbs that occupied the old *Witch House* went through it unnoticed, at least until a particular night when they began to sing late into the evening while returning from their daily labor.

It started out right in front of Cornelia's house after the four of them saw through the front window a portrait of Hitler being brightly illuminated. The men paused in the darkness beyond the window, peering in.

"Look there!" Michail said, while pointing to a porcelain vase filled with fresh fern and mimosa under Hitler's portrait, as if to further enhance it. "Herr Vogel told me the Gauleiter gave that to Cornelia in thanks after she performed as soloist at a Nazi-party concert."

The other three men stared at him, and then spontaneously a song to celebrate their coming freedom broke out from the four lusty throats while they plodded up the hill towards home. Even Dayan's warning that they'd better get inside and be safe didn't stop them from singing. Later that evening they vowed to demolish Cornelia's house after the war was over until its lowest brick became the highest.

And more songs were indeed in the air. The next day even the whole Reich couldn't have stopped the collective singing that broke out after the Polish barracks reported seeing Harder praying inside the church. That was the beginning of the end!

Finally that end came just four days later, when a white flag was seen hoisted above the city hall. Dayan noticed it as he and the others were on their way to work under August's command.

"Never mind—just keep marching," August said. "Nobody has ordered me to surrender yet."

As they passed Cornelia's house—everything was silent, and the shades were pulled down on all the windows. But everywhere along the way they saw white flags out on the rooftops, whipping in the breeze.

"You see? It's the same everywhere," Dayan told August.

"I know how to surrender!" August protested. "It's not my first time. You just keep marching. Eins—Zwei!"

As the other three Serbs continued to march along obediently, Dayan suddenly grabbed August's rifle from him. "Prisoner August Vogel. Attention!"

August's face went pale and he appeared to be in great fear while trembling, but quickly developed into an obedient prisoner —ready to do whatever he was ordered. "Forward—march!" Dayan yelled, and the new prisoner wheeled and followed, with the other three Serbs now laughing as free men behind him.

Chapter 16

In the middle of the bridge August got another order from his captor—"Prisoner! About face!" This command was obeyed. Then —"At ease!" August watched in surprise as Dayan hit the bridge abutment with his former captor's rifle, breaking it apart. He then threw the pieces into the river.

"But—I'm responsible for that rifle," August stammered. "I owe for it. I'll have to pay."

Dayan put his hand on the older man's shoulder. "Uncle August," he said, "stop worrying! Go home now and put on civilian clothes. And here—take this," he then handed him a chocolate bar. "It's for—"

"Cornelia," August said. "My niece—she likes you." He was bewildered and confused.

"Not for Cornelia," Dayan answered. "It's for Helma, your daughter. And after you've changed into some appropriate clothes, come and watch us dance the victory dance!"

In short order some French troops began patrolling Fugen—they were mostly Moroccans in white turbans riding black horses. Captain Michelet was their commanding officer, and he was greeted enthusiastically by the foreign workers when he appeared up on the balcony at the city hall, with the French tricolor being held by soldiers to both sides of him. He congratulated everyone on their freedom in the name of the Allies, and after a short speech, he announced to everyone he was ready to receive representatives of all the foreign groups.

"I regret that we have nothing to give you," he said. Unfortunately, we ourselves received all we have from les Americaines, who are advancing to the north." He then smiled and shrugged before throwing his hands up in the French manner. "We only have our French caps and French wine to sing with." He smiled again and there was a cheer from the crowd.

Dayan, who'd already been selected as the Serbian representative, called out: "And everyone down here has got the French spirit!"

Another cheer went up, and the French capitaine smiled and doffed his cap in acknowledgment. He went on to say that certain measures would be undertaken, in cooperation with the burgermeister's office and the Red Cross, to feed the people. "But first, mes amis," he said, "it's urgent that these poor Russians who wear the striped shirts marked *East*, be found some decent clothes to wear."

No one disagreed with that.

Captain Michelet was rather surprised that there seemed to be few complaints from the former prisoners about the local population. He turned to Dayan, smiling. "Perhaps a Serb has something to say?"

"A question," Dayan returned. "I've read the poetry of your Maquis, how are they faring?"

The capitaine had been a guerrilla fighter himself. He explained that news was scarce now and would be until the fighting finally ends. "The war is by no means over, my friends," he told them. "The Western Allies must continue to fight Germany until its unconditional surrender—in accordance with the Casablanca conference. And you can be sure that Stalin is keeping his eyes on that promise of theirs constantly."

Here a young Russian interrupted. "Does anybody keep account of the promises Stalin makes anymore?" he asked.

"If not," Captain Michelet replied, "they certainly should be. Otherwise, we'll have to kick him out someday, just as we're getting rid of Hitler. We can't sacrifice Europe, it's a matter of Western morale."

The delegates stood in deferential recognition of his words.

The coming of their freedom was celebrated in the small city plaza with mostly folk dances, songs and drinking all day. *La Marseillaise* was also sung, and some French soldiers were carried on the shoulders of skinny, undernourished Poles and Russians. There were many speeches ending with an enthusiastic: *"Vive la France!"* The Bordeaux wine from the Garonne Valley sent songs from the Volga into the air.

In all the excitement and commotion, the four Serbs also participated wholeheartedly and when the time came, they suffered the same consequences as the others. Years of undernourishment became responsible for a lack of alcohol tolerance, so it didn't take much wine to get the celebrants thoroughly, if happily, drunk.

Then sometime after midnight, Dayan woke up in an unfamiliar bed which felt too soft for his bony structure. He was bathed and clothed in silky pajamas. Everything smelled fragrant and fresh; he scarcely knew himself! The last thing he remembered from the previous night was ending his speech at the plaza with a toast to the unheard poetry of the French Maquis. And all the while August, their former guard who was now a civilian, stood behind a tree sniffling while he watched them celebrating.

Even the weak light shining from a corner of the room gave no clue to Dayan's whereabouts. He shouted: "Hello! Hello! Where am I?" But no one answered. He pounded on the wall next to the bed, and in a few moments a figure entered. Dimly he glimpsed a long, pale gown.

The whispering voice was soft: "My uncle brought you here." Moonlight shined gently through the window. "Everything is over now, Dayan, go back to sleep."

"Wait!" She was moving away. "Are you Frau Bechter?"

"Yes, I'm Cornelia. The other woman is my mother."

"I've never seen her before."

"She likes being in her room, reading. Last night too, before you came—but then you frightened her."

Dayan was surprised. "I frightened your mother?"

Cornelia smiled. "Yes, it was you. At first you were kind to her—you kissed her hands and called her *Mamushka*. But then you became angry. You struck the picture of Hitler and knocked it off the wall."

"I did? Really?"

She nodded. "With your wooden shoes, and Mother was frightened. She ran over to Uncle August's house with the picture."

Dayan reacted and she sensed his thoughts.

"To destroy it, of course," Cornelia added quickly. "Then August came over and put you under a cold shower, to sober you up."

"I was drunk, all right," Dayan admitted. He stretched out his arms. "But I'm not anymore."

She moved towards him without fear and laid down beside him.

He put his arms around her, holding her fiercely. "Thank you, Cornelia."

"Thanks for what?"

"For this." He seized her hungrily, but the bed seemed to almost smother them—it was too soft to hold the wild surging of his desires. He brought her gently to the floor, but Cornelia now wanted to free herself. She moved her body, not impatiently and not in fear, but with determination. He let her go and she rose, then held out her hand to him. He took it and she tugged gently, until he too was on his feet.

He put his arms around her, but her shoulders felt cold. He reached down and pulled the comforter from the bed, wrapping it around her body. Then he picked her up—she was light and slender—and started walking towards the door.

"Wait, Dayan! Where are you taking me?"

"Out to the garden—and the lilacs."

He then carried her through the hallway and out the door into the garden, towards a romantic place under the trees where the grass was dappled with moonlight. With his heart pounding now, Dayan put her down where she could lean against a tree trunk. He began picking lilac blossoms and spreading them on the ground. With a half-amused and half-tender smile, Cornelia observed these preparations he was making.

Obediently when the lilac bed was ready, she laid down amongst the flowers, her body protected from the cold by the warmth of Dayan's.

"A bed of lilacs," she murmured. "Such a bed I've never had before."

"I wish they were wild, like those in Cablo. Thanks for bringing me here."

"But you brought me."

Dayan didn't answer this—he was busy pulling the other half of the comforter over himself—for he'd suddenly realized he was naked. This also reminded him of the woods in Cablo.

"But you don't know them, Liuba and Veselinka, they're shepherdesses." He wasn't conscious of his words, for he was suspended between the present and the past. His nakedness had triggered a memory of a boyish desire for the two girls, sometimes felt when he would bathe in the creek alone back then. Now, with Cornelia, it was right to be naked.

Cornelia hadn't heard his words, for she was wholly engrossed in one sense only—that of touch. Yet she murmured, without knowing it, "You're just the second one—after Otton."

Otton was her husband, but that revelation was as lost to Dayan as his had been to her. It was much later when they both heard the trampling of a distant Moroccan horse patrol, and the chirping of a cricket in the nearby lilac bush.

The sun was streaming in through the kitchen window the next morning where Dayan stood, and he was attired in Otton's shoes and custom-tailored suit which looked hardly worn. It fit him loosely along with the collar, which was somewhat too wide. Cornelia was tying his necktie. "We'll fatten you up, and then the suit will fit better."

"Yoohoo!" Mamushka called from the hallway. She came in carrying a small bundle wrapped in paper. Dayan gave her a deep deferential bow, which was intended to convey his apologies for last night's drunken behavior. But the old lady looked happy and victorious.

"It's all here," she said. "I helped him to die!" Laughing, she displayed some ashes from Hitler's portrait, which she'd burned last night after Dayan had knocked it from the wall. "Here—I'll throw them out the window."

"No Mamushka!" Dayan said, as he quickly put his hand on her arm. "Don't do that. It's spring—his ashes would mix with the plants—it's too much of an honor for him—and bad for the flowers!"

They agreed to place the ashes into Dayan's wooden shoes and burn them together in the fireplace. Satisfied after the fire was burning brightly, Mamushka sat down by the firelight to read.

She didn't even look up when Dayan said good-bye as he went out the door.

Sadly, he stumbled down the street in the unfamiliar and tight shoes he wore. French soldiers, also wearing shiny shoes in place of their army boots, were walking in the same awkward way as they left various homes and came out into the street.

There was seen great activity within the plaza, where many Russians and Poles had gathered together. Their women wore long, slender dresses taken from some German homes, but many of them had the seams splitting over their wide hips, and their skirts collected dirt from sweeping along the dusty ground. Some tried lifting them up, revealing their wrinkled knees. Many also had three or four pairs of high-heeled shoes strung over their arms, while they still preferred to walk barefoot on the ground.

Even mink coats bundled under their arms were already being sold to French soldiers in exchange for American food. Kitchens brought from the barracks were set up outside, then butter, sugar and chocolate were dumped together into large kettles and mixed with potatoes. The energy and comfort from their full stomachs was expressed in mutual embracing; they danced, sang, hugged and kissed.

There were no more wooden shoes or printed *East* signs on the backs of any shirts. Some men in the crowd, instead, wore tuxedos along with white gloves.

Dayan left his shoes and necktie as a deposit with a Russian whose bike he borrowed, then he hurried to visit his countrymen. They'd already remodeled the front doors to the *Witch House* so they couldn't ever be used to lock people inside again. The place was unusually neat and clean, and so were the men. Their military blouses had no missing buttons; their trousers were patched and mended. A woman's apron was hanging from a hook in the corner —Dayan pretended not to notice it.

Chapter 16

After having a cup of coffee with his comrades, Dayan left saying, "You can always find me somewhere around the plaza." They all understood each other.

Although it was only the middle of the day, it seemed a long time to Dayan since he'd last seen Cornelia. In fact, the whole period since the liberation of Fugen had a dreamlike quality to it. Perhaps he'd never seen her; perhaps everything was a dream. He wanted some reality now, and needed it. He pedaled the bicycle as fast as he could through the streets crowded with everyone celebrating.

The first thing Cornelia asked him was: "Where's your necktie?" Looking down, she exclaimed: "Oh! And Dayan—your shoes are missing!"

"I didn't like them, Cornelia, they weren't comfortable."

August's niece shrugged and went to a closet in her bedroom. After some rummaging around, she emerged with a pair of ski-boots. "Here," she said, "these will surely be comfortable, little one, hungry one. What untidy people you French are!"

Dayan recognized the boots—the same ones August had offered him and that he'd returned—but all he said was: "I'm not French."

"Not French! Did I hear you right?"

"Absolutely. I'm not French." He added proudly, "I'm a Serb!"

Cornelia's face went pale. Her blue eyes flashed with anger. She backed away from him as if he was unclean. "Get out!" she screamed. "Get out and take your rags with you! They're outside in the shed!"

Shocked as he was, a voice inside Dayan said to himself ruefully: *Okay. You said you wanted reality, so here it is.* He quickly began to take off Otton's pants. "Bring me my rags, then," he commanded, "but remember, you owe me the shoes. We burned mine with Hitler's ashes and Mamushka warmed herself with the flames."

Hearing her name, Cornelia's mother appeared just as he pulled up his own ragged pants and fastened them. The younger woman faced her angrily. "Mama—he's not French!"

Mamushka looked at her daughter with a faintly contemptuous expression. "So what? I knew it already. That's why I've been reading this book." She turned the book so the title could be read: *The Serbian Revolution* by Leopold von Ranke. Cornelia glanced at the book sullenly, then turned her back, staring out the window into the garden.

"Don't mind her," Mamushka told Dayan. "She doesn't know any better. First she read *MEIN KAMPF*, then that book of Rauschning's."

"*Conversations With Hitler*," Dayan said in disgust.

"That's right. And you know all the nasty things he said about the Slavs."

"Naturally. So I have to be French to be good—to be acceptable?" Dayan directed his question towards Cornelia's angry back.

She wheeled and faced him, her face spiteful. "You can't protect me, don't you understand? You have no power!"

"I'm the representative for three other Serbs who were liberated in Fugen," Dayan said. "I talked with the French Commander Michelet only yesterday."

"You see?" Mamushka said triumphantly to her daughter. She looked kindly into Dayan's eyes. "Believe me, he has power. I can feel it."

That evening Dayan came back to Cornelia's house proudly carrying an *OFF LIMITS* sign endorsed by Captain Michelet.

"Didn't I tell you?" said Mamushka. She kissed Cornelia good night and went to August's house, leaving them alone.

Reassured now that Dayan did indeed have some power to protect her, Cornelia became playful, affectionate and happy again. She'd sit on Dayan's lap singing, *"Little one, hungry one—I'll feed you and make you a big man."*

She teased him about his wide feet. Dayan, now feeling like the master of the house he'd once vowed to destroy, exacted a punishment for such teasing—she must sit on his lap each time and sing one of Schubert's melodies.

She objected: "Schubert's melodies grew from his suffering. You're too young for that, you didn't suffer. Let me sing Strauss's *Voices of Spring* instead."

Mamushka had stayed home this evening because she wanted to discuss some details in the book *Serbian Revolution*. They all looked up startled a moment later when they heard shooting from the plaza. The sound grew louder until there was a thunder of firing from machine-guns and mortars. Bright glares lit up the mountains. Dayan moved reluctantly to the window.

"Stay back!" Cornelia said anxiously. She came to his side.

"Don't be frightened."

She took his arm urgently. "Go to the shack and change your clothes, bring this suit back to me! Put on your old clothes now!"

He was astonished. "But why?"

"Because I don't want you to be caught here, that's why!"

"My God!" Mamushka exclaimed. "What's the matter with you?"

Cornelia ignored her, and continued talking to Dayan: "Go right away as fast as you can, and if they catch you never admit to them—"

Admit to whom?" he asked.

"To our troops, stupid! Did you think they'd just sit around doing nothing—without fighting back? Now get going! Better say you're French to them if they catch you!" She pushed him towards the door. "And take that sticker off my door. I'm not off limits—not to the German soldiers!"

At the first sounds of gunfire, Mamushka had quickly knelt down. Cornelia turned to her mother, who was still on her knees listening and watching in amazement; she didn't understand at all what was happening. Cornelia now took her by the arm, and pulled her to her feet. "It's our new offensive—a new Ardennes. Victory!" The old lady looked at her, still uncomprehending and fearful.

Dayan paused with his hand on the doorknob. "The shooting is now coming from one side only," he told her. "And only one type of weapon which—"

"Hurry up!" Cornelia cried frantically. "Damn you, go, you Bolshevik!"

A few minutes later Dayan reappeared wearing his original tattered rags, with Otton's suit over his arm. He put it on the table. Suddenly the sound of shooting was replaced by the ringing of church bells, with many voices singing happily and shouting: *"Hitler is dead! Hitler is dead!"*

Mamushka looked shocked. She put her arms around Dayan and kissed him. "The war is over, at least for you, my boy," she said, hugging him tenderly.

"Yes, Mamushka—the war and everything else," Dayan replied. He turned to Cornelia, who stood speechless for once, and lifted one of his feet. He was wearing the ski-boots.

"You'll be paid for these—eventually," he told her, and let himself out the front door. Outside, he turned and looked at the *OFF LIMITS* sign, but decided to leave it where it was.

He didn't feel like going to the *Witch House,* where his three countrymen were so cozily settled in with three of the pretty town's girls looking after them. He instead wanted to be off, to go through the night. In the darkness there was no measure of distance, and perhaps for that reason, at least in his heart, the closest place was his native Yugoslavia. So it was with that thought on the first night of freedom for enslaved Europe, with peace for both victor and conquered, that Dayan spent dreaming in a ditch on the outskirts of Fugen.

In the days that followed, Dayan applied the principle of a Yugoslav proverb which said: *the wrong way is often the fastest*. Whenever he couldn't use transportation through liberated Austria because he lacked identification, he instead walked. Most of the time he avoided towns and checkpoints, walking through Alpine villages until he reached the Austro-Yugoslav border.

At last he came to a place where he recognized a church on the Yugoslav side; he'd seen it from the train while he was being transported to Germany over two years ago. He had an impulse now to pray for God's forgiveness.

He felt that he had much to account for in his prayers; he'd planned to destroy Cornelia's house—forgetting that millions of homes had already been destroyed from the Atlantic to the Urals. He'd taken August prisoner—as if there weren't enough prisoners in the world already. He'd spent two weeks with another man's wife—and even though that man was already dead, it didn't make his sin any less. Bitterly he remembered Cornelia's words; *it's the war!*

Here at the border Dayan found spring all around; in the songs of the birds, the tinkling of distant cowbells, and the color and fragrance of Alpine wildflowers moving gently in the light breeze. He wanted to wave and sway a little too, touching them with his hands, feeling the tenderness of them. He put his face down while breathing deeply, and felt the soft touch of the flowers against his cheeks. The fragrant breeze was blowing them in little waves towards Yugoslavia, and he felt that it was sending him in that direction as well.

When he stood up, refreshed and gladdened, he saw a stone marking the border on his right. There was some rusted barbed wire there also, telling him that he was exactly at the boundary line. He looked to his right and to the left. The high grass and wildflowers looked and smelled the same both ways. He first picked a bouquet on one side of the wire and stone marker—from the Yugoslav side—and then from the other, on the Austrian side. He buried his face in each bouquet; first one, and then the other. Their fragrances were the same.

He placed the two bouquets of flowers together, then separated them again into two bunches. The colors blended. It occurred to him that he could ask Thomash to carve a wooden vessel for each, and then send one bunch to the Yugoslav government and the other to the Austrian government, challenging each to establish which flowers came from which side of the border. They might consult with all of their scientists, historians, and naturalists. They could search the Czar's and King's archives, question politicians, spies, businessmen and reporters. And still they'd find no difference!

He felt assured of triumphing over all of them with such a challenge. It'd be like winning not only this war, but all the other wars for the last thousand years, and winning something for the future besides. And with just these two bouquets! Victory was his, and he wanted to share it with the whole world.

With the two trophies in his hands, and his arms spread out like the wings of a soaring bird, he pretended to fly across the waves of Alpine wildflowers. Hovering not only above his own country, torn apart as it was for thousands of years, but over the whole world in harmony with the scene before him.

In his moving, swaying primeval dance of triumph, he'd trod upon the barbed wire marking the border, pushing it deep into the soft earth with the heavy ski-boots from Cornelia. He thought of her fleetingly. She'd given him the boots which destroyed the mark of the boundary; perhaps he should've thanked her for them after all! The wire above ground was still vibrating, in contrast to the smooth, graceful motion of the grass.

He bent down, thinking that no man-made object seemed ever to attain the grace of nature, and as he did so, he thought he heard a humming coming from somewhere. He pointed an ear towards the ground; first one ear, and then the other–someone nearby was moaning. A few minutes later he found a wounded man lying in the deep grass. Behind him could be seen the long, irregular track he'd left from crawling through the meadow.

Dayan picked him up and carried him towards the church. But it was on the Yugoslav side of the border, and as Dayan went in that direction–the man indicated *no,* pressing Dayan's head weakly, turning it back towards Austria, as a rider would to a horse. When Dayan moved in that direction obediently, the man nodded his head *yes*.

At the spring where he'd bathed his face that morning, Dayan put his burden down and washed the man's wounds. In German he apologized that he had no bandages, but the man gave a look like he didn't understand him. He also seemed unconcerned with his hip wounds, all he wanted was to drink the cool water. After he'd had enough to drink, the man asked Dayan if he understood Serbian. Dayan nodded eagerly. Now the stranger began to talk, or rather whisper weakly and hurriedly.

"You must be quiet," Dayan said, "you'll use up all your strength." He picked up his countryman by hoisting him over his right shoulder with difficulty. Through it all Dayan had clung to the two bouquets of flowers, which he now thrust into the wounded man's left hand, closing his fingers around them. "Be quiet and count these. We'll get help soon."

The wounded man kissed the flowers. "They saved my life," he said. "Crawling through them—so soft—fragrant."

Dayan hurried with his burden towards a nearby Austrian village which straddled down the hill from the church. "Keep quiet," he said again, for he was afraid the talking would weaken the man further.

"I must talk," the wounded man said, with his voice barely above a whisper.

"Talk and I'll drop you on the ground!" Dayan threatened.

"Thousands murdered. Still the killing goes on. Everyone—"

Dayan realized there was no stopping him; he was obsessed. So he gave up and said, "All right then, tell me. Who's being killed? And by whom?"

As he hurried along, the man he carried on his back whispered a tale of violence. Thousands of Yugoslav refugees had attempted to escape Tito's regime by fleeing to the British troops in Austria, who'd turned them back forcibly. In the deep forests and canyons near the border they'd been massacred. This man, although wounded, had managed to escape, but his legs had given out and he'd been unable to walk further. Eventually he was able to crawl forward hopelessly, but with the last of his strength, until Dayan had found him.

At Dayan's insistence he repeated the story, giving more and more details, until they arrived at a nearby peasant's house. The peasants slowly opened their door, and let Dayan put him down on a cot in the corner of the room by the fireplace. Thankfully and gently, Dayan laid the man down, taking the now wilting flowers from his hand as he did so. The family set about bandaging the wounds, and offered them some food, but there was a noticeable lack of sympathy or compassion in their manner.

Dayan was puzzled, but the answer came as the man of the house helped him to lift the victim to a horse cart outside, to be driven to the hospital. The peasant put a tattered blanket over the injured man.

"I'll drive there as fast as I can," he said gruffly. "There may be a few bumps along the way."

"Please!" Dayan said. "Be gentle with him. You can see he's badly hurt!"

"He's not the first one," the peasant replied as he climbed onto the cart. "And he won't be the last either." He picked up the reins.

"Wait!" Dayan said. "There's something I don't understand, I have to know about it." He glanced to the back of the cart where the wounded man seemed to be comfortable enough. "You'd better tell me right now," he said urgently.

The peasant's neighbor had been standing by to lend a hand, and now the two men told Dayan a story far more shocking than anything he himself had experienced. The peasants related that during the last few days other wounded people had come or were carried across the border, telling the same story as the man in the cart.

Among the many victims were Austrians from the local area who'd been wounded by Tito's army, and Italians who'd barely escaped with their lives. They relayed how hundreds of civilians around the Trieste area were massacred with their bodies thrown into caves to rot by Yugoslav Partisans.

Another gave word of the many killings around Bleiburg. Thousands of Yugoslav soldiers and civilians fleeing Partisans were being sent back by the British to be massacred. British tanks even forced the issue, with thousands probably dead. And the Russians were being told they'd be sent back to the Soviet Union—where it was a certain death awaiting them.

"And what did you do about it?" Dayan asked angrily.

The peasant merely shrugged his shoulders and flicked at the horses with the reins. The cart lurched forward and Dayan ran after it. He thrust his arm out, handing the bouquet of flowers to the driver. "If he dies," Dayan whispered, "put these flowers in his hands."

The peasant nodded grudgingly.

Dayan thought there must be a small British garrison at Rosenbach, so he hurried off towards it. Entering the town, he managed to pass the sentry, but was met by a sergeant. The soldier saw this thin, ragged man was nearly breathless, and doubling-over while gasping from exhaustion.

"What's the matter!" the sergeant asked him.

Hardly able to get the words out, Dayan panted: "Too much to say—crimes—unheard of—for three thousand years." He attempted to pass, but the sergeant put out a hand clutching his shoulder. "Blood—blood—on your hands," Dayan whispered.

The sergeant abruptly let go of him. He raised his hands and looked at his palms, then turned them over. "Are you crazy? What blood on my hands? Here—you come with me."

He was then half-led and half-pushed into Lieutenant Greenshield's office, where Dayan collapsed on the floor. The sergeant and another soldier pulled him upright and leaned him against the wall.

"Sorry lieutenant," Dayan muttered, "a courier shouldn't fall down."

"Courier?" Greenshield was seated at his desk studying through a magnifying glass a collection of pictures showing a Nazi parade. He was evidently searching for a particular person.

"Yes," Dayan said, "I have an important message."

"All messages are important. What do you want?" He didn't raise his head.

"Nothing for myself, but for the others. Save them!"

"You mean, save the Nazis?" Greenshield looked up at last, shocked.

"No, your allies, your friends—eternal friends!" Dayan looked into the lieutenant's eyes beseechingly.

"We don't want eternal friends, they only mean obligations to defend them," Greenshield said sensibly. "Now, what's on your mind?"

Dayan gulped a deep breath of air. His voice was stronger as he said, "Thousands and thousands killed—massacred. Like Katyn. You know Katyn?"

"Never heard of it. You say thousands and thousands? My God, you could do better by saying millions and millions."

"No—I mean right now—right under your nose!" Dayan said. He was beginning to sound like a man whose reasoning was slipping away. He could scarcely frame the words with his mouth. "Out there I..." he pointed through the open window towards the Austro-Yugoslav border.

"Across the border?" Greenshield exclaimed impatiently. "Don't worry about what happens over there. Mind your own business!"

"My country! My people! Still dying. And you may tomorrow, as Hamlet said."

Greenfield ignored this and replied calmly. "If they're being killed, then they must be guilty—forget about them." He moved the photographs to one side of his desk. "Tell me, are you coming from Yugoslavia?"

"Yes and no."

The lieutenant smiled ironically. "Better make up your mind. For a *Yes,* you go to jail right now. For a *No,* I'll call you a liar."

The echoes of shooting sounded from across the border. "Listen!" Dayan said. He was somewhat rested now and pushed himself away from the wall, taking a step towards the desk. "They're dying! Please bring your English tanks and—"

The lieutenant made an angry and negative gesture motioning Dayan back. "That's enough about this, and learn to call us British!" he shouted. "Now take him to jail!" He got up and closed the window. The sergeant took Dayan away.

Chapter 16

The jail with its crumbling walls seemed the oldest structure remaining after seven and a half centuries of Hapsburg rule. A lonely policeman with a ribbon of the Austrian flag around his sleeve was the only reminder of a modern world. The other prisoners Dayan met weren't unfriendly, but seemed resigned and apathetic. *They must feel guilty of Dachau*, Dayan thought. However, they fell asleep peacefully at dusk while he remained wide awake.

Two hours later there was a commotion of trucks, cars and tanks outside. Dayan was encouraged; *the lieutenant has opened his heart*, he told himself, for the movement of the unit seemed to be towards the border. He wondered why they're not taking him along as a witness. His heart pounded with elation. Some guards were passing the window of the cell he was in, so he leaned out as far as he could and called: "Tell them to take me. I'll help!"

"You'll help to kill your own brothers? Are you a Christian?" one guard replied.

Dayan didn't understand. "I brought the message today; that's why they're going to the border."

The silence after the British unit had departed was broken by the squeaking of the old jail door. The policeman had come to give them some news of the world. Hostilities had finally ended in Europe; but Himmler, Ribbentrop and Bormann were still at large.

A tall, thin man tossed something into the policeman's pocket as he answered questions put to him by the prisoners.

Dayan asked loudly, "But what about the killing that's still going on right here around the border! Why aren't the English going to prevent it?"

The policeman looked at him almost with pity. "Sorry—I have to tell the truth," he said and sighed. "They really went to Bleiburg to help one of their units drive the Yugoslavs back home, the people who don't want to go back to Tito. There are tens of thousands of them wanting to spread out all over Western Europe."

The man who'd tossed something into the policeman's pocket quietly moved to the door and sneaked out, so Dayan followed behind him. When they made it outside there was no one in sight; they stood together.

"Shouldn't we wait for the others?" Dayan asked.

"Hell no. They've got it better there in jail than out here. They prefer it inside."

"What about you?"

His companion shook his head disgustedly. "I'll tell you," he said. "The Allies are simpletons, just like you. They always imagine the prisoners will give them information about all those in the Third Reich who committed the war crimes. So they feed them—to soften them up." He then paused, his expression becoming as serious as the words were that followed. "From me, this is all they'd get." He made an explicit, vulgar gesture and then spit, turned away and started walking towards the east.

"No! This way!" Dayan called, but he continued plodding steadily in the other direction. Dayan raised his voice. "You're confused!" he shouted. "This way is safer."

Now the man turned. "Imbecile!" he yelled. "I'm going to the Bolsheviks."

Dayan ran up and grabbed him by the shoulder. "That means you're one of them!"

"No more than you are," the thin man said.

Dayan started to push him from behind, then stopped. "What are you?"

"A scientist, just a plain scientist—unwanted by the West."

Dayan said nothing, revealing by his silence and expression that he wanted to hear more.

"It's quite simple," the scientist said. "I was captured by the West. I offered myself to them, not once or twice, but many times. They kept saying, *We'll use you when we need you*. Meanwhile, I stayed in their jails. Eventually I escaped and they captured me right here. But they don't know me—don't know who I am."

"What now, then?" Dayan asked quietly.

"Not to be used—to have one's knowledge and skill wasted is another sort of death. A scientist belongs to the world, not to a people. Bolshevik, Nazi or Democrat—he can work under any system."

"But that's not right. It's not moral."

"Only because of people like you. Idealists, whether they're rulers, or followers. The point is, what use do you put my knowledge to?" He laughed cynically. "I saw you jumping up when the British trucks and tanks roared away earlier. *To the rescue,* is that what you were thinking? Or should I say—dreaming?"

"Well, I did believe—"

"Of course. Of course you believed! So did your proud countrymen who were massacred across the border. They believed for centuries! Listen, man, I know a lot."

"Then tell me."

"No. It would only make you unhappy."

"Please."

"When they sent your people back to be slaughtered by Tito, one of the victim's last words were regret that he'd never live to fight the British. Broken pride, isn't it?"

It was too much for Dayan to take. "Sorry I pushed you." He looked towards the border.

"Go," the scientist said.

Dayan remained motionless.

"Now you want me to push you, but I won't do it. It would make you feel better, but I prefer to let you go with your own conscience to guide you. You'll be a better man for it." He patted Dayan's shoulder.

Dayan watched as the man's tall figure disappeared eastward into the darkness as he himself went the other way. Their footsteps sounded the same in the night, and in the darkness—but who could say which was the right direction?

17

After The War Ends

His journey away from Rosenbach led Dayan to eventually back-track his way towards Fugen, as he again reminded himself of the old proverb: *the wrong way is often the fastest*. It didn't bother him that he had to break the travel restrictions put in place by the occupying powers. To the contrary, he enjoyed breaking them, just as he savored the beauty of the Alps and the hospitality of the peasants along the way.

In Fugen he went back to the *Witch House*, which now sat eerily empty. He found a French artist there sitting outside on a little stool, painting a picture of it. Dayan paused near him. The artist looked up at him and smiled.

"I used to live in this house," Dayan told him, smiling back.

"Maybe you mean your great-great-grandmother did." The Frenchman laughed. "But you're a foreigner, you should go to Jenbach. All the foreigners are there—they've got plenty of American food."

"Thanks, but I can't walk any further with these ski-boots on." Dayan lifted up one of his sore feet.

"I can take care of that!" The Frenchman jumped up. "Stay right where you are."

He mounted a motorcycle and roared away. Amused and curious, Dayan waited. Meanwhile, he studied the painting. The colors were well chosen, he thought, and the composition was excellent, but most of all he liked the beautiful Alps painted in the background.

Soon the Frenchman returned carrying three pairs of good shoes. "Here," he said, "take all of them, a pair should fit you." He tried to thrust them into Dayan's hands, but Dayan backed away.

"What's the matter? They look like your size. I'm sure some will fit."

"That's not the trouble," Dayan replied. "They're not mine, I'd have to return them."

"Mais non!" the artist exclaimed. He shrugged. "Nobody gives things back any more," he said, grinning cheerfully. He tossed the three pairs of shoes, whose shoestrings were tied together, towards Dayan as he automatically reached out and grabbed them. Then taking off his worn ski-boots, Dayan selected a pair which appeared the right size, and put them on. The Frenchman watched and whistled, while occasionally looking at his painting with his eyes narrowed. When he was ready, Dayan shook hands with him, expressed his thanks again and headed for Cornelia's house.

After arriving at her house he found a limousine and a jeep parked in front of it. A new *OFF LIMITS* sign was on the door, endorsed by a Major Renard. *That foxy skunk*, Dayan thought to himself, smiling bitterly. He wrote *Thank you* on a slip of paper and slipped it into the ski-boots. Then he hung them, along with the two pairs of extra shoes given to him by the artist, over the door handle.

With that mission accomplished, he turned away once more from the scene of much grief, with some happiness as well, and started off again walking rather slowly. Was he back here in Fugen merely to return the ski-boots to Cornelia? Or was it, in actual truth, because the place represented a sort of familiar home?

An important consideration, aside from the other possibilities, was that he felt anxious to see Captain Michelet and report the incident with the dying peasants at the border. But he also wanted to avoid any more trouble having just left jail, so he pondered what to do next.

He finally decided to go to Jenbach, as the French artist had suggested. It was only eight kilometers from Fugen, and he'd often heard about the prison camp there during the war. August used to threaten to send him to it if he didn't march better, or if he dared to look at German women. "And the wild Russians will eat you up overnight," he used to say. "They're tough! They eat rawhide raw!"

The truth was, as Dayan found out, the Russians had been put to work in a nearby leather factory and if any were eating rawhide, raw or otherwise, it took place because they were starving. When he got there he found the Jenbach camp refugees in wooden shoes and their clothes were still marked *East.* Nowadays, however, its population had been expanded by the arrival of many Russians from other camps.

The new commandant of the camp had announced: *"Jenbach, American food–Elsewhere, no food."* The people had no choice but to accept this ultimatum if they wanted to eat, although they wondered why the American food was being dispensed by French authorities.

The people from the camp were holding a memorial service in tribute to all the Russians dying due to involuntary repatriation. This was being done as a result of the Yalta conference–where the Allies promised to turn over Russians to the Soviets, even against their will. A leaflet which described all of this, and which caused the people to hold this memorial service, ended with the words: *We can only cry but don't stop, for crying is a sign we live.*

The hide factory had been closed down for this occasion, but its stench was still heavy in the air. For this reason it was decided to hold the service within a distant meadow by a blooming apple tree. A bench under the tree served as an altar, with a cross made out of wildflowers placed on top of it.

The Russian people who were all gathered in the meadow watched as a column of jeeps roared towards them, then at a signal, they knelt and began singing–*Blessed One Coming In the Lord's Name.* This was in deference to the eminent Russian Metropolitan from America who was to be their guest of honor.

After the jeeps arrived, many French military police got out and formed a cordon. They did this between the kneeling people and the last two jeeps, which were loaded with Soviet officers carrying German cameras around their necks. They had a large roll of silk fabric which they were measuring into lengths and dividing amongst themselves. Then they calmly ate some oranges, throwing the peelings out of the jeeps, and finally they turned their cameras towards their praying countrymen.

By this time the service was almost over and a French policeman, shouting in Russian through a megaphone, instructed the people to return to the refugee camp where the Soviet officers would give them orders as to when and how they should return to the Soviet Union. But before these instructions could be repeated, the Frenchman's megaphone was hit by a shower of rocks, followed by wooden shoes thrown by a young Russian. There was a flurry and a scuffle, and then the service was resumed.

The eulogy was delivered by Alexey Duboroff, a Russian whom Dayan had met in Fugen. After this happened others were introduced as speakers to recount tales they had of escape or persecution by the Soviets. Dayan was included as an eyewitness with information about the massacres of many people. He told them, when given the chance, of what he'd heard of Katyn, Bleiburg, and of his experiences at the border, unaware in his excitement that some of the Soviet officers were taking pictures of him. Finally, after a last prayer the people went back to the camp, but only after the departure of the Soviet officers and their heavily armed French protectors.

The refugees were deep in discussion of what to do next when they received notification from Major Renard concerning the jurisdiction of the United Nations Relief and Rehabilitation Administration (UNRRA). With the war over in Europe, UNRRA became responsible for providing aid to all officially designated displaced persons camps like this one.

UNRRA officials were planning to conduct a thorough screening and precise census of all those in the camp seeking assistance. This bulletin ended with a typical Renard slogan*: No screening, No American food.* One enterprising refugee had already conducted a private census, and according to him there were 1,482 persons waiting to be screened and counted.

Later that day a large column of trucks moved in, with French soldiers assisting by encircling the camp. Through a megaphone, this time protected by a machine-gun on both sides, they were instructed to gather their belongings and get into the trucks. Then they'd be moved to another displaced persons camp where they had better sanitary conditions. Screenings and counting would be conducted at the new location.

Nobody had time to think, surrounded as they were by a ring of soldiers with fixed bayonets moving in closer and closer. They knew their belongings weren't a problem since there weren't many to speak of, so the only other issue was how to transport a small wooden replica of the Cathedral of Kiev; they'd constructed it as a gift to the Metropolitan who never arrived. It was finally decided that Alexey Duboroff, his wife Masha and their seven-year-old son Vania would travel with it in a following truck.

Dayan had managed to join the same truck carrying the Duboroffs. Along with the rest of the convoy they traveled uneventfully for many kilometers. Suddenly ahead of them, they saw people jumping out of the convoy of trucks which were still moving. They also noticed that other trucks had stopped along the road, with blankets thrown over the front of the cab to cover the windshield. As people jumped out they were shouting: *"They're taking us back to the Soviet Union! Get out while we're still alive!"*

Soon more than half of the trucks had been stalled and some were even driven into ditches. Russians ran through the forest calling to each other, afraid to become separated.

The Duboroffs had spread some old blankets around the cathedral to protect it, and so Masha, who'd been watching all this commotion, suddenly threw one over the front of the cab. Dayan, understanding her intent, then reached for Vania. He put the boy over his shoulder and jumped from the truck, which was still close to the jeep ahead carrying the loudspeaker.

Suddenly their truck lurched to a stop, where Masha and Alexey jumped out of the back. The jeep with the loudspeaker had stopped abruptly too, and Dayan saw an officer holding a pistol in it look around, and then say something to the passenger behind him.

Now the loudspeaker began to blare in Russian: *"Major Renard's assistant here! I hereby declare Camp Jenbach abol-*

ished. No more American food will be issued!—I hereby declare Camp Jenbach abolished. Return to the trucks everyone! It's safe to return!"

The statement—*Return to the trucks everyone! It's safe to return!*—was repeated over and over. The more it was repeated, the more the 1,482 people now scattered throughout the woods didn't believe him. They called to each other and continued moving farther away from the trucks.

Now up in the forest Dayan and Vania were reunited with the boy's parents. Dayan's forehead was bleeding; when he reached for Vania in the truck he'd scratched it on a cupola of the cathedral replica. Masha ripped off a narrow piece of her skirt to use as a bandage for him. This she applied carefully over his cut and tied securely after wrapping it around to the back.

Looking at her, Alexey said, "A skirt sure is a powerful thing," then he began talking about possible plans for the future. Dayan learned that Alexey was an engineering specialist in the lumber industry who'd successfully convinced the Nazis he was only a lumberjack. There was a lumber mill nearby where he'd worked during the war; he offered to take Dayan along with them.

"We can work there and save," Alexey said, "then one day we'll go to America."

"And leave these wonderful killing fields behind us?" Dayan quipped.

Alexey smiled tolerantly at the younger man. "Call it an arena," he said. "Do you know who built the coliseum in Rome?"

Dayan wondered where he was going with this. "The slaves and Jews," he replied.

"And what happened to those who survived the hardships while they were building it?"

There was no answer from Dayan, who looked to Masha for help. She was silent. So Alexey answered his own question: "They were thrown to the lions as we today are thrown under the steel tanks. Think it over."

After a moment Dayan replied, "I have another idea, I'm going to go to America right now, and not wait here."

"But they aren't letting anyone go there, so how will you do that?" Alexey gave Dayan a puzzled expression.

Pointing to a nearby mountain across the German border, Dayan said: "There's America now—in Germany. It's their troops. I'll go there because I have to. They need to be told about all the people being massacred."

Alexey said nothing, but he stood up and faced Dayan, who was still looking past him towards the mountain.

"I wish you'd give me the address of the lumber mill, Alexey. Maybe I'll have to come back—otherwise I'll write to you."

"Dayan, are you sure the Americans will listen to you?" Alexey was serious.

"They'd better! The Americans have ideals—look at how they imprisoned the Nazi criminals. They want people to pay for their atrocities and misdeeds right here on Earth." Dayan scraped the ground with his foot. "And if God wants to forgive them in heaven, it's up to Him."

Vania had been listening solemnly to this exchange, looking from Dayan to his father. At last he asked hungrily, "Dayan, do the Americans have sugar?"

"Mountains of it!" Dayan answered, suddenly cheerful. He spread his arms wide and Vania ran into them. Dayan carried the boy to his mother's arms. Then they all walked further into the woods together to look for some blueberries and to go their separate ways.

The Austro-German border was marked by a big cross which reached high into the sky. This served as Dayan's landmark, but its distance was misleading. As he trudged along after saying good-bye to the Duboroffs, he was certain he wouldn't reach it by dusk.

Tired and hungry, he looked towards it with half-closed eyes. It seemed to become smaller, until it appeared no larger than the size of the cross he'd drawn for Thomash in their cottage at Cablo long ago. While resting against a beech tree, he studied the distant symbol and decided this was as good a place as any to spend the night.

He'd spent many—perhaps hundreds of nights—under the open sky like this one before. He reflected on everything as he settled himself in to sleep, as best he could, with his head resting on top of his knapsack. But each night lately had been worse than the last, including the first night of official freedom after the announcement of peace. That night in the ditch outside Fugen, after he'd left Cornelia's house, had been a strange, lonely place to celebrate the end of the war in Europe.

It was cold here too, but he reminded himself of the fourteen hundred and eighty-two people who were scattered in the woods below him. They'd fare no better than he was doing now, and the thought of their presence comforted him somehow. But despite his peace of mind he was unable to sleep. He carved a cross in the trunk of a beech tree, but this didn't satisfy him. He could only redeem himself, he decided, by also carving the words he'd written for Thomash.

However, now it was dark outside. Still, he thought, Thomash's father could carve in the darkness, so why couldn't he? By midnight the words *IN HOC SIGNO VINCES* were carved under the cross. He then fell asleep and slept past dawn, for which he was sorry, since the morning dew was gone from the blueberries he'd left out for breakfast.

Shortly after eating them, he started out again and met some friendly German shepherds. They advised him to avoid the first American checkpoint which was a few kilometers distant. They'd have been surprised to know that instead of listening to their advice, he went directly towards it; he could hardly wait to meet with the Americans to make his report. He'd decided to begin with the tragedy of Bleiburg where the thousands of Yugoslavs fleeing from the Partisans had been massacred. The closer he came to the checkpoint, the stronger his heart beat.

When he arrived there, the first American soldier he met demanded his pass. Another threw him a pair of boxing gloves, which he caught. "Okay?" the soldier asked as he put up his hands, ready to box. Dayan laughed.

"No kidding," the young soldier said, feinting and dancing in front of him. His buddy put the gloves on Dayan's hands and before he knew it, he found himself in a ring surrounded by fifteen excited soldiers wearing yellowish uniforms. "Lick the Krauts, Shorty!" was the ring cry.

But Dayan didn't want to fight. He took off the gloves after the short American had hit him several times. Then he lifted the soldier by his armpits, swung him high and set him down. "God bless you, big Vania," he said.

The other soldiers laughed. Now the first soldier again demanded a pass.

"I have no pass," Dayan shouted above the noise around them. "Yugoslav! Yugoslav!"

The soldier turned to his buddies. "Yugoslav? Isn't this Germany?" They all nodded. "Okay, over there." He motioned Dayan towards a group of half-starved Germans huddled together, encircled by a rope. They also had no passes and were waiting for the military police to take them to jail in Bad Aibling.

"Lots of your countrymen are in the Bad Aibling camp," one of the Germans told Dayan. "Fine if you're not a communist."

"I'm not."

The soldiers were trying to get another man into a fight now and Dayan took the opportunity to jump across the rope and get away.

The displaced persons camp leader at Bad Aibling's Yugoslav section was a Colonel Obradovich. He handed Dayan three papers to sign, otherwise he wouldn't be allowed to stay. The first stated that he wouldn't attend a German school, the second that he'd refrain from propaganda, and the third that he'd volunteer for war against Japan when he was called.

"For the time being," Obradovich explained, "the paper about not spreading propaganda is the most important. The Americans don't like it—they call it fussy stuff—believing it reveals a sick mind—a la Hitler and Mussolini."

Dayan nodded in agreement.

"That wound on your face looks bad," the colonel said politely. "Many black marketeers come in with cuts like that, and the Americans don't like it either—they turn 'em over to Tito's Mission and they're transported forcibly to Yugoslavia."

All this gave pause to Dayan, especially the idea that a person might be sent to Yugoslavia forcibly. "Would they send someone forcibly because of propaganda? I mean, telling the truth about—"

"Nobody would be fool enough to try it," the colonel said curtly.

Life among eighteen hundred former Yugoslav prisoners of war who refused to return to communistic Yugoslavia reminded Dayan of his pre-war military life. Devotion to King and Fatherland was now stressed more than ever, also devotion to the Western Allies and a readiness to volunteer for the war against Japan. And the need for volunteers was in contrast to the statement of the UNRRA director; so far as he was concerned, it didn't matter whether the list of volunteers was thrown into the garbage can or sent to the Allied High Command.

To Dayan it appeared that the fate of all the camp's refugees was uncertain. There was no prospect for a change in Yugoslavia or the southeastern European countries under the Soviets since the Potsdam Conference. The death of Roosevelt and the resignation of Churchill didn't help matters. So he thought the best thing to hope for now was an accusation of inaction against the new regime of the Soviets and the West concerning the various massacres from Katyn to Bleiburg.

If it were only in the form of a cry coming out of the people—the alive people who still could be heard—that would be better than nothing. At least it would be a beginning. Those who raise their voices and those who weep should be heard. But how to make it so they would be?

He thought long about this problem as the days went by, and finally hit upon the idea of a hunger strike in the displaced persons camp. It would certainly be beyond the comprehension of starving Germans and cause a great deal of excitement among the people connected with the Westania Times newspaper, now busily gathering and reporting all sorts of information from everywhere in devastated Europe. For if thousands of people were to refuse to eat in these days—especially American food after years of starvation—certainly anybody in their right mind would have to wonder why?

And Dayan had the answer for this question ready: in sympathy for the massacred people and the injustice. For the Jenbach camp refugees who gave up that food and preferred blueberries in the woods; for the truth of that indomitable Russian spirit that had won the victory at Stalingrad, and that Tito wasn't a prince of the Yugoslav royal family. It would be enough, he thought, that the Westania Times mentioned these reasons. That would be the first step; the free world would begin to know what'd been hidden from them.

Rumors about the massacre at the Austro-Yugoslav border spread throughout the camp, along with whispers about the possibility of a hunger strike and a threat to pull out of the list of volunteers for Japan. This eventually reached Colonel Obradovich, who summoned Dayan to his office. "Your wound still looks bad," he said, "perhaps it's infected. You'd better go to the hospital."

Dayan started to speak and Obradovich interrupted: "That's an order. And be sure to report back to me after you've recovered."

The so-called hospital Dayan stayed at was only a large hall; it had probably been used by the Germans as a gym. It was supplied with some medicine, beds and a doctor who was a former prisoner from another camp. Dayan wasn't happy here because he thought his wound wasn't bad, and every day in the hospital was a day away from what he wanted to be doing.

Then to everyone's relief a few weeks later the Japanese finally surrendered to the Allies, which brought an end to the Second World War. Due to this the colonel assigned a committee to transcribe the list of volunteers and to give everyone a copy. He also expressed satisfaction that the rumors about *the massacred people* had disappeared, and assigned a different committee to discover the source of it.

Meanwhile, in the gym-hospital Dayan had been released as healed. Reporting to Obradovich he was instructed to provide some proof of his identity, and was then assigned to clean the camp offices, including the colonel's. He was sure this was a means of keeping him under surveillance.

One morning while Dayan was cleaning the windows in Obradovich's office, he heard the colonel shouting at a frail, bent man who had white hair and a bristling mustache: "What now? This is the third time you've come in here."

"No, sir. It's the fourth time."

"Well," the colonel said impatiently, "what do you want? You went to Yugoslavia after the war?"

"Only back to the border, but I couldn't stay there. A Russian with a red star slapped the other officers and shot at me, so I ran away. I was sure I'd be killed by them, so I came back here."

"But you were with the Partisans during the war. Isn't that so?"

"Yes, that's true."

"Right! And the Ustashis as well?"

"True again."

"And now you'd join the Western Army?"

"Not anymore. No to that one."

"Tell me then, altogether how many people have you killed?"

"Let's see. I started at Caporetto as an Austrian soldier, so that's one." The old man continued counting on his fingers while talking. "And that was forty years ago! So by now, including Bosnia—" At this point he lost track. "Let's just say—very many."

"And what about Bosnia? Who did you kill there?"

"Mostly prisoners, but the last one I killed was a Commissar." The old man crossed himself, and his eyes turned upward. In this position his eyes fell on Dayan, who was standing high above him on a ladder cleaning a window.

Dayan had been listening to this conversation, uncertain what to do. Now there was no doubt in his mind. He dropped the cleaning cloth, jumped to the floor and put his arms around the little man's bent figure while shouting: "Tell! Tell! It's you!"

The colonel stared at this sight in astonishment. Dayan half carried Tell's thin, old body to a bench, where the old man clung to him sobbing: "Mutan! Mutan! Mutan, my boy!"

In their joy, neither of them was aware of what Colonel Obradovich was doing. He'd taken out a paper and a pencil, and was quickly writing an order. It was to assign a special committee with the task of discovering the identity of the young man, and finding out the truth about his much older friend—and why he'd been pestering him so much.

18

In A Kangaroo Court

"According to this report, you've been the source of rumors which have been circulating concerning some nonsense about massacres," Colonel Obradovich said to Dayan sternly. This confrontation was taking place in the colonel's office on the day the special committee had finally confirmed the identities of Dayan and Tell.

"Maybe you should be looking for the source of the massacres themselves," Dayan retorted. "You won't need to look very far either—it's the communists and their Western Allies. And you hope to join them, I know. But you'll find out they don't like you."

"Rubbish."

"Yes, there's plenty of that being tossed around, but stick to the facts, Colonel. Tell heard about the same massacres as well." Dayan looked more squarely into the colonel's eyes. "Surely you remember your Shakespeare: *Truth will out!*"

Obradovich chose to ignore that last remark. "Actually, the worst thing that'll happen is when the Allies summon us to join forces with them, half of our people will be under the skirts of these German frauleins," Obradovich said.

"So, it's been a hard winter—and our hungry fellows haven't had much fun in years." Dayan noted the colonel's glum expression, but went on: "You of all people should know about that, Colonel. And don't forget how in Albania the relatives of a dead man will fill a bottle with his blood, and if it starts to boil—that means it's time to look for murder. Just like the blood over these massacres is boiling harder by the thousands."

The colonel swallowed hard.

Dayan continued: "Once word of this gets published in the Westania Times newspaper, the boiling blood will rise up in the throats of all those who participated in this horror, and also for those who remained silent."

The colonel tried to swallow once more. "You can't prove it so get out of here," he shouted quickly. He mopped his brow, jumped up and strode to the window.

Dayan casually left the room, content that he'd made his point. He then went in search of Tell, who'd been assigned the job of cleaning the gym-hospital.

Once there they reflected on their meeting in Bosnia with Dayan's escape, and their conversation became somewhat lengthy. Dayan told of his capture by the Germans and of his experiences at the border. The old man also reinforced his story, he especially couldn't get over the cruel attitude of the Partisans. Once when he'd killed a German soldier, they'd taken out his kidneys and hung them on the dead man's ears. "That was the last real soldier I killed," he said, shaking his head and sighing.

"And what about Edo?"

"Edo wasn't a soldier—not even a man. He was a beast!"

Just after celebrating the Greek Orthodox Christmas, Mr. Bronton, who was the director of UNRRA, invited all the leaders of the displaced persons camps to attend a tea. Here he expressed his thanks for the various Christmas parties to which he and his staff were invited to attend. As the others began leaving, he signaled that Colonel Obradovich should remain.

When they were alone together, Bronton brought up the subject of eligibility to stay in the camps. "We're being pressured to get your camp's size down again," he said. "They keep harping on me to expel more of the refugees." He paused, rose, and began to pace slowly in front of the colonel. At last he said, "That means we'll have to have another screening to keep them off my back, and you'll have to devise another excuse for holding it."

Obradovich now jumped up, facing the director. "Another excuse already!" he exclaimed. "My God—we've already been screened five times in six months!"

Bronton looked around carefully, checking the doors and windows. They were closed. "This one will be different," he said in a low tone. "Top security, led by American specialists. Once they give those they want a clean bill of health, the refugees can stay for another round. These American men are top experts—they know everything! They can even tell you how deep the Danube is at any given place or how many seashells are to be found along the Adriatic Coast. Just follow along and you'll be rewarded as usual!"

Obradovich listened intently, but reserved judgment, while the director told him that he was a former shipping agent left jobless when Germany sank all the ships during the war. "I hope to see it again someday, but this is too rewarding to leave," he said. He sighed, put out a hand and patted Obradovich on the shoulder. "The screening will take place in Munich," he said. "The sooner you get going, the better for us all."

The colonel nodded, opened the door quietly, and walked down the hall. But his heart was pounding. He and his staff began immediately to make preparations for the move, but they were careful not to alert the camp refugees just yet. They didn't want them to know about their eventual destination.

Early on a snowy January morning in 1946, the camp was evacuated to the Munich area, where they all arrived before dawn. The camp yard—formerly the military drilling grounds—lay under a continuous blanket of snow, so a few refugees began shoveling this away while others were busy settling things inside. Under the snow a thick layer of ice was found instead of the usual frozen earth. There was nothing the men could do but leave it: it was too thick to be chipped away.

The new occupants were given no breakfast, and the explanation given was that their arrival wasn't anticipated by anyone except for the highest ranking U.S. Army officers. Many of them refused to believe it.

The camp itself was the usual complex of German barracks, partially damaged by war planes. The high wooden watchtowers indicated that it had been used for German war prisoners after the war. However, the bleakly familiar surroundings failed to dampen anyone's high spirits; rumors about a possible acceptance into the

Western Army had again spread to everyone thanks to Obradovich.

They speculated as to what sort of weapons they'd be issued by the military. It was then suggested that they take a nap, but with all of this anticipation combined with their starving hunger—they were unable to sleep, and eagerly awaited the screening.

When the call to assembly came, Obradovich was delighted by the orderly lines which quickly formed, while traditional Serbian marches were played by a few of the men who had flutes. But the music was drowned out when a column of armored cars and tanks roared through the opened gates, followed by a long limousine.

Colonel Obradovich stood at the forefront of the mass of people and shouted: *"Long live America!"* The eighteen hundred other voices joined in the salute. Meanwhile, soldiers wearing helmets and carrying fixed bayonets left the armored cars and stood in front of them, while the occupants of the tanks stayed near their vehicles.

An American lieutenant stepped forward. *"We're here,"* he shouted, *"to protect the representatives of a country whose regime we recognize. Don't attempt any foolishness, like your people did in Naples."* This was a reference to an incident where a representative of Tito had been lynched at a camp in Italy.

The lieutenant now signaled to the men in the limousine. By this time the refugees realized who they were—Tito's men—who let the American officer know they refused to emerge from the limousine until they had more U.S. soldiers between them and the crowd. When this was accomplished, they finally came out, but none too eagerly.

Dayan was never sure afterward about the following events. There was no previous planning, for until Tito's representatives arrived his people hadn't known they'd be coming. Finally, he concluded that it was a case of spontaneous combustion—the conditions required for it were all brought together at an exact moment and the men's spirits were inflamed.

Suddenly the camp refugees broke into many groups, each forming a circle. Alarmed, the American soldiers moved forward, but the lieutenant stopped them. The circles began to whirl to the music of the flutes in the Balkan dance, the hora. Voices were raised in songs, mingling with the flute music; there were loud exclamations with shouting of anti-Tito slogans.

Soon the heavy mass of ice underfoot gave way. Under the beating of many hundreds of feet pounding out the traditional dance, it was turned to slush. The gray skies, the bleak camp, the gathered tanks, the uniformed officers and enlisted men, in contrast to the emaciated but wildly moving dancers and the fiery music—it created a scene the watchers knew would be impossible to describe. A number of men clambered out of their tanks and took pictures with their German-made cameras.

The American lieutenant and Obradovich faced each other. "Why in hell did your people unpack?" the lieutenant, whose name was Grey, complained. "They'll only have to pack up again before leaving here."

"They'd rather die under your tanks than return to what's left of Yugoslavia," Obradovich answered. "Besides, they have almost no belongings to speak of. Remember, they were war prisoners."

Grey responded only to the first sentence: "You mean they're not dancing for joy? For going home again?"

"To the contrary, they're dancing to defy Tito's officers and to protest the way your people arrived; with guns and tanks."

Grey was confused. "We were told that they all wanted to go home." He then looked at Obradovich's uniform. "No red stars—no hammer and sickle?"

Obradovich just laughed.

The lieutenant turned and gave an order to the soldiers with Tito's men. Upon hearing this they all withdrew, then the armored cars and limousine backed up and moved away until only two tanks remained. Lieutenant Grey turned and faced Obradovich again. "Okay," he said, "let's hear it." He looked intently at the other man's uniform.

Obradovich straightened his shoulders. "To answer your question, sir," he spoke somberly, "no hammers, no sickles, no red stars—all of us are against communism, including me."

With this Grey studied him for a moment. "Well, it's my country's belief that everyone's opinion deserves respect. But I'm here on orders. You've been accused by a country recognized officially by the United States. This could mean a threat to the peace we've strived for."

At this Obradovich couldn't restrain himself, and he laughed bitterly.

"This is a serious matter, sir," the lieutenant said. "Those of you who refuse to go home can't wear those uniforms."

"Look," Obradovich said with resignation, "our uniforms are at least five years old. We fought the Germans and Partisans in them. We spent years as prisoners in them. See for yourself!" He turned out his elbows to reveal patches, and then tapped his knees; there were patches there also. "Don't these show you we fought for peace?"

"Everything is for peace: the U.S. cooperation in the Nuremberg Trials, UNRRA food, the United Nations—and that you're forbidden to wear your uniforms, especially your caps without a star, hammer and sickle."

"Our caps are much older than the uniforms," Obradovich protested. "We have worn such caps for over two hundred years without red stars. They're part of our national attire."

"Sorry—I've got my orders," the American said curtly. He then reacted as a commotion was heard from one of the tanks, and a voice shouted: "For God's sake—Butch, get me out of here!"

Grey wheeled and ran towards the tank. He stood by while some soldiers, at his signal, helped a fat man to squeeze out of it. Speaking in Yugoslav, the disheveled, portly man in an UNRRA uniform introduced himself to Obradovich and his staff. He said he was the chief clerk from the main UNRRA office in Munich, and had arrived with the American unit to organize the departure of the camp's refugees for Yugoslavia, as ordered by his superiors.

As a former cook in a pre-war Yugoslav western embassy, he knew the language and had intended to address the people in it. But when he saw their reaction to Tito's officers, he'd become frightened and hid himself in one of the tanks.

"You don't know these people," he told Grey. "They're dynamite!" This was an expression he'd picked up from the West and he thought it was very sophisticated. Privately, Grey was beginning to believe it was true.

That evening a dozen trucks brought some authorized uniforms for everyone to wear. They were old American G.I. uniforms previously dyed black. They'd been worn by already released German war prisoners; there was a large *WP* in white on the backs of the military blouses.

In the daily bulletin he issued, Obradovich praised the people's discipline and described the incident earlier that day as nothing more than a matter for final screening. "Our connection with the U.S. Army, through the Eisenhower blouses," he ended, "is the best indication that the West depends on us." He added that the uniforms had been properly disinfected and were expected to fit on everyone nice and loose.

Unfortunately the shortage of food in this new camp wasn't any different, and it was explained away as a result of the transition from being a displaced persons camp to becoming a military unit, when it would receive regular army supplies. Meanwhile, the undernourishment of the people was revealed in their faces and their postures. Even the smokers were jumpy and nervous because of fewer cigarettes.

Altogether it was in bleak contrast to Bad Aibling's camp where there were German children looking through the fences trading in black market items. No more were German cameras and wristwatches exchanged across the fence for sugar, identity papers and chocolate. Here, the fence was lined with desolate, hungry crows who sat for hours, undisturbed.

When delegations went to the officers requesting a reason for the delay in screening, they were told the questionnaires were still being prepared, and it was taking longer because of their extra importance to all concerned.

Despite strict orders to remain on camp property, some refugees managed to sneak away to Bad Aibling for a few days—to continue friendships and to enjoy additional food. These people brought back an explanation for the switching of camps earlier. Director Bronton and his staff, the story went, kept the old camp's supplies and were selling things off slowly into the black market. Every night a truck arrived to take more of it away, they said, where it then ended up being traded or sold elsewhere.

The story was so persistent from enough sources that it caused a lot of internal discontent. For this reason Dayan decided it was a strategic time to bring up the question of having a hunger strike. This would be to protest the screenings and the silence in the free world about the massacres at Katyn, Bleiburg and along the Austro-Yugoslav border.

His plans were shattered though by the news that General Mihailovic had been captured in the mountains of Yugoslavia. Particularly sensational to the Western world was the fact that the announcement of his capture had been delayed for two weeks. It was speculated in the Western press that the general had been transported to the Kremlin's Lubyanka prison for brainwashing; where new chemicals were being used for such persons—by injecting them into the brain and nerve centers apparently.

The Soviet press made no bones of the fact that in trying the general, Tito would also be putting the West on trial too. His power had already become obvious to everyone; he was appointed Prime Minister of Yugoslavia through a rigged election creating his new communist republic, and he'd successfully abolished the monarchy to enforce his total control over the Yugoslav state.

For Mihailovic's trial, Tito brazenly denied entry to dozens of American Air Force men who wanted to bear witness in support of Mihailovic. While on their missions to the Eastern Front from Italy, their planes had been hit and damaged by the Germans. These men had parachuted into Yugoslavia's free territory held by Mihailovic's Chetnik forces, who helped them return to their bases back in Italy. Their petition ended: *If Mihailovic is on trial, we want to be on trial too.*

When the time came for the general's stance, in contrast to the defiance displayed by his followers who'd shouted the slogan—*Freedom! Democracy!* before a firing squad, his was one of stoicism. This was explained by some in the press as proof he'd been brainwashed by the Soviets, and also because he was disappointed with the West having abandoned him. Otherwise, the question was asked, how could this man—as Europe's first guerrilla leader —who struggled against Germany and Italy when they were at the heights of their powers, sit quietly before a kangaroo court with his life on trial?

The mystery of Mihailovic's strange fatalism hadn't been solved when the tragic results of his so-called trial became known; death by firing squad. His execution was swiftly carried out only two days after sentencing and before any foreign country could ask for clemency. The place of his execution and the location of the general's grave remained a top secret. In Munich, the Yugoslav displaced persons camp was the first in the area to hold a commemoration service in his honor.

In the improvised chapel at the camp, next to the holy icons, they placed a painting showing Mihailovic receiving bread and salt on a wooden plate offered by a Bosnian peasant, their symbol of welcome to a national leader. Behind him stood the peasant's barefoot daughter holding a bouquet of flowers. In the picture Mihailovic wore a tunic and moccasins, while an American Tommy gun hung from one shoulder and an ammunition bag from the other. His traditional cap bore the emblem of Yugoslav unity.

This service was conducted by Greek Orthodox priests from other Munich area camps, headed by a Russian bishop. Colonel Obradovich stood at the gate to welcome representatives from these East European camps. He was surprised by the arrival of two American jeeps carrying seven soldiers and an officer, who introduced himself as Captain Tucker.

"You've been expecting us?" Captain Tucker asked. He offered Obradovich a cigarette and lit one for himself.

Obradovich refused, pointing to the large gathering of people around the chapel where incense fumes billowed up around them.

"What's going on?" the captain asked, startled. "Is that a fire?"

"No, a church service. In commemoration of..."

The puzzled American interrupted him. "How come you're wearing an outfit like that to a church service?" He indicated the colonel's black-dyed uniform, which had previously been worn by an SS man, long-since released and sent home. "But hold on!" he exclaimed. "This isn't Sunday! Are you Jews? Or Muslims, maybe?"

"We are Orthodox Christians, sir," Obradovich replied. "We're holding a memorial service for General Mihailovic."

The captain looked at Obradovich in amazement. "Are you saying that General Mihailovic is dead?" Abruptly he extinguished the cigarette.

"Yes, sir. He was executed by Tito's regime."

"But isn't Mihailovic—wasn't he in power in Yugoslavia?"

"By no means. Tito now governs that communist country. Mihailovic wanted to but was abandoned by the West."

"Are you saying that we betrayed the man who fought by our side? You've got to be kidding! Why, we even filmed a Hollywood picture about him and the Chetniks—he was the hero!"

Obradovich listened somberly without replying.

Tucker went on with a tone of defensiveness in his voice now. "Actually, we knew nothing about Tito until we got to Italy—when Germany was already half-defeated." The captain hesitated, apparently feeling he was getting into deep water. He straightened up and his voice became more formal. "Colonel Obradovich," he said, "I wish to inform you that we've arrived here as a screening team. I believe you've been expecting us for some time."

Obradovich nodded and saluted. "First, would you care to join in our services?"

"Gladly. I welcome the opportunity to express my own and my country's sympathy. I deeply regret what's happened."

"Americans have already conveyed their feelings," Obradovich told him. "Your Secretary of State has termed the execution of Mihailovic a legal crime. Which it is."

"Words—empty words," Tucker said impatiently. "Actions means something!" He gestured to the crowd of people standing outside the chapel, crossing themselves. "Crossing themselves won't help. Look at all those pacifist men!" he told his soldiers.

Obradovich replied to this obvious criticism: "We have no weapons—nothing. We're even forbidden by your superiors from wearing our traditional caps, part of our national attire." He took off his black-dyed U.S. military cap, revealing a scar which ran from his temple and disappeared under his hair.

Tucker reacted to seeing this and his expression became solemn.

"A souvenir of the First World War," Obradovich told him. "And today, I can't even cover it with my *real* cap."

Captain Tucker looked around. "Where are the shovels—you must have used them for the snow last winter?"

"No, we've had to shovel the snow with our feet. We even broke a thick layer of ice dancing to defy the communists and your country's collaboration with them. That's all we can do. Dance and sing."

"In America, we'd cut the throat of anyone who tried to deprive us of our freedom to wear what we like—to say what we believe. We'd even use a shovel for a weapon if we didn't have anything else. Right, boys?"

His men, who were standing at ease while listening, chorused back: "Yes, Sir!" and "You're damn right, sir!"

As Tucker and his seven soldiers fell behind Obradovich, the worshipers made a lane so they could enter the chapel. They stood at attention before the painting of Mihailovic, giving a formal salute of respect. To Dayan, seeing them through the thick incense made them look like any other worshippers. As a matter of fact, one soldier reminded him of a man who used to come to the camp. He always had bags full of chocolate bars and small cans of coffee which he'd sell on the black market; he also gave Tell a package of cigarettes when he came.

Word had already spread that the American soldiers were members of the screening team—the very people who were authorities, they'd been told, on Yugoslavia and Eastern Europe. The ones who supposedly knew the exact depth of the Danube at any location, and the exact number of seashells along the Adriatic Coast.

After the hymn *Eternal Glory* was sung in memory of the late general, the eulogy was delivered through a loudspeaker by a man with deep, sunken eyes under lowered eyebrows. Although his voice revealed tension with anguish of spirit, the eighteen hundred listeners were deeply moved, listening in total silent respect.

He attributed the fate of Mihailovic to an international conspiracy whose actions often took place in the Balkans. "No people worthy of their name," he said, "could retaliate with the brutality imposed on them by the communists during the war." He continued that for this alone, if not for anything else, it was the duty of civilized mankind not to extend help to the communists. He finished by saying that the very executioners of Mihailovic had in turn been murdered by Tito's closest aides in order to preserve the secrecy of the general's grave.

At the conclusion of the ceremonies, Captain Tucker told Colonel Obradovich that his team would delay beginning work until the next day, out of respect for their betrayed ally. "This whole service has been very impressive," he commented. He said prior to being a soldier, he was a farmer who'd never paid much attention to work politics until being drafted. But he promised that when he returns to his native Kansas he'd petition his congressman and both state senators on behalf of Mihailovic's name.

Dayan was standing in front of the chapel when the man who'd given the eulogy emerged nearby. With his heart beating fast, Dayan addressed him: "Captain Radovich?" Dayan recognized the strong hand falling onto his shoulder, it was the same whose pressure had encouraged him—over four years ago—to volunteer for the Adriatic mission. But now he could feel that the hand was more tired.

"Dayan, you're alive!" Tears quickly came to his deep eyes. "Where have you been? What's been happening to you? Tell me!"

"You first!" Dayan said. "You must have far more to tell me." He saw the dark eyes close wearily, and added gently: "Please, Captain. You know everything that's been happening."

"Not quite everything." Radovich's smile was rueful. He took Dayan's arm and pulled him to one side, which was somewhat apart from the crowd milling about outside of the chapel. They stopped and Dayan looked at the older man eagerly. Radovich sighed. "You're right, Dayan. I've been everywhere and have seen more than enough."

"Then you'll help us here? We need you! We must tell the world about the massacres."

They were walking along a little path now, right between the buildings. Radovich stumbled like a blind man and Dayan saw that his eyes were actually closed. "Captain, you'll fall! Open your eyes," he said urgently.

"Yes, I must. It's such a temptation to close them."

Dayan's heart went out to the war-weary man, who seemed temporarily at least to have lost his will to see anymore.

"Take me to the nearby watchtower, Dayan," Radovich whispered. "All of my belongings are up there."

By *belongings* he meant his counterfeit passport which was hidden inside of a crevice in the concrete tower's walls—with the fake passport bearing the name of a White Russian. "It's the only safe place I could think of to hide it," he told Dayan. "It's too dangerous to leave it in Obradovich's office, he's the only person who knows where it's hidden."

At the mention of Obradovich, Dayan smiled cynically. "That fool, always expecting something!" he said.

"Don't judge him like that, Dayan—he hasn't had our experiences. Someday, perhaps he will. Then he'll know better." Radovich then began to tell Dayan of his wanderings, starting with the time Mihailovic sent him to the West after the conquest of Southeastern Europe by the Reds.

His mission had been to convince high officials of the Western Allies that the people of the enslaved countries weren't communists, although they'd been conquered by the communists. As a result, he was labeled an international troublemaker and said to be working against peaceful relations between the East and the West.

He was arrested in the Austrian British zone, but as he was being carried off to jail, he managed to fall down in the prison yard—pretending to be dead. In the ensuing confusion, he'd managed to escape, and became one of their most wanted men. He made his way via France to the Low Countries, where he kept in touch with some staunch Western anti-communists and émigré leaders from Eastern Europe, traveling occasionally to some large émigré centers.

Dayan was greatly impressed with Radovich's experiences. "Tell me, what happened to your friends at the Saint-Cyr Academy?" he asked.

Radovich sighed. "Only a few survived the war, and they're in Indochina now, dying like flies for the same cause from which you and I are suffering." He paused for a moment, then said almost in a whisper: "I should say the same cause from which you and I are escaping."

"Yes, escaping, always escaping," Dayan said. "I'm ashamed when I think of all those who've been lost! And here I am—escaping too!"

"But you must escape, Dayan." Radovich gripped his shoulder. "Please, for the sake of your mission, let them be ashamed who forced us to escape." He explained that he was in constant danger of death at the hands of the Allies, although he was one of them, in the same way that the Yugoslav people were enslaved by the communists. "You will understand what I mean. I remember your poetic nature."

Dayan had been listening intently. "So you're saying in a way, I think, that we must *imagine* the faces of those we belong to, because they have lost their real identities."

"That's it! I see that you do understand." Captain Radovich looked searchingly into Dayan's eyes. "You're a poet, Dayan. Tell me—what happened to the poem you told me about concerning the disappearing people. Now there are so many more of them, with the people being massacred at our very border, trying only to return to their homes."

It was now Dayan's turn to close his eyes. He thought of his promise to the professor at the Danube fisherman's wharf, and of the lines he'd read to Tobo which had made him weep. Just as Goritza had loved the poem, *I will return, Mother*. He was ashamed to never see it published. How pleased she would have been! He pressed his body against the edges of the tower now in self-punishment.

As if sensing Dayan's trouble, Radovich said, "It's time for me to leave."

"Take me with you!" Dayan begged. "I want to confront those with the lost faces, and die doing it—if I have to."

"There's no need to be killed, that's too much of an honor for the killers. And satisfaction too, even profit. It's better that the victim lives!"

Dayan leaned against the square wooden pillars and looked cheerfully back at his companion.

Radovich smiled and held out his hand. "One more thing—"

"Wait a moment!" Dayan said quickly. "You know Nell? Dickens' Nell?"

Radovich shook his head.

"Well, Dickens, the English novelist, wrote for the magazines a lot. One story was about this imaginative little girl named Nell. It was written in six installments, and in the last one, little Nell died. So many people had been following the story, as it appeared month by month, that the reading public from London to Calcutta went into mourning for the fictional little girl. London churches announced her death, and bells tolled everywhere. And just think —all for a little girl who never really lived. How would the world mourn for real people, thousands, hundreds of thousands of real people, if only they knew what had happened to them?"

The other man saw Dayan needed to talk, to have some means of expressing his horror and to plan some practical and definite action. But unfortunately it was absolutely necessary for him to leave. "One last thing," Radovich said urgently.

"Yes?"

"You ought to know this—the Soviet Mission took your picture in Jenbach, while you were at the eulogy talking about the massacres with the Russians."

"I'm scarcely surprised, but thanks for telling me."

"It's very important, Dayan. Remember that, and watch out for Max Barrack. Try avoiding him in your section, I hear he's very dangerous."

19

On Cardboard Sandals

Finally the long-awaited screening by the Americans was starting to take place. Seven tables were lined up in the camp yard, and at each one they had a G.I. and an interpreter seated together. Long lines of displaced Yugoslavs waited their turns to answer questions, and to show the proper identification at the various tables.

Luckily for the refugees, word had gotten back to Director Bronton about the Bad Aibling camp supplies and their knowledge of them being sold into the black market. This made him ease up on the screening so nearly everyone would pass. The younger refugees turned the occasion into a lark, laughing as they displayed the names of their sweethearts carved onto their prisoner-issue tags, now plated with silver procured from the black market.

Meanwhile, Captain Tucker was relaxing inside Obradovich's office, studying a map that showed the course of the civil war in Yugoslavia. He was there because he wasn't needed outside; the screening had become a fairly routine matter.

During this time the lines of people outside were moving through the process quickly. When it was Dayan's turn, he showed his paperwork and was asked the name of his sweetheart. "Angeli —" he started saying and then broke it off, regretting that he'd even answered him.

The G.I. who was questioning Dayan toyed with a small mirror with a colored picture on the back. It was of a pretty German model who, like most G.I. girls, used heavy mascara and brightly colored lipstick on her face. She wore a jacket made from a U.S. military blanket. The soldier looked at her approvingly.

"I'd gladly tell you the name of mine." He studied the name *Brunnhilde* written under the picture and sighed. "But unfortunately, I can't pronounce it. So I'll just call her Bunny." Suddenly the soldier looked up from the picture into Dayan's face. Abruptly he asked: "Don't you have a prisoner's number?"

Dayan looked at the roughened skin on his wrists where he'd burned the rope in Bosnia to untie himself and escape. "No," he said.

The soldier whistled. "Here's another one for you, Jimmy!" To Dayan, he said: "Go to table number 7. Jimmy's our college type. He deals with offbeat guys like you."

Dayan obediently went to table 7, joining the others who hadn't officially been war prisoners. Tell was there too at the front of the line, and he was arguing with the soldier in charge. Apparently he was refusing to swear to the truth of the information he'd given about himself. His reason was that he'd sworn to the truth so many times in his life, beginning in 1914 as an Austrian soldier, and every time he'd been forced to go back on his word.

"Now that I'm an old man, there isn't much time left before I must account to God. So I don't want to have more added to my conscience."

Captain Tucker was summoned from Obradovich's office and listened to all this, then wrote *O.K.* on Tell's papers to keep the line moving.

Later, when it was Dayan's turn, Jimmy the College Man, as he was called by his team, looked up smiling. "You're just the guy I was hoping for," he said. "A man with an education. And to start out with a straight question—why in the world don't you go home? You and these comrades of yours? What's holding you here?"

Before Dayan could answer, the soldier continued: "Your country's free—no violence recorded by our Third Army. I myself—"

Now Dayan had to interrupt: "But sir, you never went to my country except on Easter Sunday—when you dropped your bombs on it. On Belgrade!"

"Don't tell me where I've been!" Jimmy said, getting red to his ears.

"I'm not trying to. I'm just telling you where you haven't been."

"Oh! That sounds like a Nazi talking." It was Dayan's turn to blush with anger, which his antagonist noted with satisfaction. Jimmy continued: "In my opinion, two reasonable men should make sense."

"That's my opinion too. Then why don't you begin?" Dayan challenged.

"Okay. Now it says here you were sent on a mission by your general."

"That's true."

"Well, where's your proof? We need something written on paper."

Dayan shrugged.

"Look—even myself. I'm here today on official business and I've got a paper to prove it. That's military efficiency."

Dayan looked again at the burned scars on his wrists. "Well, I haven't got any efficient papers. None at all."

"Tell me, to whom did you leave your life insurance before you undertook your dangerous mission?" Jimmy was trying anything to place things into a focus he could recognize. "To your father?"

"Life insurance?" Dayan laughed. "I drew a cross on a stone tablet with the Latin words—*IN HOC SIGNO VINCES*—for my father."

"Then your father would have received some money if you'd been killed?"

Dayan gave up, since this whole conversation seemed senseless. He decided to remain silent, or try to. But he knew the next question must be answered.

"Are you a communist?"

"No, I'm not." Then Dayan said it firmly. "No. N—O—Period!"

Jimmy then studied him for a moment, and nodded his head slowly. "O—K—Period. I'll grant you status here as a displaced person. You're lucky. Now you can enjoy food from the good old U.S.A."

"Food and what else?"

"What more do you want? Two-thirds of the world is starving."

"True. But I have seen fourteen hundred and eighty-two White Russians choose to eat blueberries and grass instead of your food, so they could enjoy their freedom."

"I've got my duty to perform." The soldier shook his head regretfully. "Evidently it's impossible for you and me to come to terms. It's a waste of time for us to talk."

"I agree. It can't be otherwise."

Jimmy pounded the table in frustration. "But why, for God's sake? Why can't two intelligent men arrive at some sensible agreement?"

"Let me ask you a question then," Dayan said. "Why didn't your Third Army enter Prague?"

"We had an agreement with the Russians."

"So you honored your obligations. Is that it?"

"Right. We Americans are honest. We kept our word."

"In my country," Dayan said, "we have a saying that people who raise pumpkins with the devil will break them over their own heads. But you've been lucky so far, since the pumpkins you're raising aren't ripe yet."

"Look wise guy. Let's get together after all this screening stuff is over. I'd like to *talk* with you."

"Sorry," Dayan told him, "I'm too busy. I'm writing a poem." He then left and went to the chapel, where he found an honor guard standing before General Mihailovic's painting. Instead of shouldering arms, he held a wreath of flowers, similar to those the barefoot Bosnian girl in the painting was handing to Mihailovic.

"Here—I'll take over," Dayan whispered. The guard left and Dayan kneeled. "Forgive me, General," he whispered. "I became a displaced person. I wrongly tried to carry my country out on the soles of my shoes like you refused to do. My own country, which lost one hundred and six people for every German they killed there during the war!"

Feeling better, he rose to his feet and hurried to the abandoned watchtower, which he now was using as a writing area. Climbing up into the lookout station, he was finally content to be alone.

The human heart is the arsenal of the most destructive weapons, he wrote on a board, *created by the lack of feeling for our fellow man and ignorance of the life around us—thus forming a vicious circle.* He read the words over and over again; they always sounded and meant the same to him.

Just below the board on which he'd written this, some lonely G.I. had scrawled the words: *Kokomo, I love you so.* Dayan liked those words too. They must've been written, he decided, by an unskilled man, perhaps a farmhand. Most of all he liked them because they were words of love, the simple love he himself had for Cablo and for his country; for Poland, and for all the vanished and massacred victims. Then, on the same board above, he wrote the first verse of his poem.

When the two days of screenings were over at the camp, only 12 unlucky Yugoslav's were evicted. And like those evicted from earlier screenings, they often were allowed into other camps after obtaining fake identification on the black market. Some even chose free living and stayed outside of the camps, being fed through the German ration system.

Captain Tucker made a short speech praising the remaining refugees for their courage in standing by what they believed in. He repeated what he'd said the day he arrived, that Americans would use a shovel if that's all they had to defend themselves against anyone who attempted to deprive them of their freedom.

He was pleased, he said, to meet so many peasants, and proudly identified himself and his ancestors with the farmers. Those who fed the world by plowing the soil with tractors, mules, or even a single ox. Those who asked for nothing more than rain and sun for their crops, and gladly gave their strength and sweat in return for simple rewards. "If people everywhere would be content with such a way of life," he declared, "the earth would never again be soaked with blood."

But naturally, he failed to mention anything about them joining their Western Army. All summer in the camp they'd waited for the screening so they might hear word of this—thanks to what Colonel Obradovich had been promising. They'd also looked forward to being issued official I.D. cards which would enable them to travel freely. Since neither of these things materialized, the refugees now looked reluctantly towards winter with frosty misgivings.

They'd also heard reports earlier giving the total number of war victims in Yugoslavia as 1,750,000 citizens—a figure confirmed by Radio-Belgrade. This number compared to the announcement of 16,500 Germans killed or missing in their country, revealed a staggering disproportion never before recorded in human history. Such as it was, the question as to what the war was really about—and who'd won it—remained unanswered. Certainly Yugoslavia couldn't call it a victory with the loss of 106 citizens for every German lost.

These numbers confirmed to everyone in the camp the severity of the war's injustice, which lead to more and more talk. An excerpt from a Westania Times newspaper was printed in the camp periodical stating:

The United Nations unanimously condemned Spain's Franco regime for sentencing seven communists to death earlier this year. After their executions, Spain was further isolated when France closed off their border, effectively blocking Spain's access to all of Europe.

Anyone in their right mind would conclude that if the United Nations condemned Franco for only seven deaths, they should be raising all hell over the massacre of almost two million Yugoslavs!

The article then went on to wish the readers a Merry Christmas and a Happy New Year, recommending patience and brotherly love in the sense of Jesus' teachings, with the hope that everyone will be able to celebrate the next Christmas by their own fire-places.

An optimism inspired by the warm hopes for the New Year kept people together in a bearable atmosphere for months. Their spirits rose even further with the arrival of Australian and Belgian teams to recruit a limited number of workers from the displaced persons camps in the Munich area.

The periodical in the Yugoslav camp, however, admonished the refugees to remember their devotion to the King, Fatherland and the Western Allies as soldiers, and not to immigrate to other countries and become civilians. This also kept them together, but with the coming of warmer spring days in 1947, nothing could prevent them from wandering farther away and strolling into the country, where they offered their virility to German farms regardless of low wages or camp regulations.

As this excitement slowly died down, a worse problem arose: there was a drastic reduction in food allotments. This was combined with an encouragement each week from German Munich Radio stating the only salvation left for displaced persons was to return to their homelands.

Meanwhile, a number of industrious former shoemakers were joining forces in the camps to manufacture sandals out of the emptied thick cartons which their camp supplies arrived in. The heavy cardboard proved to be an excellent material which wore well on the feet. In this way, the refugees were able to save their heavier footwear for when winter arrived. That spring, the sandals were so popular, they even appeared through the black market on the feet of German frauleins, to the delight of many.

However in the Yugoslav camp, the empty cartons were cut up and used mostly as bulletin boards, on which various announcements were printed with charcoal. Colonel Obradovich made no objections to this; so instead of world news, the inter-camp bulletins now had the priority.

The remaining number of cartons not used for bulletin boards were utilized by the Yugoslav camp's Art Association as canvases that were shown in exhibits, with the latest one being held in a barn formerly used by the Germans for their horses. Opening day of the exhibit was a huge success, attended by hundreds of people from other camps, including camp children and displaced families.

Colonel Obradovich even delivered a speech Dayan had written for him. The colonel, who was being criticized for his lack of personal courage, had worn all of his First World War decorations, which were proudly pinned to the front of his black Ike military blouse. He stated with pride that they showed he'd been ready to die fighting for what he believed in, and would again if given the chance.

The art exhibit inside the barn was arranged into three galleries. Along the wall in the first gallery was a huge painting of Karl Marx's skull, which was easily recognized by his long hair and beard. Two barbed wires were drawn from beneath his jawbone through the eye holes, and then transformed into big horns. Some workers were depicted passing by and turning their faces away from him. Next to Marx was a painting of Lenin's skull with a goatee, covered by a beret. Ears had been added showing him listening for anyone who disagreed with communism.

Hitler's portrait was next to Lenin's, but with an unusual expression: he was laughing and revealing his broken teeth, which were all pillars of the Victory Gate in Munich. His neighbor was Ana Pauker, the Romanian communist, and on Ana's right was Ilse Koch. Then came Stalin and Goebbels. Stalin was laughing like Hitler, but nevertheless sending a dirty look towards Ana Pauker. Ilse was protecting Ana from Stalin by holding out her umbrella made with human skin.

Molotov was there preparing a vodka drink for his Western visitors, while keeping a wary eye on the poison dripping from Goebbels' mouth. Tito was pictured in a cave in the remote Bosnian mountains counting Allied money, surrounded by sophisticated girls lounging on top of oriental rugs.

The second gallery was titled: *Man in God's Service.* It had subtitles such as: *Man Feels for his Fellow Man, Man Fights and Dies for his Fellow Man, Man Keeps his Promises* and a few others. The first painting showed the British poet Byron, with the quotation: *Man's love is of man's life—a thing apart.* This was placed over a large map of Greece.

Above the map was another painting with the American, William T. Washington, who died heroically fighting for Greek freedom at Nafplio in 1827. Then came Lord Tennyson with his poem to Montenegro, William Ewart Gladstone, Lafayette, Kosciusko, Pulaski and others who gave their lives. The only person among them still alive was Helen Keller, shown weeping for the South African Boers who'd lost their fight for freedom.

At the end of the gallery was a painting of displaced persons. In the center it had many hungry skeletons playing a game of baseball with the bats and gloves sent by UNRRA. At the edges were other skeletons watching them while holding lanterns into the sunshine looking for anyone who might at least understand them.

In the middle of the barn was shown the third gallery. First the Empire State building was seen standing sixteen feet high, next to which American people with strong hands were piling up parcels of food. The pile grew three-dimensionally until it reached the size and shape of the building. Then it was shown on a ship sailing out of the harbor, with the Statue of Liberty in the background. Next it was seen at a West European port. Then, in a succession of paintings while it traveled to a displaced persons camp in a Bavarian town, it could be seen diminishing in size as it passed in front of many UNRRA distributors. At its final destination the pile ended up being the size of a matchbox.

Unfortunately for the camp artists, when the UNRRA staff came through and saw this last depiction, it was the final straw that did in the exhibit. Completely fed up with the camp's attitude towards them, UNRRA sent in solders to remove all the paintings. This was carried out by a sergeant who led a squadron into the big barn.

Dayan was up in the watchtower working on his poem when this occurred, and from there he could hear all of the soldier's laughing. Inside they were sticking bayonets into the dozens of paintings and boxes, and were piling them up outside. Dayan now watched this from above, seeing one soldier put Molotov's picture with Goebbels on the pile. Another soldier stuck Lenin, Hitler and Tito together and dumped them onto the same pile. But someone else took the Statue of Liberty and Helen Keller off of the pile, and went over into the chapel with them. He'd taken off his cap, and Dayan recognized him as Jimmy the College Man.

The idea that Jimmy might've learned Hitler and Tito were soldiers of one army in the First World War, hostile to the West, pleased Dayan. And that it was the German army who'd brought Lenin inside of a sealed train from Switzerland to Russia, to both promulgate the revolution and to ease their own front, was equally important. Or maybe, Dayan thought, he'd realize that Molotov's vodka, prepared for the Western guests, might prove to be as poisonous as Goebbels' own poison. But Jimmy was too late in saving more of the paintings. Other soldiers had finished piling them up outside and, after drenching them with gasoline, they were set on fire.

It grieved Dayan to see the efforts of the camp's artists destroyed like this. He turned away to watch the gathered refugees as they danced in defiance. Here again, he had something to regret, for this hora wasn't like the one he'd watched with Angelica in Belgrade at the spring dance. This ground, almost as hard as concrete, wasn't shaking under the pounding of these men's feet, and neither did their wavy hair shake as they jumped.

Instead, these men were gray at the temples, and their foreheads were damp with sweat at the effort of dancing on empty stomachs. Their cheekbones were larger and their eyes were sunken. No white handkerchiefs were waving, no hands were holding young girls around their slender waists, and no children shyly tried to imitate the adults here—just like they did in Cablo at the dances under the oak tree.

But Dayan had no questions, no *why* as Jimmy the College Man did. He knew why Jimmy, with his brave Third Army, had been stopped at Pilsen, and why Stalin's armies waited at the Vistula river until hundreds of thousands of brave Poles died heroically in the Warsaw uprising. It was all because the devils were at work. And when the devils work, as his mother had told him long ago, they laugh and the angels weep. That's why Hitler and Stalin were shown laughing in the paintings which were now burning fiercely, and why inside the chapel Helen Keller's painting wept in contrast.

There's not much one can do at such a time, but sharpen a blackthorn branch to a point and stab the devil in his heart as one does to a vampire. This was the advice the peasant gave Dayan on the train, when he made his first trip to Belgrade as a student. But the blackthorn branch wouldn't help him here as long as the bayonets protected the devils. Perhaps he should close his eyes, as the sexton had once advised him to do in Cablo. He even said it was sweet to sleep while the devils are at work. Dayan decided to try.

Dayan felt better with his eyes closed, and he started to imagine himself dancing on the watchtower platform whose edge hung over the street. The music was playing and as he danced alone, he envisioned a gathering of enslaved people, including some from the USSR and Poland, still wearing striped clothing and wooden shoes as they had during Hitler's time. They were dancing too.

But when he opened his eyes, he saw the soldiers with their fixed bayonets protecting the devils around the tables. He hated bayonets and hated the devils even more, so he closed his eyes again. Now the dancing circle was much longer, and in the crowd he could recognize many people.

Children were getting their honey from the sexton at the St. George Church in Cablo. Thankfully, they weren't being asked to become a Tito's Pioneer, the preparation for selling their souls as adults. And then there was Thomash, he held his crutch in one hand and Angelica with the other, and she was looking for someone—for Dayan. Thomash was getting old; his crutch was almost worn out. He offered it to a Polish cripple, a veteran from Monte Cassino.

"But you're older, and you still need it," the veteran Pole said.

"Please, this is all I can do for your country," Thomash said. "I also have a son, he'll help and bring me a new one."

The Pole listened to him while Angelica stood alone. She was tender and shy as always. Rushing to join her, Dayan stretched out his arms and lost his balance. He was falling and falling, Angelica was falling too. He tried to grab her. He was afraid to open his eyes, for then he'd lose her. But it was too late and she disappeared.

"You're much better," a voice said after Dayan slowly opened his eyes. But neither the words nor the white object before him meant much, so he closed them again. Then he felt a soft hand gently grab his, so he again opened his eyes. There was nothing to see at first but that whiteness, and now it gradually assumed the shape of a young woman in a white gown.

Then he saw some of her features, the red lips and blue eyes. He began pulling her towards him and his mind became clearer. He remembered the flames from the burning paintings, the shiny bayonets and the platform he was on in the watchtower.

"Where am I?" Dayan asked cautiously.

"In St. Joseph's Hospital in Munich," the nurse answered. "You've been here three days now."

"In Germany?"

"Of course." She showed him a printed questionnaire in German. "I have to fill this out, but for now just give me your name and native country. Otherwise, no food."

"I'm a gardener," Dayan said. "From Bulgaria."

"Yes, you talked about giving violets to someone, in your delirium. But first—your name!"

"Write Salashef. Mitko. Mitko Salashef. Now what's happened?" He then looked puzzled at her.

"My name is Olga Urban. I'm a refugee from East Germany, a Biology student. I live with my mother, my fiancé—"

"No, no! What's happened to me? Why am I here?" He knew he was being self-centered, but couldn't help himself.

"You were brought here three days ago, it was at night. A dog apparently found you lying on the street unconscious near a displaced persons camp, and it started barking. Then an ambulance picked you up. They thought you'd been struck by a car—maybe you'll remember something soon."

Dayan thought for a moment. "I already do. Thank you, Olga." And it was true; while she was speaking, he remembered the watchtower, and how he'd closed his eyes as the sexton had recommended. He also remembered grabbing for Angelica.

Chapter 19

Meanwhile, Dayan must get well again. The doctors took five x-rays; they showed that one shoulder was broken and four ribs were cracked. Olga tended him well and apologized for the room, which was formerly used for storage. He said the room was fine, and since it was too small to include another bed, he had his privacy. The diet consisted mainly of starches without any meat, yet he couldn't complain. It was as good as anything else he'd eaten lately.

Strangely though his nurse occasionally asked him whether it was a sin to change one's name. To this Dayan finally answered that yes, it was a sin. "It might create confusion in the heavens," he said. He then pulled the blanket up over himself while laughing.

Dayan was planning to ask her jokingly whether certain deeds were sinful in her opinion too, but noticed that she had a habit of standing at the window fixating her eyes to a certain place on the street. She never allowed him to get up except to use the bathroom, but after she'd left the room—he did, and he looked out in the same direction. Nothing unusual was to be seen outside.

Although Olga knew nothing about him, Dayan knew a lot about her. She talked freely, telling him about her younger brother missing at the Eastern Front, and of her dead fiancé. She even admitted that the reason she'd been assigned to his room was a scheme of the Sister Superior, Donata, who worried about there being five million more German women than there were men.

Olga mentioned she planned to visit her mother who stayed in a camp for German refugees in Frankfurt, and she hoped to attend either the Frankfurt or Munich universities. She urged him to recover soon, and to leave the hospital as quickly as he could, saying she'd take him to the streetcar station.

"Would it be regarded as an escape?" Dayan asked. "I don't want to jeopardize you."

"No, not at all. They can't feed the patients anyway and the doctors are unhappy. They're actually starving too, just as we are."

She moved closer to him and whispered in his ear. "I'm going to get out the same way."

"Then let's leave together," Dayan suggested.

She agreed willingly.

After five weeks, Dayan's bones were finally healed. So as he'd planned, Dayan escorted Olga to the Munich North railroad station, leaving his records behind at St. Joseph's Hospital, with the papers and files still under his false name.

"Maybe you'll come to see me sometime," he told Olga as she was about to leave. "You can find me in my camp." He helped her get into the train, with her few possessions in a bag slung over her shoulder. He waited for her answer, but she only stared at him.

"You're in the Bulgarian camp?" she finally asked him, as the train began to move away.

"No. No. There's no Bulgarian camp!" The train was quickly picking up speed, and he was angry with himself for wasting time. "Yugoslav!" he shouted. "The Yugoslav camp!"

Did she hear him? He couldn't tell, and now that the train had pulled away—it was too late to find out.

20

Throwing Gold Coins

During the five weeks that Dayan was in the hospital, UNRRA officials became much more desperate about the situation in the Yugoslav camp. They had allowed members of Tito's Mission to enter the camp four times, and four times the displaced persons danced in front of the embarrassed armed soldiers, defying them. Meanwhile, each time this happened their daily food allowance was reduced, and after the fourth time—it was down to nearly the starvation point.

People who were earlier advised to avoid work on German farms were now encouraged to do so, in the hope that the remaining refugees at the camp would have more food. There was also a push to be more open about having the displaced persons immigrate to overseas countries, since at this point it was obvious there was no end in sight for them. They even made an order setting aside any non-perishable food for the absent people, in the hope that many would leave voluntarily knowing they could recoup the food later if needed.

When Dayan returned from the hospital, his share of non-perishable food was waiting for him. It consisted of two dried plums, five tablespoons of peas, six peanuts, twenty-three grains of beans and six pieces of potato chips, with two of those broken in half. From the other items officially termed as *basic needs,* he received only a single used shoe lace.

The skinny supply clerk who issued these items to Dayan made him sign three copies of documents, while warning him not to take his riches to the black market. "This is in accordance with the Allies' strict policy," he stated grandiosely, "which should put Germany once more on its knees."

He pointed out how he was the only skinny supply clerk in the modern world, boasting it was a simple matter of pride to him.

And he was skinny; as skinny as Dayan was. Dayan was impressed. An honest supply clerk?

All those eligible in the Yugoslav camp were now encouraged by Colonel Obradovich to register at Munich University, following an announcement that they were going to accept a 10% student quota of displaced persons as new students. It was also stipulated that they'd receive school meals just as the German students did. Since the University buildings were partially destroyed and there was a shortage of teachers due to the war, the exact numbers would be relatively small that they could accept.

Applying at the University registrar's office, Dayan was asked for his school papers. "I have none," he said. "I even came to Germany under a false name from Yugoslavia."

"False name! That's against the law!"

"It was against the law."

"It's as illegal now as it was before," the clerk said. "Just try to put something false in the questionnaire and the Amis will take you straight to Dachau. But perhaps not you. After all, you won the war. We were the losers."

Dayan laughed mirthlessly.

"Sure, we lost," the clerk insisted. "Anyway, why don't you write home for your papers? The Post has just been reopened between Germany and Yugoslavia. Or you could go and get them yourself. It won't take you that long."

"Were you in the war, sir?" Dayan asked quietly.

"Who, me? Thank the Lord no. Never! Neither Hitler nor Kaiser Wilhelm, God bless his soul, drafted me."

Dayan said nothing, but something in his expression put the clerk on the defensive. So the clerk went on to say that he could have been killed here at any time, just like anyone else. He pointed through the open window at the completely destroyed medical school with the Roentgen statue in front of it. "I could happen to be passing by with some files, or having lunch in front of Roentgen, as I usually do. I worship Roentgen—a great man. He showed us how to look into people."

"So he did. Pity we don't look," Dayan replied. "Well, now can I see my professor?"

"You won't have one until you register. No one will believe your status without seeing it in black and white. And apparently—"

"Remember, sir, you just said that you worship Roentgen. Try learning from him; try looking inside of people occasionally."

Dayan then left and as he passed by the university hall, he saw the initiation ceremony for some new students taking place inside. He decided to go in. He wanted to forget the clerk's words, *no one will believe you*, but he was unable to, even though the Graunke Symphony Orchestra was playing Wagner's *Tannhauser* opera.

As he went out, his eyes moved up to the marble plaque which hung above the main door, dedicated to the professors and students who'd given their lives while fighting Hitler's Nazis. Silently, Dayan gave symbolic respect to the seven names engraved on the plaque; even the number was symbolic to him. More than ever the dead were close to him, part of himself. And for this closeness, he turned to them. "You believe me," Dayan whispered, "and I believe you."

His spirits rose further when his registration with the Department of History was later granted, upon the recommendation of Professor Weisner, based on a paper he'd turned in entitled: *Contributions of Suppressed People to Mankind*.

Dayan's lot now was truly improving; Professor Weisner, himself an émigré—having fled to Switzerland during the Nazi regime —urged him to develop it as a thesis with the possibility of publication later. Also, a school meal was added to the comfort of a room with a German family somewhere in Munich, plus a regular ration of food coupons as a German citizen. He wasn't assigned to cleaning the ruins or rebuilding the university's destroyed buildings—as the German students were. This exclusion, unofficially known as a German intellectual reparation, was a privilege generously offered to displaced persons who were accepted as students like Dayan was.

For Christmas, in addition to the regular meals, Dayan received two jars of lard donated by the Red Cross from Holland. And with the beginning of the New Year in 1948, a twenty-two pound CARE package purchased by a group of Antioch college students in America arrived for him. Everything here was conducive to his disciplined scholastic work. Although he was no longer on the Yugoslav camp's list for food, since he was receiving the German ration coupons, he often visited the camp to see his old friends.

One Sunday while at the camp, Dayan climbed up the abandoned watchtower and with a string, measured the height of the place to where he'd fallen to the ground. It was something less than seven meters, which he considered not especially high when compared to the boulders along the creek near Cablo—from which he used to dive into the water. He wondered what had made him lose consciousness and fall, and also why did a dog find him? Why not a person? The words were still there on the board where he'd written them, so perhaps they'll give the answer. Then he thought of his poem, and was ashamed at its slow progress.

That evening there Dayan went to sleep, still thinking about the poem he'd now named *KATYN*. In his dream Tobo appeared. The fisherman seemed to be floating on icy blue water, surrounded by a lot of shapeless white marble images of some sort; he wasn't swaying as he'd been on the streets in Belgrade, while saluting imaginary generals, but moved now with the grace of a born nobleman with his eyes closed. Burning candles fell from the dark sky around him, creating a magical light. The shapeless marbles reminded Dayan of the churchyard in Cablo where there stood the block of granite from which Thomash was to have carved a monument for his grandfather.

"Open your eyes, Tobo!" Dayan cried out in his dream. "I'm here. Dayan—your professor!"

Tobo paused, looking towards Dayan with the expression he'd worn so often; like that of a troubled child, still eager to please. "Dayan!" he said, "I'm still looking everywhere for your people. And mine too."

"You mean the missing people? The people I told you about on that day behind the mule stables, when I brought you the fish from the Danube?"

"Yes, and many, many more!" Tobo replied gravely. "The world hides them." He closed his eyes again. "But no need for my eyes to seek them. The heart is enough."

"Where is the heart?" Dayan demanded to know. "Where is the heart, Tobo?"

He waited, and it seemed the fate of the world hung on Tobo's answer. Dayan hoped he'd draw closer, that they might clasp hands and embrace like comrades. But Tobo had disappeared, merging with the misty white marble. The icy blue water began to murmur, the sound increasing until it became a roar like that of an angry sea. There all of the falling candles flickered into the rising mist and spray. Dayan quickly woke up sweating. At the tower of the neighboring nursing home, the clock was close to striking 2:00 AM.

He rose slowly and began to work on his poem.

~

On a late snowy evening, Dayan left the Yugoslav camp to return to his room in Munich, when he suddenly heard some footsteps crackling behind him. As he stopped, so did the footsteps. This made him feel uneasy, so he decided to find out who was there. He wheeled around angrily, and at seeing it was Tell, Dayan moved towards him. "Tell! Why are you following me?"

Tell stepped back, and acted alarmed. "Don't be angry with me, please," he said cautiously, "I need to ask you something." He took a few steps forward towards Dayan. "I need to know what a mission is."

"Come on, we might as well walk," Dayan said, "it's too cold to stand here." He struck off again through the snow, while Tell fell into stride with him as best he could.

"Now, a mission," Dayan started saying in a scholarly, rather perfectionist way. "Well, there are various interpretations of the word, and a great deal depends on its context."

Tell listened attentively.

"It may hinge on who's saying what to whom," Dayan continued. "Suppose we start with the word democracy. The West has had it for centuries, but today the East calls it bourgeois democracy. Then the East claims what they have is democracy too, while the West says what the East has is tyranny."

"Yes, but a mission? I keep hearing about it."

"From whom?"

They both stopped and then faced each other. Tell looked around fearfully. The falling snowflakes that had frozen on his mustache glistened in the moonlight. His eyes shined with an expression Dayan knew and trusted; he spoke softly. "From Max Barrack. You know him?"

"Sure, he's a handyman from our country. He repairs everything." Dayan replied casually, but his heart had skipped a beat as he remembered Radovich's warning.

"Yes, but first he breaks them so he'll have them to repair," Tell warned.

"What on earth for?"

"So he can listen and spy," Tell said, obviously very worried. "And on you too."

Dayan wanted to change the subject. "Back to what a mission is, Tell. When I was captured in Bosnia, I was on a mission. I was doing what I believed was right and I still believe it. Our people will never be enemies of the West."

"I had a mission too, once. I think God likes what I did," Tell said immodestly.

"Such as?"

"I buried a man."

"Buried?" Dayan was curious. "Where?"

"In Austria, when I returned from the border. I followed his last wish."

Now Dayan was the one worried. "And what was his wish?"

"That I get a letter back to his family, which I did later."

"Was this man wounded?" Dayan asked quickly.

"Badly of course, in both hips. And he wasn't the only one," Tell continued. "Many more were wounded and even murdered at the border."

Now Dayan wanted to avoid this subject too. "What has all this to do with your question about what a mission is?"

"This Max. He always knows when Tito's men will come with the Americans." Tell broke off abruptly while a couple was passing them by, arm in arm, despite their bulky overcoats. After they were gone, Tell said urgently: "Listen, Dayan, I want to kill him!" He brought his hands together in a choking position. "At night!"

"No, Tell! Murder is against God and there's already been more than enough killing. You yourself told me that Edo was the last man you ever wanted to kill."

"But this Max spies on you and the others."

"Let him. You already killed Edo for me. Didn't you?"

"Yes, and for me too."

"Look, Tell. Go back to camp and cross yourself before you go to sleep, like a good old grandpa. Promise?" Dayan held out his hand.

"I promise," Tell said at last, the trustful gleam dimming in his eyes as he looked solemnly at Dayan while shaking his hand. There was more frozen snow on his mustache as he walked away, leaving Dayan to continue on his way to the city alone.

~

For weeks the Student Welfare Committee at Munich University, with a representative from each department, had been reviewing applications for harvest jobs in Switzerland for the summer. There were 26 jobs and 358 applicants. The committee considered them chiefly on the reasons they gave for wanting the job.

"Listen to these everyone!" one of the committee members said:

"Applicant #1. Sick and tired of ruins all over, especially the disfigured Roentgen statue in front of that bombed-out medical school. The statue is so badly machine-gunned that pigeons fly in and out through the holes."

"Applicant #2. I wish to send a globe to the school by my native town so the pupils can understand the size of the free world and not lose all hope for their future. This method worked once during the war when I painted an Easter egg with a representation of the world."

There was a slight rustle, and the reader paused. The committee members had listened attentively to the request from Applicant #2, and several then whispered with their colleagues. After a moment the representative of the Biology Department, Margaret Neuman, spoke up.

"I believe that request should be given first class consideration," she said.

The chairman for the day replied: "This is from one of the first foreign applicants to apply, colleague Neuman. What are your reasons for the recommendation, please?"

Margaret Neuman rose, and then replied modestly: "I don't know many of the foreign students. Since some of these students came in on the displaced person quota, perhaps we should extend that among these applicants too. I feel consideration of such an application would indicate our desire to participate in the free world more effectively, it's better than merely changing our street names from Bismarck, Richthofen and so on—to names with peaceful connotations. In other words, the occupation powers will never accept us as a democratic nation if we don't take steps in that direction ourselves."

A member from the department of Political Science spoke up. "Imposed democracy contradicts itself," he intoned.

"They have no right to talk about our democracy while they fraternize with the Soviets," a different voice shouted from the floor, followed by applause.

"Ladies and gentlemen, please!" the chairman appealed. "Let's not contradict ourselves either. This plan is subject to the final approval by the occupying powers, who will or won't approve the exit permits and passports for Switzerland."

Chapter 20

The group applied itself more calmly now to continuing on with the reviews. The remainder of Applicant #2 was read, revealing that the student sympathized with the professors who spoke only one language and the parents who failed with their children. His request said it would, if granted, remove him from the German ration list, making his food available to others.

It was finally decided to accept Margaret Neuman's proposition that the application be accepted. Also accepted was a proposal that since Miss Neuman had chosen this foreign student, it would be her duty to contact the applicant and bring him in for their final decision later next week.

A couple of days later, after Dayan had left church that Sunday, he again was approached unexpectedly from behind. When he turned around to see who it was, there was Tell looking like he had the last time, and now he had more news. "He wants to talk to you now, Dayan. That spy, Max."

"I know you don't like it, but I'll see him. I'll meet him anywhere, then we'll go to a place that I pick out."

"Good! And I'll follow you."

"No, Tell. Please don't worry—I'll take care of him if necessary. Let him know for me, and ask him where he wants us to meet."

It was arranged, and a few days later Dayan boarded a streetcar at the first corner behind the camp to go to the Prinz-Regenten bridge. Once there he strolled on a lonely path by the Isar river, where he saw Max sitting on a log up ahead.

"All right, Max. What's on your mind?"

Max sighed once, and then twice. He stood up and lowered his eyes. "Mr. Costovar," he began, but then he stopped and drew in another deep breath.

"Call me Dayan."

Max appeared to be struggling, but got right to the point: "Would you believe me if I told you I'm a spy?"

"You mean a traitor!" Dayan struck him across the face so hard that his blonde hair bristled and his eyes opened wide. He looked straight at Dayan without fear.

"I deserve that, Dayan. Hit me again." He turned the other cheek, but Dayan dropped his hand.

"No, not until we talk some more."

The imprint of the blow was fading from Max's cheek while he sat back down with his arms resting on his knees. "I know all about you," he said.

"What? And how?"

"I was trained long ago as a prisoner. Did you ever hear of the Soviet NKVD?"

"Of course. They're as bad as the German Gestapo were."

"That's the agency I spied for. The communists."

The blow Dayan struck now on the other cheek was much stronger than the first. Its sound was lost among the crashing waves of the Isar river, and there was no apology this time.

Max acknowledged the blow and thanked him for it, but opened his coat so Dayan could see his holster with a pistol. "I took those two for what I deserve, now don't push your luck again."

He went on to say his guilt went far back; he'd been the victim of a well conceived communist prisoner indoctrination. Proud of his Bosnian origins, whose revolutionaries fought Turkey and the Austro-Hungarian Empire—including the assassination of Archduke Ferdinand in 1914—he'd learned even more than his masters had planned.

Convinced that for this reason he'd been left in the prison camp by Tito's men, Max started to work towards even a low rank. And he did so well that he gained the confidence of the chief of the Soviet Mission in Munich. For all this a rank of captain in the Secret Police was promised if he agreed to stay in Germany for one more year, and in Yugoslavia he had a major's rank waiting for him.

He'd always wanted to become a major above everything else in the world; the Austrian officer who took his father to a concentration camp during the First World War had been a major, and at the time seemed like the most powerful man anywhere, next to Franz Joseph.

"I know you've been talking to others about the massacres," Max continued. "Here is something else about those grave sites at Katyn that the Nazis discovered in the spring of 1943. Goebbels became very excited about finding them, even though the Gestapo and the NKVD had secretly coordinated activities early on in Poland. Goebbels even tried later to use the Katyn discovery against the Soviets to help break up the Western allies. However, nobody would believe Nazis considering their own history, so the Soviets blamed the Nazis for the massacre, and that decision was approved by the very top leaders in the West."

"That's impossible. You mean Western leaders too?" Dayan was shocked.

"Yes, President Roosevelt and Churchill." Max continued. "That's why there wasn't an investigation into this by the Polish Government in exile or the International Red Cross. The Polish military intelligentsia were shot and massacred at Katyn to remove any resistance to Soviet control by Stalin. Then they lied about who did it and the Western leaders knew this!"

Dayan quickly shook his head and said, "I never would have believed it."

"I can see why you think that, even the Nazis successfully hid many things. Like the secret drugs given to German soldiers going into battle to make them more alert and aggressive. Or the testing they did on nuclear weapons in Thuringia, it's all just the tip of the iceberg."

"Go on, tell me more," he urged Max.

"It's all past history now, we were used just like pawns on a chess board by everyone. Even the British had something they called the Special Operations Executive, our Yugoslav King never had a chance against all this. I wish I had more time to talk, but I must hurry now Dayan. Duty awaits me."

Dayan grabbed Max's shoulders after he stood up. "Duty? You mean spying?"

"No. Not anymore. It's probably death. They murdered my sweetheart in a Bosnian village, so I'm going to avenge her."

Dayan was convinced Max was telling the truth. "Who killed her?"

"The communists. She was totally illiterate, but I kept getting letters supposedly written by her. She said they'd taught her to read and write under the new regime. What a lie! Instead she'd been dead for years." He pounded his thighs with his clenched fists. "But I answered the letters. Now I'm going to kill one of the leaders, so I won't be back. This is why I wanted to meet with you." Max pulled a bundle from under his coat. "Take this gold, I earned it from spying. You can live on that much money in Germany, or it'll even take you as far as America. Our grandfathers fought together, so I wanted you to have it."

Dayan untied the bundle full of golden coins. Max watched as, one after the other, Dayan tossed them into the waves of the swollen river. When they were all gone, the two men were silent, each experiencing a moment of exhilaration. Then Max leaned towards Dayan. "If only I could be as close to God as you are."

"But you can't be, Max, because you're on your way to murder. Please wait. There will be punishment. God is sometimes slow, but..."

"How can I wait?" Look!" Max took a photograph out from his pocket and handed it to Dayan, who stared at the husky girl with long blonde hair.

"When I was in Bosnia, Max, I saw someone like her killed, but she looks younger and the one I saw was with some other peasants."

"Weren't you captured in Bosnia? I didn't want to tell you this, but that's why they found and drowned your father in Gradina."

Now Dayan seized Max by the arm. "My father? Drowned???"

"For that slate they found, since his name was on it. And a cross."

Dayan's knees sagged and he almost fell. Max clasped him tightly around his shoulders, while supporting him. "I can't believe it, Max. We both know so much that we must tell each other everything."

While supporting Dayan as best he could, Max led him back to the log so they could both sit. Now that they'd exchanged the chief burdens of their knowledge, they could talk more freely together.

Max had learned from Tito's Mission about the finding of Dayan's slate with the cross drawn on it, and what had happened to Thomash. He even knew about their tossing his corpse wrapped in an UNRRA sack from the bridge. And Dayan could scarcely satisfy the questions Max asked about the girl he saw killed. He wanted to keep hearing the details of it over and over again, and Dayan realized that he was fueling Max's hatred to better prepare himself for the murderous task he had assumed.

"Don't do it," Dayan begged him. "Don't kill. Our people have fought for years. The wars, the killing and the bloodshed were always supposed to bring a better life for us; to bring us freedom. But it never turned out that way, all we got was the self-destruction. A great English writer once said—*it's the life that counts*."

"But she has no life now, Dayan."

"No, and neither do the almost two million dead Yugoslavs. Remember, we lost one hundred and six for every German killed in our country. Will adding another death even up that score?"

"No, nothing can. But I still have to go."

"Alright then Max, but will you do something for me?"

"Anything. I'd even die for you."

"I only ask that you somehow pass the word to my village that I'm still alive. That'll make my mother very happy. She's in Cablo."

"Yes—in the Gradina district. I'll do it, of course." Max stood up. "Time for me to go."

Dayan rose and held out his hand. "Just think it over, Max. Remember—life is what counts."

The two men shook hands and Max turned to go. But Dayan couldn't tell from his expression what he intended to do.

Later that day when Dayan was back at the university, he still had thoughts of Max and what he might do to get his revenge. But then he was surprised to see someone he recognized standing before him at the door to the history department.

"Miss Urban!" Dayan said cheerfully.

"Mister Sal—asheff." She stumbled over the pronunciation. "What are you doing here?"

"I'm here in the Department of History."

"As a gardener?" Olga Urban, who'd nursed him after his fall from the watchtower, gave him a quizzical smile.

"Everybody tells a little white lie every once in a while," Dayan said while smiling. "What are you doing here?"

"I'm looking for a certain foreign student." She then unfolded a document and read: "By the name of Dayan Costovar."

"At your service!"

They both laughed, and then she quickly said: "Call me Miss Neuman. Margaret Neuman. It's my real name."

"Your sin is my sin, I take it upon me," Dayan promised. "Thus, no more confusion in the heavens. Besides, we intend to live, don't we?"

She smiled, and without coaxing, gladly told him why she'd taken an assumed name: because it sounded more Slavic to use while fleeing from East Germany at the end of the war. "Many girls had papers in assumed names, they could use them to get out of trouble more easily if they ended up caught by the Soviets." She didn't ask why he'd used an assumed name, neither did he try to explain it.

"It looks promising for your application to work in Switzerland," she told him, then explained the next steps towards acquiring the necessary permission. As they strolled along the path, talking like old friends, they came to the statue of Roentgen. Dayan went around and peered at her through one of the holes left by the shooting during the war.

"Try it," he instructed. "Look at me!" He pushed one of his hands through a large hole. "These holes allow us to see through Roentgen just like the x-rays he discovered." Her expression showed he was right, and she smiled at how ironic it was.

Chapter 20

That afternoon she took Dayan to the Munich Pinakothek. The exhibition impressed him, but he preferred to watch her as she moved around, especially while standing before Rubens' *Garland of Fruit*. Before they separated, she invited him to meet her mother the following evening, which turned out to be snowy and cold. New snow had covered the path from the gate to the house where she lived with her mother. Margaret was wearing some low, flimsy shoes.

"Let me carry you," Dayan suggested. "I'm wearing my military shoes." In spite of her resistance, he took her in both arms, then lifted her up and held her close. "All sins are mine from now on," he said happily. He felt her lightness and warmth filling up all the emptiness inside of him.

Christine Neuman was coughing as she opened the door. "Don't be worried about Mother's cough. She always does it when she gets excited," Margaret told him. "It's a nervous thing. Ever since she got news that my brother Hans was killed."

"This is not home," Frau Neuman apologized to Dayan after they were introduced. "Few Germans have a home here anymore. But such as it is, consider it yours. And perhaps Margaret told you that my husband was a Nazi. But—" Here she had another coughing spell.

Margaret interjected quickly: "No, Mother, I didn't."

Her mother went on, looking up at Dayan. "My husband was a first-class baker, believe me, but jobless until they took him. I swept the Palace of Justice to feed the family. Maybe Margaret told you about our darling Hans." Then she began coughing again.

"Yes, I did. Everything."

Dayan was looking from one to the other.

Frau Neuman was eager to talk to someone. Evidently through the lonely years, she'd been repeating the history of their little family to herself, and now she wanted to tell this attractive young man all about it. It took a long time. Dayan heard about Margaret's grandfather, also a baker, whose brother died as a young priest. On the maternal side, her great grandfather was first to introduce Wagner's music in his native town. One of his two sons owned a valuable microscope, which was lost during the war, along with all of their other belongings. The other son was a professional soldier, who was killed at Verdun.

The story would have been even longer, but Margaret intervened. "Mother, let's find out something about Dayan," she suggested. This embarrassed Dayan, and as the two women looked at him, his mind went so blank that he could scarcely even remember his own name.

Realizing this, Frau Neuman began asking questions, but before he could answer them, she made her own answers in the form of comments. First was the matter of the Allies hatred for Bismarck, Nietzsche and even Wagner. Then the justification of the Nuremberg Trials. She asked whether the rumors were true that the Polish General Anders was forbidden to appear as a witness at the trial.

"It must be true," she answered herself, "because he was showing up Nazi-Soviet relationships against the West. And once our Demontage is over, new fighting will start, mark my words!" She gave this a semi-official tone of voice.

Margaret disagreed. "Who'll do the fighting, Mother? The war is over for good."

"We can't fight, obviously," her mother replied. "It's up to the Allies themselves. You'll see I'm right."

Dayan noticed a collection of Goethe's works on the bookshelf.

"They're the only books we saved," Margaret said, glad to change the subject. "You can borrow some of them if you like."

"An American lecturer in Munich's American house," Frau Neuman started again, "said that Hitler was going to proclaim Goethe a Jew."

"I never heard of that," Dayan said diplomatically.

"Neither did I," Margaret agreed.

"Nobody ever did," Frau Neuman added, "until that American came."

Margaret looked at Dayan. "Mother, I think we've heard enough now!"

21

The Church Bell Rings

Hillarich, the former commandant from Gradina and now a general in Tito's Army, peered through the window of a villa in a Belgrade suburb. The Danube seen below glittered in the early morning sun. Looking through the windows on the other side of the room, he could see the casernes, seat of the kangaroo court which had sentenced General Mihailovic to death.

He shook his head, grabbed a small pair of scissors and went up to the curtains of a window. Carefully he cut off a piece of the heavy material and put it into his mouth, chewing it slowly—almost solemnly—while he stared at the silver river. The curtains were ragged and uneven at the edges where other pieces had been cut off. After a while, he spit out the present chew and selected a new piece to cut out.

Juliana, his typist, was sleeping nearby on a large mahogany desk. Her beautiful blonde hair was spread out amongst the empty coffee cups, the nearly-full ashtrays and the stacks of typed pages. Those papers, Hillarich had been told by his superiors, represented the most important task of his life, and Hillarich had agreed with them. The report was being specially prepared to be read by Tito at the upcoming Warsaw meeting with all the communist countries, and was to be translated into all the Slavic, Baltic, and Hungarian languages.

The subject of the report involved the history of the Communist Party, with an emphasis on proving the battle of Stalingrad was won through the use of Soviet artillery, and not because of any awakened national spirit, nor due to the material help of the Western warmongers and plutocrats, whose shrewd diplomacy had turned Hitler against them.

A tremendous task, the report was the result of painstaking work over many months by some of the highest intellectuals in the Yugoslav Communist Party. It had even involved linguists and semanticists whose job it was to find sufficient derogatory words and phrases to use in reference to the West. These experts even included a man who was an authority on Sanskrit.

Since Hillarich had been active in Stalingrad, and his military career stretched longer than any of Tito's other aides, he was in charge of evaluating the plausibility of it. He also served as co-author on that portion which dealt with the Soviet artillery. Compiling its contents was a sleepless all-night job for him and Juliana, who'd fallen asleep some twenty minutes earlier after becoming completely exhausted. But now it was time to arrange the papers into their proper order and perhaps make a last-minute check of things.

"You did a splendid job, Juliana," Hillarich murmured. "Without your cooperation the Marshal wouldn't be able to go to Warsaw." Juliana was breathing evenly, yet he realized she was still sound asleep. "My little one," he whispered. He touched her fair hair with his trembling, crooked fingers.

Juliana stirred and yawned. With her eyes still closed, she said: "I'm still so very sleepy." Reluctantly she opened them. "I should probably get up now," she said, and then she raised her head. "But oh!" She put her head back on the desk and closed her eyes again.

"I'm tired too," Hillarich said sympathetically. "There's no other I'd have worked so hard for during all these months, except for our Marshal." He then looked respectfully at Tito's picture hanging on the wall, but Juliana had kept her eyes closed so his effort was meaningless.

Hillarich was determined to arouse her so he raised his voice. "Now, Comrade," he said loudly. "Whether Marshal Tito sends you to the Riviera or St. Moritz, it's up to him. Maybe the Crimea. But I've got something for you, a present!"

That did the trick. Juliana sat up on the desk and watched as Hillarich opened a drawer and pulled out a special bottle of perfume. "The last one," he said. "I mean, the only one left for you." She watched as he opened it and brought it to her nostrils.

Breathing deeply, she exclaimed with delight: "It's French! How marvelous!"

Hillarich was pleased. "I got it last year on that mission to Paris. Actually, there were four bottles, but two had to be sent to my ex-wives."

Juliana smiled. "Comrade, two and one makes three," she said.

Hillarich gave her a silly, half-sheepish look. "Oh well, we're all human. I gave one to——never mind."

Juliana said nothing, but looked at him curiously.

He felt compelled to defend himself. "Somehow it's strange about women. Once you start, it's like striking a soldier." He laughed self-consciously. "You feel sorry for the first one, and maybe even the second one. But then."

"Yes? Then what?"

"You don't feel sorry for it anymore."

Juliana slipped off the desk and went to the window, while not understanding him, since the perfume wasn't her idea of a way to wake herself up. She preferred the fresh morning air before the sun heated up all the city streets. But now she suddenly drew away from the window and turned to Hillarich. "Soldiers!" she whispered. "Lots of them—all around us!"

Hillarich smiled. "You're so very young and inexperienced." He stretched out his arms as if to embrace her, but she backed away from him. "In a few weeks it's Vidovdan, a traditional holiday on June 28th for the Serbian reactionaries. Each year it's held in memory of the day when the Serbs clashed with the overwhelming army of the Turkish Empire in 1389. No doubt there will be many demonstrations here, and the soldiers are practicing on how to handle them."

Juliana was unimpressed, so she crept back over to the window. She stared down fearfully as heavy tanks began rolling through the streets and soldiers in helmets marched in close order around them.

"But our new social order doesn't recognize this holiday," Hillarich told her. "Yet the last remnants of the Serbian bourgeoisie will try to go to church, so the soldiers will be monitoring them too."

Hillarich looked back at all the paperwork on the desk. He then remembered two things they needed to check on before the report was finally assembled, so they started working again, when a short time later there was a banging on the office door, which was then kicked open. Two soldiers stepped inside.

"You see," Hillarich said calmly to Juliana, "they're here to see the progress we've been making."

"Get out woman!" said a rough voice as the soldier pointed his Tommy gun towards Hillarich. Behind him was another soldier with slick black hair, wearing a uniform decorated with many red ribbons and stars. He pulled out a revolver.

Hillarich rubbed his sleepy eyes, while Juliana quickly left through a side door, leaving the French perfume behind on her desk.

"Yes, I know!" Hillarich looked up. "How things change! It's you, Perun Novak, and you're a big success now. Congratulations."

"Shut up!" Perun yelled. Other soldiers then entered the room and encircled Hillarich. Perun grabbed him by the shoulders, and ordered the soldiers to collect all the papers and carbon copies on the desk.

"Fun is fun, but it's not quite ready," Hillarich quipped, showing surprise.

"We want your Stalingrad papers anyway!" Perun moved his hands to Hillarich's neck and began to shake him. "You'll sign now, won't you?" He shook him harder.

Hillarich was nearly choking. "Sign what?" he said, his voice strangled.

An officer handed him a blank sheet of paper, indicating where he was to sign. Perun released him.

"What's this all about? You know my standing here!" Hillarich shouted. A soldier thrust a pen over to him and he grabbed it reluctantly.

"Comrade Tito isn't going to Warsaw after all. It's a split with the Kremlin," the officer stated flatly. "We're taking a new direction." Perun nodded his approval.

"Thanks to God," Hillarich exclaimed. He placed his right hand on Perun's shoulder. "Everyone wanted this day to come." Perun stepped back from him. "Any fool knew what communism stood for," Hillarich went on. The soldiers still surrounding him now formed a line, while facing him. Taking this as a sign of respect, Hillarich promised to Perun: "There will be many perks after we're in power together. You'll get a high—"

A burst of Tommy gun fire quickly cut off Hillarich's voice, and his falling body crashed by Perun's legs, thrashing convulsively. It then straightened out stiffly.

"Wrong again, no coup. You've changed sides for the last time!" Perun said to his lifeless body. He then instructed his soldiers: "Do just as you did in the war." He then shot a bullet into Hillarich's head. "You and your Christ," he said. The others followed his example.

When Tito's change of policy towards the Soviet Union actually happened, it brought a rush of Westania Times reporters and observers into Belgrade. The majority felt that the recent loss of Czechoslovakia to total communism was compensated for by Yugoslavia's move away from obeying the instructions of Stalin, while the Soviet's expulsion of Yugoslavia as one of the Eastern Bloc communist countries further solidified this move.

Even religious freedom was potentially in sight, with the stipulation that the American born and educated Serbian Bishop Varnava be released from prison. And to compensate for the cruelly murdered Jan Masaryk, the West was now talking with Tito as its possibly ally in Southeastern Europe again.

The observers pointed out that Tito needed the West's help to bring Yugoslavia into the Western orbit, which he vigorously wanted to accomplish. They cited as an example the killing of Tito's closest aide, General Hillarich, at the Yugoslav-Bulgarian border while covertly trying to escape back to the Soviets.

The experts said that Tito needed unlimited credit for more modern jet fighters, tanks and all the other advanced military equipment he could acquire. During the following day, another close aide and a spokesman for the Marshal declared that in case of military conflict between the Soviets and the West, Yugoslavia might still stand shoulder-to-shoulder with the Soviets—depending on negotiations. For this reason more details about Tito's needs couldn't be reported as announced, but would be given out soon, the report ended.

Meanwhile, back in Yugoslavia, things under communism since the war ended were as bad as Dayan had imagined. Even though Tito had openly split with the Soviet Union, the newer economic system was left styled as before. By this time nearly all of Yugoslavia's wealth had been nationalized, including the confiscation of all church lands. Wages and prices were set by the state, and the political purges of many who'd returned, whether by force or voluntarily, still continued.

In Cablo, everyday aspects of the villagers' lives was monitored as well, from the moment they awoke until the sun set at night. The villagers had for a long time even been forbidden to ring the church bell. This was after the old priest from a neighboring village had been sentenced to death for giving communion to Aladdin before his suicide.

Now only the newly-established police militia could ring the church bell, which was rung in certain ways to provide information or present demands in a sort of code. For instance, one pattern of ringing meant they were to bring chickens for the soldiers' rations; another that they were to assemble with all their available tools ready to work on the road; a third that they were to attend a lecture on social reeducation, and so on.

Villagers who returned from Gradina after a year or more in jail, often carrying marks of torture all over their bodies, obeyed these regulations strictly. Others hearing about the horrors of torture were obedient too.

Everyone, that is, except for Lazar for a brief time, who'd bravely returned from a German prison camp after the war. The police knew of the rumors he had a rifle with a hundred cartridges hidden away up in the hills above Cablo. Even worse, he'd talked about meeting up with some English and American war prisoners from the German camps, where throwing a few beans, a half cigarette, or some rotten potatoes during their head counts often cemented a friendship between nations.

Lazar even went further, telling the villagers what Americans had taught him about their freedom and form of government. He even knew about the American people's right to petition, and to impeach their highest officials. One day, Lazar rang the church bell on a Sunday in defiance of everyone over this, and before the police militia could muster enough men to capture or kill him, he'd shot at them and gotten away.

But now it was over a full year since Lazar had left Cablo, and only a few days after Yana had returned from spending two years in jail. Like many other young women and brides, she too belonged to that third of the Yugoslav population which went through the jails and prisons. According to the official declaration of Tito's Secretary of Police, this was to counteract the fact that the reactionaries still were lifting up their heads.

There was still no news about the Cablo young men who'd joined General Mihailovic's Chetnik guerrillas during the war, only random whispered tales of massacre at the Austro-Yugoslav border had circulated about them. And the church bell still hadn't been rung by a villager since Lazar's departure, except for once last year on St. Peter's Day, when it was officially allowed.

Then one morning in the middle of summer in 1948, a militia member rang the church bell for an early assembly. It was just after dawn and despite the early hour, the villagers carried their road-working tools and rushed to gather within the churchyard. There they found a whole company of soldiers, officers, and mules loaded with heavy machine-guns and mortars waiting for them.

After observing that the youngest children and the old people were missing, an officer ordered that everyone must attend. "Young ones and old ones!" he insisted. Couriers were sent out to round up those that were missing, while the remaining men of the village were instructed to form a line along the churchyard wall.

"What's this about?" a slender woman asked.

"It must be St. Peter's Day," a harsh woman's voice answered. "It's my Nashko's birthday too, he's twenty-eight today," It was Auntie Stephanie, the lucky mother who'd learned that her son was working on a commercial Mediterranean ship. On hearing this people crossed themselves for St. Peter's Day and for Nashko's life.

"St. Peter my foot, you missed it this year!" the officer shouted. "And what's this, you're still crossing yourselves?" He ordered the soldiers to shove the men against the wall. "Go ahead. Try and cross yourselves now."

The men were so jammed together that they couldn't even raise an arm, and the sharpened tools in their hands were hurting those standing next to them.

"We can't cross ourselves," someone finally answered to the officer. "We can barely breathe."

"Then ask St. Peter for help!" To his men he said: "Give them another shove!"

They obeyed, and the men rocked back from the blows.

"An old man has fainted," said a smothered voice from within the crowd.

"Did he fall down—at least to his knees?"

"He can't fall, we're too close together," the voice moaned.

"Then don't worry. You'll all fall to your knees along with him."

Nobody understood that the officer was speaking figuratively, but someone in the crowd encouraged them to press harder than the soldiers were demanding.

"And how? We're practically smothering," a voice protested.

"Come on!" the other voice insisted. "Press back against the wall, everybody! One, two, three!" The centuries-old stone wall couldn't withstand so much pressure—so it gave way and the noise of the tumbling stones frightened the loaded mules. From over the mountain range east of Gradina, the sun beamed down on the scene while the villagers breathed in the blessed fresh air. Crossing themselves, they prayed for God's forgiveness in having knocked over the churchyard wall.

Meanwhile, Angelica's presence in Cablo had still been confusing the officials, while only the villagers knew of her story and they'd kept it to themselves. But when the church bell rang this morning, she'd gone along with Goritza to the churchyard assembly with some caution.

Suddenly an officer called to them. Yana, who was next to Goritza and Angelica, moved forward. "Not you!" the officer told Yana. Then he looked at her and said casually: "Did you know that your sweetheart Lazar has married a Nazi war widow and has escaped to Argentina?"

Yana had heard these lies before. The words had lost meaning, except that they still made her blush. She said nothing.

Now four soldiers came up carrying a heavy burden wrapped in a military tent and they put it down on the ground. Then they danced the Kozara around it, a Partisans' circle dance created during the war for celebration.

"Don't you know how to dance this?" the officer asked Goritza.

"I'm too old for that," she answered. "But maybe when my son marries."

"Your son—you expect him to marry?"

"Of course."

"How long since you've seen him?"

Goritza started to count on her fingers, while whispering to herself.

"Let me help you," The officer suggested. "Today is July the twelfth, nineteen hundred and forty-eight."

"I don't know how to count that way," Goritza responded, still figuring on her fingers. "Let's see—seven years 'til St. Sava. Then —" She appealed to Angelica for help in figuring out the weeks and days.

"To St. George is always fourteen weeks," Angelica told her.

"You've got too many saints, no wonder you're both confused," the officer interrupted them. "We haven't time for all that." He then ordered the soldiers to uncover the load on the ground, and when they obeyed him—the body of a man was exposed. Angelica grabbed Goritza's shoulders and hugged her, trying to shield their eyes from the shock of seeing the dead corpse.

"Well, do you recognize your son?"

Goritza went over and knelt by it, with Angelica still by her side, with her arms still encircling her. The soldiers then formed a circle, forbidding the villagers who'd gathered to watch. The face of the cadaver they saw was covered with patches of frozen blood, so that it was impossible to see the features.

Goritza said urgently to Angelica: "Go fetch me a bucket of water from the well."

"But I don't want to leave you," Angelica answered, so a soldier left for the water.

"I must talk to my son now," Goritza said while wanting to disengaged herself from Angelica's embrace. "Let's be strong together."

When the soldier returned with the water, Goritza worked gently to remove the blood from the face of the corpse, while the officer waited by impatiently, tapping his feet and looking at the ruins of the churchyard wall nearby.

When some blonde hair appeared at the man's temple, Angelica exclaimed: "This isn't Dayan!!!"

Goritza continued to wash the dead man's face. "Thanks to God!" she said, "but he's someone's son."

Now a soldier came up on a trotting horse. He handed a paper to the officer, who read through it carefully, then looked annoyed. After reading through it again, he ordered Goritza to get up and move away. Angelica helped her to her feet until Goritza stood above the corpse, looking down at it.

At last she said loudly: "This isn't my son!" The officer nodded his head angrily. Tears in her eyes, Goritza made a sign of the cross over the body, which was then wrapped up again in the same tent and loaded back onto a mule.

Before he rode away with his soldiers, the officer ordered the villagers to disperse, after first warning them not to believe any rumors they might hear regarding Yugoslavia's future policy. "Unless," he said, "you all want to repeat the experiences of the last three years!"

In Gradina, *The Progressive Voice* newspaper had become a daily publication, instead of a weekly, almost two years ago. On the following day, it commented favorably on the rebuilding of what had been Shark Street, which was now renamed Marshal Tito Boulevard. That section of Gradina was being turned into a tourist attraction as part of a five-year reconstruction program, and was promised to bring in a lot of hard currency from the many eager Western visitors they were expecting.

Even the mining of newly-discovered bauxite from the hills around Cablo was discussed, and much credit was given to the Westania Times observers and experts for finding the needed Western assistance, which was now trickling into Yugoslavia after Tito's break with the Kremlin.

A special bulletin in the same edition of *The Progressive Voice* read as follows:

The key figure of a Western spy operation, who was sent to our country with orders to assassinate a fellow comrade, was recently found and liquidated near Cablo. His accomplice, a former villager named Dayan Costovar, remains at large.

***

"I only wish I'd done something against God," Angelica told Goritza after she heard why the man was murdered from the newspaper.

"But why would you want to do something so terrible?"

"Then I'd know why these things happen—all the hardships and torture. But perhaps I do anyways," she said to Goritza, while beginning to tear up.

Goritza refused to believe her. "You don't know, Angelica, only the devils do."

"What do you mean?"

"Dayan will tell you when he comes home; I've told him many times. Man has an angel on his right shoulder and a devil on his left one. The world does too, the whole world."

Angelica dried her tears with her handkerchief. "Then the devils sing when the angels cry?"

"No. The devils don't know how to sing."

"Well, do they know how to weep?"

"Never, angels only. Like you," Goritza said. Small tears had come to Angelica's eyes again.

"I must go and look for Dayan now." Angelica said. "He's alive, I'm sure of it."

Goritza listened, but was worried by her sudden determination.

Angelica went on: "That murdered man must've had a message from Dayan, so it was all my fault. I never should've left him in Belgrade."

"Wait a while longer," Goritza pleaded. "Don't go yet, he may still come home." She patted Angelica's shoulder and kissed her cheek.

"No, he won't! I'll ask Yana to go with me to Belgrade, we'll find Dayan eventually."

"Must you go so far, and leave me alone?"

"I'll send Yana back to take care of you, I only want her company for the trip. Auntie Sandra can hide me in what's left of her house."

"Then get married as soon as you meet him," Goritza begged. "Promise me!"

The two women embraced, holding each other close.

22

As Bones Are Buried

With the switch-over from UNRRA to the IRO (International Refugee Organization) a few months later, the lower administration for all the displaced persons camps became dissolved along with the higher UNRRA echelons due to a lack of funds. Many of these directors, according to the rumors, were now retired and relaxing at their villas or on their yachts in the warm Mediterranean sun.

The Yugoslav camp was also dwindling down, and it was now nearly half-deserted. The refugees who remained were still searching for work in the area, preferably finding it on large German farms, while others had moved on to other camps with better living conditions.

One day Colonel Obradovich, now chief of the fire team for the last remaining Munich camps, summoned Dayan to check on the identity of a stranger who'd just arrived. The man turned out to be Paul, from a neighboring village near Cablo, but Dayan scarcely recognized him as he stood before Obradovich in his shabby uniform of post-war Yugoslavia.

However Paul still resembled his father, a man Dayan remembered well. It was his father's job to castrate the peasant's horses and oxen back in the villages—he thus became a symbol of terror for all the small boys in the communities, and adults sometimes threatened that he'd do the same to them if they didn't behave properly.

The horror Dayan felt now was nearly as bad, as he listened to Paul's account of life in Yugoslavia before his escape across the Austro-Yugoslav border. This was during the period when Tito's popularity was being boosted by the Westania Times observers from Belgrade, who considered him an ally. They reported that his leadership, along with Yugoslavia's thirty-two military divisions, constituted the greatest equalizing military force in the region.

And everything Max had told Dayan about the death of Thomash was confirmed now by Paul. He also told Dayan about the suicides of Dr. Vedrano, Aladdin, and many others. Paul said he'd been on furlough when Max was killed in the Cablo hills. He then gave Dayan a tattered excerpt from a Belgrade newspaper, even though he did so reluctantly. It stated:

A car carrying some foreign spies was machine-gunned while evading the soldiers on duty at a checkpoint last week. None of the occupants survived, however a lot of subversive material was retrieved, including flags representing some Western countries. It's been established that these flags were distributed by a certain Philip Moravaz from Belgrade, a former Western spy killed in 1944. The items found in the car were being delivered by Angelica Moravaz, his daughter, who was a passenger acting as his replacement courier between a Western country and some local reactionary elements. The investigation continues.

Dayan read through it twice, and then crushed the paper in his fists. "I can't believe this, it's obviously not true."

"I'm very sorry, Dayan," Paul said, "but unfortunately, it is."

Dayan looked at him bewildered. "Yes, yes, I believe you. It's just—I can't accept it with my heart since I wanted to marry Angelica. But my mind knows it has probably happened, at least about the killing." Dayan went silent for a moment while he tried to compose himself, then looked at Paul with an expression of sincerity. "But they always have to exaggerate things, don't they?"

"I know they do, but your mother told me more—that Angelica was looking for you."

"You talked with my mother?"

"It was just before leaving. I promised her I'd try to find you."

Dayan took Paul's hand in his. "Thank you." Then he said with an effort: "When you were in the village, did you ever see her? Angelica?"

"Only briefly. She lived in your mother's house and helped care for her, but finally she went back to Belgrade. There she found the ruins of her former home, and learned that her father had died on Easter morning—the day of the big Allied air raid. She also looked for you and your father before returning from all the devastation to Cablo."

Dayan put his hands over his eyes, and Paul threw an arm across his friend's shoulder. After a moment Dayan straightened himself. "They couldn't even treat dogs worse than that," he said. "I remember you never liking them."

"No—that was Smilko," Paul said, "my brother."

"So it was. He'd always run away—and the dogs were chasing after him. Where is he now?"

"He's lost, along with the other men Lazar was searching for." Quickly Paul's eyes teared up, so he brushed them away. "Let's sit down, there's so much to tell you."

Dayan was glad to sit, still weakened by the news of Angelica's death. But there was so much more to learn. Paul told him about Lazar's death at the Austro-Yugoslav border, where his corpse had been left on a hill within sight of patrols, becoming prey to vultures and foxes. It was soon a skeleton used as a symbol by the Titoists to intimidate anyone suspected of planning to flee. Brought to the spot of his bones, they could see that nobody escaped the people's justice.

Paul had been a frontier soldier then. He couldn't bear seeing the dishonored skeleton of the man who'd been killed while searching for his own brother and other countrymen. One night while on duty, he seized the arms of Lazar's skeleton and managed to escape with them to freedom.

"And where have you buried Lazar's arms?"

"Let's go and I'll show you," Paul said.

After a long walk, the two eventually reached inner Munich and the ruins of St. Peter's Church. Paul pointed to a chandelier shattered when the church was destroyed by exploding bombs, and it lay amongst the many fragments of the stone walls. "There," Paul whispered. "It's Lazar—covered with flowers. But not his fingers, they're still at the border."

Dayan motioned Paul to lead him to the exact spot. They uncovered Lazar's whitened arm bones, and on one of them was the place where the bone had mended after he'd fallen from a pear tree when he was still a young boy. Thomash had put a cast on it.

Dayan crossed himself. "You're right," he said, "I can tell it's Lazar." They bowed their heads and prayed silently.

After the long walk back to the Yugoslav camp, Paul and Dayan found Colonel Obradovich in great distress while holding a letter in his hands. "What happened?" Dayan whispered to Tell, who was standing beside the colonel.

Tell leaned forward. "It's word from his children."

"Colonel, I hope your children aren't ill, are they?" Dayan asked sympathetically.

"No! It's worse than that! Much worse!"

Dayan was shocked. "My God! I hope they haven't died—"

"It's even worse than that!" Obradovich said while springing to his feet and pacing back and forth. He walked to the window, stood looking out a minute and then turned, his expression distraught. "They're calling me Comrade!" he shouted. "My children! My own children!" He then tore the letter into pieces and dropped it into the wastebasket.

Dayan didn't know what to say. After a moment he said hesitantly: "Sir, I hate to change the subject, but I can testify to this young man here with me. He's from a neighboring village to my own. Please let him stay, he wants to emigrate when he can."

"Yes!" Paul broke in eagerly. "To Australia! That's where my friend is on a ship somewhere. I want to go and see him."

"To Australia? That sounds like a grand idea," Obradovich quipped. "And I'd love to send my children all the way to Australia with you."

As the days passed by, Dayan suddenly felt an eagerness to finish his poem now. He was holding a deep emptiness within him, and had taken many wounds to his heart. This somehow made his writing come easier too—as it translated better into words. For this reason he didn't want Margaret to be too close to him right now, since he was afraid she'd heal all his internal wounds, and thus he'd lose his impetus to work on *KATYN*. Schubert's saying that his music was born out of sorrow served Dayan now as a guide.

Margaret, still unaware of what was happening, moved innocently towards him while he retreated. And not knowing his past, she pressed him with invitations to visit her home. These notes were signed with the nickname Mutti. They even included tickets for a concert, the theater or an opera too, which she'd bought for the two of them. They also made enough time for deep conversations where Margaret finally became aware of some of the sources to his troubles.

Later Dayan was grateful when she insisted they attend the class annual dance together; for he knew she was only trying to help him. But although such distractions offered a minor escape, they were still only temporary. Soon he would be swept up in events that made dances and operas seem as remote as the faraway moon.

It all started when some posters appeared on the bulletin boards in Munich announcing the upcoming celebration for 100 years of freedom of the press in Germany—dating back to 1848. Dayan decided this would offer him the perfect opportunity to make known all the murderous crimes that were committed in the meantime, which had been merged together into his poem *KATYN*.

Since there were no more Missions of Tito or Stalin visiting in Munich area camps, and no UNRRA rats were there either, Dayan believed it would be an advantageous time to try it. It would be the first real attempt he'd be making to the outside world on this; and he wasn't doing it for himself, but for all the innocents who had vanished helplessly. It was his job to see that their deaths weren't forgotten in vain.

He also got and idea to try something different, so he carefully made a bed of daisies for the arms of Lazar's skeleton, then swathed the bones in a clean cloth, and went to the Westania Times office building—where he told them about an interesting case he wanted to discuss. It concerned a man's attempt to escape from across the border. Dayan was sure such an explanation would arouse their curiosity.

And he was right. They mentioned a case where a man had recently escaped from Czechoslovakia in a self-built plane, and said they wanted to hear his similar story.

"My case is much more sensational than that one," Dayan told them. "And in addition, I have a living witness to prove it."

He told them of the French Captain Danjou, commander of Legionnaires at the Camaron battle in Mexico, 1863. While he lay dying, his soldiers swore on his wooden hand to never surrender. "One member of the surviving Legion," Dayan told his impressed listeners, "retrieved Danjou's hand and it was later taken back to France."

"It now rests in the Hall of Honor at Legion Headquarters in North Africa." Dayan paused while taking a moment to compose himself. "Similarly, I also swear on the bones of a friend—on his very arms—not to stop until I make known the hidden crimes committed at Katyn, Trieste and the Austro-Yugoslav border."

The men leaned forward, staring in fascination as he revealed Lazar's snow-white arm bones, which had been cleansed and bleached by the Alpine sun and rain. There was silence as the men waited for him to control his emotions and go on.

"All I'm asking for, gentlemen," Dayan's voice was stronger now, "is that you help me bury these bones in dignity at any Allied cemetery in Western Europe. Greek Orthodox priests should officiate, for that was this man's faith. When you come to the service, you'll be able to interview the man who brought these bones from the border and hid them in the ruins of St. Peter's Church."

After a whispered discussion, his listeners told him they'd hold a conference with some higher authorities, and get back to him with their answer.

When nothing was heard back after ten days, Dayan returned to the newspaper office. But the man in charge professed not to know anything about the matter, and said they were too busy packing boxes to move to a new building. When Dayan gave him a short resume of his request, the man reluctantly remembered and said the authorities had decreed such a request must be officially issued from the Yugoslav government in Belgrade.

Too full of anger and frustration to make a reply, Dayan turned to go. "But wait!" the man said. "All of us here were impressed by your story and," here he looked down with embarrassment, "we did a little something on our own. Not much, but it might help a little."

Dayan reacted joyfully. "On your own?" he said. "Yes—that's how it should be!"

The man handed him a thick manila envelope. "We collected this money amongst ourselves as a gift to the man's family. It's for his burial, you don't need much space really. As I remember you're talking only about the man's arm bones."

Meanwhile, some of the men from his last visit were drifting into the outer office. They listened curiously to the exchange, but they could see that Dayan was displeased.

"I'll take this, gentlemen," he burst out angrily, "so that I can throw it right back in your faces." He slashed open the envelope and, removing some paper money, flung it towards the surprised men, who stepped back more puzzled than alarmed.

"I threw twenty times as much into the swollen Isar river not too long ago, and that was pure gold. It's obvious you're hoping to absolve your feelings of guilt by giving me money, but you can't."

The staff remained speechless as Dayan turned around and raced out the door. A moment later, before anyone had moved an inch, he was back in again. "I'm sorry I lost my temper," he said. "I apologize, let me tell you a story about a wise man of long ago."

"Go ahead," someone said. The others looked bewildered at this, wondering what he had to say.

Dayan told them that before anyone understood anything about physiology, there was a scholar whose wisdom was challenged by some people who knew him. Thinking to expose him as a charlatan, they propped up a corpse before him and went away. When they returned later, the corpse had fallen over freely. Now angry about it, the people taunted the wise man, and asked him why it had happened. He replied, "Because the man lacked something inside."

"And that applies to us today," Dayan told the men gathered in the newspaper office. He then left and this time he didn't return.

Dayan had also been deeply disturbed by the casual words said by the Westania Times newsman. Any arms which died while stretching across a border between tyranny and freedom, and had sought to break across the Iron Curtain, needed a vast, open space. Their rattling should be heard as far as free men can reach.

He went to St. Peter's Church and there, above the shattered chandelier, he swore that he'd never surrender, just as those brave French Legionnaires had also done over Danjou's wooden hand. This new oath committed him to work on *KATYN* day and night.

Meanwhile, he read in the newspapers that due to the switch from the Reichsmark to a new German currency, there were funds available to be spent on restoring the Munich area churches. Accordingly, he and Paul hurriedly gathered up Lazar's bones and hid them inside the chapel at the Yugoslav camp.

For the following nine days, Dayan didn't see Margaret while he worked urgently on his poem. When they did meet at the university, she begged him to visit with her mother if he cared anything at all for the feelings of others. He was fond of Mrs. Neuman, so this plea touched him and he agreed to go, but insisted that the visit must be kept short.

"Mutti only wants to see you," Margaret told him. "She's beginning to think she only imagined there's someone like you."

As they walked towards her home, Margaret sensed that Dayan was under some terrible pressure she didn't know about. By the time they'd reached her front gate, she was urging him to be strong.

"I am strong," Dayan replied. And suddenly he did feel strong and young, and almost carefree. "As proof of it, I've been staying away from you for nine days!"

When they came in through the front door, Frau Neuman held Dayan's hands in hers for a long time. "I told you, Margaret, he'd come back—I said it over and over again. These hands tell me the truth."

That evening it was agreed that Dayan and Margaret would take a summer trip to the mountains soon. She had a bicycle of her own and Dayan could use her late brother's.

A few days later, Paul asked Dayan to help him fill out his papers for emigration to Australia. He had some worries about going. "Are you sure Australia is as far away as I can go?" he asked.

Dayan assured him that it was.

"You see," Paul said, "my mother told me that if I didn't find Smilko, I should go as far away as I could and forget the whole world. If it weren't for her," he admitted, "I'd stay here in Munich and join the new Western army."

"Forget it," Dayan told him, "such an army doesn't exist."

"Yes, it does," Paul insisted. "Ask Colonel Obradovich. The Americans and Germans were here today, talking to him."

Dayan hurried off to find out what was going on. He found Obradovich and the former supply clerk, now even skinnier than ever, with Tell carrying their fire safety equipment. They were inspecting some buildings. They told him that the Yugoslav camp was to be rebuilt soon for the new German Army, and that last Sunday's service had been the last in the chapel.

"Big bulldozers will come in and crush everything into rubble, it's closing," Obradovich declared. "The experts in psychological warfare say this location has a sentimental meaning to the Germans, and they want their army headquarters to be on this site." He pointed to an area already leveled with some workers busy surveying there.

Dayan wasn't paying much attention to the details. "Has anybody gone over to the chapel since last Sunday?" he asked anxiously, while hoping to disguise his feelings.

Obradovich thought a moment. "Of course, but I don't know how many. I saw a few of the regulars go in and an American with a young woman, a pretty refugee from Czechoslovakia, I believe."

Dayan's heartbeat quickened. "What did he look like?"

"Oh, like all Americans do. Easy-going and happy." Obradovich then thought for a moment. "There was one unusual thing though, the girl asked for the general's portrait, so we gave it to her."

"Was the American's name Jimmy?"

"Maybe, but I didn't pay much attention," Obradovich said rather impatiently while looking at the fire equipment hanging around his waist. He wanted to get on with his inspection. "But they must be kidding about a German army happening so soon, even I wouldn't make that lie up." He turned and started checking wastebaskets.

Sensing Dayan's disappointment, Tell added, "I think that American looked familiar to me."

Dayan quickly nodded and rushed off to the chapel. He was relieved to find undisturbed the place where Lazar's arm bones were hidden. However, the paintings of Helen Keller and the Statue of Liberty had been taken away, along with the portrait of Mihailovic.

Later that evening, Dayan and Paul removed Lazar's bones from their hiding place. Dayan untied the wire which bound them together and handed that to Paul. "On your way to Australia," he said, "where the ocean is the deepest, throw the wire in. Your mother would like you to do that."

Paul stuck the bent wire into his pocket, crossed himself and then kissed the white bones, now in Dayan's hands.

The mountain trip Dayan and Margaret were following was arranged hurriedly; Dayan was able to borrow a rucksack from his landlord. Their plan was to go by train and then ride their bikes, which were in the baggage car, while following the same route Dayan had taken three years earlier.

"I want to ask you something, but don't get mad at me," Margaret said after they'd left the train at Kiefersfelden and started to pedal away.

Dayan knew she was sensing something already.

Chapter 22

"Why did you wear that pack even on the train? People were laughing at you." They were pedaling side by side and Margaret put her hand on Dayan's arm—intending to convey that she was only curious, while not being critical.

Dayan hesitated, then replied, "Well, I wouldn't laugh at them under the same circumstances." To change the subject he added, "Margaret, look at how beautiful it is here!"

They stopped for a moment to relish feeling the cold, clear air of the nearby Alps. They marveled at the slopes which were thick with colorful wildflowers, and gazed high into the distant snow peaks. Then they went on, eventually turning into a narrow road with a tiny hut up at the end, the home of a cowherd's family. Here they left their bikes and walked to it, the highest around, near the Austro-German border. The family they found outside was eager to talk to strangers and invited them in.

Dayan was glad they found hospitable people with whom he could leave Margaret while he went on his lonely mission—it was right for it to be lonely, he believed—to give Lazar a proper burial. With Margaret safely inside the warm, pleasant cottage—he set off with the pack on his shoulders, assuring her that he'd return in a few hours. A pick was leaning against the wall of the hut; he took it along with him.

After an hour's climb, he came to the big cross at the Austro-German border, and a little while later he was at the foot of a tall beech tree on which, over three years ago, he'd carved the cross with the words: *IN HOC SIGNO VINCES*. The mountain silence was all around him as he recalled the memories of that night. The carved cross was larger now, for the bark had died back as the tree had grown, and with it so had the letters. There was no trace of human life within sight.

"This beautiful place is what you deserve, Lazar," he murmured. He thought about the man in the Westania Times newspaper office who said that Lazar's bones wouldn't need much room, since they were, after all, only the arms.

The day was clear now, and the distant views of both Germany and Austria lay before him. Dayan began to dig a deep grave, the size of Lazar's arms, right in front of the cross with the devout words on the tree. He placed the bones into the recess, and covered them with the fresh wildflowers and the dried daisies taken from the other border, and covered the soil carefully so the grave couldn't be noticed.

The serenity of the distant Alps along with the glorious vistas here, he thought, made it a fitting resting place for Lazar's arms. Here they *would* have enough room.

When he returned to the hut, he found the cowman's wife giving Margaret a lesson in cow milking. The two women laughed together as Margaret managed to squeeze a thin trickle of milk from the patient animal's udder. Dayan replaced the pick against the wall and stood watching them for a moment, forcing himself back to the present sunny day and the sound of laughter, and away from those dark memories of the past.

After thanking the peasants for their hospitality—and for the jar of fresh milk—the young couple set off in the opposite direction from which Dayan had just come. He'd taken the precaution to put some wildflowers into the gap in his knapsack created by the removal of Lazar's bones, hoping that Margaret wouldn't notice any change. But he shouldn't have bothered since she was absorbed in the beauty of the alpine mountainside, of being out of the city—while feeling free and young.

Agile and swift, she followed Dayan easily as they peddling along the path, which was becoming fainter as they climbed higher. "Where are you leading me?" she asked. "There's almost no trail here."

"Every way leads somewhere," Dayan answered. He turned from her smiling, rosy face to look at the mountain peaks. Hearing her pedal behind him up into the mountain silence gave him an impulse to keep going forward, faster and faster. Without realizing it, he'd increased his pace so that when he reached a small plateau, he discovered that Margaret wasn't in sight.

A single pine tree stood at the edge of the plateau, which was also thick with wildflowers. Dayan hurried to it, careful to tread lightly on the flowers and the surrounding grass. He took off his pack and was about to go in search of Margaret, when she finally appeared. Slowly, with his arms half-outstretched, he went to meet her. She too had slowed her steps as she walked waist deep through the tall grass. She was smiling radiantly, but the smile didn't entirely hide her inward shyness and confusion. To Dayan, her smile was as bright as the sun was over the distant Alps.

The wildflowers were taller here; they even touched her breasts. Now Dayan's arms spread wide and his steps were faster, until there was nothing left between them; nothing except for the desire to be even closer. Feeling that her body was relaxed and happy in his arms, he gently brought her down until their bodies were hidden deep within the sweet-smelling mountain flowers—which swayed violently at first, then with a gentle rhythm, and at last they were as still as the two bodies which had disturbed them.

Margaret broke the silence long after the flowers above them were motionless. Lifting her head off his arm, she brushed his hand with her cheek and asked, "Where have your hands been all these years?"

"Always busy," he said, stroking her hair with his fingers.

"Doing what?"

"Well, gathering kindling for my mother when I was a child. Have you ever seen, far away in the night, the light of hearth flames shining through an open door?"

"Never. Go on, tell me more!"

"Let's see. I taught the girls how to write on their slates. And Tobo—I taught him how to carve letters on a piece of wood."

She ignored the last words and focused on the first ones. "Girls? What girls?"

Thinking of Liuba, Veselinka and of Yana, he replied, "Not girlfriends, Margaret. Just girls. They were shepherdesses in the hills near Cablo, my home." He looked away towards the mountain peaks, remembering the innocence of that peaceful time. Then, sensing Margaret's feminine need for absolute assurance of his devotion, he took her into his arms again. The wildflowers swayed more rhythmically now, for these desires didn't need words and they both let them take over the moment.

The sun was just going down beyond the highest peaks when he again picked up the conversation, prompted by Margaret's question earlier about his hands. He thought of telling her about the poem *KATYN*, but knew he could only hint at writing since it wasn't finished. Meanwhile, Margaret was waiting for him to speak. "Once I made a wreath," he said, and he pulled a bundle of flowers together and buried his face in them.

Margaret leaned forward, trying to see his hidden face. "A wreath for war heroes?"

"Yes, for heroes. But not those the world knows of as such. People think of heroes as those who are the conquerors in battle, but my heroes are the victims. They remain unknown, because their heroism lies in their faith for which they died for." It was an effort to disclose his deepest feelings to Margaret as he was nervously putting together more and more flowers, unaware of what his hands were doing.

Margaret held out her hands. "Let me hold them for you, Dayan." Taking the flowers, she buried her face in them as he'd done earlier. The fragrance wasn't like that of the flowers cultivated in a garden. It was a fresher smell captured from the sun and the clear mountain breezes.

"Let's stay here tonight, I won't let you freeze," Dayan whispered.

Taking her silence as consent, he held out his arms. He gently pulled her up and they went to the lone pine tree for shelter during the night. Once there, they laid down and snuggled together to maintain warmth, then slept as the last rays of the sun fell upon them, before disappearing behind the distant, darkening mountains.

In the morning, they toasted each other with the milk the cowherd's wife had given them, before starting on the trail downward and then back to Munich, where they went directly to Margaret's house to announce their engagement to her mother. She was overjoyed to hear the news, and blessed them while standing by the bookcase which held the works of Goethe.

Chapter 22

Later that day there was one last thing Dayan hoped to do—he must remind Paul of his promise to dispose of the wire which had bound Lazar's arm bones together. So after searching through an atlas, he went to see him, out to one of the last displaced persons camps still open in the area.

"You must throw the wire into the sea when you come to this area on your trip through the Indian Ocean," Dayan showed him on the map. "The waters there are very deep and it will never be found in any fish."

He related the story of how the tyrant Polycrates' precious ring was thrown into the ocean to preserve his good fortune, while the next day it was discovered inside the stomach of a fish that was caught, showing how lucky the tyrant was.

Respectfully, Paul agreed to carry out this final assignment. Then Dayan threw an arm around his shoulder. "And that's it for you," he said. "For me—I still have more work to do."

While walking down the barracks on his way out, Dayan heard a noise, and through the opened doorway he saw Obradovich. He was busy doing one of his duties as a fire inspection officer, and emptying the ashtrays in the offices. The former colonel greeted him sullenly. "These damn Germans," he said, "they smoke like chimneys now that they're getting American cigarettes." Angrily he dumped a large ashtray filled with cigarette butts into a bucket, sending up another ash cloud which set him to coughing loudly.

Dayan lightly slapped him on the back to ease his cough. His eyes wandered around the office, and suddenly he exclaimed, "Look, Colonel!" He pointed to a photograph on one of the desks. "It's Masaryk!"

Obradovich continued to cough and sniffle while Dayan went over to the desk and studied the picture. In it, the great statesman was bending over a printed text while another man stood next to him.

The words—*Our First Constitution*—were printed in large letters on top of it. On the bottom it read—*Philadelphia, U.S.A., 1918*. Tucked into the frame at the left was a snapshot of a young G.I. with a pretty girl.

"It's from when Czechoslovakia gained its freedom," Dayan said, "and now it's left with communism. The same thing has happened to our country, so what was the West thinking?"

"You think they were thinking? Don't be silly, now let's go." Bent with age and burdened with his heavy fireman's equipment, Obradovich hurried Dayan out through the door.

***

To Dayan, the loss of Angelica while Margaret became a part of his life was proof of the words Thomash had used so often: *God takes with one hand and gives with the other.*

Dayan believed this, but he still felt the need to influence those events which cut deeply into his very being. He wanted to participate and contribute to the fullest extent of his power. His strength seemed to be growing, nourished by the warmth of his relationship with Margaret.

They were discussing plans for marriage now. For a year there had been rumors about a mass-immigration to the United States —to be sponsored by the Truman administration. Some 200,000 people would be in on the first quota, and Margaret and Dayan hoped to be a part of it.

The two talked for hours about this glorious possibility; they'd be welcomed by the Statue of Liberty, assured for the first time in years that they wouldn't become suppressed or needy. They'd become citizens of Captain Tucker's country, and of Jimmy's too, whose greatest problem had been—*why can't two reasonable men talking together make sense?*

Dayan's own problem, to make the destiny of thousands of Katyn-like victims known to everyone, seemed equally important too. And he believed his best opportunity to accomplish this was at the centennial celebration for German's having freedom of the press. It was the perfect setting, he thought, the best way to prove how truly free they are!

23

Who Will Listen

Eagerly Dayan walked through the streets of Munich. His poem *KATYN* was in the breast pocket of the second-hand suit he wore, an engagement gift from Mrs. Neuman. It fit surprisingly well considering she'd taken it from her late husband's closet.

"Bring your poem and we'll record every word," a man had said to him yesterday in the Munich University employment office, who identified himself as a member of the opening committee. Now as he walked to the new Westania Times building, recently renovated and rising seven stories high, the man's invitation seemed to hold great promise for *KATYN*.

Dayan was told they were looking for students with good voices to test-read before some recently repaired Magnetophon sound equipment. It was apparently developed during the war in Germany and used by Hitler to give faked *live* broadcasts. This allowed him to be safely away somewhere else as the recordings were being played over the radio.

This session they'd scheduled for today was in preparation for the grand re-opening of the building tomorrow on Armistice Day. "Be on time," he'd told Dayan, "as it's our renewed commitment to freedom of speech." It would also be for a great occasion; not only was it the hundredth anniversary of freedom of the German press as proclaimed at St. Paul's Church in 1848, but it would provide a semi-official meeting place for politicians and journalists under the auspices of the city of Munich.

Dayan looked forward to the opportunity to read *KATYN* and have it finally heard. In contrast, nearly all of the German students had turned down the same chance, considering the words *freedom of speech* to be a trap.

As he entered the Westania Times building, Dayan straightened his shoulders and strode between the two lines of marble pillars. The bent shoulders of his student days, he reflected, when as a young scholar he'd sought the truth, were gone. Now he knew the truth. He'd seen it and lived it, and was ready to make it known before the world. He only wished his black-market military shoes with worn heels and wrinkled leather were like those worn in Fugen during the war. Then what a brave sound they'd make as he marched forward to read his poem!

At the entrance to the main hall was a banner that read: *Is It Live or Is It Recorded?* Once inside, he was met by the man he'd talked to yesterday at the university. He thanked Dayan for being on time and directed him to go into the recording room through a side door.

After entering the next room, one of the technicians was there waiting and said he'd record Dayan for ten minutes while he spoke in the sound booth. "When you see the green light you start to speak, and when the red light comes on it's finished recording. Talk clearly into the microphone, there's a clock inside to keep track of the time," he said.

Once the technician prepared the recorder, he had Dayan go into the sound booth and wait for the green light. After it turned on, Dayan took a deep breath and began to read the opening stanzas of his poem, which recounted the atrocities of the Second World War. They were carefully prepared verses that sounded dithyrambic, like those of Serbian epic poems so admired by Goethe.

He watched the clock and finished just before the red light came on, perfect timing he though for what he needed. He stepped out of the sound booth as the technician re-wound the tape. Here the technician played it from the beginning through their loudspeaker system so others could listen throughout the office building. The recording of his poem sounded amazing, it had no hissing or crackling noises, and it sounded just like Dayan was saying it in person.

Dayan and the technician listened intently to the entire poem. They both nodded at how great it was, and as it finished three other men came into the recording room. One introduced himself as the chairman, while the other was his assistant. The third was the committee man who'd directed Dayan here.

"It sounds very impressive. Now tell us something about yourself, young man," the assistant said.

"Sorry," Dayan apologized, "one reaches that stage in life where he lives for others and can't talk about himself." He was offered a chair.

"Your country has given a lot already," the chairman said when they were all seated. "That was proven by her concessions after the war." He smiled at Dayan. "The Big Three at Tehran and Yalta were wrong about her future role."

"I'm Yugoslav, not German," Dayan said. "But I agree they were wrong, and about lots of other things besides that."

"So you're not in favor of progress?"

"How can you call any of that progress?"

"Well, progress of—recording itself." The chairman seemed to be at a loss, and none of the others came to his rescue. He gestured rather uncertainly to the recording machines.

Dayan remained silent. Then he rose, facing his listeners. "Didn't you hear—didn't I just read about the most inhuman events which took place in man's recent history? About lampshades being made from human skin in Buchenwald? About thousands of soldiers and civilians disappearing?"

He paused while looking at them somberly, and then went on in a lowered voice. "It was Katyn—in fact, many Katyns." He was clenching the poem tightly in his right hand, but now he opened it. "The poem *KATYN* isn't really finished. There must be an epilogue."

There was an uncomfortable silence. At last the committee man said, "Apparently we don't speak the same language." He gestured towards the acoustical equipment. "We're dealing with the development of a new recording system here, testing these products for improvement. It's going to be a huge industry, as it will allow for the taping of commercials and radio programs entirely."

"Are you telling me that you're not interested in poems, mine or anyone's?"

"We're interested in recording sound, to make it the best it can be." He picked up a magnetic tape and looked at it like it was printed money. "This tape that goes into the Magnetophon recorder is the future—it's what the world has waited for, and now they will have it!" He went to hand Dayan some of the recording tape. Dayan shook his head.

"I came here to be heard, for my words to have meaning beyond just sound," he said. "So who will listen now, if all your focus is on the sound alone. A sort of new Babylonian Tower—the meaningless babble of voices—so long as they're sufficiently loud and clear."

"They will listen when you come back tomorrow to recite at the celebration! This was done just to prepare the recorded tape. I thought you already understood that?"

Dayan could scarcely believe his ears. "Gentlemen," he said grimly, "what I just recited was about the massacre and murder of thousands and thousands of people, and you barely even seem concerned!" He turned towards the door.

The men looked at each other puzzled and confused. They felt they'd offended him, but didn't understand why.

"Wait, sir." the chairman offered. "Please don't take it this way, we're only doing our jobs."

Dayan couldn't suppress a cynical laugh. "That's what they all say, even at the military tribunals like the Nuremburg trials," he said. "And who are those three men wearing heavy boots who've been peering in from the halls? They seem to signal with their eyes, never talking out loud."

The chairman looked puzzled so the assistant answered. "Oh," he said, "those are some Russians here for training. You see, the Soviets sent their own technicians, they're just as interested in recording sound as we are." The others all nodded in agreement.

The chairman then stood up to leave, and told Dayan that their time was up. "Tomorrow you'll be able to see this in a better light.

We're on the cusp of an amazing technology, where taped sounds live. Thanks for coming in!"

As Dayan left, he felt resolve having put his words into their recording machines, and perhaps tomorrow would be another opportunity to get his voice heard. It reminded him of a ballad he'd heard in which a weeping angel asked God not to create steel for chains. But God said he'd give man enough sense to break those chains, and steel has enough good uses to justify its existence. Here Dayan must put this opportunity to good use himself, he thought.

Now, as nighttime was approaching Dayan welcomed it; he wanted it to be pitch black so he could hide himself in the darkness. But outside the street lights came on, so he turned and went in the direction of an isolated park, which was lightly covered with the first snow of the season. It was deep enough to show footsteps as he trudged along, but it wasn't so deep like in Gradina ten years ago, when his mother followed behind him in her moccasins.

He walked up and leaned against a chestnut tree, his eyelids closed against the snowy night until, at last, from the complete silence on the street, he knew it was empty. There he wondered why he hadn't been able to get his point across earlier about *KATYN*, until giving up and continuing on home. It was late into the night before Dayan eventually made peace with himself, before drifting off into sleep.

Although the city of Munich had won a citation for clearing the war ruins and widening its streets, the one Dayan took on his way back to the Westania Times building the following night was scarcely passable. With the poem *KATYN* under his right arm, he casually walked along while reciting some new verses for its epilogue.

The cold evening came without a trace left of last night's snow, but there was a dense mist that hung in the air. It was occasionally pierced by strong lights beaming from the Westania Times building, which also illuminated the ruins of the street. It wasn't unusual to see people digging in them in search of furniture, important papers—even the skeletons of their beloved ones. But there was something odd about the three men he saw digging in one of the piles; they were too fat and heavy to be Germans, whose starvation during and after the war had reduced their shape and stature.

Dayan was chanting verses to himself now in his thoughts. He became aware of some steps behind him; someone was walking at the same pace. Annoyed by their intrusive insistence, he quickened his own steps, only to hear the other steps quicken as well. He tried to ignore them while concentrating on the verses.

Suddenly the steps behind him were much closer and then there was silence. He felt a sharp pressure under his left shoulder blade, which at first felt warm, even hot, but then cold. There was an agonizing pain. Holding his breath, he stopped—rigid and yet shivering. Heat and cold were streaming through his body. He swayed to the left and saw blood on the hard ground.

Dayan's vision blurred and it seemed to him that he was surrounded by a huge crowd of men, who changed from giants to dwarfs, all fat and wearing boots. They pressed close to him, uttering a single Russian word: "*davai.*" Moving his right arm painfully, he tucked the poem under his left armpit and then pulled a knife from his shoulder blade.

The legion of men, now the size of giants, encircled him closer chanting over and over: "*davai, davai.*" He felt a hand on his chest and swayed to the right, striking with the knife at a blurred figure. The thrust was followed by a long scream like that of a strangled goat. He jabbed again and heard a weakened moan.

His hands still firmly on Dayan's chest, the attacker toppled, his mouth gaping and his eyes wide open. Dayan was falling with him, but two pairs of heavy hands grabbed his elbows. The man on the left was pulling at the rolled pages of *KATYN*. Dayan cast the knife away, but before it could be heard rattling on a nearby pile of concrete, he threw his body to one side, and discovered that of the entire poem, only a single bloody page remained. He grabbed it as blood trickled through his fingers.

Now a car with—*PRESS, Do Not Delay*—signs backed out from a side-street blowing its horn. Two of the attackers began dragging their dying accomplice towards it. The woman driver screamed harshly at them from the backing car. She jumped out, and hastily the three of them managed to lift and push the limp body into the car's trunk. The woman snatched the bloody pages from the man who clutched them. Furiously she took off her gloves and slapped the two men each twice across the face.

"Fools!" she said in her harsh voice. "You were ordered to stab him at close quarters and get his poem to shut him up. I come back and you messed it up!" She made to slap the face of the corpse as well, but changed her mind and spat at him. Then she gestured to her followers to slam down the trunk lid. She hurried around to the driver's seat, the two men jumped into the back of the car and it shot off, leaving a trail of dirty exhaust in the cold night air.

Painfully Dayan crawled to the corner, mostly on his right side. The street was empty. His progress was slow as he dragged himself along until the bulk of the Westania Times building could be seen. But now he didn't want to crawl any more.

This is no way for a man to end up, Dayan thought to himself, even when he's dying. So, with sweat dripping down his face and his armpits, slowly, with agonizing pain, he managed to pull himself to his feet. He began to walk, staggering, stumbling, and it seemed that the walls were leaning away from him—everything was moving, leaving him behind. He tried to call for help, but was unable to utter a single word. Every breath brought more pain.

Leaning against a wall with his right arm, he beckoned towards any passersby he saw with his left hand. No one responded and he wasn't surprised; the hand was bloody and twisted around the only remaining page of his poem, just as everyone remembered the twisted hands that Hitler and his Gauleiters had used to destroy Europe.

A moment later an old couple with a dog on a leash passed by and the dog stopped and sniffed Dayan, who naturally smelled of blood. The animal let out a strange little yelp, and its master quickly pulled it away. For a moment Dayan wanted to hit the dog as a means to attract the owner's attention, but decided against striking an innocent pet.

No, there was only one way left for him, and that way was forward, like Jesus on Golgotha. And once Golgotha was reached, the people could be reached; one could speak to them and they'd listen—and God as well. This thought kept him moving forward while staying on his feet. He hastened towards the Westania Times building as best he could, and despite the pain.

At the corner of the building, exhausted, he leaned back against its smooth marble wall. It was time for the evening news which appeared each night at the top of the building, moving across in large electric letters. People stood in scattered groups, looking up.

"They lie with their news," an elderly man said to the people clustered around him. "Heard the latest joke?"

They all looked at him expectantly. "Tell us, Doctor," somebody prompted him.

"During Hitler's time," he began, "the wagons were rolling on the rails, and now the rails are rolling away on wagons. You know where to?"

They shook their heads.

"To Stalin Dzhugashvili!" the Doctor said, laughing, and his audience obediently laughed with him. "The West called him *Good Uncle Joe,* but even if they baptized him in Westminster Abbey, he'd still be the same!"

His listeners nodded in agreement.

"The West better watch out," the Doctor continued, "they might think they've got us on ice, but just when they need us, we won't be waiting here anymore."

The scrawny, hungry-looking group laughed again. Dayan was so weak that even these thin, miserable Germans, who hadn't had proper food for three long years of occupation, looked like towers of strength to him. He was suddenly afraid he'd fall over, and felt himself sliding down the smooth marble wall. Steadying himself, he teetered towards the iron fence which enclosed the grounds of the building. The straight poles, each topped with a pigeon holding an olive branch in its beak, were connected by square rings at the bottom and the top.

While hanging onto the fence, Dayan looked back and saw that he'd left a large smear of blood on the smooth white wall, a smear as big as his body. Not too far above it were the windows of the hall where delegates of the seventy-two countries were taking their seats. Meanwhile, people hurried past him to the entrance. It seemed impossible that no one could notice him—or the dark-red smear of blood on the wall, but they didn't.

Hoping to attract their attention, he took off his gold ring and threw it towards the street. Surely someone would see the gleam of the circlet as it flew through the air and rolled on the ground. Again, no one noticed a thing, and he was so weak the ring landed only a few feet away, the sparkling diamond turned towards him.

He put his arms through the iron rods of the fence to support himself. The sharp edges cut into his flesh, but he didn't notice it. The weight of his body was pulling at his arms until they formed the letter V. Slowly he turned his head to the right, as Jesus was shown on the holy crucifix in Cablo's St. George Church.

As he did so, he saw all the windows above him alight. It was now packed with delegates holding a stormy session. Wounded and bleeding outside while feeling crucified against the iron fence, Dayan could hear angry voices raised in accusation and protest. He even caught words and whole phrases of it, as the shouting back and forth continued from the meeting hall.

A voice in Russian said, "You and your bourgeois democracy! You want to dominate the world economically—while we strive to free the last slaves of capitalism, wherever they may be." The sound of frenetic applause followed, with cries of "Bravo Devourin!"

Another voice said, "I protest in the name of the world! I especially denounce the shooting down of passenger planes, the killing of innocents. Democracy! and Freedom! translates into Tyranny! and Slavery!" Then more applause, but restrained without bravos. The listeners weren't eager to involve themselves in further bickering.

During the lull, with less of their discussion reaching him, Dayan sank deeper into his semi-conscious state. He was aroused as a renewed bustle took place nearby. Only dimly aware of the cold darkness around him, his delirium was concentrated on the nearest window above. There he imagined a fantastic scene taking place at the meeting, the same one on which he'd placed such high hopes for the future of men.

Each person present—all the delegates and newsmen, famous statesmen, and representatives from the East and West, had been given a pile of papers. However they became apprehensive when they observed the forbidding look of the people distributing the papers. Then as they began to read them, their hands started trembling because the letters were written with the human blood from many thousands of innocent, tortured, and massacred people. Most came from the bodies of peasants and shepherds killed in the Caucasus, the Carpathians and also the Balkans.

The end of each letter produced a cry from the massacred person, and the readers put their hands over their ears to ward off the horrible sounds of anguish being heard. To Dayan they sounded familiar, but far more real than the words he'd recorded last night on the magnetic tape. These were stronger, so strong that they created cracks in the very walls of the newly-reinforced Westania Times building. The fissures went straight down to the ground and below, all the way to its hardened foundation.

Horrified at this, the men in the hall hurried to the main desk to stack the letters on it, saying it was none of their fault. But even as they spoke new missives kept arriving. The stacks back at their desks grew and grew towards the ceiling. New cries were heard and the cracks in the walls widened, until finally a huge bundle containing twelve thousand notes hurtled through and landed in the middle of the chairman's desk.

Dayan wished he could throw the bloody sheet from his hand, all that remained of his poem, so it landed at the very top of the pile. At first it would be dripping with blood and then it would pour out, until it covered them all in blood as they ran away.

Chapter 23

The cracks in the building widened now and merged with the enlarged horizon he saw. In Cablo years ago, he'd seen the high hills with deep gashes in them after lightning struck them; Goritza had told him they were formed from a saint who was chasing the devil. If those had been created by a saint, then these were surely formed through God.

Still feeling crucified in the cold night with his arms stuck through the railing, Dayan continued to see visions. An hour ago, stumbling along the ruined walls, everything seemed to be receding. Now the whole globe was moving towards him with its vast intricacy of configurations: people, cultures, cities, temples, shrines, churches and especially graveyards. All rushed towards him, and he watched from a great distance above. Goritza would be happy to see him so tall and high.

Everything was speeding along, yet moving the fastest were the people going in all directions. Scientists from the West ran towards the East to whisper formulas; poets from the East hurried towards the West to murmur verses. Only one, a man in a white toga wearing tiny sandals, moved slowly and with great and modest dignity.

Stepping as if he was afraid to harm the earth on which he walked, he wore spectacles and his eyes were directed towards the temple he approached. This was Gandhi. Dayan wanted to shout, to warn him of the killer who awaited him, but was unable to because his throat was parched and he had no voice. He turned his head away; he didn't want to see Gandhi killed. Then he heard the great teacher's words spoken to his killer: *"You're too late."*

"You're too late," Dayan whispered. It meant to him that Gandhi, like Jesus, had accomplished his mission on earth, shedding no blood but his own. "But what about me?" Dayan asked himself, grieving the loss of *KATYN* and all the victims written into it. He decided to throw the single bloodied page down in front of him.

More than that he wanted to throw it straight into the face of the whole world—except for Gandhi. He tried to raise his arm, to release his fingers which clutched the single sheet of paper, but found that he couldn't. Was his arm paralyzed? He didn't think so.

No, it was God's design to keep him straight now and not let his arms take the shape of the letter V anymore, the false symbol of victory. The Poles and Yugoslavs hadn't lived under any real sign of victory, nor did half of the other people. Instead, they were betrayed by so many.

Then his eyelids closed heavily and firmly so he couldn't reopen them. But even with his eyes closed these pictures and thoughts still raced through his mind, while remembering the hundreds of thousands betrayed in many countries. He was all the more enraged because he knew it had happened to them exactly as Hitler and Goebbels had predicted all through the war.

Now he felt at ease and victorious over the whole scene, whose images were fading and dimming. Nothing mattered any more, neither his left hand, now stiffening like the iron fence he grasped, nor his fierce thirst. The muscles in his neck ached ever since he'd turned his head away to avoid witnessing Gandhi's assassination. But these discomforts he felt were a great blessing, for they brought him closer to Jesus. He too had been thirsty on the cross.

Dayan had reached Golgotha, and could talk to God.

24

To *KATYN*

The Southeastern news division at the Westania Times building was being addressed by its chief journalist: "Gentlemen," he said, "the news of this stabbing overshadows everything else being reported on for Armistice Day and the Centennial of the German Press."

"Maybe it's something we can make sensational," proposed the reporter for the Mediterranean area, who was nicknamed *Plato*.

"No, Plato! Can you imagine the headline: *Westania Times walls covered with innocent human blood!* We can't have it reflecting badly on us!" He squeezed the arms of his chair. "What would the East say? They're already gunning for us as it is."

"Do we know if the victim was innocent?" Plato asked. "Why was he here?"

The chief looked up from some briefing notes he had. "How strange. This morning in East Berlin," he said, "they're burying a Soviet technician who worked in our building, apparently rumored to be a spy. They say newly-formed East-German units will serve as his honor guard, maybe this is somehow related to the fellow who was stabbed outside yesterday."

The group remained silent for a moment, while they contemplated what to do next.

"Wait a minute," the chief said after looking over another report. "The stabbed man is fighting for his life right now on the second floor of St. Joseph's Hospital." He spread out a map of Munich. On it, the hospital was marked with a red cross. The others gathered around while he pointed with his thumb. "In room 21. Street cleaners found him this morning hanging on the fence outside our building, his body was as rigid and straight as a railing."

There was an incredulous murmur from the others.

The chief stared at the red cross on the map for a moment, as if it could tell him something; then he looked up. "The point is, gentlemen," he said, "it does appear this man came here to this building for some reason. But why? What does it mean?"

"Nothing at all, most likely," Plato responded.

The East European man chimed in: "There are lots of fights around here—soldiers and civilians mostly. Over black-market items or those German girls."

"Not to mention just plain holdups," Plato agreed.

"The motive wasn't robbery," the chief replied. "There was a gold ring found lying near him on the ground. It was evident he had something more on his mind. His hand was clenched so tightly they had trouble removing something from it." He looked at them with an odd expression. "What do you think was in that hand?"

Plato hazarded a guess. "Another ring?"

The chief shook his head. After opening his briefcase, he pulled out a manila envelope and removed the single bloody sheet of paper it had inside. At seeing the dried blood which saturated it, a wave of curiosity and revulsion went through the cluster of men.

"Since it happened outside our building, they gave me this to investigate. There's only one barely legible word here," the chief said, holding the paper up for all to see. "It says: *KATYN*."

"Katyn? Katyn?" the others repeated it to themselves and to each other, trying the word on their tongues and listening to it. The shape of the word left each man with his lips parted and his teeth revealed, as they appear on those who've suddenly died.

"Katyn," the chief echoed after them. "But what is Katyn?"

No one knew. The men stared at the bloody sheet which may have held an answer, but could no longer give it.

"Well, I'm going to find out," the chief said. "Any volunteers for St. Joseph's?" Carefully he replaced the paper in its envelope and slipped it back into his briefcase.

"Count me in!" both Plato and the East European reporter said as the three men hurried out. They got into the chief's car and headed for the hospital, discussing various possibilities as to the meaning of the attack on the unknown man. It was the chief's theory that the victim must be a scientist. Perhaps the Soviets had managed to steal a formula he'd written, all of it but this single page, code-named *KATYN*.

"It's our job to find out what the formula is about before this man dies."

The East European reporter spoke. "I've got a hunch this business has something to do with nuclear physics."

"Sure." Plato scoffed cynically. "Just like in the comic strips."

"In these days," the chief said, "it's a question of whether the comics reflect life or life reflects the comics. Either way, the idea is not so far-fetched considering atomic weapons already exist. This certainly isn't a joke, it may be the most serious task we've ever attempted. Think for a moment what would happen if the East managed to improve on these formulas before us."

His companions nodded solemnly. The chief stepped on the gas.

Dayan was in a hospital bed at the other end of the hall from where he'd stayed three years ago. He was forbidden to talk, let alone move. Nevertheless, hearing a noise outside his small room, he managed to move his head enough to see two hands fumbling at the window near the bottom of his bed. He tried to hold the catch down with his foot to keep the intruder out.

"Let us in!" The words were muffled, but he did his best to keep the window from being opened. Then he saw one of the hands hold up a bloody, wrinkled sheet of paper. *KATYN*!

He released the catch on the window and sank back into the pillows, exhausted by his effort, while a stranger climbed into the room. He tied a rope to the bed and threw it out the window. Soon another man clambered in. There were dirty footprints on his shoulders. He watched as a third man climbed in the same way, then pulled up the rope and closed the window.

The three news reporters showed Dayan their identification cards. "This paper that was found in your hand, it's covered in so much blood. We can only read one word, *KATYN*. What does it mean?"

"Did you find—the other—pages?"

They looked at him shaking their heads.

Tears came from Dayan's eyes and started flowing down his cheeks. "All the same—God has sent—you to me." His voice was surprisingly clear, but he stammered. "Forgive me—usually I'd look into your eyes—when I speak. But the doctor says to look—only at the corner—of the window. Don't move."

"Can you talk more? Tell us." The chief looked at him urgently.

"Not supposed to. I'll bleed—again."

The three men stared at him, worried and frustrated.

"But I'll talk," Dayan told them. "Even if—I bleed."

"We'll take care of you," Plato promised. "The best doctors—Nobel prize winners! Just tell us the meaning of *KATYN*."

"Don't need doctors. Maybe priest."

"We'll take you to Switzerland," the chief said, not understanding.

Dayan's words still came slowly and blurred. He was obviously in great pain. But it seemed his mind was still lucid, for he answered: "Wanted to tell the story—had arm bones—to provide a witness—you didn't help me."

"We didn't? We've never seen you before!" Plato stared at him, though Dayan's eyes were turned away towards the window.

"Your brothers—suppose to be in service of man." Remembering these things that had happened to him earlier, a sudden surge of panic overwhelmed Dayan's body. He suddenly couldn't speak as his breathing became too shallow to control.

The three reporters were impatient—his mind was wandering, they thought.

"What about *KATYN*?" Plato demanded harshly. "Now's the time to tell us."

Yes, tell them! It's now or never. Dayan was unable to utter a single sound.

Chapter 24

"Katyn! *KATYN*! Is it a formula?"

The voices were all the same to him by this time; anxious, irritated, urgent; Dayan couldn't see the three men, but they seemed to be pulling at him, digging into him, working frantically to uncover some hidden treasure. Now his chest filled with air, and more rushed in as he began to talk.

"If it's used for a good purpose," Dayan answered. "Unlike steel pens that wrote lies to everyone. Millions killed, and by God's great gift to man through words."

"All right, all right. Maybe so, but about *KATYN*. What kind of formula is it?"

"You have paper—write down?"

It was strange to the men, for though Dayan spoke urgently his face was still turned from them towards the window. "Sure, sure," one of them answered. "Go ahead. Talk!"

"Soon won't be able to."

"Then speak now. Hurry!"

If he heard the last sentence, Dayan didn't acknowledge it. He signaled the men to open the window for more air and began a deliberate slow, steady breathing. The room was quiet except for the rustling of notepaper as the three men prepared to take down every word. The silence was broken by Dayan's voice. It was strong and renewed by the fresh air blowing from the window and, more important, by this final opportunity to speak the truth.

"You're right," Dayan said, "*KATYN* really is a secret formula, it was all recorded the other night in the Westania Times building using the tape recorder they have under development. A few who heard it stole what I carried after stabbing me. It's written in a dithyrambic code and is being covered up. It must be published to be understood."

Dayan hesitated for a moment to catch his breath, then continued. "The Russians know about it, I'm sure. Even the Americans know. You must find it."

For the first time he turned his head towards the listeners as he heard the sound of fading footsteps, and they were gone! The room was empty. The door was half-open, and close to his hand on the blanket lay the last sheet of *KATYN*. Now he pulled it to him and grasped it, as he had when the chief reporter had first given it to him.

From the doorway he heard a nurse's warning to someone: "Only a short visit."

"I told you to find it!" Dayan protested, assuming the three men had returned.

"It's an official here to see you," she said to him gently. Then she said to an unseen person. "Make it short!"

A policeman in uniform appeared at the door. He walked stiffly towards the bed and showed Dayan the gold ring he'd thrown on the street outside the Westania Times building. It was placed on a piece of paper which contained printing.

"Sign this," the policeman said. He offered it to Dayan with a pen, who took the ring and looked up at the plump man with a pasty complexion.

"Where's the diamond?"

The policeman blushed. "That's how it was when they turned it over to us," he said defensively.

"Still, my diamond is missing." He wanted to throw the ring through the window, but lacked the strength. "Once I threw a whole bundle of gold coins into a river. How happy I was."

The policeman simply stared at him.

"But at that time I had a real life. A whole one." He signed his name on the paper, then placed it and the ring in the policeman's hand. "Take it. The gold is yours too."

"Mine? What do you mean, Mr. Costovar?"

"It came from your brothers in Christ by way of my grandfather. Now it goes back to its origins."

The confused policeman was looking in wonder at the gold ring.

"Only the blood is mine now," Dayan said. "Look inside—those small bloody spots. All mine." He felt his wound getting warm again. "Now I'm giving the last drops," he said, "please go."

And the policeman did—carrying the signed paper with the gold ring.

After that there was a silence for a few minutes, until steps could be heard in the corridor. These footsteps seemed familiar to Dayan. He'd known them near the high Alps, and had heard them echo on the floor of the Munich Pinakothek. They were Margaret's footsteps, and they came sure and unhesitant, while still light and feminine. He wondered if he was having a dream.

When they were quite close he realized that he had, in fact, been sleeping, but the reassuring sound of her approaching footsteps had awakened him.

He looked eagerly towards the door as she appeared. Her face was pale, however she smiled bravely as she approached the bed to take his hand. He remembered her warm touch from when he first stayed in the hospital before, after falling from the watchtower. It was when they'd first met.

Now she looked intently into his face. Unobtrusively, he slid the sheet of *KATYN* under the blanket. *Have I told her lately how much I love her?* It wasn't too late; not quite. "Margaret, I love and admire you."

Gently she caressed his head. "Dayan."

"I'm sorry I kept so many secrets from you. I always wanted to surprise you some day."

She smiled, and despite the small hospital room, there was a joyful radiance about her. "I have a surprise for you right now."

"Is it about the jasmine blooming again?"

"This is much better. Much, much better!" She carefully sat on the bed next to him. She was light; the bed barely sagged under her weight.

Dayan was now thinking of flowers, with sunlight and green hills. He'd never see them again, he thought. "Better? But I forgot. Spring is so far away." His voice was faint and her expression changed to one of worried apprehension.

"Dayan, let me find the doctor. You need—"

"No, Margaret!" He stretched out his hand and she grasped it. "I need only you."

"I'm here. But please don't talk. Let me do the talking."

"I'm in a hurry. You have more time."

Gently she stroked his face, running a finger across his forehead, tracing the outline of his eyebrows tenderly. When he started to speak, she put her fingers over his lips. "Wait! You must listen to me, Dayan. We're going to have a child."

Now she clasped his hands again, both of them, bent her head and kissed his lips. Dayan's eyes had been closed. A child! After all the deaths, the bloodshed, the people lost, hunted, destroyed—a child! He opened his eyes and tears welled in them as he looked into Margaret's face.

"Margaret! How happy—" Again she put her finger over his lips to silence him.

"Perhaps I should have waited until you're well. But I couldn't wait, Dayan. I wanted you to know. So we could share it."

She didn't understand how short their time might be, and that he must talk now, more than ever before. His wound no longer pained him. Or if it did, that feeling was submerged by the joyful knowledge of having started a new life. One that surely would be a better one than his own, and to which he owed everything, including himself. He was overcome by the feeling that every moment was priceless and so fleeting!

He tried to sit up and Margaret quickly doubled his pillow to support him. "Good. Now we're closer and you'll hear me better," he said.

When she tried to quiet him again, he paid no attention. She must listen. No more secrets! "Margaret," he whispered. "Remember what we've talked about so much."

"About the beauties of nature, the colors. Yes."

"And also about valor. How to be brave. And should the need come, I know you will be!" He was pulling the bloody sheet of *KATYN* from under the blanket. "My parents wouldn't approve..."

"Why not?" She was puzzled. All this wasn't how she'd imagined the scene, even though he was ill. There should be joy at such a time.

"To be showing you something like this." Holding the sheet in his right hand, he went on, "But now you'll understand my secrecy." He lifted the hand and revealed the bloodied sheet. Margaret looked down at it, her face suddenly pale.

But she said in a steady voice, "I'm brave enough. Just tell me what I must do."

He spread the paper out and smoothed it so she could read the word *KATYN*. "There are more words underneath this blood. Many words, and then more blood again and more words. So goes the long story of my people. And my own story as well."

Margaret nodded slowly.

"The Greeks took women with children to look at their statues. You too must go to the Pinakothek."

"We'll go together," Margaret whispered. "I know what you want me to see."

"Rubens."

"Yes. *The Garland of Fruit*."

He smiled, closing his eyes. "Remember the dance? You will fall in love?" Then, while sinking into a coma, he continued. "My dream—we were sailing to America."

Again Margaret answered, "And we will some day."

"We stopped at a place—Atlantis—watched a play. *Symphony of Fear*. But no audience, actors only. The whole world acting, a never-ending show. Somebody called it *Prelude to Drowning*. I was worried for you—you had violets from the monument in France."

"Dayan!" Margaret whispered urgently. "Open your eyes!" She wanted to bring him back to the present, to reality. Back to her.

But Dayan was still far away. "I'm sleepy—Pulitzer brought you to me—we were going to dance—I fell down." He tried to sit up and Margaret grasped his arms. The touch of her hands, warm and alive, was like sunshine through a mist.

"Perhaps you've written about all this Dayan."

"Yes. It's all there, under the blood." He pushed the page of *KATYN* towards her. "It's real," he said. "But if only I'd written a book instead, maybe."

"Of course. Yes, yes." she soothed, trying to press him back, to make him relax against the pillow.

"In my dream I waved the poem—from the ship in the first American port. Everybody saw it." He held the paper up. "Like this! Even Captain Tucker. Remember him?"

Margaret shook her head.

"From Kansas, a farmer. A good man—like Lazar. Or Aristides, the Greek shepherd I met on a train." He pointed to the word *KATYN*. "People asked me what it means. *Everything* I said."

"Yes, yes. But now you must rest." She was very worried and afraid to leave his side even to summon help.

"No, you must listen, Margaret! If the child is a boy, teach him to stand tall. All his life. A girl—to sing Beethoven's *Ninth*."

"We'll do it together," she assured him.

"You think the reporters can discover it—*KATYN*?"

"Of course they can. All of them." She stroked his face gently.

"I told them they must reach out and find the truth." He tried to stretch his arms out again, but was too weak. Sinking back into the pillows, he felt a chill move through his body. No more blood flowed from his wound and he murmured to himself, "Perhaps I've finally given the last drop. I knew they'd get me sometime. If only we'd made it to America."

Margaret started towards the door to summon the doctor.

"No. Come back!"

Torn, she moved back to the bed.

"That's better. History repeats itself Margaret, it always does. More massacres will happen," he whispered, almost defiantly. He was glad to have given the last drop of his blood. And very slowly, so that Margaret wouldn't notice it, he crossed his arms up on his chest with the sheet of *KATYN* held there. "I promised my father to do this for him. Margaret, are you sure the reporters will learn about *KATYN*?"

"Yes, yes, Dayan! I told you!" She was strained to the point of collapse, determined to call a doctor, but he didn't let her.

Dayan's heavy eyelids closed, and he couldn't reopen them. He tried to move his hands lying on his chest, but they only trembled with the page of *KATYN* clasped between them.

It seemed like he was shaking the jasmine tree in Margaret's garden again, just as he'd done last spring, and the flowers were falling down on him, just as they'd fallen on Margaret at that happy time. The blossoms seemed to drift gently to his face, but it must be raining, for the petals were wet.

They were Margaret's tears, dropping on his face, and as he felt their pattering touch he smiled peacefully.

"They would understand you, Dayan. Sure, all of them."

"You mean *KATYN*? Many—many—Katyns."

"Yes," she was assuring him.

"And—child—life—life—"

Dayan's smile remained as the tears fell. Then his face stiffened and he couldn't see a jasmine tree shake, or feel its wet blossoms anymore. But the tears continued to fall, and Margaret's voice still murmured words of reassurance and new life.

Then the words too ceased, until there was only the tiniest sound left of the tears falling on the bloody sheet in Dayan's hands. There the single word became more and more legible as the blood washed away, until the word stood out clearly again—*KATYN*.

THE END

www.ingramcontent.com/pod-product-compliance
Lightning Source LLC
Chambersburg PA
CBHW030624310726
48979CB00003B/869
9780998541624